FROM THE MANSIONS OF BEVERLY HILLS
TO THE GLITTER OF MANHATTAN, TO THE
POWER PLAYS AND POLITICS OF
WASHINGTON, D.C., FOUR WOMEN STRIVE
FOR THEIR AMBITIOUS DREAMS . . .

. . . AND RUN FROM A NIGHTMARE
OF THE PAST.

Helene Galloway . . . Beauty and talent made her a brilliant actress. But her hidden heartaches made superstardom an empty promise.

Diane Henderson . . . She made it to the top as a TV producer in a glamorous world where one shocking secret could be her downfall.

Rachel Weiss . . . A dreamer, a fighter, she had to choose between her family's wishes and the man she never expected to love.

Augusta Tremain . . . She lived in the cutthroat world of politics, where a scandalous passion could shatter a career overnight.

SECRET SINS

LORRAINE STANTON

DIAMOND BOOKS, NEW YORK

SECRET SINS

A Diamond Book / published by arrangement with
the author

PRINTING HISTORY
Diamond edition / May 1992

ISBN: 1-55773-703-7

Diamond Books are published by The Berkley Publishing Group,
200 Madison Avenue, New York, New York 10016.
The name ''DIAMOND'' and its logo are trademarks
belonging to Charter Communications, Inc.

PRINTED IN THE UNITED STATES OF AMERICA

10 9 8 7 6 5 4 3 2 1

To my husband, John, and my daughter, Alison, for all the love and support and for believing in me long after I stopped believing in myself.

SECRET
SINS

Prologue

Los Angeles, 1980

SUCKING IN A NERVOUS BREATH, RHETTA GREEN UNOBTRUSIVELY SLIPPED into the crowded conference room at Cedars-Sinai Medical Center. A haze of cigarette smoke hung over the room like a shroud, and the earthy scent of too many bodies crammed together in one small space assailed her nostrils. But what most unnerved her was the anticipation in the air, an almost tangible aura of ghoulish curiosity that left her feeling weak and vulnerable. She wondered how the hell she would survive the next ten minutes.

As she glanced at the reporters milling around the coffee machine, her entire body tensed. They reminded her of vultures circling a bloody carcass. How ironic that their presence here was a testament to her own success as a theatrical agent. Ten years ago these same people would have laughed her out of town for daring to call a press conference. Now they came running, salivating like a pack of hungry dogs that had scented a meaty bone. They all knew Rhetta Green had power, and in Hollywood power was the only currency more valuable than money.

Rhetta smoothed her hands over her rumpled Dior suit, fleetingly wishing she had taken the time to go home and change her clothes. Even on her best days she looked every one of her forty-eight years—ten pounds overweight with enough sags and wrinkles to make her a prime candidate for some creative plastic surgery—but today the mirror in her tiny gold Cartier compact reflected the face of a hag.

But her appearance hardly mattered now, when she was about to tell the world the news that had shattered her life, when she was afraid even to contemplate her own future.

After slowly moving to the front of the room, Rhetta

1

assumed her position behind the lectern. As she looked out at the sea of eager reporters, she repressed a surge of panic. Only a few minutes, she told herself, and she would be free to slink away into the shadows and mourn in private.

Clearing her throat, she gripped the microphone with trembling hands. "I have a brief announcement," she said quietly. "Helene Galloway was pronounced dead at eight o'clock this morning."

There was a moment of stunned silence as the members of the press turned to one another in disbelief, than a single shout escalated to a roar.

"What happened?" yelled Hank York from *Variety*.

"Was it suicide?"

"Were you with her?"

Gripping the sides of the wooden lectern to steady herself, Rhetta managed to mouth her well-rehearsed lines: "I have no further information. The results of the autopsy haven't been released yet."

Liz Baker, a stringer for one of the weekly tabloids, elbowed her way through the crowd and stopped directly in front of Rhetta, her bright red lips twisted into a cruel smile. "Come on, Rhetta. We all know Helene's been on the skids for months. What pushed her over the edge?"

Rhetta stiffened at the callous words. Just the thought of that ghoulish bitch writing lurid stories about Helene made her skin crawl. But all she could do was delay the inevitable for a few more hours. By tomorrow the whole world would know the truth. She fixed Liz with a withering glare. "Watch what you print, Liz. That's just speculation."

"Then tell us what happened."

Several reporters echoed her demand, and the atmosphere suddenly became charged with hostility. Rhetta clung to her faltering composure by a thread. "You'll have to wait for the medical examiner's report. Until then I have no further comment."

A chorus of loud protests filled the room, but Rhetta held her ground, standing immobile at the lectern until the reporters slowly began to disperse. As she watched them disappear into the corridor she realized she no longer cared how they treated her in the future.

Once she was alone, Rhetta slowly sank down onto a metal

chair and surrendered to her raging grief. Tears flooded her eyes as she imagined Helene lying still and cold on a slab in the morgue. She let out a shrill cry of unspeakable pain; there was no one to hear it.

PART
One

Summer 1968

CHAPTER
One

GUSSIE TREMAIN SLIPPED INTO HER PALE PINK JACKET AND PADDED ACROSS the room to study her reflection in the mirror. Her blond hair hugged her head like a sleek cap and her green eyes perfectly complemented her fine features and flawless complexion. Suddenly she was glad she had defied tradition and chosen a Chanel suit instead of a frilly dress. Everyone else would look dowdy beside her—dowdy and unsophisticated.

In just a few short hours her four years at Brentwood College for Women would be behind her forever—the dreary hours of study, the endless rules and regulations, not to mention the shabby rooms and slimy shower stalls. She supposed there were a few things she would miss about Brentwood, but the grungy communal bathrooms were definitely not among them.

A sharp rap on the door distracted her and she turned away from the mirror as her friend Rachel burst into the room. "Have you talked to Helene this morning?" she asked.

"Not since breakfast. Why?"

"Diane and I have been looking all over for her."

Gussie shrugged. "You know Helene. She's probably off by herself somewhere."

Rachel shoved a leather suitcase aside and flopped on the cluttered bed, heedless of her delicate white linen dress. Her wiry brown hair was skimmed back in an unflattering knot at the nape of her neck that made her sharp features seem even more prominent. Even today she was completely indifferent to her appearance.

"If she doesn't show up soon she'll miss graduation."

As Gussie started to reply, Diane popped her head into the open doorway. "Have you found her?"

"Not yet," Rachel said.

Diane entered the room and perched on the edge of an upholstered chair, carefully smoothing her hands over her inexpensive green dress. The daughter of a Methodist minister, she was one of the few scholarship students at Brentwood. "I can hardly believe we're really graduating," she said. "Last month I was counting the days, but now I'm a nervous wreck. What if I starve to death before I find a job?"

"Are you having second thoughts about moving to Manhattan?" Gussie asked.

Diane absently threaded her fingers through her curly auburn hair. "My father has been pressuring me to go back to Kansas with him. I hate making him so unhappy, but I want to work in television, and he refuses to understand that the best opportunities are in New York. All he talks about is the crime rate and the high cost of living."

"You can always come home to the Bronx with me," Rachel said. "Try living over the deli with my parents for a few months."

Diane laughed, and her vivid blue eyes twinkled. "At least you won't go hungry and maybe you'll be too busy studying to argue with them."

"Maybe," Rachel said grimly. "But sometimes I'm sorry I decided on Columbia. Who knows? I might have been just as happy somewhere in the Midwest."

Gussie felt a knot of anxiety tighten in her stomach as she listened to them discuss their futures. Although it was heavenly to imagine returning to her luxurious family home, she had yet to figure out what she would do to occupy her time—a fact that was beginning to gnaw away at her like the pain of a sore tooth.

And when it came right down to it, her choices were rather limited. She could either join her mother in her endless charity work or help her father with his reelection campaign, but luncheons and fashion shows bored her. Despite the fact that she was the only daughter of the senior senator from Virginia, she had never acquired much of an interest in politics. She was graduating at the top of her class, and for what? It hardly took a degree in fine arts to beg for campaign contributions. And that was precisely what her parents had in mind. Not exactly a stimulating prospect.

Gussie was so engrossed in her own thoughts that she was

startled when she noticed Helene standing in the doorway, her dark eyes filled with tears.

"Helene, what's wrong?" she said.

"My mother's . . . not coming to graduation."

"Why not? What happened?"

Helene shrugged as she slowly entered the room and slumped against a maple dresser. Her silky black hair accentuated her pale skin and delicate features. She looked vulnerable, almost fragile. "She says she has a migraine. But I'm sure that's . . . just an excuse."

"I'm sorry," Rachel said softly.

"It's no big deal. I never really expected her to come. I mean, it's not as if my mother and I have ever been close or anything."

Gussie felt a rush of pity. It must be terrible to be the daughter of a famous movie star. Brenda Galloway seemed much more interested in creating new scandals than maintaining any sort of relationship with Helene.

"I just wish we all weren't going to Hyannis," Helene said. "Right now I never want to see my mother again."

"So let's call it off," Rachel said. "We'll do something else."

Helene shook her head. "I have to face her. Besides, this is our last fling—we've been planning it for weeks."

"Whatever you want," Rachel said. "Just remember we'll all be there if you need us."

Helene smiled wanly. "I know, I'm okay now. I'll meet you in the auditorium in a few minutes."

As Helene left the room, Gussie turned to Diane and Rachel and helplessly shrugged. They were all such close friends, bound by four years of shared dreams and confidences. But they had no words that could ease Helene's pain.

CHAPTER
Two

AS BRENDA GALLOWAY GAZED OUT HER BEDROOM WINDOW AT THE sweeping view of Nantucket Sound, she felt a fierce stab of possessiveness. This was all hers, the sprawling white house and the manicured lawns, the raised beds of zinnias and marigolds, even the barren sand dunes that stretched all the way to the clear blue water. Everything as far as she could see belonged exclusively to her.

She watched the man running along the beach and suddenly felt uneasy. Even though she had paid dearly for him, Rick Conti would never belong exclusively to her. As she watched him skim gracefully over the sand, his bronzed skin gleaming in the sun, her uneasiness turned to anger.

She had to do something about Rick. Great sex was hardly a reason to let a conniving young actor play vicious games at her expense. She had plucked him out of obscurity; she would dump him right back on the dung heap, right back on the stinking pile of male whores who scavenged Hollywood looking for a free ride. And he would be dumped *sans* his bright red Porsche and designer wardrobe.

Rick had been a mistake from the beginning, she thought, too stupid to figure out that once he'd sold himself to the highest bidder he was temporarily off the market. Well, now he was about to learn just how little he was worth.

Smiling, Brenda allowed herself the pleasure of imagining his shock when she sent him packing. He was planning on accompanying her to Spain next week, no doubt anticipating a few discreet affairs while she filmed her latest movie on the streets of Madrid. Too bad he had underestimated Brenda Galloway. Too bad he had dismissed her as an aging star starved for a virile young lover.

11

She *was* a star; that was undeniable. But that was all he'd gotten right. Turning from the window, she peeled off her voluminous silk caftan and stood naked in front of the mirror, critically appraising her reflection.

God, how she wanted to be young again, a gorgeous starlet with a million-dollar body and a wild mane of flaming red hair. But time was catching up with her. Any day now she would have to make that inevitable appointment with a plastic surgeon. There were spidery lines around her mouth, and the tender skin under her wide gray eyes was just the slightest bit puffy. Even her famous breasts were beginning to sag—not much, but she could see it.

Furious, she picked up a silver-backed hairbrush and hurled it at the mirror, shattering the glass. God damn Rick Conti. She was still gorgeous, still a fucking star. Who the hell was he to screw around behind her back?

"Miss Galloway, are you all right?"

Brenda swung around as her housekeeper rapped on the open door. "I had an accident. Get in here and clean it up."

Accustomed to immediate obedience, Brenda turned away and slipped the caftan over her shoulders, but the woman hovered in the doorway. "Miss Galloway, you promised the staff the rest of the day off. With all your company, we haven't had a day off in almost two weeks."

Disgusted, Brenda was tempted to fire the housekeeper on the spot, but, God, it was hard to find good help in Hyannis. These damn locals all thought they were above domestic work. With thirty guests arriving the next day, she had no choice but to negotiate. Flashing her award-winning smile, she turned on the charm.

"I'd forgotten about that, Mary. Is everything ready for the party tomorrow night?"

"Oh, yes, Miss Galloway. I checked with the caterer this morning. He ordered all the food from Boston, just like you wanted."

"What about the cleaning crew?"

"They'll be here by noon tomorrow."

"All right, you can leave after you clean up this mess."

"Thank you, Miss Galloway." The housekeeper smiled ingratiatingly. "I fixed a nice cold supper for your daughter and her friends. They'll be here any time now."

Brenda clenched her fists in frustration. She had forgotten about Helene and her friends—just what she needed right now, another emotional encounter with her daughter.

"That's fine, Mary," she said briskly. "I'm sure we can manage on our own for one night."

"Yes, ma'am. I'll just get this cleaning done and be on my way."

Dismissing the housekeeper with a curt nod, Brenda swept past her and made her way out of the room and down the massive oak staircase, her thoughts on Helene. Why had the girl insisted on this ridiculous reunion? What the hell did she want?

As she crossed the marble foyer to the living room, she had a sudden craving for a stiff drink. Seeing Helene again would be pure hell. She could almost feel the chilling force of those wounded black eyes mutely accusing her—those god-awful hungry black eyes. She wasn't cut out to be a mother, she'd been telling Helene that for years. The kid was just too needy.

Shuddering, she hurried to the teak bar and downed a hefty shot of scotch in one gulp. Maybe Helene had every right to accuse her. She had never been much of a mother, never felt any kind of maternal stirring for the delicate little girl who had always reminded her so much of Carlo. Never even tried. But Helene should have accepted that by now. Why was she still wasting her time searching for something that had never existed?

Brenda poured herself another shot, then sat on the edge of the white leather sofa. Now that her daughter had blossomed into a beautiful woman, it was absurd to think they could establish any kind of relationship. All women were natural enemies. Someday Helene would understand that. Someday she would look in the mirror and see the shadow of her rival hovering behind her like a ravenous spider.

Distracted by the sound of footsteps padding across the redwood deck, Brenda looked up to see Rick saunter through the French doors. He was naked except for the swatch of bright green fabric stretched tight across his hips and the thin gold medallion hanging around his neck. Beads of perspiration glistened on his skin, trickling from his throat to the thatch of golden hair on his chest. She caught a whiff of a sweaty odor that should have been repugnant but was arousing instead. Christ, he made her salivate like a bitch in heat.

She silently counted to three, then fixed Rick with the cold stare that had taken years to perfect. "Where the hell have you been? I didn't bring you here to roam off by yourself all day."

His rugged features registered surprise. "Sorry. I didn't think you'd mind."

"You don't think at all, do you, Rick? One of these days we'll have to have a little talk about what bothers me."

It pleased her to see a trace of anxiety flicker across his insolent face. Maybe the bastard wasn't made of steel after all.

"What's wrong, babe?" he said joining her on the sofa. "Why are you so uptight?"

Since she had already decided to keep him around until she left for Spain, she swallowed the ugly words she was saving for their final confrontation. "I'm just on edge. Helene and her friends will be here any minute."

"So what?" He trailed his fingers across her shoulder, expertly massaging her rigid muscles. "Forget Helene. Relax."

Even as she loathed him, she still craved his touch. He lowered his hand to her breast and rubbed one of her nipples through the silky fabric of her caftan. Never a gentle lover, he fondled her with rough fingers until the fine line between pain and pleasure became indistinct. He was the guide now, slowly leading her through a maze of sensation.

She groaned low in her throat as he lifted her caftan and skimmed his hand over her smooth white belly. She was already wet and quivering when he slipped his fingers deep inside her, and she writhed against him, desperate for release.

But he refused to let her come. He stroked her until she thought she'd lose her mind, then pulled his hand away. He was punishing her. The fucking bastard was punishing her. Enraged, she bared her teeth like a rabid dog, sank them deep into the soft flesh of his arm, and held on until she tasted blood.

Rick made a guttural noise that was somewhere between a moan and a grunt of animal pleasure as he twisted free of her mouth and roughly pushed her down on the sofa. As he shed his trunks, she greedily reached for him, but he shoved her hand away and entered her in one savage thrust, then began brutally pumping and grinding, quickly driving her to some depraved place beyond the edge of sanity.

She came in a violent burst of energy, then felt Rick shudder and collapse on her chest. As she gradually returned to awareness, she recoiled at the sickening taste of blood. Why. had she let him drag her into that black pit of lust and violence again? But when she looked into his eyes, she saw the truth written in his mocking blue gaze. No matter how much she pretended she could live without him, she was a hopeless addict, hooked on a release only he could provide.

Under any other circumstances, Diane Henderson would have reveled in the unaccustomed luxury of riding in a Rolls-Royce limousine. How far the minister's daughter from Kansas had come! But every time she caught a glimpse of Helene crumpled on the seat like a broken doll, her spirits plunged. Her friend had seemed fine during their college graduation reception, but when the limo arrived to whisk them away to Hyannis, her mood had steadily deteriorated.

Unfortunately her glum mood had been infectious; even Rachel and Gussie had barely uttered a word since they left Brentwood. Gussie looked bored as she deftly applied another coat of rose-colored nail polish. She always seemed so cool and detached that it was impossible to guess her thoughts. Her life of privilege showed. Growing up a senator's daughter had taught her the value of discretion. Rachel Weiss was much easier to read. She had been covertly watching Helene for the past hour, concern clearly visible in her eyes.

They were all so different, Diane thought. Such unlikely friends. And yet they had been drawn together at Brentwood, each adding a different dimension to the close-knit group.

"Will we be there soon?" Diane said, responding to a familiar need to break the tense silence. It was an annoying legacy of her childhood—always assuming responsibility for smoothing over every rough spot.

Helene turned away from the window, shrugging indifferently. "At least another hour."

"Are you sure you want to go through with this?" Rachel asked, glancing at Helene. "It's not too late to change your mind."

"What would I tell my mother?" Helene's voice was flat. "She's expecting us."

"So what? After the way she treated you, you don't owe her any excuses."

Helene shook her head, her dark eyes thoughtful. "Brenda would love it if I just disappeared. I think that's what she's always wanted. Why should I make it easy on her? Anyway, it's not as if I expected her to show up for graduation. I know better."

There was a brief silence. Then Gussie said, "Well, that's fine if you can handle the pressure, but there's no point in punishing yourself just to prove something to your mother."

Helene stiffened defensively. "Stop treating me like a basket case. I'm fine now, really."

Shrugging, Gussie elegantly waved her fingers in the air, then shifted on the seat and rummaged in the limo's compact refrigerator. "Then we may as well start the party. I'm sure your mother has something much better in here than that awful punch they served at the reception."

A few seconds later she triumphantly produced a tapered amber bottle. "*Voilà*! Cristal."

Diane, suddenly feeling like an outsider, watched Gussie expertly uncork the champagne. Though no one had ever been cruel enough to remind her, she knew she was an impostor, a scholarship student mingling with legitimate heirs to wealth and privilege. Luxuries like Cristal and limousines were so far beyond her reach that she felt almost guilty for enjoying them. In fact, it took a tremendous amount of control for her to appear nonchalant as Gussie passed her a delicate fluted goblet.

"To best friends," Rachel said, raising her glass.

As crystal chimed against crystal, Diane tried to capture the moment in her mind. Much as she wanted to believe their glib promises to keep in touch, life had a way of subverting good intentions. Glancing at the others, she wondered if they felt the same way. "Do you really think we'll keep in touch?"

"Of course we will," Rachel said adamantly. "We'll always be friends."

Gussie nodded in agreement. "A toast to friendship," she said, raising her glass to meet the others, then downing the champagne. "Anyone join me for another?"

"What else are friends for?" Helene said softly, yielding to the mood.

But by the time the limousine whooshed to a halt in the center of a sweeping circular driveway, Helene had lapsed into silence again. She wore a wary, melancholy expression, which her friends quietly noted. Feeling ill at ease, Diane shifted her gaze to the elegant white house in the distance.

It looked like something out of a Hollywood fantasy, a towering contemporary mansion surrounded by vivid gardens and plush green lawns. Matching bronze fountains sprayed streams of sparkling water into a stone-paved fish pond, and a thick crescent of pine trees curved around the landward side of the house, creating an aura of intimate seclusion. Diane had never imagined such opulence, such a palatial monument to money and success.

Gussie and Rachel had already climbed out of the limousine and were standing in the driveway watching the chauffeur retrieve their luggage, but Diane remained seated beside Helene, transfixed by the majestic house. Then she saw Brenda Galloway crossing the lawn, and her breath caught in her throat.

She had seen Helene's mother countless times on the movie screen, but in person the woman radiated sheer magnetism. She exuded power and a raw sexuality that was both fascinating and disturbing. Diane felt an odd sensation in the pit of her stomach as she followed Helene out of the car.

Brenda Galloway seemed to glide over the thick carpet of grass, her scarlet caftan whipping around her legs in the brisk ocean breeze. When she reached Helene, she smiled and lightly embraced her.

"I'm sorry I missed your graduation, sweets," she said, her voice a throaty whisper, "but I had one of those terrible migraines."

Helene shook free of her embrace. "Forget it, Mother. I didn't really expect you to come."

Brenda looked shocked and angry as she dropped her arms to her sides. "That was unnecessary, Helene. I've already apologized."

"Of course, an apology solves everything."

Shedding the last traces of her genial facade, Brenda slowly advanced on Helene, pinning her against the side of the car. "If you've come here to cause trouble, you might as well leave right now. I have no intention of enduring any nasty little scenes. Do you understand?"

Helene had become accustomed long ago to being embarrassed by her mother in front of friends and strangers. She averted her eyes and nodded.

"Good," Brenda said, backing away a few steps. "Now, why don't you introduce me to your friends?"

As Helene stumbled through the introductions, Diane tried to curb her escalating sense of dread. The idea of spending three days at the beach house had already lost most of its luster, and she wondered why Brenda Galloway had ever agreed to let them visit. She obviously had no interest in salvaging her relationship with Helene—her attitude toward her daughter bordered on overt hostility. And what about Helene? Why did she *want* to spend time with a woman who looked at her with such loathing?

"Well, girls, I hope you'll enjoy yourselves while you're here. Please call me Brenda," she said, her affable mask in place again. "Tonight it will be just us, but I'm having a little party tomorrow evening. Please feel free to join us."

Diane let out a nervous little laugh, then blushed profusely. "That sounds lovely, thank you."

After giving her a cursory glance, Brenda shrugged and abruptly turned toward the house. "We might as well go inside. I'm sure you'd like to freshen up before dinner."

Try as she might, Diane was unable to repress her apprehension as she exchanged wary glances with Rachel and Gussie. So far nothing had turned out quite the way she had imagined, and all her glowing fantasies about the Cape Cod weekend now seemed like foolish pipe dreams. She could tell from their faces that her friends were feeling the same way. Instead of a glamorous fling, this little vacation was fast becoming a disaster.

Several hours later Rachel squirmed to find a cool spot on the white leather sofa. Just like everything else in the spacious living room, the couch had been designed strictly for appearance. Brenda must have been trying to duplicate some photo spread from *House and Garden*, with the low-slung furniture and stark black and white color scheme. The abstract paintings looked like the scribbles of a demented child. In fact, the only appealing thing in the entire room was the glass wall that provided a fantastic view of Nantucket Sound.

Feeling slightly woozy, Rachel swallowed a last gulp of champagne and set her glass on a glossy black end table. Suddenly the night air seemed hotter and stickier, heavy with the pervasive scent of the sea. Glancing around the room, she felt a tingle of alarm. Diane and Gussie were sprawled out on the white wool carpet, obviously tipsy, while Brenda Galloway silently watched as Rick Conti played seductive games with Helene.

Despite the lavish amount of champagne coloring her senses, Rachel was keenly aware of the dramatic change in Helene. She had been distant and forlorn until Rick fawned over her during dinner, completely altering her mood. Now she was curled up beside him on a love seat, whispering and giggling, oblivious to the crackling tension in the air and to the way her mother was stalking her with smoky gray eyes. Or maybe, Rachel thought, annoying her mother was just what Helene wanted.

She was still pondering the idea when Brenda Galloway suddenly sprang to her feet in a whirl of red silk.

"That's enough champagne, Helene. You're drunk."

Smiling faintly, Helene slowly refilled her glass and raised it to her lips. "Not yet, Mother, but I'm working on it."

Brenda Galloway froze, her mouth twisted in a grimace of pure rage. Then in a flurry of motion she flew across the room, wrenched the glass away from Helene, and flung it into the marble fireplace.

"I warned you not to create a scene, but you had to defy me. You *had* to cause trouble."

Helene seemed to shrink, her brief spurt of rebellion crushed by the sight of her mother towering over her. Brenda was relentless. "I've had enough of your silly games," she hissed. "Now take your friends upstairs."

"But I—"

"Did you hear me, Helene? Go upstairs right now."

Clutching the arm of the sofa, Helene struggled to her feet, tears gathering in her eyes. As she stumbled toward the foyer, Rachel nodded at Diane and Gussie, and they all rushed to help her.

"Now do you see what a bitch she is?" Helene mumbled. "She hates me. My mother hates me."

"Come on, Helene," Rachel said gently. "It's late. Let's go to bed."

Brenda managed to contain her fury until she and Rick were alone in the living room. Then she viciously turned on him. "You bastard! You miserable perverted bastard! What the hell were you doing crawling all over my daughter?"

"Give me a break, will you? Your daughter's a fucking kid. I was only fooling around."

"You were coming on to her, the same way you come on to every other bitch in heat."

Rick extricated himself from the love seat, ambled over to the French doors, and stared out into the night. "You want to know the truth?" he said finally, turning to face her. "You're not enough, baby. I need something young on the side to keep me going."

Brenda began to shake uncontrollably. Rick Conti, an ignorant peasant from Brooklyn, had effortlessly exploited her. She could almost taste her hatred, her hunger for revenge.

"Then find yourself another meal ticket," she snarled. "Go on out there and sell yourself like a whore. That's all you've ever been, a cheap hustler."

She watched him closely, experiencing a surge of triumph when she saw the realization creep into his calculating blue eyes. His whole act with Helene had been just another cruel game, but this time he had gone too far.

"Pack up your things and get out, Rick. And be sure to leave the keys to the Porsche. I'd hate to have to send the cops after you."

"Come on, Bren. I didn't mean what I said. I was just fooling around."

She paused for one last look at his supple body. Rick Conti was a sadistic predator, and unless she found the strength to expunge him from her life, he would ruthlessly destroy her.

"Get out, Rick."

As she turned her back on him, Brenda Galloway wondered where she would find another man capable of appeasing the dark hungers he had awakened in her.

— — —

After a few hours of sleep, Helene awoke completely sober, a stream of sweat trickling between her breasts. Only the soft sound of Gussie breathing punctuated the silence, a silence that became more oppressive by the minute. Restless, she kicked the sheet aside, thoughts of her mother reigniting the powerful anger of the night before. Once again Brenda had rejected her, and humiliated her in front of her friends.

Shivering beneath a patina of sweat, she tried to dispel the disquieting thoughts by forcing herself to concentrate on the way Rick had blatantly come on to her. But she kept remembering that Brenda had spoiled even that paltry victory.

Too upset to sleep, Helene crawled out of bed and groped her way through the darkness to the stairs, intent on escaping the smothering closeness of the house. Maybe the night air would clear her mind.

As she crossed the living room to the open French doors, she noticed a flickering orange glow and the shadowy outline of a man sitting on the redwood deck.

At first he seemed unaware of her presence as he sat looking out over the water. Every now and then he inhaled a deep drag of the joint he held between his fingers, and as Helene breathed in the sweet scent of marijuana, she felt a wave of longing wash over her. She craved someone to fill the emptiness, to want her, to make her feel whole again.

Rick's voice came out of the darkness, stroking her like a caress. "What took you so long, babe? I've been waiting for you."

Helene slowly crossed the deck, then lowered herself to the floor beside him. Moonlight cast a silvery glow on his blond hair, softening the harsh lines of his face until he looked almost gentle.

Snuggling against him, Helene relinquished herself to the pervasive warmth that seemed to seep through his skin. His gold medallion pressed against her breasts as his mouth opened over hers, soft and persuasive. She reflexively slid her arms around his shoulders, silencing a faint inner voice of protest. She was tired of thinking. Tired of fighting.

Slowly Rick lifted her flimsy nightgown and took one of her breasts into his mouth while his hands explored her naked body, pressing and stroking. She groaned and arched against him.

"Easy," he murmured. "We have all night."

"No, now. I want you, Rick."

How many times had Brenda stroked this man's skin, as she was doing now? Helene wondered. At first the thought repulsed her, but as Rick entered her, she felt a savage pleasure, a jolt of excitement that surpassed any sexual gratification she had ever known. Helene had won.

CHAPTER
Three

DIANE AWOKE WITH A JOLT. HER EYES SNAPPED OPEN, AND AN ODD SENSE of alarm shot up her spine. Inching herself up against the headboard, she listened intently, but there were no unusual sounds, only the steady murmur of the sea. She rolled to her side and closed her eyes, hoping to go back to sleep, but her drifting consciousness was pierced by a scream.

"My God, what was that?" Rachel whispered from across the room.

There were several more shrill cries and then a dull thump.

Rachel sprang out of bed, opened the door, and peered into the dark hallway. "Something's wrong. Let's see if Helene and Gussie are awake."

Still slightly dazed, Diane rose and followed her across the hall, then cautiously entered the room Helene was sharing with Gussie. Moonlight filtered through the bamboo shades, casting eerie shadows on the walls. Gussie was sitting up on one of the twin beds. The other was empty.

"Gussie, you're awake, too," Rachel said, inching closer.

"Of course I am. What the hell was that?"

Flicking on the overhead lamp, Diane blinked at the sudden glaring light. "Someone was screaming. Where's Helene?"

"I have no idea. She was gone when I woke up."

"Maybe we should go downstairs and find out what's happening," Rachel said.

Diane hesitated, reluctant to encounter Brenda Galloway again. "It's really none of our business."

"Helene is our business."

"What does that mean?" Gussie sounded nervous.

"Nothing. I just think we should have a look around."

After a brief pause Diane nodded, and Rachel immediately

started for the door. Huddled close, they made their way down the stairs.

As soon as they reached the first floor, they realized something was terribly wrong. A light shining on the deck revealed a scene from a nightmare. Helene was crouched in a corner blankly staring into the night, and Rick Conti was lying motionless in a pool of blood, a knife embedded in his chest.

Gussie screamed, slumping against Rachel as Brenda materialized out of the shadows like a ghostly apparition. "There's been an accident," she said. "Come in the house, and we'll decide what has to be done."

"What about Helene?" Rachel said. "You can't just leave her out here."

"I'll give her a sedative in a minute. Right now we have to talk."

Brenda led them into the dining room, and as they silently took seats around the table, she said, "Rick is dead. I found him . . ." Her voice faltered, and there was a discernible twitch over her right eye. "I found him making love to Helene. We quarreled, and . . . well, she snapped. He was just using her, for God's sake. I . . . She . . . she ran into the kitchen and grabbed a knife . . . and she killed him."

"What? Oh, my God. Brenda, are you sure he's dead?" Gussie asked shrilly.

Brenda used the back of her hand to wipe a film of perspiration from her flushed cheeks. "Believe me, he's dead. Now we have to decide what to do."

"Call the police," Diane whispered, chilled by Brenda's calmness.

There was a lengthy silence while Brenda inspected their faces with probing eyes. "If I do that, Helene will spend the rest of her life in prison. She's my only child. I can't let that happen. Now, pull yourselves together, girls."

Trembling, Rachel reached for the pack of cigarettes in the center of the table. "So what are you planning to do?"

"You're her best friends. I know you want to help me protect her." She smiled serenely at the stunned faces before her. "I want you to help me dispose of the body."

Gussie and Diane gasped incredulously, but Rachel nodded mechanically.

"Too many people know Rick was here. We'll have to

report him missing. In the morning I'll call the police and say he got drunk and took a late night walk on the beach. We haven't seen him since.''

''They'll investigate,'' Rachel said, watching Helene rock back and forth in an unrelenting rhythm.

''Maybe, but eventually they'll assume he either drowned or ran off. Rick was a drifter; there won't be any pressure to find him.''

Rachel nervously dragged on her cigarette. ''What about his family? They'll demand to know what happened to him,'' she said.

Brenda shrugged. ''The only family he ever mentioned was a mother in Brooklyn. As far as I know, he never bothered to keep in touch with her.''

''This is crazy,'' Diane said. ''We can't just . . . bury a man.''

Brenda stared at her intently for a moment, then shifted her gaze back to Rachel. ''There's something else you should consider. If we report Rick's death to the police, you'll be involved in a murder investigation.''

Gussie moaned, suddenly alert. ''My God, my father's running for reelection this year. A scandal could ruin him.''

''A scandal could ruin all of us, not just your father, Gussie,'' Brenda said. ''People are vicious. They twist the truth. I know; I've been there.'' She lapsed into silence and again studied their faces as if trying to look into their minds.

Diane closed her eyes, but the vision of Rick lying naked and bloody on the patio was still flashing in her mind like a neon sign. Clutching her throat, she tried to subdue a violent wave of nausea. This couldn't be happening.

''I don't think you girls are prepared to face the publicity of a trial,'' Brenda went on. ''You have your futures to consider. Being even remotely connected to a murder investigation would be a black mark against you for the rest of your lives.''

Gussie absently ran a hand through her hair. ''Do you think . . . I mean . . . Can we really get away with this?''

''If we're careful, if we plan every detail,'' Brenda said. ''But first we have to be in agreement.'' She gazed around the table, her gray eyes intimidating. ''Will you help me?''

Diane felt as if her heart, beating wildly out of control, had plunged into the pit of her stomach. Gripping the edge of the table to steady herself, she looked directly at Brenda. "No, we have to call the police. Helene needs help! You're crazy, all of you, to even think of doing this. I'm going to call the police."

"And ruin our lives?" Gussie cried.

Rachel lit another cigarette, her hands shaking violently. "We have no choice, Diane. We have to protect Helene. Nothing else matters. Brenda's right."

"It's wrong," Diane said. "Rick was a human being. We can't just toss him away like a bag of trash."

Rachel flinched at the gruesome image, but she refused to retreat. "Are you willing to send Helene to jail?"

Massaging her throbbing temples, Diane realized that her emotions were circumventing every attempt at reason. "No . . . I don't know. . . . I can't think straight."

The beams from their flashlight were a frail glow in the darkness, not nearly bright enough to exorcise the shadows distorting the landscape as Brenda led them to an abandoned well obscured by a stand of pine trees. They moved silently through the hot night, frequently pausing to redistribute the weight of the inert body they carried. When they reached the safety of the trees, Brenda wordlessly motioned to the well, as if silence would in some way mitigate the horror of what they were about to do.

Rachel took one look at the crumbling stone wall and froze, like a rabbit blinded by the lights of an oncoming car. She had been so certain that this was the right thing to do, but now she hesitated, imagining the nightmares that would haunt her for the rest of her life. There was a vast difference between her abstract vision of concealing a body and the reality now confronting her. Suddenly she was no longer sure she was capable of consigning Rick Conti to eternity in an unmarked grave.

"Rachel, we have to hurry. It's almost dawn," Brenda said, her eyes gleaming ferally in the darkness. "Help us lift him."

Shivering, Rachel cradled Rick Conti's head in her hands as the four of them slowly lifted him to the open chasm of the well. Her nails carved deep grooves into the hollows of his cheeks, disfiguring his flawless skin. Transfixed, she stared at his eyes, certain they would open at the last moment to condemn her. Then suddenly her arms were empty and a sickening thud was reverberating through her skull.

"It's done," Brenda said.

Gussie gagged. "I'm going to be sick."

"Not now," Brenda said. "We have too much to do. Let's get back to the house."

Rachel found herself unwittingly murmuring a half-forgotten prayer as they trailed Brenda through the grove of trees. When she realized what she was doing, she clamped her mouth shut. Invoking the name of God at a time like this was a travesty.

By the time they reached the house, the night was fading into the horizon and Brenda seemed driven by an increased sense of urgency. Helene was still sitting on the deck, vacantly staring into the distance, the dark stain on the redwood floor offering silent testimony to the mortal struggle that had transpired there.

Kneeling beside Helene, Brenda gripped her shoulders. "I'll need some help getting her upstairs."

"I'll do it," Gussie said.

Brenda nodded and turned to Diane and Rachel. "You two find some cleaning supplies and scrub the deck. We have to finish before the help arrives."

Once they were alone, Rachel looked at Diane, tentatively touching her hand. "Are you okay?"

Diane burst into laughter, a shrill cackle that chilled Rachel to the core. "That's priceless. We just buried a man and you're asking if I'm okay." She wrapped her arms protectively around her chest. "Of course I'm not. I'll never be okay again."

Rachel longed to offer some sort of comfort, but the reality of what they had done was too brutal. There were no words to erase the memory of a body thudding to the bottom of an abandoned well. Shrugging helplessly, she said, "At least Helene is safe."

Diane seemed lost in thought until she suddenly whispered, "Do you really believe Helene killed him?"

Rachel tensed, unnerved to hear Diane echo her own suspicions. "I'm not sure," she murmured. "At first I did, but I've been thinking that it could have been Brenda."

"And she lied so we'd help her cover it up," Diane said flatly.

Fighting an almost overwhelming fatigue, Rachel sank down on a yellow canvas chair and wearily rubbed her eyes.

"Maybe. I don't know. You saw how jealous she was. Finding Helene and Rick together might have pushed her over the edge."

"My God, what have we done?" Diane gasped.

Rachel leaned forward in her chair, her sharp features illuminated by the first rosy streaks of dawn. "We protected Helene," she said fiercely. "She might have killed him, Diane. We couldn't afford to take that chance."

Tears glistened in Diane's vivid blue eyes. "So what happens now? Do we just go on as if nothing happened?"

"I don't know," Rachel said softly, but as she watched the new day brighten the sky, she knew the memories would never fade.

Late that afternoon the coffee shop at Logan airport was hot and stuffy, rife with the scent of too many warm bodies. Diane joined Gussie and Rachel at a chipped Formica table, ordered an iced tea from a frazzled waitress, and then wearily closed her eyes. She felt nervous and edgy, drained by the ordeal of being questioned by Chief Ralph Edwards of the Hyannis Police Department. Every bit of her energy was focused on controlling her anxiety, but Rachel seemed oblivious to her struggle.

"I wish Brenda had let us see Helene," Rachel said. "I hated leaving without talking to her."

"She was still sedated," Diane said listlessly.

Rachel stirred her coffee, her movements quick and jittery. "I know. That's what bothers me. Why was Brenda so determined to keep us away from her?"

Though she had been troubled by the same unsettling thoughts all afternoon, Diane was irrationally angry at Rachel for voicing them aloud. "I'm sure she was just trying to protect Helene. It probably would have upset her to see us."

"Maybe," Rachel said. "Or maybe Brenda was protecting herself by preventing Helene from telling us what really happened."

"Will you lower your voice?" Gussie said. "People are staring at us."

Rachel glanced around the crowded room, then lit a cigarette. "You're getting paranoid."

"I am not, but I don't want to talk about this anymore. I just want to go home and forget."

Diane laughed bitterly. "Forget? We'll never be able to forget this. Someday we'll have to face the truth; someday it will all come out."

"That's ridiculous," Gussie said shakily. "You just love being the voice of doom."

"And you live in a dream world, Gussie."

There was an uneasy silence; then Rachel tamped out her cigarette and reached for her canvas tote bag. "We have to go, Diane. They just announced our flight."

Diane stood and embraced Gussie in a mute gesture of apology, but she knew things would never be the same. They now shared a deadly secret, a secret that bound them irrevocably, a secret that would insidiously erode the foundations of their lives.

On a hot night in late July, Police Chief Ralph Edwards slid into one of the scarred pine booths in the Harbor Lounge and sat back to savor a frosty Budweiser, his mind fixed on thoughts of Rick Conti and his strange disappearance. Though there was no evidence to suggest foul play, the idea of a grown man vanishing into the night bothered him. And after thirty years on the force, he had learned to trust his gut instincts.

Lost in thought, he was shocked when finally he looked up and saw his old friend, Mick Travis, slide into the booth across from him. "What the hell are you doing here, Travis?" Travis had left Hyannis years ago to become a ruthless Hollywood biographer, but Edwards still remembered the hungry reporter who had spent his nights hanging around the police station looking for a hot scoop.

"I'm on vacation, but I'm curious as hell about the Galloway case. What's the word? Any leads on Conti?"

"Nope. He disappeared like a fucking phantom. According to Galloway they were having a party and he wandered off and never came back. I ran a make on him, but all I turned up was a dishonorable discharge from the Navy for beating up an officer. The guy is a loner. His own mother hasn't seen him in years."

"Now what? Where do you go from here?"

Edwards drained his beer in one long gulp, then shoved the bottle aside and restlessly drummed his fingers on the table. "Nowhere. Right now he's just another missing person."

"Bullshit. I'll bet my ass there's a story here, a damn good one. Keep in touch, Edwards. Let me know if you come up with anything."

Edwards nodded, but as he watched Mick slip out of the booth and make his way to the door, he silently cursed himself for being so indiscreet. Mick Travis was a crack investigator and the last thing the department needed was a nosy writer poking around in the Galloway case.

PART
Two

Fall 1968

CHAPTER
Four

IT HAD BEEN A BRUTAL SUMMER, THICK WITH HEAT AND HUMIDITY, THE metallic stench of the subway rising through the pavement to accent the smells of the city streets—unwashed bodies, hot pretzels smeared with mustard, exhaust fumes wheezing from the sagging backsides of ramshackle buses. For Diane it had been a discouraging initiation to the realities of life in Manhattan.

Her minuscule Chelsea apartment was grossly overpriced and poorly maintained. She had felt isolated, overwhelmed by a sea of unfamiliar faces. But the most alarming aspect of her new life was her inability to find a job in the television industry.

After three months of interviews with condescending male executives, she had concluded that she would either have to adjust her expectations or seek another type of work.

Unwilling to give up her dream, she had begun combing the *Times* for something that would offer at least a hint of incentive. And today, just two weeks later, she had accepted a job as secretary to Jordan Carr, the executive producer of the glossy television magazine "On Target."

Now, as she left the studio after spending her first workday filling out personnel forms, she felt elated. The job would offer her unlimited opportunities to study the inner workings of the network, and perhaps there would be a slim chance to move ahead if she convinced Jordan Carr she was capable. She smiled as she imagined her name stenciled in gold on one of the heavy oak doors in the executive suite.

Completely immersed in her dreams, Diane remained unaware of the man walking beside her until his hand briefly

33

brushed her elbow and she tensed, reflexively clutching her purse.

"I'm harmless, I promise," he said, grinning at her. "But you aren't very observant. I've been following you for three blocks."

Diane ignored him and increased her pace. She had been living in the city long enough to have acquired a defensive mentality, particularly with men.

"Hey, slow down, I'm running out of breath."

Without thinking she looked at him and he laughed softly, a warm gurgling sound that threw her off balance.

"Thanks. All I want is five minutes of your time, and then I'll leave you alone."

The street was crowded with shoppers, businessmen, and tourists, an unlikely place for any sort of attack, but Diane was wary as she met his eyes.

"There, that's much better," he said. "I knew you'd have blue eyes. That's one of the reasons I followed you; I'm a sucker for blue eyes."

His own eyes were an intense, vibrant green that was at once startling and appealing.

"You're making me very nervous," she said.

"Why?"

"Because I don't make a habit of talking to strangers."

"That's probably smart, but this time it's okay. I'm completely reliable. I put on clean socks every day, I always pay my rent, and I've never been arrested."

A smile touched the corners of her mouth, and that seemed to be all the encouragement he needed. "How about a cool drink? I'm on the verge of a heat stroke."

"I don't think so. I have to get home."

"Just a quick one? If you'll settle for a Coke there's a coffee shop right across the street."

Diane hesitated. There was nothing sinister about him. He had a very open face, animated and expressive, and she didn't really have any friends in the city. "All right, but I only have a few minutes . . ."

He beamed at her. "Let's go, bright eyes."

The coffee shop was dark and narrow, squeezed between two office buildings. An unpleasant odor of stale cigarette smoke and the greasy residue of hundreds of hamburgers lingered in the air. The few men hunched over the counter had a downtrodden look, as if they had exhausted their supply of possibilities and were now consigned to the ranks of the defeated. Even the brassy blond waitress was lethargic, too bored to waste a smile on her customers.

"Obviously not one of the most gracious dining spots in the city," he said, leading her to a booth. "People put up with incredible crap just to live in Manhattan."

"But it's worth it—at least I think it is," Diane said. "I've only been here three months."

He looked at her thoughtfully, then smiled. "You're from the Midwest."

"Kansas originally, but I've been at school in Massachusetts for the last four years."

His eyes flickered with curiosity, but Diane fell silent, irritated by her compulsive need to babble.

"Why New York?"

She shrugged, then gave in to an impulse to share her excitement. "I plan to work in television. Actually I just got a job today."

"And that's why you were grinning like an idiot when I saw you coming out of the Preston Building."

The waitress shuffled over to their table and, while he ordered, Diane discreetly studied him. His nose was too large for his face, and his curly brown hair had already started to recede. The only word that came to mind was "homely," and yet he possessed enormous charm and an irresistible smile that had penetrated her defenses. She felt surprisingly at ease.

"All right, where were we?" he said.

"I was grinning . . . like an idiot."

His lively eyes momentarily clouded with confusion; then he laughed. "Sorry. I shouldn't have said that. But when you hang out with a struggling comedian you have to put up with a few rough edges."

"Are you really? A comedian, I mean?"

"That all depends on how you define the word. If we're talking dingy bars in Hoboken, I'm the next Charlie Chaplin, but the sad truth is, I have to wait on tables at Sardi's to keep from starving."

"There's nothing wrong with making a few compromises,"

she said softly, "as long as you never let yourself forget what it is you really want."

She tentatively met his gaze and was stunned by the understanding that immediately flowed between them.

"Who are you?" he said softly. "I feel like I've known you forever."

"Diane Henderson."

"Diane, I think we just bypassed months of trivial conversation."

She nodded, elated that he felt it too. "What's your name?"

"Joel Elliot. Will you have dinner with me tomorrow night?"

"I'd like that," she said simply.

He smiled again and, reaching across the table, took her hand. "What do you say we get out of this dump?"

The moment she entered her Chelsea apartment, Diane stripped off her clothes and plugged in a small fan that was virtually useless against such an onslaught of heat. Then, flopping on the sofa in her underwear, she allowed herself to think about Joel Elliot and their odd encounter. She had never experienced such an immediate connection. Their conversation as he had walked her to the bus stop had been so easy and familiar.

Late afternoon faded into evening, and the flickering neon lights of the bar across the street painted streaky patterns on the walls. As the encroaching darkness permeated her tiny living room, Diane became newly aware of her acute loneliness. Instead of celebrating her new job with friends in a brightly lit bar or restaurant, she was secluded in a dingy fourth-floor walk-up, starved for the sound of a human voice.

She considered calling her father, but he viewed long-distance calls as a frivolous extravagance, and his unspoken disapproval would dampen her mood even more. Then she thought of Rachel. It had been weeks since their last conversation, and yet she hesitated, remembering the unfamiliar strain that had underlain the frequent silences. Though they had pretended things were the same, Rick Conti had floated between them like a restless ghost.

After several minutes of indecision, Diane picked up the receiver. Rachel was her best friend. If the barrier between them had thickened to an impenetrable wall, she would try to break it down.

"Rache, it's me, Diane."

"I don't believe it! I've been thinking about you all day."

"Why?"

Rachel sighed. "I wanted to call you, but things have been so lousy here, I decided to wait awhile."

"What's wrong?"

"Living here, it's driving me crazy. My parents expect me to . . ."

"What?"

"Live the way they do. We fight over what I eat, where I go on Friday nights. They can't accept that I'm not who they raised me to be. The dutiful Jewish daughter."

Though Diane was relieved that this time there were no painful silences, she felt for her friend. Ever since Diane had known her, Rachel had struggled with her Orthodox upbringing. "Maybe you should talk to them, tell them how you feel."

"I have, but they don't want to hear it." Rachel paused, then changed the subject. "So what's happening with you? Is everything okay?"

"You mean . . ."

"Yeah."

"Sometimes I have trouble sleeping. You know . . . nightmares."

"So do I. Have you heard from Gussie or Helene?"

"I wrote to both of them, but I didn't get any answers."

"I'm not surprised." There was another silence; the awkwardness was creeping back. "Look, I have to go," Rachel said. "I'll call you in a few weeks."

"Sure."

Diane replaced the receiver before she realized she'd never even told Rachel about her new job. She stretched out on the tattered sofa, knowing it would be hours before she slept. She wondered if the fear would ever fade.

Ed Blake sat in his expensively decorated office assessing his losses. Now that Jordan Carr had hired a new secretary, Ed no longer had access to privileged information. It had been relatively simply to manipulate office politics when Julie

Rivers was hand-feeding him Carr's secrets. Now, without her help, he was at a distinct disadvantage.

Slumping back in his chair, he laid his hands flat on his desk, absently smoothing his thumb over a rough spot in his otherwise perfectly manicured nails. He wondered if it would be worth the considerable trouble to cultivate Carr's new girl. She was an unknown quantity, and there was a certain risk in approaching her. Julie had been an easy conquest, a young woman living far above her means, who appreciated an occasional dinner at an exclusive East Side restaurant or a pair of theater tickets. This Diane Henderson might not be quite so malleable. Much as he hated indecisiveness, he decided to proceed with extreme caution.

When Jordan Carr appeared in his doorway a few minutes later, Ed automatically adjusted his tie and raked his fingers through his sparse brown hair. "Morning, Jordan. I checked those tapes on the illegal gambling segment. You were right—the picture's a little grainy. I don't know how the hell that happened."

"We'll go over it later," Jordan said, frowning as if he, too, was dismayed by such an elementary error. He stared intently at Ed for a moment. Then a shutter seemed to come down over his eyes and he turned to introduce Diane.

"Ed, this is my new secretary, Diane Henderson." He turned to Diane. "This is Ed Blake, my assistant. He'll show you around the studio."

Ed stood and extended his hand, his smile somewhat condescending. "Glad to meet you, Diane. I think you'll be happy here. We treat our girls pretty well."

Diane managed a polite response, but her insides were churning. She had never experienced such an instantaneous animosity, a kind of bone-deep revulsion that she would have dismissed as impossible an hour ago. There was something oily and slick about Ed Blake, but there was also a cunning intelligence in his too-earnest eyes. She instinctively recognized him as a ruthless opportunist.

After a few minutes of stilted conversation, Jordan patted her shoulder and left her alone with Ed. She was uneasy, and Blake seemed to enjoy her discomfort, ignoring her as he stacked the papers scattered across his desk into an orderly pile. When he finished he finally looked at her. "How well do you know Jordan?"

Surprised, Diane returned his avid gaze. "Not at all. Why?"

He shrugged. "I thought maybe you were a family friend. It happens all the time here. Girls are hired just because they have a few connections."

"Well, that's not what happened with me. I saw the ad and applied for the job."

His expression was inscrutable as he walked around his desk and gripped her arm. "We might as well start with the file room. Eventually you'll need to become familiar with the filing system, but for now we'll just have a look."

They took the elevator to the ninth floor where the actual production work was done. Diane knew absolutely nothing about the technical aspects of television, but she listened attentively as Ed briefly described the filming, cutting, and editing of a videotape. His manner was abrupt, but he obviously possessed a great deal of expertise.

After two hours of touring the various labs and sound stages, he led her to the cafeteria. A few executive types were gathered at the far end of the room having a late breakfast, but most of the tables were unoccupied. Ed brought their coffee, then joined her at a table overlooking Fifty-eighth Street.

"Well, what do you think?"

"I have a lot to learn."

Laughing, he dug in his pocket for a cigarette. "Believe me, no one expects you to understand anything technical. The tour was just to give you a vague idea of what goes on here."

Annoyed by his superior attitude, Diane gulped a swallow of hot coffee, wincing as it scalded its way to her stomach. "I plan to study the whole production process."

"There's no need; you're only a secretary."

When she saw the thinly veiled hostility in his narrow eyes, Diane realized she had made a serious error. Jordan Carr had offered her subtle encouragement, but Ed Blake seemed to view her as a threat, a potential competitor. Disgusted with herself for allowing him such an unobstructed glimpse of her ambitions, she tried to divert him by staring out the window, letting their conversation lapse.

But Ed persisted. "What exactly are you looking for, Diane?"

This time she carefully considered her words before she spoke. "Right now I just want to learn enough to be a good secretary to Mr. Carr."

"And later?"

"I'm not sure."

"Do you have any idea how hard it is for a woman to get ahead in this business?"

She nodded, stirring her coffee, fixing her eyes on the little eddies left in the wake of the spoon.

"But you're not discouraged. That tells me how ambitious you are."

Unwilling to contradict him, Diane remained silent while he examined her face. His inspection made her jittery, suddenly conscious of her physical flaws and imperfections, and again she felt a surge of animosity.

Ed continued to stare, not at all disconcerted by her silence. After a time he said, "Be careful, Diane. Jordan's pretty inflexible. If he figures out what you have in mind, you'll be waiting in line for a government check."

Diane knew then that she had made a powerful enemy, but why had he used Jordan to threaten her instead of simply admitting his own obvious contempt for women? She had sensed an undercurrent of animosity between the two men, and now she wondered what kind of devious game Ed Blake was playing and how she could avoid becoming a casualty in a corporate power struggle.

By the time Diane arrived at Umberto's Clam House, Joel had already claimed an outdoor table and was sipping a glass of inexpensive red wine. When he saw her, he smiled. "Thank God, I was beginning to think I'd imagined you."

"I'm sorry, I had trouble finding the right train." She sat across from him, glancing around the dimly lit courtyard. "I like this. It feels like New York."

Grinning, he reached across the table and took her hand. "What does New York feel like?"

"Busy, exciting, too much to take in at once."

"And dirty and dangerous and . . . do you want to hear more?"

She shook her head. "Tell me about your audition."

His grin abruptly faded. "I was a flop, bright-eyes. Three

minutes into my act the club owner kicked my butt off the stage.''

He tried to mask his pain and humiliation behind a wobbly smile, but his green eyes were too eloquent to mask his dejection. ''So it's back to Hoboken,'' he said, still smiling. ''I guess my act needs more polish.''

''Maybe the owner just had an off day.''

Joel squeezed her hand. ''Don't be kind to me. I was lousy, I could feel myself losing it, but the harder I tried, the more I fucked up.''

''You must have been nervous.''

''Hell, I don't know.'' He looked at her, then motioned to the waiter. ''Enough about me. Let's order. Then you can tell me about your first day on the job.''

Afraid of draining his obviously limited resources, Diane insisted he order for both of them. His pale blue shirt, she had noticed, was frayed around the collar, and his cheap summer-weight slacks bagged at the knees. Clearly he was short of money, but somehow she knew he would resent it if she offered to buy her own dinner.

Once the waiter disappeared, Joel let go of her hand and leaned back in his chair. ''So how did it go?''

''Not too badly. I felt useless and stupid, but Mr. Carr went out of his way to help me.''

''So what went wrong?''

''How did you . . .''

''Your eyes—they're unhappy.''

Again Diane was stunned by the understanding that seemed to flow between them like an electric current and by how easy it was to open herself to him. ''Mr. Carr has a slimy assistant named Ed Blake. I foolishly let him see how much I want to move ahead in television.''

''Why the hell should he care?''

''Partly because I'm a woman—he clearly has a problem with ambitious women—but mostly, I think, because he has his own plans.''

''How much clout does he have?''

Her stomach muscles clenched. ''Plenty, and he's devious enough to cause trouble between Mr. Carr and me.''

''Then you'll have to learn to play his game and stay one

step ahead of him. This is the big city, bright-eyes. If you let him, he'll swallow you whole.''

His eyes were suddenly hard green points, cynical and cruel, and Diane experienced a moment of doubt. She wondered if she had misjudged Joel Elliot, if his warmth was only a veneer, but then he smiled and she relaxed. Joel was exactly what he appeared to be, a fascinating man who for some inexplicable reason seemed able to intuit her thoughts and feelings, a man worthy of her trust.

After weeks without any visitors, Diane was startled by the unfamiliar sound of her own doorbell. As she crossed the living room to the narrow foyer, she had visions of a violent maniac lurking in the shadows of the hallway. Then she peered through the peephole and gasped when she saw the intense brown eyes of the Hyannis police chief, Ralph Edwards.

Shocked, she stared at him, certain that he had come to arrest her.

"Miss Henderson, are you in there? Please open the door."

Diane froze for a moment. Then, instinctively responding to the authority in his voice, she slowly opened the door.

"Hello, Miss Henderson," he said. "I don't know if you remember me. I'm Chief Edwards from the Hyannis Police Department. I'd like to ask you a few questions."

Diane mutely stared at him. Although there was nothing menacing about his genial smile, waves of panic engulfed her. She thought she might strangle on the knot of fear clogging her throat.

"Are you all right, Miss Henderson?" he said. "I didn't mean to alarm you."

"I . . . I was just surprised to see you. Please come in."

As Edwards followed her into the living room, Diane struggled to compose herself. Obviously he had no intention of arresting her—not unless she lost control and blurted out the truth.

"Do you mind if I sit down?" he said. "It's been a long day."

"No, of course not."

She watched him sit in a rickety armchair and fish in his pocket for a battered notebook. On the surface he looked like a country bumpkin visiting the city for the first time, harmless and naive, but she knew that was just a clever ruse. Ralph Edwards was anything but naive.

Diane eased herself down on the sagging sofa and waited for him to begin. He seemed lost in thought until finally he looked at her and said, "Rick Conti is still missing. I know we've been over this before, but I'd like you to tell me exactly what happened the night he disappeared."

"I'm not sure I remember *exactly* what happened. I mean, it was three months ago. I might have forgotten something."

He smiled affably. "Just do the best you can."

Diane stifled an impulse to shrink away from his probing gaze. She tried to recall the precise details of her statement, but her mind was like an attic cluttered by too many versions of the tragedy. Which were real? Which were lies? She was no longer certain.

After a long silence she stumbled through what she hoped was an accurate version of her original story. She glanced frequently at Edwards, but his weathered face remained impassive. When she finished, he said, "What makes you so sure Conti was drunk?"

"Well, he . . . he drank a lot of champagne, and he seemed wobbly . . . disoriented."

"Do you know why he went for a walk on the beach in the middle of the night?"

She felt trapped. "Maybe he was trying to sober up?"

"Or maybe he left the house because of an argument," Edwards said. "Was there an argument, Miss Henderson?"

Inhaling sharply, Diane shook her head. "No. No argument."

Edwards leaned forward in his chair, his eyes seeming to bore holes in her flesh. "Some of the hired help claimed that Brenda Galloway and Rick Conti fought a lot. Is that true?"

"I . . . I don't know." Her voice quavered. "We were only there one night. I never saw them fight."

Still fixing her with his relentless stare, Edwards asked softly, "Why are you so nervous, Miss Henderson?"

"I'm not. I . . . ." Then, realizing it was futile to deny that she was nervous, she said, "I've never been involved in anything like this. . . . With the police, I mean."

He continued to study her, and she sensed that he was weighing her words, critically examining them for a flaw that would brand her a liar. At last he said, "Miss Henderson, what do you think happened to Rick Conti?"

"I don't know," she whispered. "I assume he drowned."

Edwards shook his head. "Not likely. Most drowning victims eventually wash up on the beach."

"Then he . . . he must have run off or something."

There was a protracted silence. Then suddenly Edwards sighed and extricated himself from the chair.

"All right, Miss Henderson. I appreciate your cooperation. Please contact me if you think of anything else."

Feeling boneless and rubbery, Diane stumbled to her feet and escorted him to the door, hardly daring to breathe until he became an indistinct shadow in the hall. Then as relief washed over her, she began to shake uncontrollably.

She was safe for now, but how long would it be before Edwards returned to interrogate her again, his piercing eyes paring away her defenses and peering directly into her soul.

Two days later Edwards checked out of his Manhattan hotel and headed back to Hyannis. Normally the forced inactivity of such a long ride would have driven him crazy, but he had too much on his mind to feel claustrophobic. The wall of silence surrounding the Conti case was finally showing some signs of weakness—nothing conclusive, just a few fissures in an otherwise impenetrable facade.

A thin smile creased his leathery face as he recalled his interviews with Rachel Weiss and Diane Henderson. On the surface their stories remained essentially the same, but this time he had picked up on a few inconsistencies. The Weiss woman had insisted that Conti was fairly sober when he left the beach house. More important, she had also admitted that there might have been some friction between Conti and Brenda Galloway—an admission that led to all sorts of intriguing possibilities. Not enough to help him solve the case but certainly a reason to continue the investigation.

As he guided his car through the tollgate and merged with the heavy northbound traffic on the Connecticut Turnpike, Edwards mentally debated his next move. A visit to Augusta Tremain—the one they called Gussie—was probably the most logical step, but he was too cautious to risk the wrath of a U.S. senator. Only a fool would tangle with a powerful man like

Tremain without any concrete evidence to back him up, and Edwards was no fool.

That left the elusive Helene Galloway. At first the idea of flying to California to interview her seemed absurd, but the more he thought about it, the more plausible it became. Though he was fairly certain the town councilmen would never agree to pay for the trip without a body or at least a few pieces of hard evidence, they did owe him a sizable chunk of vacation time. And he could always cut expenses by bunking in with Mick Travis once he arrived in Los Angeles.

Suddenly Edwards felt a tingle of anticipation. After years of investigating countless petty crimes, he finally had a case that would challenge his abilities as a cop. Finding Rick Conti would be the pinnacle of his career.

CHAPTER

Five

STILL DISTURBED BY MEMORIES OF HER ENCOUNTER WITH CHIEF EDWARDS, Rachel stood on the steps of Butler Hall at Columbia University handing out anti-war leaflets. Suddenly she became aware of a lanky blond man sitting on the steps eating his lunch, his eyes riveted on a textbook. She had seen him there before, always immersed in his studies, apparently unconcerned with the tension between the protesters and the minority of students who had chosen to ignore the campus rebellion.

It was strange, but she now found herself looking for him the moment she arrived at Butler Hall each day. He had an interesting face, an angular bone structure that was softened by a sprig of freckles across his nose. His eyes were clear blue and very direct. Usually she was content simply to enjoy his silent companionship, but today she decided to approach him.

He glanced up at her as she sat on the step beside him. "Are you going to the peace rally this afternoon?" she said.

He shook his head and began to peel an orange.

"Why not?"

"I just signed on with the Humphrey campaign."

Rachel cringed. It had taken only one terse sentence to establish them as adversaries. "You mean you actually support the war?"

"It's not that simple. Nobody wants war, but we have a commitment to help those people. If we pull out, the Vietcong will overrun their country, their whole way of life."

Groaning, Rachel rummaged in her purse for a crumpled pack of cigarettes. "That's nothing but government propaganda, an excuse to justify what we're doing over there."

He reached into his pocket for a gold lighter, then smiled as

47

he lit her cigarette. "What do you say we talk about something else? I'm not a very good candidate for conversion."

Rachel was disarmed by his smile. It glowed all the way to his eyes, warm and inviting. She tried to look away, but an odd curiosity kept her gaze locked on his face. "Then we have nothing to talk about."

"Sure we do. You're a student here, right? What are you studying?"

"Education. I'm working on my master's."

He nodded, passing her a section of his orange. She held it in her palm, staring at it as if he had just offered her thirty pieces of silver. Then, feeling ridiculous, she popped it into her mouth.

"You were an easy conquest," he said, grinning. "Never compromise the cause by taking sustenance from the enemy."

Rachel's head snapped up. "How did you know what I was thinking?"

"It was written all over your face."

The orange was sweet and wet in her mouth and as she savored the taste, she covertly watched him, surprised at how much she was enjoying their peculiar conversation. She had never been especially comfortable with men; her two intimate relationships had been more cerebral than passionate. Puzzled that he had evoked thoughts of past lovers, she slid across the step, increasing the distance between them.

"I was only teasing," he said. "Here. Have another piece of orange."

This time she accepted readily. "I've seen you here before. This is a strange place to eat lunch."

"Not really. I like being outside. It clears my head."

Again she avidly studied him. He seemed a bit old to be a student, and unlike the others at Columbia, he was wearing an expensive-looking double-breasted gray suit. "Are you a professor?"

He smiled and shook his head. "What gave you that idea?"

"Your clothes."

"I'm in my last year of law school. Suits are required for moot court."

"So you're going to be an establishment lawyer. That explains a lot."

"Like what?"

"Like why you're working for Hubert Humphrey, why you support an immoral war. You want a chance at all those big government bucks."

His body visibly tensed. "Money has nothing to do with the way I feel about the war, not a goddam thing."

Rachel laughed derisively. "Then why crawl into bed with killers?"

"Because I spent two years in 'Nam." His eyes blazed with anger, but there was something more, a soul-wrenching anguish. "I saw it firsthand, lady. I saw the Cong wipe out whole families. I saw little kids tossing fucking grenades. I saw things you can't imagine, so save your preaching for your pacifist friends. I'm not interested."

Stunned by his outburst, Rachel shivered in the warm afternoon sun. She felt a sudden urge to touch him, to absorb some of his pain. Suddenly they were no longer antagonists; they were simply two human beings caught in a moment of naked emotion. Tentatively she touched his hand. "I'm sorry. I had no idea you were over there."

He raked his fingers through his thick blond hair, clearly bewildered by his outburst. "Forget it. I had no right to strike out at you like that."

They lapsed into silence, and Rachel began to relax. After a while he said, "What's your name?"

"Rachel Weiss."

Her hand still rested in his palm, and he squeezed her fingers in an approximation of a handshake. "I'm Brian McDonald."

The name struck an immediate chord, evoking a clear picture of a superior court judge known for his law-and-order stance. "Any relation to Cleatus McDonald?"

"My uncle."

He squared his shoulders as if to brace himself for another attack, but Rachel bit back her sarcastic reply, reluctant to sever their tenuous bond. "So the law's a family tradition, then?"

"In a way," he said, relaxing his posture. "My father and two of my brothers are cops. I thought about joining the force, but after 'Nam I wanted something more. I've already signed on with the Manhattan D.A."

Rachel sucked in a mouthful of air, imagining what it would be like to face Brian McDonald in a courtroom after being publicly accused of conspiring to conceal a murder.

"What's the matter? You look a little pale."

She blinked in an attempt to clear away the disturbing vision. "I just had a weird thought. Nothing important."

"I figured maybe it was a sudden aversion to a future assistant D.A."

Smiling weakly, Rachel shook her head, then glanced at her watch and sprang to her feet. "I have to go. It's almost time for the rally."

Brian looked up, raising his hand to shield his eyes from the sun. "Same place tomorrow?"

She felt suddenly threatened by the vitality of his smile, and by the timbre of his deep male voice. "That's not a good idea."

His eyes reflected a shadow of disappointment, but he seemed to understand and accept her rejection. "Well, I enjoyed talking to you, Rachel Weiss. Maybe we'll run into each other on campus sometime."

"Sure, see you around."

As she hurried down the steps, Rachel noticed a group of students gathered in front of Low Library. Even from a distance she could feel the vibrations of their discontent. Many of the signs they carried were crude and gory, vehement expressions of their contempt for a government engaged in a war they despised. Their irate voices shattered the quiet of the sunny afternoon.

By the time Rachel reached the fringes of the crowd, the speaker had already assumed his position at the microphone. Ironically, his subdued manner seemed to increase the belligerence of the protesters. As he delivered his fluent indictment of the war, a gripping psychic energy surged through the crowd feeding the tension. Then suddenly a young black man shoved the speaker aside.

"Listen up, brothers and sisters," he shouted. "You belong with your own people."

A black woman beside Rachel raised her fist in the air, fervently chanting her support as the man paused to look out over the crowd. His face was lean and hard, radiating an almost fanatic passion.

"You hear me now. No more kissing white ass. No more playing games with the man. We want power—black power." Several white students began to protest, and the speaker struggled to regain control of his audience. Rachel turned to the woman beside her. "Who's he?"

"Cal Hawkins. He organized the Black Brotherhood."

Rachel nodded, recognizing the familiar name. Cal Hawkins had been a medical student until he became disillusioned with the Great Society and left Columbia to agitate for racial equality. His Black Brotherhood operated out of a storefront in Harlem, providing essential services to the community while he prepared for revolution.

As the crowed stilled, Hawkins resumed his speech: "Today I made a promise to some kids in Harlem. I promised them a school—a school where they can learn about black pride, a school where the teachers care if they learn to read and write. But I need your help. I need money to buy books. I need brothers and sisters to teach our kids. I need black solidarity."

A rumble of approval swept through the crowd as the students fell under the spell of his magnetic voice.

"Take a look beyond this campus," Hawkins commanded, waving a hand toward Harlem. "Those are your people. Their poverty is your poverty, their hunger your hunger. As long as one black man cries out for justice, none of us are free."

When his speech ended, a few black men passed among the students asking for donations. Rachel tossed a ten dollar bill into the bucket, then pushed her way through the crowd until she reached Hawkins's side.

When Cal Hawkins met her eyes, Rachel felt a panic that electrified every nerve in her body. His assessing gaze seemed to penetrate her thoughts, reducing her to a terrifying state of mental nakedness. Their eyes remained locked until he spoke in a low menacing voice. "What can I do for you?"

"I want to help out at your school."

"Forget it."

He started to turn away and Rachel realized she had been arbitrarily dismissed. "I came to volunteer," she said quickly. "I'm a licensed teacher."

He faced her again, listening.

"I believe in what you're doing," she said.

He stared at her intently, then shook his head. "You can believe all you want, but you'll never understand what it means to be black in a racist white country."

"Maybe not, but right now you need my help. I'm a damn good teacher," she pressed on, ignoring the lingering crowd.

Hawkins smiled. "Where do you get your balls, lady?"

"You think you need balls to have a brain?"

"You're a stubborn woman."

She nodded.

"Come to the Brotherhood headquarters tomorrow morning at nine. You can make your pitch to the committee."

Rachel smiled and held out her hand, certain she had found a way to contribute to the future—and maybe atone for the sins of her past.

CHAPTER
Six

ELIZABETH TREMAIN SAT ON THE PATIO OF HER ELEGANT GEORGETOWN home sipping her morning coffee. A light September breeze ruffled the abundant displays of mums and late-blooming roses surrounding the patio, but she was much too preoccupied with the details of her husband's reelection campaign to notice the exquisite fragrance of the flowers. She seldom paid attention to such mundane pleasures. Elizabeth had been bred for only one purpose—to assist her carefully chosen mate in navigating the complex waters of an affluent and privileged society—and she devoted her life to excelling at her assigned role.

An extraordinarily beautiful woman, Elizabeth placed tremendous value on her physical appearance. She stoically endured a rigid exercise regimen to protect her slim body from the ravages of a life-style fraught with excesses. When her natural blond hair began to fade, she avoided the brassy shades of yellow common to middle-aged women and chose a soft silver-gray that accentuated her flawless complexion. Her wardrobe was expensive but simple, each garment carefully chosen to enhance and flatter. Everything about Elizabeth Tremain spoke of old money.

When the sound of light footsteps disturbed her concentration, Elizabeth looked up and was surprised to see Gussie standing at the edge of the patio, cradling a cup of coffee in her hands. "What are you doing up so early?"

Gussie joined her at the wrought-iron table. "I didn't sleep well again."

Frowning, Elizabeth tapped her pen on her saucer in a quick rhythm that betrayed her impatience. Gussie's chronic discontent had become a vague worry lurking on the fringes of her

53

unconscious, popping up at inopportune moments to distract her. "Tell me what's wrong."

"I feel useless. I don't want to spend the rest of my life having lunch. I want to get a job."

Elizabeth's frown intensified, carving a slight arch between her brows. "What sort of job? It would have to be something suitable, you know."

"I have no idea, but I'm sure my degree from Brentwood qualifies me to do more than work on your inane committees."

The unfamiliar contempt in her voice both annoyed and troubled Elizabeth. Gussie had always been compliant and eager to please, but lately her mild rebellion had created a schism in their normally harmonious relationship. "Exactly what do you have in mind?"

"I thought maybe . . . There's an opening for a research assistant in the poli sci department at Georgetown University."

"That's totally inappropriate. Suppose you were asked to investigate your father? Can you imagine how the press would react?"

Gussie sighed. "Then I'll find something else, but I can't abide another day of boredom."

"Why don't I talk to your father? I'm sure he can—"

"What?" Robert Tremain crossed the patio and eased himself into a chair, taking care not to wrinkle his blue linen suit. "What do you have me doing now?"

Elizabeth smiled at her husband, pleased as always by his distinctive good looks. Tall and broad-shouldered, his body was still lean and trim. His steel-gray hair had been artfully styled to conceal the small bald spot at the crown of his head, and his stunning blue eyes were direct and sincere. He had cultivated the perfect public persona, an image of competence and stability.

"I thought you might help Augusta find a suitable job."

Robert turned to Gussie, his lack of enthusiasm evident in his tightly compressed smile. "Aren't you happy working with your mother on my reelection campaign?"

Forced to defend herself twice within the space of just a few minutes, Gussie shifted in her chair, anxiously fingering her opal ring. "I want a job of my own."

"It's not that simple, Augusta. Any position you take will open you up to public scrutiny. If you do a less than creditable job, I'll be expected to defend you and to explain your failure."

Gussie flushed. "I appreciate your confidence."

"That's not what your father meant at all, dear," Elizabeth said quickly. "But we do have to be careful. You know how the press distorts the truth."

"Why should the press or anyone else care if I have a job?"

Robert started to respond, but Elizabeth placed a restraining hand on his wrist. "You're right. The press is hardly the issue here. I'm much more concerned about you. If you're unhappy, then we have to do something about it. What do you suggest, Robert?"

The senator's annoyance was almost palpable. "I'll ask around," he said stiffly. "In the meantime you can make yourself useful at campaign headquarters."

Gussie agreed, but Elizabeth noticed the flash of resentment in her eyes and resolved to find her an appropriate job before her discontent had an opportunity to fester. In an election year there was no room for even the slightest hint of scandal.

A week later, Gussie found herself cataloging bits and pieces of Americana at the Smithsonian Institution. The job was incredibly tedious, and her supervisor, a tyrannical man, went out of his way to point out her deficiencies. Her dream of a stimulating career seemed totally out of reach, but at least she was free of the endless charity luncheons and fashion shows. The staff of the Smithsonian included many people her own age, so she now had a chance to establish a social life apart from her mother—and she was too busy to dwell on the death of Rick Conti.

The tragedy had been creeping in and out of her thoughts all summer, distracting her at odd moments, turning her dreams into grisly nightmares. But now she had a job and some new friends to occupy her mind.

One young woman particularly appealed to Gussie. Alice Monroe was a secretary from an unpretentious middle-class family, not the type Gussie normally would have associated with. But there was something about Alice and her hunger for adventure that fascinated Gussie, and the two women began taking lunch hours together. Alice had a ready laugh and an irreverent sense of humor that reminded Gussie of Rachel

Weiss. She offered an intriguing respite from Elizabeth's rigid social conventions.

One day during their afternoon coffee break, Alice dragged Gussie to the cafeteria, her face flushed with excitement. "What are you doing tonight?"

"Nothing special. Why?"

"Some of my friends are getting together at Harvey's after work. Why don't you come along?"

Gussie knew all about Harvey's, the noisy singles bar that catered to young professionals. She had driven past it several times, always curious but too inhibited to walk through the heavy oak doors alone. "Why would I want to go to a pickup place?" she said, afraid to admit even to herself how much the idea appealed to her.

Alice gulped a mouthful of Coke directly from the can. "Because it's fun . . . hordes of gorgeous rich men on the make."

"Have you ever been there?"

"Sure. That's where I met Kip, the guy I lived with last summer."

"You *lived* with a *man*?"

Alice laughed. "It's no big deal."

"What happened to him?"

"Nothing. I just got restless. I'm too young to get hung up on one guy."

"But what about . . . I mean, you slept with him?"

Again Alice laughed in a way that left Gussie feeling like an outsider. "Sure. I've slept with lots of men. Wake up, Gussie. It's a new world out there."

A new world—how often had she heard those same words from Rachel? Often enough to know that they expressed only a portion of the truth. Not all women were able to toss their fears aside so easily. Freedom was scary. It left you on your own without any clear rules. It made you vulnerable to mistakes that might irrevocably alter the rest of your life. Freedom meant choices, and choices were risky.

Alice waved her hand in front of Gussie's face. "Hey, are you listening?"

Startled, Gussie realized that Alice must have been rattling on for some time without her. "I'm sorry. What were you saying?"

"I was trying to persuade you to stop living like a nun. Come with us tonight. It'll be great."

"What happens if you meet someone? I'll feel ridiculous sitting there by myself."

"I won't leave you alone, I promise."

"All right," Gussie said slowly, almost grudgingly. "But if you take off with some man, I'll never forgive you."

Grinning, Alice pitched her empty can into the trash and slid her chair away from the table. "Who knows? Maybe you'll end up taking off on me."

"That's one of the stupidest things you've ever said. I'm not interested in meeting a man. Not at a bar, anyway."

Harvey's had a rather unimpressive history. For years it had been a nondescript watering hole frequented by harried government employees wanting a quick drink on the way home from work—an unassuming place with comfortable leather booths and a long oak bar. Then it was accidentally discovered by a few upwardly mobile attorneys, and within weeks Harvey's became the favorite haunt of Washington's young professionals.

The amazed owner thoroughly appreciated the whimsical stroke of fate that had turned his modest bar into a sensation, but instead of squandering his profits on renovations, he left the place exactly as it was. The brass railings around the bar were perpetually tarnished, the ancient tin ceiling buckled slightly in the center, and the noticeable hump in the dance floor challenged the dexterity of the dancers. Only the updated record collection in the jukebox reflected prosperity.

Gussie was disappointed in her first glimpse at the interior of Harvey's, but after a few minutes she succumbed to the hum of anticipation in the air. Everyone seemed to be up, shouting greetings to old friends, eyeing new conquests. The men were well dressed and successful-looking, obviously interested in connecting with a compatible woman.

Ignoring the booths along the wall, Alice nudged Gussie toward the bar, whispering that it was much easier to attract a man if you were easily accessible. Gussie frowned at her, but she followed willingly, afraid of being left alone.

While they waited in line to order drinks, Gussie was only mildly uncomfortable, but once she held a vodka gimlet in her hands, she began to feel conspicuous, as if she were inviting some nameless man to approach her. The muscles around her mouth tensed, making her appear grim and prudish.

"Ease up, will you?" Alice said. "You're just nervous about meeting someone. Once you dance a few times you'll feel better."

Until that moment Gussie had been unaware of the crowded dance floor to the rear of the bar, but as she saw several couples sensuously moving to the slow rhythm of the music, her stomach began to ache. There was something flagrantly sexual about the way their bodies fit tightly together, as if their dancing were merely a prelude to other, more intimate acts. On one level she found it obscene, but on another more primitive level she was aroused. She felt an awakening jolt somewhere deep inside her, a lascivious curiosity that shocked her. How would it feel to have a strange man slide his hands over her hips, pressing her closer? She imagined the sensation and then, disgusted by such prurient thoughts, looked away.

Most of Alice's friends were already attached to men and wore smug smiles that proclaimed their relief at having been rescued from the ranks of the undesirable. As Gussie watched them possessively guard their newly acquired prizes, it occurred to her that a woman had a great deal to lose at a place like Harvey's. What was the price of failing to attract a man? A battered ego? Would she have to endure the pity of her friends, their well-meaning but humiliating assurances, and the devastating knowledge that she was somehow deficient? A few minutes in the arms of a man hardly seemed worth such degradation.

"I'm leaving," she said, putting her untouched drink on the bar and turning to Alice. "See you in the morning."

Alice tugged at her sleeve. "You're not going anywhere. Things are just warming up. Have another drink."

Gussie shook her head and began to elbow her way through the noisy crowd, but suddenly there was a man blocking her path, gently touching her shoulder. "Please don't leave. We haven't danced yet."

Perhaps it was his slight accent or his deeply resonant voice, but something made Gussie pause to look at him. "I don't feel like dancing."

"Then let me buy you a drink. Come, we'll find an empty booth."

His grip tightened on her shoulder as he led her to a booth. Once they were seated, he smiled and beckoned to the waitress. "What would you like?"

"I . . . a vodka gimlet."

While he ordered, Gussie admonished herself for being so easily manipulated, but instead of simply getting up and walking away, she sat there staring at him.

He remained silent for the few minutes it took the waitress to return with their drinks, and Gussie couldn't stop herself from staring. He had an interesting face, dark olive skin and sharply carved features that might have been harsh without the mitigating softness of his smile. His lips were full, and his teeth seemed incredibly white against his bronze complexion. He looked foreign, slightly mysterious. Even his black silk suit contributed to the illusion of a dashing but dangerous man.

After he paid the waitress, he focused his full attention on Gussie. "Tell me why you were in such a hurry to leave."

"I don't like this place."

Amusement flickered in the depths of his black eyes. "You've never been here before?"

Shaking her head, Gussie took a sip of her drink, unaccountably hurt by the realization that he was laughing at her. "I have better things to do with my time."

"Then I consider myself very lucky."

Puzzled, she glanced at him.

"If you hadn't come here tonight our paths might never have crossed."

He was too smooth, she thought, too confident. "Is that your standard line?"

He closed his fingers around her hand. "Would you believe this is my first time here, too?"

"Probably not."

"It's the truth. I was having a drink with a business associate when I noticed you at the bar. Until then I had no intention of approaching a woman."

Gussie shrugged. "Am I supposed to be flattered?"

"Not at all. I was just trying to make you understand that I'm not a barroom Romeo. I like women too much to enjoy seeing them degraded this way."

For some odd reason Gussie believed him, and her hostility diminished. "It *is* demeaning. That's why I was in such a hurry to leave."

"Do you feel more comfortable now?"

She nodded, and he smiled again.

"Comfortable enough to tell me your name?"

"Augusta Tremain. Most people call me Gussie."

"Gussie, I like that. I'm Tony De Costa."

His accent intrigued her; it was so slight, and yet it added an almost musical quality to his voice. "Where are you from?"

"I was born in Italy, but I spent most of my childhood commuting between New York and Venice."

"Why?"

"My family has extensive business interests in this country, and my father wanted me to become familiar with the entire operation at an early age."

Gussie averted her face, wondering just what the family business was and feeling vaguely guilty for being curious.

"Will you dance with me?" He stood and held out his hand.

"All right, I'd like that."

The dance floor was dark and intimate. Tony held her in a close embrace, and it occurred to her that she was way out of her element. Tony De Costa was no fumbling college boy who would be satisfied with an hour of petting in his car. Tony De Costa was a virile man who would just naturally assume she was interested in a sexual relationship. The thought simultaneously terrified and excited her.

They danced for what seemed like hours. Tony occasionally whispered something in her ear, but mostly they remained silent, concentrating on the feel of their bodies moving together in an erotic rhythm. Until tonight Gussie had experienced only a mild awareness of herself as a woman, but now she felt an inner blossoming, a visceral longing that raged to be assuaged. Her face grew flushed, her breathing labored and shallow. She had to get away from Tony De Costa before she committed an unthinkable indiscretion.

"I have to leave now," she said abruptly.

"Have dinner with me."

"No, thank you. My parents are expecting me."

"Tomorrow, then."

"I don't know. Maybe."

"Meet me at Antonio's."

Gussie knew she would be inviting disaster if she saw him again. The potent physical attraction between them was dangerous, and her parents would be horrified if they discovered she was dating what they called an immigrant, especially an Italian who might have all sorts of unsavory connections. But in spite of the numerous complications, she wanted to have dinner with him.

"All right. What time?"

"Seven."

She disentangled herself from his embrace and smiled faintly. "I'll see you then."

He nodded, and as she made her way to the door, she felt his eyes following her, and again she reminded herself that her parents would consider Tony De Costa totally unsuitable.

A month later Gussie was still seeing Tony De Costa on a regular basis, dining at the swankiest restaurants and then dancing until the early-morning hours at one of the exclusive private clubs in Georgetown. Each night their kisses became more urgent, the heat of their bodies more intense until Gussie ached with wanting him. Yet each night she denied her hunger and returned to her bedroom alone.

She would lie awake for hours, her body crying out for release while her mind coolly insisted on dredging up an endless list of reasons why their relationship would never work. Her parents were one obstacle. They had no idea she was involved with Tony, and it bothered her that her deceit was becoming almost second nature. The imaginary law student she had manufactured to explain her late nights had a limited life expectancy. Eventually Elizabeth would demand to meet him to gauge his suitability, and then Gussie would be forced either to compound her lies or to introduce Tony to her parents. And the thought of subjecting herself to their vehement disapproval was more than she could contemplate.

It was ironic that while Gussie found Tony's European charm and polish attractive, she also viewed those same attributes through the critical eyes of her parents—as reminders of his "inferior" origins and "peasant" roots. Her parents would be suspicious of his olive skin and everything it represented, but Gussie was totally infatuated with him, an infatuation that went well beyond a transitory sexual interest. For the first time in her life, she was indulging in impossible fantasies, tenuously applying the word "love" to the unfamiliar feelings that threatened to overwhelm her.

She spent hours searching for some sort of compromise, a temporary solution that would appease her parents and allow her to continue seeing Tony. But the problem seemed insurmountable, and she decided to go on with her schizophrenic existence until she was discovered. Then circumstances would force her to make a decision.

Preoccupied with her thoughts, Gussie was rudely jarred back to reality when her cab lurched to a stop at Washington National Airport. As she paid the driver, she glanced out the window at the gray horizon, wondering if the weather in New York was equally dismal. All week she had been anticipating her flight on the De Costa company jet and a day in the city with Tony, but the bleak sky and steady rain had dampened her enthusiasm. Even the prospect of having lunch with Diane and Rachel failed to elevate her mood.

Tony was waiting just inside the terminal, his dark hair ruffled by the wind, droplets of rain glistening on his cheeks. He looked incredibly handsome, and Gussie shivered when he drew her against his chest and kissed her.

"Even in the rain you're beautiful," he whispered.

Totally inept at the language of love, Gussie blushed profusely.

"Why do you blush when I compliment you?"

"It makes me uneasy."

He seemed on the verge of saying something, but after a momentary pause, he looped her arm through his and led her down the long corridor reserved for private planes.

They boarded immediately, assisted by a steward who treated Tony with deference. The interior of the plane resembled a suite in a luxury hotel—several plush chairs and sofas upholstered in varying shades of pale blue and a bedroom at the rear of the cabin done in the same calming colors. Everything had been designed to cater to the comfort of the passengers, with no apparent concessions to cost, and Gussie was awed by the elegance. Her only experience with private planes had been a few trips on government jets, which tended to be utilitarian rather than lavish. She had never even imagined such extravagance was possible on a plane.

The moment they were airborne the steward served them drinks and canapés, then disappeared. Tony spread a toast point with caviar and passed it to Gussie, but she shook her head.

"The weather seems to be getting worse," she said. "I hope we won't have any trouble getting back tonight."

"We can always stay over in New York."

"No, I have to get home. My parents have no idea where I am."

Frowning, Tony met her eyes. "Why haven't you told them about us?"

Gussie squirmed. "I've been waiting for the right time. It just hadn't come up."

His frown deepened, creasing the flesh between his brows. "Are you afraid they'll object to me because I'm an Italian?"

"No, I . . . They're just involved in the campaign right now. I'll tell them after the election."

"I'm too old to play these games, Gussie, and I care for you too much to sneak around like a teenager. I want to meet your family."

Gussie felt weak as she drew a mental picture of a meeting between her parents and Tony. He had accurately perceived the truth: Robert Tremain would never accept an Italian immigrant as a prospective son-in-law. His ethnic tolerance was limited solely to public occasions. In the privacy of his own home he seemed to derive perverse pleasure from using words like "wop" and "nigger." The fact that Tony controlled a vast importing business would mean nothing to Robert Tremain.

Then there was her mother. Elizabeth would be appalled, mortified, to learn that her daughter was associating with such a socially undesirable man. After taking to her bed with a migraine for a few hours, she would emerge like affronted royalty, her ice-cold stare capable of wilting Gussie in her tracks.

Clearly a meeting was impossible, but Gussie was not yet ready to endanger her relationship with Tony by being honest. Instead she looked up at him, her large green eyes deceptively innocent. "Please, just give me a few more weeks. They're very protective; I need to prepare them."

Sighing, he reached for her hand and smoothed his thumb over her wrist. "A few weeks, no more."

Gussie offered him a radiant smile, then leaned back and closed her eyes, her heart pounding an erratic tattoo.

Rachel and Diane were already seated when Gussie arrived at the Café des Artistes. She had insisted on the pricey restaurant, hoping the ambience would encourage Rachel to behave sedately, but as she looked around at the Christy murals and the romantic thirties decor, she decided she had probably overdone it. Even Diane, who fit in almost anywhere, looked out of place. But it was too late to alter their plans. Plastering an artificial smile on her face, Gussie followed the maître d' to the table.

"It's about time," Rachel said. "Do you know what a drink costs in this place?"

"You could have waited in the lobby."

"For an hour?"

Gussie shrugged. "The traffic coming in from La Guardia was terrible."

Always the peacemaker, Diane squeezed her hand. "I'm glad you're here. I've missed you."

Then, as if they had exhausted their supply of conversation, they descended into an unnatural silence. Gussie picked up her menu while Diane and Rachel sipped their drinks. It was several minutes before Rachel said, "Has anyone heard from Helene?"

"I've written three times, but she hasn't answered," Diane said.

Gussie feigned an interest in the menu, but Rachel persisted. "What about you?"

"Once, a few weeks ago. I called her. She was . . ."

"What?"

"Incoherent. Drunk, I think."

"Oh, God," Rachel said. "What did she say?"

"Not much. Brenda's still in Spain. She's involved with a Spanish count and plans to stay away indefinitely."

"Poor Helene," Diane said. "Is she working?"

"I don't know. We never got that far. She was barely able to talk, and it was only three o'clock in the afternoon."

Rachel swallowed the rest of her drink, then lit a cigarette. "I wish there was something we could do."

"We're not her guardians," Gussie said abruptly. "And besides she's three thousand miles away."

"So we just let her drink herself to death? How can you be so cold?"

"I'm not cold," Gussie said, feeling hurt. "I'm just mature enough to realize I can't save the world."

Diane audibly cleared her throat. "This arguing isn't helping Helene. I'll call her. Maybe I can get through to her."

"You'll be wasting your time," Gussie said. "Helene needs a psychiatrist. We always knew she had problems."

Again they lapsed into silence, and again it was Rachel who finally spoke. "She would have been all right . . . but she can't handle what happened."

Gussie gripped the stem of her water glass, fighting to repress her memories of Rick Conti. "I thought we agreed not to talk about that."

"I can't help it. I think about it all the time," Rachel said. "And I still can't believe Chief Edwards never came to see you. He must have been afraid of your father."

"Thank God," Gussie said. "Now can we please change the subject?"

The waiter appeared to take their order, and after that the conversation centered on their jobs and the changes in their lives since they had last been together. Gradually their restraint vanished in the glow of the wine and the gourmet food.

"So stop holding out on us," Rachel said. "Who's this guy with the private jet?"

"Just a friend."

"Some friend. He has you grinning like a cat in heat."

Gussie lowered her eyes, repelled by such crudeness, but then she wondered if she might be giving off some sort of scent, like an animal in dire need of mounting. "That's disgusting."

Rachel laughed, then slouched back in her chair as the waiter poured another glass of wine. "Come on, Gussie. Tell us about him."

"There's nothing to tell. He's a businessman I met last month. We've been seeing each other, but I'm certainly not serious about him."

"Are you spending the night in the city?" Diane asked, grinning.

"Of course not. He had a business meeting in town, and he invited me to come along to do some shopping. We're flying home after dinner."

Diane nodded. "What's he like?"

After a long hesitation, Gussie mumbled, "He's an Italian immigrant."

Rachel immediately tensed. "So what?"

"My parents would have a fit if they knew I was dating him. It's an impossible situation."

"You mean Senator Tremain has a thing against Italians?" Rachel said.

Gussie realized what she had been implying and quickly withdrew. "Why are you interrogating me? I already told you, there's nothing serious between us." Then, glancing at her watch, she picked up the check. "I have to go. I'm meeting Tony at Bloomingdale's."

As they divided the bill, Gussie had an absurd impulse to talk about Rick Conti, but instead of admitting her guilt and fear, she forcibly shoved them to the back of her mind as if they were lethal explosives, too sensitive and destructive to handle.

CHAPTER

Seven

EVEN BY BEVERLY HILLS STANDARDS THE GALLOWAY MANSION WAS ostentatious. Designed in the fashion of a French château, it had been built in the twenties and contained eighteen rooms rich with Carrara marble and sparkling Baccarat chandeliers. The lush grounds were protected by an electronically wired fence that concealed the heart-shaped pool and the tennis courts from the prying eyes of tourists. It was undeniably beautiful, and yet there was a noticeable absence of warmth, as if the entire estate had been purchased intact from a museum.

Helene had always felt lost in the rambling house, and now there was an added element—a strangling fear that haunted her nights. She was terrified of living there alone. At times she imagined an evil presence stalking the halls, crying out in the darkness. She slept with a light on and the windows locked, but her fears persisted and after a time she discovered there was only one antidote to her panic—a bottle of scotch.

When Diane called, Helene was sleeping off the effects of another night of blind indulgence. She heard the telephone, but her body refused to respond to the insistent ringing. Eventually one of the maids answered and timidly entered her room.

"There's a long-distance call for you, Miss Helene."

Helene opened her eyes, then quickly closed them. The bright light made her dizzy, and her mouth felt dry and cottony.

"Miss Helene, do you want me to say you're not at home?"

"Who is it?"

"Diane Henderson."

Blinking, Helene slowly lifted her head. "Ask her to hold on. I'll pick up in a minute."

As the maid left, Helene cautiously sat up, supporting her

head with both hands. Her body ached and her mind was fuzzy, but she desperately wanted to talk to Diane. After a moment of hesitation, she picked up the phone beside her bed.

"Hello."

"Helene, is that you?"

"Yes."

"What's wrong? You sound funny."

"I had too much to drink last night."

There was a long silence, and then Diane rushed ahead, obviously mouthing a well-rehearsed speech. "Whatever's wrong, drinking won't help. You're just making things worse."

"It's the only way I can sleep."

"That's dangerous. You'll end up an alcoholic."

Helene wanted to explain about the nightly horrors, but she was too dazed to coherently describe the eerie feeling that someone was watching her, waiting to seize her and drag her into a dark bottomless pit.

"Listen to me, Helene. You have to get yourself together. What about Brenda? When is she coming home?"

"Never, I hope." Helene laughed, but it was a brittle imitation of amusement. "She has a new lover, a Spanish count."

Diane drew in an audible breath. "Are you drinking because of what happened?"

"What do you mean?"

"Rick Conti."

Helene felt her insides go liquid. She never consciously thought about Rick Conti, though at times he seemed to float into her mind, a vague swirling image that frightened her. "Please, I don't want to talk about him."

"Are you sure? Maybe it would help. I have nightmares, too."

"I'm sorry . . . I'm sorry you have nightmares, but there's nothing . . . Please let it go."

"All right," Diane said, but her voice echoed uncertainty. "Will you write to me?"

"In a few weeks, after I make some plans. I'll write and let you know what I'm doing."

"Take care of yourself, Helene."

"I will."

— — —

Later that evening, Helene sat at the edge of the pool dangling her feet in the water. She had spent the day ruminating on the emptiness of her life and was now determined to exist without the numbing oblivion of alcohol. But as the sun sank behind the distant mountains, her fears slowly crawled out of the shadows and settled like a shawl around her shoulders.

Feeling the familiar panic rise in her chest, she impulsively ran to the house, shrugged into a pair of jeans, and hurried to the garage. She needed bright lights and the sound of voices, the reassurance of human contact. She threw herself into Brenda's vintage Jaguar and raced through the quiet streets of Beverly Hills, then cruised down Hollywood Boulevard and finally stopped at a run-down bar.

Inside, the bar smelled of stale tobacco and sour beer. Several bikers were shooting pool in the corner, their coarse laughter occasionally rising above the country music blaring from the jukebox. Helene ordered a Coke and carried it to one of the tiny black tables. A few minutes later a lanky man dressed like a cowboy sat down beside her.

He had an arrogant grin and hard blue eyes, but when he led her to the dance floor and pulled her against his chest, she felt better. Her fears receded. She had no desire to drink, only to press herself against the rough planes of his body.

After an hour of frenzied dancing, he followed her to the parking lot and smiled when she invited him to slide behind the wheel of the Jag. As she watched his craggy features come alive with appreciation for the powerful car, Helene settled back in her seat and relaxed.

He drove nearly all night, racing through mountain canyons, careening along steep winding roads. Helene was intoxicated by the danger, which pulsed along her nerve endings like a burst of sexual energy. When he finally stopped the car in front of the mansion, she took his hand and wordlessly led him to her bedroom.

Their lovemaking was quick and urgent, a primitive act of release. Helene met each brutal thrust, but the instant her shuddering orgasm abated, the fears returned and she clawed at his arm. "Stay with me. Don't leave me alone."

He laughed low in his throat. "Sure, honey. I'll stay as long as you want me."

Helene snuggled against him and closed her eyes, but in the morning he was gone. Only the semen stains on her legs and a slight internal soreness assured her that his presence had not been a dream, and she finally understood that she was slowly disintegrating.

She tried to erase her humiliating memories of the cowboy with increasing quantities of scotch, but instead of disappearing, the mental images became more lurid. After days of dissipation, she dragged herself out of bed and confronted her reflection in the mirror. She was shocked by the deterioration she encountered. The skin beneath her eyes was puffy, and her complexion had grown sallow and waxy. She looked like a lush, a woman well on her way to self-destruction.

It took Helene nearly a week to purge herself of the effects of her binge. She still had difficulty sleeping, but she resisted the temptation to sedate herself with alcohol. Each morning she swam several laps in the pool, then forced herself to eat a hearty breakfast before she began making the rounds of talent agencies. She spent a great deal of time fantasizing about a career in the movies, and her fantasies became her lifeline, though her search for an agent turned out to be an exercise in futility. She was determined to succeed without using the Galloway name, but on her own she met with repeated rejections.

Rhetta Green sat at her desk, gazing out the window at the seedy landscape of lower Sunset Boulevard. Each time she looked at the view something inside her died. She had been forced to locate her fledgling talent agency in a less than affluent section of Hollywood, and she hated being reminded of her precarious financial situation.

Rhetta had grand dreams of becoming a successful independent agent. After years of backbreaking work at the illustrious Standish Agency, she possessed the connections and know-how to make it on her own, but success took money, and Rhetta was just breaking even.

The sound of her secretary knocking at the door distracted her from her morose thoughts, and she looked away from the window. "Come on in."

Millie wiggled into the room, her skintight skirt forcing her to take tiny mincing steps that made her look like a parody of a dumb blond. "There's a girl to see you. She looks good, Rhett."

"Terrific. Does she have any credits?"

Tucking her gum against the inside of her cheek, Millie shook her head. "But I'm telling you, this one's got potential, a great face and one of those dynamite Twiggy bodies."

Rhetta sighed, anticipating an encounter with still another kid from Michigan who was hot to see her name in lights— never mind that she had no talent and shared a brain with three other aspiring actresses. "Why do they all end up here?"

"She's probably been turned down everyplace else."

"Thanks. You do great things for my ego."

Millie laughed. "So what do I tell her?"

"Send her in. I'll try to talk her into hopping the next bus back to Kalamazoo."

As Millie left her alone, Rhetta raked her fingers through her drab gray hair, wondering why she felt such an absurd sense of responsibility for the star-struck kids who wandered into her office. They were all alike—big bright eyes and hopeful smiles—and they never listened, never believed that Hollywood would chew them up and spit them out like bits of garbage. Every one of them thought she had that special glow, that indefinable spark that would light up the Hollywood skies, and all but a few were destined to fail. Some would figure it out in time and go home to their high school sweethearts; others would find jobs on the fringes of the film industry; a few would return home in a pine box. And that was why Rhetta could never quite bring herself to send them away without first trying to rescue them from their dreams.

Millie ushered a young woman into the room. Rhetta immediately noticed she was wearing a Blass original and felt an unexpected twinge of curiosity. Most struggling actresses arrived in faded jeans or an ensemble from Sears spruced up by a scarf or a good piece of jewelry. Her interest piqued, she focused her full attention on the girl.

"Rhetta, this is Helene Gregory," Millie said.

Offering a professional smile that intentionally lacked warmth, Rhetta nodded. "Take a seat, Helene. Let's have a look at your bio."

Helene dropped down onto one of the cheap upholstered

chairs and immediately began to fidget. "I'm sorry. I didn't bring a bio."

"Then you'll have to tell me about yourself, but give me a minute to look you over." Rhetta dismissed Millie, then fixed her assessing gaze on Helene. There was something familiar about that exquisite face, though at the moment whatever it was eluded her. Then Helene smiled and Rhetta froze. Her smile was spectacular, a beaming burst of light shadowed by vulnerability, a smile that would evoke instant sympathy and love from an audience. And it was at that precise moment that Rhetta recognized the young woman seated before her, though she concealed her awareness behind an impassive nod. "Do you have any professional credits?"

"A few college productions, nothing impressive."

"Any acting lessons?"

Helene shook her head, appearing even more nervous than she had when she arrived. "This probably sounds crazy, but I know I can act. I feel it inside."

"So does every other kid in this town. What makes you so special?"

Her narrow shoulders sagging, Helene wordlessly shrugged.

"Look, I don't know what the hell kind of game you're playing but I'd say being Brenda Galloway's daughter makes you pretty damn special."

"How . . . how did you know?"

"It's my business to remember faces. I met you once at a premiere. But I don't understand—why the masquerade?"

Helene swallowed convulsively. "I don't want anything from my mother, not even her name. I can make it on my own."

Picking up a pencil, Rhetta tapped it against an overflowing ashtray, trying to remember everything she had ever read about Brenda Galloway and her daughter. But as far as she was able to recall, even the scandal sheets had never hinted at an estrangement. "Why make it hard on yourself? One phone call from Brenda and you'll have twenty agents begging to represent you."

"Because I hate my mother," Helene said simply.

Rhetta knew by the quiet vehemence in her voice that this was no temporary feud. Helene Galloway was driven by more than a shallow desire for fame and recognition. She wanted to triumph over her mother in her own arena. "There's no way you'll be able to keep your identity a secret. Once you start getting some publicity, the press will have a field day exposing you."

"Maybe, but for now I want to be Helene Gregory."

Lapsing into silence, Rhetta considered her options. She had a feeling deep in her gut that Helene Galloway had star quality in enormous proportions, but there was also an air of tragedy about the girl—and an aura of instability that might destroy her chance of success. It would take a tremendous amount of time and money to cultivate her innate talent, an investment that could easily go sour, and Rhetta was in no position to survive a critical financial loss. Yet her well-honed instincts told her to gamble on Helene, to risk everything she had on this one chance to reach for the brass ring.

"All right, Helene. Let's talk a few realities. Right now you're a liability. You have no training, no experience. The only thing you've got going for you is your name, and you refuse to use it. Why should I risk a bundle on you?"

"Because I have what it takes to be a great actress. I'll work hard. I won't disappoint you."

Rhetta leaned over her desk, avidly looking at Helene. "That's not enough. I want complete control of your life. You don't make a move without consulting me first. If I tell you to shave your head, you buy a razor. If I tell you to parade down Sunset Boulevard in a plastic bag, you do it with no argument. That's the only way I'll represent you."

Helene smiled, and the sunlight streaming through the window seemed momentarily brighter. "Does that mean I have an agent?"

"I'll have Millie type up a contract."

After the contract was signed and notarized, Helene left the office in a giddy daze while Rhetta poured herself a stiff shot from the bottle of bourbon she kept stashed in her desk drawer. She projected an unflappable public image, but at the moment her nerves were gyrating. Her elation at discovering Helene Galloway was compromised by a growing sense of apprehension. What if she had just committed the most monumental blunder of her life, jeopardizing years of work on the basis of one lousy hunch?

The thought of risking everything she had accomplished

chilled her to the core, but the alternative was just as numbing. If she passed up this roll of the dice, she might never have another chance to shoot. The odds of another Helene Galloway strolling into her office were infinitesimal. Fate had finally offered her a break. Only a fool would slam the door in the face of such an opportunity.

Still feeling unsettled, Rhetta lit a cigarette and wandered over to the window. The shabby view summoned unbidden memories of her dismal childhood in Sweet Water, Alabama. She still felt the pain of being the sixth unwanted child in a family of shiftless drunks and petty criminals. Her father had been brutal and abusive, terrorizing her mother to the point of complete submission, beating his daughters whenever he felt the need to assert his diminishing masculinity. By the time Rhetta turned sixteen, she had already decided that love was a worthless commodity.

But everything changed the day she met Gilly Jones. She was just out of high school and working as a waitress at the Sweet Water Café when Gilly ambled in for lunch, bold and cocky as a rooster. He used his blond good looks and liberal doses of flattery to charm her into a night at the drive-in, and by the end of the evening, she had willingly given him her virginity.

Rhetta adored Gilly. He made her feel good about herself, as if she might someday overcome the unfortunate fact that she had been born into the wrong family. She ignored his smug grin when they ran into one of his friends, and she paid no attention to the way he avoided sitting beside her in church. He was her first boyfriend, and even if his behavior seemed peculiar, she was simply too grateful to criticize him.

Their relationship might have continued indefinitely, but after three months of urgent sex, Rhetta discovered she was pregnant. Certain that Gilly would marry her, she wasn't particularly upset when she snuggled against him and told him the news.

"I went to Doc Hardy this morning," she whispered. "You're going to be a father."

Gilly tensed, and a crimson stain spread over his round face. "The hell I am."

Laughing uneasily, Rhetta stroked his cheek. "I know we didn't plan on a baby yet, but things'll work out. You make good money down at the mill, and I'll be able to work right up to the end. We'll get by.''

"No way, Rhetta.''

"What do you mean? I'm having your baby.'' She repeated her announcement, thinking that perhaps he hadn't understood her the first time, but his answer shattered her illusions.

"Who's to say it's my kid?''

"You know you're the only one. Why are you acting this way, Gilly?''

His expression had turned mean and nasty. "I'd never marry a girl like you. I'd be laughed right out of town.''

Devastated by the terrible realization that she had been used and discarded, Rhetta lashed out. "Then I'll tell everybody what you did.''

He dug his fingers into her arm, squeezing until she whimpered. "Try it. I'll have ten guys say they banged you.''

Rhetta dissolved into tears, her dreams of love battered into oblivion, her future too horrible to contemplate.

Eventually she mustered the courage to strike out on her own and, after months of traveling, settled in Phoenix to await the birth of her baby. She had already decided to relinquish her child to a Methodist adoption agency, but when it came time to part with her little girl, she felt an emptiness that would never be filled, a hollow space in the center of her being.

It took her a long time, but once she accepted the fact that her baby was irrevocably lost to her, Rhetta migrated to California and found a clerical job at the prestigious Standish Theatrical Agency. Since she was totally alone in the world, her job became the focus of her existence, and she received several promotions in rapid succession. By the time she was thirty, Rhetta was a full-fledged agent, known for aggressively pursuing the best possible deals for her clients. But in her own mind she was still Rhetta Green, the dregs of Sweet Water society.

A few years later it came to her that she might have a greater sense of accomplishment if she opened her own agency. It seemed foolish to go on contributing to the already vast wealth of Dan Standish when she had enough connections to go into business for herself. After thinking it over for another year, she resigned from her position and took the biggest gamble of her life.

And her gamble was just beginning to pay off. While she was far from rich, her business had gradually prospered, attracting new clients every month. But now she was on the verge of taking another perilous risk. Launching Helene Galloway would require an almost fanatical commitment, a singular devotion that would surely alienate other clients. She was investing her entire future in one very vulnerable-looking young woman. But Helene had evoked a latent instinct to nurture. Already Rhetta was feeling a maternal desire to protect and shelter. She wondered if Helene in some way represented the baby she had abandoned so many years ago, if this was her chance to redeem herself.

Annoyed with her futile speculations, Rhetta returned to her desk, picked up the telephone, and dialed a number. When a heavily accented voice answered, she smiled. "Nadia, Rhetta Green here."

"Ah, Rhetta, it's been a long time. How has life been treating you?"

"Not bad. I still have a roof over my head."

Nadia laughed, a rich, husky sound. "Stop toying with an old woman. I know all about your successes. You've done well, Rhetta."

"Reasonably, but I'm about to bet everything I have on a gut hunch, and I need your help."

After a lengthy silence, Nadia said, "You know I'm retired."

"I also know you're the best acting coach ever to work in Hollywood."

"That was years ago. Not now."

"Bullshit. You're the only one I trust. Helene Galloway signed on with me this morning, and with the right training she'll bring this town to its knees."

Again Nadia retreated into silence, but Rhetta could hear the almost imperceptible quickening in her respiration. "What do you say, Nadia? Are you willing to have a look at her?"

"Tomorrow, but I make no promises. We'll see if she is more talented than her mother."

The next morning Helene impatiently paced in a wide circle while Rhetta coached her on how to impress Nadia Rostoff. "She'll ask you to read for her—probably something classical.

She knows you have no training, so don't try to con her with any flashy techniques. Just go with what feels natural.''

''Why are we even bothering with this? Nadia Rostoff's a legend, she'll never agree to work with me.''

Rhetta smiled. ''She will if she believes in you, but I had to be honest with her, Helene. She knows who you are.''

''Why? Why did you tell her?''

''Because she would have figured it out anyway. You can't deceive a woman like Nadia. She's too perceptive.''

Intrigued despite vague feelings of betrayal, Helene stopped pacing and sat on the edge of Rhetta's desk. ''What's she like?''

''Brilliant, demanding. She refuses to settle for anything less than perfection.''

''Then I have no right taking up her time. She'll laugh at me.''

''Maybe, but what have we got to lose? Now come on. She hates to be kept waiting.''

Helene followed Rhetta to the parking lot, not at all comforted by her blunt response. As they drove up Sunset Boulevard toward Bel Air, she tried to write possible dialogue in her head, but everything sounded either ingratiating or insipid. Nadia Rostoff began to take on an almost supernatural existence in her mind. She imagined that the woman would be able to look right through her, gleaning an unobstructed view of her most private thoughts, discovering every one of her inadequacies.

When Rhetta pulled her dented yellow Volkswagen to a stop in front of a delightful stone cottage, Helene was surprised to see such a simple home nestled among so many pretentious mansions. Bel Air was the undisputed gem of Hollywood real estate, surpassing even Beverly Hills in price and prestige. Helene decided that Nadia Rostoff must be a complex woman to have chosen to live so modestly amid the glitz.

A wizened butler greeted them at the door and directed them to the parlor, where a silver tea service had been set out on a mahogany sideboard. ''Miss Nadia will join you in a moment,'' he said.

Helene nervously roamed around the room, occasionally pausing to examine one of the photographs that covered every available surface. She was looking at a faded picture of a man in a foreign military uniform when she felt Nadia Rostoff's presence.

"Be gentle. Those are an old woman's precious memories."

Spinning around, Helene flushed, feeling like a child caught in a shameful act. Nadia was staring at her, her pale gray eyes alert and probing. "I'm sorry. I . . ."

Nadia waved her hand, dismissing the apology. "It is good that you are curious. Already I see that you are more intelligent than your mother." Then, turning to Rhetta, Nadia opened her arms. "And you, you have been neglecting me."

Rhetta stepped into her embrace, kissing the tissue-thin flesh of her cheek. "Never deliberately."

"I know, you are too busy making money to cater to a doddering old lady."

"Doddering my ass, you're the slyest old lady in Hollywood."

The two women laughed, their eyes locked in a mutual expression of affection; then Nadia broke away. "Come over to the window, Helene. I want to see you in the light."

After parting the fragile lace curtains, Nadia gripped Helene's chin in her withered fingers, studying every facet of her face. "You are beautiful," she said simply. "But here in Hollywood beauty is everywhere. We must see if you can act. Sit and have some tea while I decide what I want you to read."

While Rhetta poured tea into delicate china cups, Helene covertly observed Nadia Rostoff. She seemed so frail, her body hunched and withered, but there was nothing feeble about her penetrating gaze or the agility of her mind. Working with her would be a rare privilege, a chance to learn from a master, and suddenly Helene wanted to earn her approval more than she had ever wanted anything in her life.

Nadia chose the death scene from *Romeo and Juliet*. The role was perfect for Helene, a tormented young woman about to tragically end her life rather than endure the loss of the man she loved. Helene took several minutes to reach inside herself and dip into the vast reservoir of pain and loss that had shadowed her own life. Then as raw emotion flooded her senses like a raging river in a spring thaw, she began to read the timeless lines.

When her voice quietly faded away, there was a moment of almost religious silence. Then Nadia slowly stood, her gnarled hands trembling. "We will begin tomorrow. You will be my greatest triumph."

The sweet scents of juniper and honeysuckle lingered in the warm evening air as Chief Edwards glanced back at the Galloway mansion and reluctantly climbed into his rented Ford. He felt frustrated and irritable, discouraged by numerous futile attempts to interview Helene Galloway. Her efficient staff had been carefully trained to protect her from unwanted intrusions. And he was clearly an unwanted intrusion.

Disgusted, Edwards started his car and headed down the long driveway. As he rounded a slight curve he spied a sleek black Jaguar barreling toward him and instinctively swerved to avoid a collision. A second later the Jaguar screeched to a halt and a young woman jumped out and ran in his direction.

"Are you all right?" she gasped.

Edwards knew beyond a doubt that he was looking at Helene Galloway but he forced himself to remain calm as he slowly climbed out of the car. "I'm fine, Miss Galloway."

She seemed unaware of his use of her name. "Thank God. I never expected to meet another car. I'm sorry."

Edwards smiled. "There's no reason to apologize. Actually I was hoping to talk to you."

She visibly retreated, shrinking away from him like a wild creature confronted by a predator. Her black eyes glittered in the shadows, wide and vulnerable. "Who are you?" she asked. "What do you want?"

In a quiet voice calculated to reassure her, Edwards introduced himself and explained the reason for his visit. When he finished, she remained absolutely silent, barely seeming to breathe. "Miss Galloway, is something wrong?"

Her slender hands began to tremble, and again Edwards was reminded of a delicate woodland creature, fragile and defenseless. He felt like a brute for frightening her, but then he remembered his investigation and hardened his resolve. "Please, Miss Galloway, I want to ask you a few questions about the night Rick Conti disappeared."

Helene slumped against the car, shaking her head. "I don't remember," she said softly. "I was drunk . . . stoned. . . . I don't remember anything."

Edwards stared at her, surprised by her strange response. He

had anticipated a carefully rehearsed story or even a rude
dismissal, but he was totally unprepared for such naked
vulnerability. After a long silence he said, "This is no place to
talk. I'm sure you'd be more comfortable in the house."

"No, you don't understand. I have nothing to tell you . . .
nothing. I passed out and Rick was . . . gone by the time I
woke up the next day."

"You didn't see him leave?"

She shook her head again, her silky mane of raven hair
tumbling over her shoulders. "I'm sorry. I can't help you. I
have to go now."

As she turned and ran to her car, Edwards remained rooted
to the ground, enthralled by her ethereal beauty. Then, horrified
at his lapse, he hurried after her. "Wait, Miss Galloway, please
wait."

But the Jaguar seemed to vanish into the darkness, leaving
him alone in the driveway.

A few hours later, Chief Edwards poured himself a cup of
black coffee and joined Mick Travis in the living room of his
lavish Malibu beach house. A warm breeze filtered through the
windows, and the gentle sound of the surf lapping at the shore
echoed in the distance. As Edwards sank into a burnt orange
chair, Rick shot him an inquisitive glance. "How did it go?
Any luck cornering Helene Galloway?"

Edwards shrugged, not quite sure how to describe his bizarre
encounter with Helene. He felt vaguely guilty for letting her
slip away from him, and his voice was strained as he described
their brief meeting in the driveway. "She claims she was
totally out of it the night Conti vanished."

"What the hell does that mean?"

"She says she passed out, doesn't remember a thing."
Edwards absently rubbed his fingers over his lower lip. "But
it's funny that the others never said a word about her passing
out."

Mick leaned forward in his chair, his eyes bright with
curiosity. "Looks like the ladies might be hiding something."

Edwards nodded. "Yeah, but what? If Conti really ran off
they have nothing to hide."

There was a long silence, and then Mick said, "Suppose they
killed the poor bastard."

Edwards had been kicking that possibility around in his head for months, but it was still a shock to hear Mick voice his own suspicions. There was something unnatural about the idea of four decent young women committing a murder, something repugnant and deeply disturbing. "Why would they kill him?" he said. "As far as I can see they had no motive."

"Maybe it was an accident. They had a fight and he ended up dead."

"Maybe, but Conti was Brenda Galloway's boyfriend. What if she killed him and the others are covering up for her?"

Mick nodded, thoughtfully chewing his lower lip. "Without a body this is all just idle speculation. Where do you go from here?"

Sighing, Edwards shook his head. "I'm heading back to Hyannis in the morning. I'll never get close to Helene Galloway again, not without a warrant."

Clearly surprised, Mick arched his sandy brows. "So you're just giving up?"

"I'll probably dig around some more in my spare time, but you're right, I have no case without a body. And for all I know, Rick Conti could be alive and well, sunning his ass in the Caribbean."

"You don't believe that any more than I do."

"No," Edwards said quietly. "But right now I'm out of leads. This might turn out to be one of those cases that never breaks." He pinched the bridge of his nose, suddenly looking years older. "The hell of it is, I'll still be wondering what happened to Conti the day they give me my gold watch. Loose ends drive me crazy; they always have."

PART
Three

Winter 1969

CHAPTER
Eight

THOUGH THEY HAD BEEN SEEING EACH OTHER FOR SIX MONTHS, JOEL HAD never invited Diane to watch him perform. He claimed the bars he worked were too seedy, but she suspected he was actually protecting himself from the humiliating possibility of failing in front of her. She had discovered that his bravado was merely a mask for his underlying insecurities. Now at last, after countless arguments and weeks of subtle persuasion, she was seated at a table in a sleazy Hoboken club waiting for him to appear on stage.

The Red Rooster was even more squalid than she had imagined. The crowd was rough and crude—hard-drinking men and a few brassy-looking women—not the type of audience to appreciate Joel's cynical humor. She found it difficult to believe that appearing in such a place would in any way bolster his career, but Joel never turned down a gig; he was addicted to the applause.

When the owner of the club, a fat, balding man in a shiny blue suit, materialized from behind a frayed curtain and muttered a cursory introduction, Diane curled her fingers around the stem of her glass, feeling an unbearable tension. Then Joel stepped out onto the stage and her heart began to race. She tried to catch his eye, but he seemed blinded by the smoky haze of the spotlight.

His routine only lasted thirty minutes, but Diane knew she would remember each agonizing moment for the rest of her life. When he finally left the stage to a chorus of obscenities, she quickly followed him to his shabby dressing room, fumbling in her mind for the right words to console him. But the owner of the club had gotten there first. He fired Joel.

85

—   —   —

Diane fully intended to pursue the matter of Joel's disastrous
performance, but three days passed and she had yet to find the
right moment. He seemed to be deliberately avoiding any
discussion of his faltering career. Each time she tried to
maneuver their conversation to his next gig, he cleverly
diverted her. And because she loved him, she detested the idea
of being excluded from such a major portion of his life.

Maybe their relationship had progressed too quickly, she
thought. They had just drifted into a steady thing, spending all
their free time together, exploring the city, having dinner at
cheap little out-of-the-way places, seeing foreign films at artsy
theaters in the Village. In just a few months Joel had become
the center of her life, and she now wondered if it had been a
mistake to devote herself so completely to a man who seemed
either incapable or unwilling to express his feelings.

Frustrated by her thoughts, Diane checked her watch, then
hurried to the kitchen. She was planning a special dinner,
hoping a bottle of cheap Chianti would relax Joel enough to
open up to her. There were things they had to discuss—where
they were going, what he wanted from their relationship. Much
as she loved him, she wasn't prepared to squander the rest of
her life on a man who refused to commit himself.

Dinner had gone well until the subject of Joel's career had
come up. They'd finished in silence.

Now that she had found an opening, Diane was apprehensive
about offering advice. He was looking for someone to blame
and might deliberately misconstrue her words. But there was
no way she could go on pretending to support what she
considered to be his disastrous career choices. "Maybe that
guy was right to fire you."

"What the hell does that mean?"

"You're too good for a place like that."

"Since when are you a critic?"

"I was there; I saw what happened. You're wasting your
talent."

Sighing, Joel gently led her to the sofa. "You're wrong,
bright-eyes. I'm strictly bush league. Either I change my act or
I get out of the business. I'll never be a headliner."

"You *will*," she said fiercely. "All you need is one break, one chance to prove yourself at a decent club."

Joel's eyes implored her to convince him she was speaking the truth. All she could think of was a dying patient pleading with the doctor to offer one last shred of hope, and she was assaulted by doubts. Maybe she was wrong to encourage him when she loved him too much to be objective, but the alternative was to crush his hopes and there was no way she could bring herself to hurt him.

"Keep working on your act, and look for a new agent. I know you can make it."

Groaning, Joel slipped his arm around her. "God, I love you. Marry me, bright-eyes. Spend the rest of your life with me. I need you."

As his mouth came down over hers, hard and demanding, Diane melted against him, feeling as if a great weight had been lifted from her chest. Everything would be all right now. Together they were invincible.

In the six months she had been working at the television studio, Diane had seen Ed Blake attempt numerous schemes to discredit his competition. He played all sorts of dirty tricks—spreading unsavory gossip about other producers, eavesdropping on private meetings, sabotaging creative ideas for new proposals—and Diane suspected that his final goal was to oust her boss, Jordan Carr. The consensus around the office was that he would eventually succeed.

As Diane added milk to her coffee, Andy Cathcart tapped her on the shoulder. An easygoing bear of a man, Andy was one of the few production assistants who had attained his position simply by virtue of his competence.

"Have you got a minute? I think we need to talk," he said.

Diane turned to look at him and was unnerved by his peculiar expression. Then she noticed that the other people near the coffee machine were slowly backing away, retreating to their offices. "What's going on?"

Andy shifted his weight from one foot to the other. "Christ, I hate telling you this, but we all thought you should know."

"Know what?"

"Jordan Carr has filed for divorce. There's an ugly rumor going around that you're responsible."

Stunned, Diane stood there with her mouth open.

"Diane, are you all right?"

"That's a vicious lie!"

"Of course it is, but you know how the goddam gossip mill works around here. Somebody's really doing a job on you."

"Ed Blake," she said flatly.

Andy nodded, his mouth set in a grim line. "Probably. Something sleazy like this is right up his alley."

Diane began to tremble as her shock subsided and she was able to think coherently. If this rumor reached the boardroom it would mean her job. The network was unbelievably prudish about any kind of moral indiscretion. Jordan probably had enough leverage to survive a scandal, but she was only a secretary; she could easily be replaced.

"What am I going to do? If I deny it, I'll only look more guilty."

"Talk to Jordan. Maybe he can shut Blake up."

The idea of talking to Jordan made her stomach churn, but Diane knew it was the only solution. If she just closed her eyes to the gossip it would continue to escalate until it finally reached the wrong ears. After thanking Andy for having the decency to warn her, she crossed the hall and knocked on Jordan's door.

The moment she saw his face, Diane knew he had already heard the rumor. His complexion had a grayish cast, and the lines around his mouth seemed deeper, more prominently etched. At first her anxieties had all been for herself, but now she felt an extra measure of concern for the man who had become her mentor. Jordan had taken the time to teach her about preparing a budget proposal, editing a tape to achieve the maximum impact, and assembling the best possible production crew. Now he was being persecuted for encouraging her.

"Have a seat, Diane," he said. "I assume you've heard the latest gossip."

"Just now, at the coffee machine."

He smiled, but his eyes were weary. "I never dreamed my divorce would give Ed this kind of ammunition. He's been angling for my job for years, but he's never attacked me this directly. I'm afraid that means I've lost some footing around here."

Jordan had always been noncommittal about network politics and she was surprised by his sudden frankness. "Then you think Ed's responsible?" she asked.

"I'm positive. The question is, how do I deal with him? This is a delicate situation. I don't want to risk losing you."

She was pleased by his concern, which reinforced her conviction that he was an honorable man, but she was well aware that he might be forced to sacrifice her in order to save himself. "Maybe we should just ignore it," she said, "let it die on its own."

"Things have gone too far for that. I've already been called upstairs for an emergency meeting."

"You mean they'll formally accuse you?" she said, horrified by the thought.

Jordan shook his leonine head. "I imagine they'll fish around awhile, give me a subtle warning. Then if I'm not able to get control of the gossip within a few days, they'll come after me. Obviously that's what Ed's counting on."

"Is there anything you can do?"

Steepling his hands beneath his chin, Jordan sighed heavily. "I can make Ed back off for the moment, but his retreat will be only temporary. In another year he'll have my job."

Diane gasped, and he offered her a wan smile. "That's the way it goes in this business. There's always someone younger and hungrier nipping at your heels, plotting to be rid of you. Ed Blake happens to be a ruthless bastard, but that doesn't change the fact that I've outlived my usefulness here. It's time for me to move on to something else."

"You can't let him push you out!"

This time his smile was more genuine, reaching all the way to his eyes. "I'm not ready to throw in the towel just yet. I intend to see you promoted to assistant producer before I go. You have great ability, and I'd like to look back someday and know I played a part in forcing the network to recognize you."

"What about Ed? He'll never . . ."

Jordan silenced her with a wave of his hand. "Let me worry about Ed. You just concentrate on learning everything you can. Are you willing to stay late and work with me?"

Diane thought of Joel and the toll her absence would take on their relationship, but she quickly subdued her misgivings, certain that he would understand. "I'll be here whenever you want me."

"Good, then I think I'll have a little talk with Ed."

CHAPTER
Nine

"CAL WANTS TO SEE YOU AS SOON AS THE KIDS LEAVE."

Rachel was on her knees, struggling to buckle a fidgeting little boy into a pair of boots that were a size too small. She looked up at the angular black woman hovering above her, troubled by her abruptness. "What's going on?"

Mary Bevins shook her head. "Not now. I'll be in the kitchen when you're finished."

Prodded by an inexplicable sense of urgency, Rachel quickly bundled the rest of the children into their bulky winter coats, then stood in the doorway watching them until they blended into the crowd moving along 125th Street. Normally it bothered her to see them trudging home unsupervised, but today she was too distracted by Mary's odd behavior to dwell on the dangers of the city streets.

Though they had been teaching together in the church basement for nearly six months, Mary remained an enigma. Rumors regularly circulated through the ranks of the Black Brotherhood—stories about Mary's migration from the Deep South and a life of abject poverty—but it was all idle speculation. Mary never discussed her private life. She seemed to cultivate an aura of inaccessibility, particularly around Rachel.

When the last child had disappeared, Rachel locked the door and made her way through the empty classrooms to the kitchen, where Mary stood at the sink scrubbing the children's paint jars, her movements quick and jittery.

"What's happening?" Rachel asked.

"Trouble. Two white cops gunned down an old black woman."

"My God, when?"

91

"A few hours ago. Cal wants you out of here right now."

Rachel lit a cigarette, sucking the smoke deep into her lungs. "Why?"

"Once the word gets out, there'll be violence. We don't want your blood on our hands."

Turning away from the sink, Mary walked to the stove and poured herself a cup of coffee. Sunlight streamed through the window, illuminating her rich ebony skin. Rachel had never seen a more striking woman.

"What about you? Do you want me to leave?"

"I never thought you should be here at all."

"Because I'm white?"

Mary smiled, but her luminous brown eyes were infinitely sad. "Yeah, because you're white. You don't belong, Rachel. This is our fight."

"I'm a human being, and I hate seeing other human beings abused. That makes it my fight."

Cal Hawkins had been silently standing in the doorway, but as Rachel continued to protest, he crossed the room and took a seat at the cluttered table. "She's right, Rachel. Go home and stay there."

"What are you planning to do about that shooting?"

"We march on City Hall tonight."

"I'm coming, Cal. There's no way you can stop me."

Sighing, Cal shook his head. "This is no Sunday afternoon peace march. There'll be nightsticks and riot helmets. Are you ready to bleed in the street? Maybe die?"

Rachel swallowed, tasting the caustic acid of her own fear. Nothing frightened her more than physical violence, and yet she knew if she hid behind her fears tonight, she would always regret it.

"Where shall I meet you?"

Brian McDonald, the law student Rachel had met in front of Butler Hall, was waiting for her in front of Low Library, his lanky frame braced against the bitter wind. Seeing him standing there in the shadows evoked an instant barrage of conflicting emotions—anticipation mingled with guilt, boundless joy tempered by the realization that their relationship was inherently wrong, that they were thieves greedily stealing forbidden fruits.

She had sensed their mutual attraction the moment he offered her a section of his orange, but instead of being frightened off by the differences that separated them like a gaping chasm, she had allowed herself just a taste of illicit pleasure. And that taste had led to an addiction, a craving that raged through her bloodstream like a potent narcotic.

Now, six months later, they were still straddling an immutable fence, meeting to take pleasure in each other's company, then returning to their separate lives, enriched by their time together, impoverished by their inevitable parting. So far they had not consummated their relationship, afraid such total intimacy would irretrievably bind them together, but Rachel wanted him with a hunger that was insidiously eroding her resistance.

As she approached the library steps, Brian opened his arms, and she felt a warm glow seep through her body as he brushed his lips over her cheek. "You're late."

"I was talking to Cal. Did you hear about the murder in Harlem?"

Brian nodded, his smile waning to a grim line. "It wasn't a murder, Rache. The woman was drunk. She went after the cops with a knife. Those cops had every right to defend themselves."

"By shooting an old lady? Come on, Brian, it was just plain murder. If it had been a white woman on Riverside Drive, there's no way the cops would have shot her." Then she thought of Brian's father and brothers—all city cops, "My God, it wasn't one of your—"

"No, thank God."

They mutely stared at each other for a protracted moment; then Brian took her hand. "Let's go someplace and get a cup of coffee; it's freezing out here."

They crossed the campus in silence. Again they were on opposing sides of an issue, pitted against each other in what seemed like an eternal war, a conflict of values that was so extensive it defied compromise. Rachel fleetingly thought of begging Brian to run off with her to some magical place where their differences would be meaningless, where they would be free to love without guilt. But that was only a fantasy, quickly blown away by the raw winter wind.

Once they were settled at a table in a quiet coffee shop on

Amsterdam Avenue, Rachel reluctantly resumed their discussion. "Cal's organizing a march on City Hall tonight. I'm going along."

"You're out of your fucking mind. There'll be a riot."

Brian rarely swore, and as Rachel's gaze flew to his face, she read the anguish in his eyes, the disapproval in the taut set of his mouth. Why were they torturing themselves like this? Why couldn't she just turn her back on him, erase him from her life? The answer brought tears to her eyes. She loved Brian McDonald, loved him enough to risk her own destruction.

"Rachel, why are you crying?" he said softly.

She shook her head as if to deny her tears, but when he gently touched her cheek, gathering a film of moisture on the tip of his finger, she lost the last vestiges of her control. "Us . . . It's so hopeless. I feel . . . like I'm being ripped apart."

"I know, but would it be any easier if we stopped seeing each other?"

"Not for me."

"Me either."

Rachel roughly wiped away her tears. "Sometimes I just want you to put your arms around me and promise me that everything will be okay."

He smiled tenderly. "I love you. That's the best I can do."

"I'll take it," she said, forcing a smile from trembling lips. "Who needs promises?"

Three hours later Rachel found herself in a cell that reeked of urine and body odor, a cell she shared with several other women.

Her jaw throbbed, and she carefully opened and closed her mouth, testing for broken bones. Once she was fairly certain her jaw was intact, she sat up and tried to remember what had happened, but her memory was fuzzy and the only thing she could focus on was somehow escaping the narrow confines of the cell. Just then a guard appeared, directed to escort her to a phone to make the one call she was allowed.

It took Brian nearly an hour to rouse his uncle, Judge Cleatus McDonald, and persuade him to intervene. By the time Brian arrived at the police station with the release forms, Rachel was

glassy-eyed and mute with exhaustion, but the instant she saw him waiting in the lobby, she regained a measure of vitality. She signed a sheaf of papers without even glancing at them. Then, when a bored cop told her she was free to leave, she stumbled into Brian's embrace.

"My God, your face. What happened?" he said.

"Later. Just get me out of here."

Wrapping one arm around her shoulders, he led her out the door and across the street to his ancient Chevy. As she settled herself on the seat, she felt a bone-deep chill, a pervasive cold that had nothing to do with the bitter February night. She wondered if she would ever be warm again.

"We'll have your jaw checked at the hospital. Then I'll take you home."

Her head snapped up. "I don't need a hospital, and I can't go home like this. Not now. Not in the middle of the night. Besides, I told my parents I was staying with a friend."

"Come home with me, then."

She nodded, then closed her eyes and rested her head against the window.

Brian had a studio apartment in a converted brownstone on West Seventy-eighth just off Columbus Avenue. There wasn't much space, and the tenant upstairs played the French horn all night, but it was relatively cheap and convenient to Columbia. As Rachel followed him through the door, she felt strange, unsure of herself.

After flicking on the overhead light, Brian drew her against his chest. "Hey, take it easy."

She looked up at him, her eyes wide. "God, it was so awful. The smells, the filth. I can actually *feel* the grime on my skin. I'll never be clean again."

Brian kissed the top of her head, gently stroking her back. "It's all right. It's over."

She clung to him, absorbing the comfort of his arms, the shelter of his body, but the horror remained right at the surface of her mind. Her ears rang with the sound of sirens, screams, the hollow thud of nightsticks connecting with bone. Even with her eyes closed she could still see the cop who had hit her. The memory was so sharp, permanently impressed upon her senses.

"Come on," he said, slowly nudging her toward the bathroom. "You're freezing. You need a hot shower."

She wordlessly allowed him to remove her clothes and help her into the tub. Then as she stood immobile under the spray of hot water, she noticed a deep purple bruise discoloring her thigh like a grotesque tattoo. Repelled, she looked at it for a moment, then began to ruthlessly scour her flesh, desperately trying to scrub away the stain of human brutality.

Later, snuggled against Brian in his narrow bed, she listened to the steady beat of his heart, and slowly her terror abated. A silvery stream of moonlight softly illuminated the planes and valleys of his face. She saw the lingering worry in his eyes, the tense set of his mouth. Gently she touched his lips. "Thank you for taking care of me."

"I was half out of my mind not knowing where you were. When I heard about the riot, I tried to get through the police lines, but it was a mob scene. The cops had everything barricaded. Finally I just came home to wait. I felt so fucking helpless."

She pressed herself against him, wanting to reassure him, to reassure herself. "I never knew it would be like that, so much hatred and violence. My God, we were just demonstrating."

"What now?" he asked. "Will you stay the hell out of Harlem?"

"You know I can't. I have to be there for the kids. I want to be there."

"Enough to get killed?"

Again she was reminded of their differences, and again she felt hopelessness wash over her, but this time she refused to listen to the inner voice of caution. Instead she slipped her arms around his neck, succumbing to a fierce need to become one with him. "Love me, Brian."

He groaned, pulling her closer, running his fingers along her spine. "Are you sure? It won't change anything, you know."

"It doesn't matter. I want you. I want you so much."

There was no hesitancy in his movements. He touched her as if they had been lovers for a lifetime, and she cried out at the pleasure, a low animal cry of satisfaction and desire. It felt so good to be held, to have his hands, warm and sensitive, caressing her. Then, responding to their mutual need, he thrust inside her, filling her completely.

The sensation of having him buried deep within her was like nothing she had ever known. They moved in perfect harmony, their bodies instinctively knowing how to please, how to prolong each exquisite motion, but somehow as they simultaneously convulsed in orgasm, the physical thrill became a spiritual bonding, a merging of their souls.

Afterward, she lay gasping in his arms, tears flooding her eyes. She was no longer a separate entity. Brian McDonald had touched a secret part of her, a previously unknown recess of her heart that had been starved for love. She realized there would be no going back, no scurrying retreat to safety. But where would she find the currency to pay the price of loving a man so totally wrong for her?

CHAPTER
Ten

GUSSIE LISTLESSLY PICKED AT HER VEAL MARSALA, BORED TO DISTRACTION by the conversation at the dinner table. Her parents seemed fixated on the details of the party they were hosting the following evening. Elizabeth's preoccupation was understandable— she believed her reputation hinged on her ability to orchestrate the perfect dinner party—but Gussie was amazed to see her father involved in something he considered essentially female. She almost wanted to laugh at his sudden and incongruous display of interest in the seating arrangements and the quality and quantity of the canapés. Obviously there was something special about this particular party, but rather than risk being dragged into the conversation, she swallowed her curiosity and devoted herself to her dinner.

She was lost in thought when Elizabeth said, "What do you think, dear?"

"About what?"

"Really, Augusta, I wish you'd pay attention. Do you have any idea what an honor it is to entertain the President?"

Gussie tried to mask her indifference behind an expression that reflected an appropriate amount of awe. "I didn't know Nixon was coming."

"Only for cocktails, but that's just as well. People are too nervous around the President to enjoy themselves. This way we'll have something delightful to talk about over dinner, after he leaves."

"Too bad I won't be here to meet him."

Robert sprang to attention. "What the hell does that mean? Of course you'll be here."

"I have other plans."

"Change them."

99

Setting down her fork, Gussie debated the wisdom of arguing with her father. It might be easier to just slip away tomorrow night and face the consequences later, but a perverse need to assert her independence goaded her to say, "I really can't do that. My friends are counting on me."

Robert slammed his fist on the table, rattling the delicate Rosenthal china. "Are you out of your goddam mind? I don't give a—"

"Robert, please," Elizabeth said. "We don't want the servants gossiping."

Gussie noticed her mother glancing nervously toward the kitchen and thought about the countless conversations that had been aborted because Elizabeth was absolutely paranoid about concealing family disagreements from the servants. She depended on them for virtually everything, and yet she continued to view them as vastly inferior beings, incapable of loyalty or discretion. Even as a child Gussie had been warned against becoming too friendly with any of the maids. She could still recite almost verbatim her mother's lecture on the moral frailties of the lower classes.

Robert looked as if he might explode, though he managed to subdue both his temper and his voice. "I insist you be here tomorrow night. Do you understand me, Augusta? No excuses."

"All right, but I don't see why it matters. Nixon won't miss me. He doesn't even know I exist."

Elizabeth sighed. "I never knew you were so selfish. This is one of our greatest triumphs, and all you can think of is yourself. How could your plans be more important than family loyalty?"

Realizing that she had resoundingly lost the argument, Gussie lowered her eyes in defeat, but Elizabeth wasn't about to be put off. "Where exactly were you going?"

"Out to dinner with friends."

"What friends? Are you still seeing that law student you told us about?"

Gussie nearly choked on her wine. "Occasionally."

"Then I want you to invite him to Sunday brunch so your father and I can meet him. This secrecy has gone on long enough."

"What secrecy? We're just friends."

Robert's complexion was still suffused with color and he seemed intent upon a demonstration of his authority. "Who is he? There must be something wrong with him if you're afraid to bring him home."

"That's ridiculous. I just don't want him to think I'm panting to marry him."

Gasping, Elizabeth fanned her face with her hand. "What a crude expression. I certainly hope you don't speak that way in public." She looked to Robert for support, and when he vigorously nodded, she continued. "At any rate, we'll expect your young man on Sunday."

"And you're to be here tomorrow night," Robert added. "Your mother's arranged a dinner partner for you."

Gussie groaned. "Who?"

"Senator Chandler. His wife died last year," Elizabeth said. "He's a charming man. I'm sure you'll enjoy his company."

Feeling trapped, Gussie nodded, then excused herself and escaped to the privacy of her room where she immediately collapsed on the bed. Her head throbbed, pulsing with each beat of her heart. She pictured herself enduring an evening of stilted conversation with Richard Chandler, and the pain in her skull intensified. It would be utter torture, especially since she suspected that the party was a thinly disguised effort to fix her up with a suitable man.

Only Elizabeth would regard Richard Chandler as a "suitable man." He was at least forty with prematurely gray hair and a chilling smile that looked as if he spent hours in front of the mirror trying to appear human. His brown eyes were narrow and suspicious, and there was something repellent about his fastidious grooming. He seemed fussy, almost feminine. How could Elizabeth consider him even marginally acceptable?

The answer of course was his money and position. He possessed all the necessary attributes to become the consort of the heiress apparent to the Tremain legacy. Gussie had always known her parents expected her to marry a socially prominent man, but the thought of sharing a bed and a lifetime with a man like Richard made her shudder. Then she thought of Tony, and tears flooded her eyes.

After months of denial, she was finally ready to admit she was wildly and passionately in love. But her parents would never accept Tony, and once she brought him home for their inspection, her beautiful fantasy would be over.

Gussie spent an hour staring at the ceiling, trying to come up with an excuse to avoid Sunday brunch. Then, realizing how pointless it was to oppose her mother, she sat up and reached for the phone. Tony answered on the first ring.

"I can't make it tomorrow night," she told him. "My parents are having a dinner party, and they insist I be here."

"Can you bring a guest?"

There was a note of quiet determination in his voice, and Gussie knew what was coming next. Her refusal to introduce him to her parents was a constant source of friction between them.

"Not this time. It's a formal dinner, and I—"

"You're afraid I'll eat with my hands or pinch your mother's ass?"

Gussie squeezed the receiver until her knuckles turned white. "What a horrible thing to say. You know that's not true."

"Then why the hell have we been sneaking around for the last six months? Be honest, Gussie. It's fine to play around with an Italian, but you know better than to bring him home."

"Tony . . . please." Her voice caught in her throat. He sounded so bitter, and somewhere in the deepest reservoir of her mind, she recognized a faint glimmer of truth and flushed with shame. "Will you just listen for a minute? I want you to come to brunch on Sunday. My parents are expecting to meet you."

Tony expelled a gust of air and said, "I love you, *cara*."

"And I love you. Maybe now you'll believe me."

As she said the words, Gussie felt guilt lick at her insides like a scorching flame. Her love was worthless, rooted in deceit. She was destined to betray the man she adored.

Elizabeth had spared nothing in her effort to create a social event that would be the talk of Washington for months. There was abundant and sumptuous food, just enough liquor to blunt anxieties without fueling any unpleasant incidents, and a staff meticulously groomed to provide impeccable service while remaining virtually invisible. But those were only the superficial elements of a successful party. Elizabeth went a good deal further to ensure a perfect evening.

She had carefully considered each guest before deciding on a seating arrangement, balancing personalities the way an accountant might balance a ledger—making the best of assets and diminishing liabilities. She had kept careful records of which china and table linens had been used at previous dinners and took care never to use the same pattern twice. But her most clever strategy was to avoid inviting anyone who was even remotely controversial or belligerent. She knew it took only one nasty guest to taint the complexion of an entire party.

As Gussie stood in the doorway sipping a glass of wine, she grudgingly admired her mother. Dressed in a stunning black Dior gown and surrounded by a cloud of Joy, Elizabeth seemed to float among her guests, chatting and laughing, the perfect hostess presiding over the perfect party. At one time Gussie would have been impressed to the point of reverence, but at the moment she found the whole scene rather nauseating. There was an almost carnivallike atmosphere, and her parents were working the crowd like hucksters.

A flurry of activity at the front door caught her attention, and she watched several Secret Service agents escort the President and Mrs. Nixon into the house. Conversation momentarily ceased as the guests tried to maneuver themselves into advantageous positions. No one wanted to appear too conspicuous, but they were all clearly competing for the inside edge.

Gussie waited for the first tide of excitement to subside before she joined her parents and the Nixons in the living room. As Robert made a grand spectacle of introducing her, she discreetly studied Richard Nixon, finding him even less appealing in person than on television. He had the most evasive eyes, and when he shook her hand his skin felt dry and cold, almost reptilian. Pat Nixon, however, evoked her sympathy. Beneath her polished facade, the first lady seemed nervous and uncomfortable. Her posture was unnaturally stiff, as if she had to brace herself to keep from crumbling, and Gussie felt a twinge of compassion. On a much smaller scale she had experienced the same panic at having her actions dictated and judged by outside forces. She knew precisely what it was like to be constantly on display.

The Nixons stayed only an hour, but their presence elevated

the excitement to a manic level. By the time dinner was served, even the most dour guests were feeling giddy after such a close brush with power. When Richard Chandler took his seat beside Gussie, he was visibly exhilarated.

"This has been quite an evening," he said. "It was a real coup getting Nixon here."

Gussie nodded politely, hoping her silence would discourage him. Unlike that of the rest of the guests, her mood had progressively deteriorated, her thoughts continually straying to Tony and their doomed relationship.

"I'm really looking forward to the next eight years," he went on. "It'll make a hell of a difference having our man in the White House."

"You sound just like my father."

Richard smiled. "I'll take that as a compliment."

"Of course."

Lowering her eyes, Gussie stared at her glazed Cornish hen with distaste, finding both the meal and the company unappetizing. Then as she delicately speared a bit of asparagus, she felt her father watching her. Perhaps because she had always craved his approval, she was able to sense his annoyance from across the room. He was sending her a silent reproach and an order to treat Richard Chandler with more deference. And because she had been conditioned to be a dutiful daughter, she turned to Richard and offered him a brilliant smile.

"I understand you just bought a horse farm in Maryland."

"It's quite a spread; you'll have to see it sometime. Horses are fascinating creatures, much more interesting than politicians."

Gussie heartily agreed. She hated riding and had learned to sit a horse only because Elizabeth had physically dragged her to the stables, but right then she would have preferred the quiet company of an Arabian to the agony of being forced to cultivate Richard Chandler.

"Do you ride?"

"Not very well. I never learned to appreciate the outdoors."

"Then I insist you visit me at the farm. Once you've ridden a prime piece of horseflesh, you'll be addicted. Are you free next Saturday?"

Glancing at her father, Gussie realized she had no choice. He was shooting her a beaming smile bursting with love and pride.

"Next Saturday's fine," she said. "I'd love to see your farm."

"Wonderful. I'll pick you up at noon."

The rest of the evening seemed interminable. Richard hovered at her side, assuming she returned his interest when she actually found him pitifully dull. In spite of his attempt to be genial, his mechanical smile revealed his cold and calculating interior. Gussie tried to avoid comparing him to Tony, but every time she looked at him she was reminded of their vast differences. Tony was warm and open, his conversations stimulating, his lean body capable of arousing her to mindless passion. He had taught her to laugh, to forget her inhibitions, but tomorrow it would be all over.

Tony De Costa occupied the penthouse apartment in a luxury high-rise that was owned and operated by De Costa Enterprises. A decorator commissioned by the company had taken optimum advantages of the magnificent view, leaving the floor-to-ceiling windows unobstructed. The furniture was sleek and masculine, done in shades of beige and brown. But in spite of such gracious amenities as thick hand-woven carpets and priceless paintings, Tony felt like a transitory visitor just passing through.

He would have preferred a rambling old house in the Virginia countryside, but the apartment was convenient, and its impersonal character had never particularly bothered him until he met Gussie and began thinking in terms of the future. Now the place struck him as a barren mausoleum echoing the sounds of loneliness. He had a sudden desire to establish roots, to build something permanent in his life and Gussie was the key.

As he set aside his razor and patted his face dry, Tony was irritated with himself for feeling so apprehensive at the prospect of meeting the Tremains. He was acting like a pimply-faced adolescent anticipating his first date, but he had been around old American money long enough to know his Italian background would immediately brand him an undesirable outsider. He also knew that he would be crazy to sacrifice his pride by groveling for the Tremains' approval—the De Costa name commanded respect all over the world, after all, and he was sole heir to a financial dynasty—and yet he had foolishly fallen in love with Augusta Tremain and was now about to humble himself before her aristocratic parents for the simple privilege of dating her.

Shrugging at his own perversity, Tony padded through the quiet apartment to the spacious den and picked up a manila folder. He had less than an hour to study the report his investigator had compiled on Robert Tremain, less than an hour to prepare himself for what would inevitably be a brutal attack.

Comfortably settled in plush armchairs in front of a crackling fire, Elizabeth and Robert Tremain sipped their morning coffee as they reviewed each delicious detail of their party. Only in the privacy of their bedroom did they permit themselves such casual intimacy. Elizabeth was still in her nightgown, looking slightly older without the sheen of carefully applied cosmetics. Robert wore his favorite terry-cloth robe; his hair was tousled, and the skin beneath his eyes looked puffy from lack of sleep. They would have been mortified to have anyone see them in such a state of disarray, and yet they thoroughly relished their Sunday morning ritual. In a life dominated by public exposure, it was their singular concession to unguarded simplicity.

Gussie stood in the hall listening to the muted sound of their voices, knowing her intrusion would be unwelcome, but afraid to let her deceit continue. After nervously wiping her sweaty palms on her skirt, she softly knocked on the door.

"Who's there?" Robert shouted.

"It's me, I need to talk to you."

"Come in, dear," Elizabeth said.

Moving into the room, Gussie felt like a crude invader. The satin sheets were rumpled, and there was a musky odor in the air. She had a positively disgusting vision of her parents having sex, and her face turned beet red as she pictured them naked and grunting.

"What is it, Augusta? Are you ill? You look feverish."

"I'm fine, Mother, but I have a few things to tell you about Tony."

Robert perked up like a hound on the hunt. "I knew it! You've been hiding something. What's wrong with him?"

"Nothing, but he's not a law student. He's older, a businessman."

"How old?" Robert persisted, looking very much like a prosecuting attorney.

"Thirty-two. His name is Tony De Costa, he's vice president of De Costa Enterprises."

"And a goddam Italian. My daughter's running around with a greasy dago."

"That's not fair. You've never even met him. You never—"

"I know all about his kind. They're crawling all over the Hill like slime, trying to pass themselves off as legitimate businessmen. Your boyfriend's nothing but a two-bit mobster."

Gussie blanched, sinking down on the bed. "You're just saying that because he's Italian."

"That's right, and I won't have him in my house. You get on the phone and tell him I don't want anything to do with him or his goombahs."

Elizabeth had been quietly listening, the muscles around her mouth taut with distress. Now she intervened. "Do you really think that's wise, Robert? De Costa Enterprises is a powerful company."

Shooting to his feet, Robert began to pace, his breathing hard and ragged. "So what the hell am I supposed to do, let some crude peasant run off with my daughter?"

"No, of course not, but let's try to get rid of him with as little unpleasantness as possible."

Enraged that they were discussing her future without even consulting her, Gussie shouted, "What do you mean, 'get rid of him'? I happen to be in love with him, or doesn't that matter?"

"Calm down, Augusta," Elizabeth said. "I'm sure you have deep feelings for this man, but we can't allow you to make a mistake that will ruin the rest of your life. A good marriage is essential for a woman. There's no room for romantic fantasies."

Gussie was close to tears now, nearly choking on her words. "Please . . . just give him a chance. Meet him. Get to know him."

Elizabeth shook her head. "It's over, Augusta. You're not to see him again after today."

"But I—"

"You heard your mother. There's nothing more to say."

Feeling like a mortally wounded animal, Gussie retreated to her room, hurting in a way she had never imagined.

The brunch was a gruesome affair served in the formal dining room and accompanied by a pretentious display of Elizabeth's finest Baccarat crystal and Sèvres china. Morning-fresh orchids graced the center of the table. The champagne was French and very expensive—a lavish spread calculated to intimidate a social inferior.

"I hear your company's been applying some pretty heavy pressure over on the Hill, trying to swing the vote on the foreign trade bill," Robert said.

"We've hired a lobbyist to protect our interests. I'd hardly call that heavy pressure." Tony smiled, but his black eyes were alert. "After all, lobbyists are a way of life these days."

"As long as they stay within the law."

"Are you implying that my company has done something illegal?"

Robert shrugged. "There's a fine line between suggestion and coercion. You people don't always play by the rules."

Leaning back in his chair, Tony smoothed his fingers over his spoon, his expression inscrutable. After an uncomfortably long silence, he said, "I'm sure you didn't mean that the way it sounded, Senator."

His cheeks florid, Robert wiped a bit of spittle from the corner of his mouth, then threw his napkin aside. "Come on, De Costa, you know what I'm talking about. You foreigners are muscling in where you're not wanted. This country belongs to honest Americans, not to a bunch of wild-eyed hoods."

Gussie recoiled with shock, frantically struggling to speak, but it was Elizabeth who finally attempted to avert a disaster. "This is certainly no place to argue politics. Augusta, why don't you show Mr. De Costa the greenhouse while I see about fresh coffee?"

Tony rose and, with a formal bow, extended his hand to Elizabeth. "That's not necessary, Mrs. Tremain. I'll be leaving now. As your husband so clearly reminded me, I'm not welcome here."

Her poise totally deserting her, Elizabeth limply clasped his hand, her eyes wide with panic. "I . . . There's no need for you to leave."

"I'm afraid there is. I'll be in touch, Gussie."

He smiled briefly, then left the room with quiet dignity.

Gussie spent the afternoon and early evening raging against her parents. Every time she closed her eyes, she felt an acute emptiness, as if some vital inner substance had been scooped out of her and destroyed. In the space of just a few moments her dreams had turned to ashes. She had simultaneously lost Tony and been stripped of the childish illusion that her parents would never intentionally hurt her.

Over the years she had in many instances been forced to sublimate her own wishes to those of her parents. She had always done so with a minimum of fussing because she'd possessed an unshakable belief in their love and benevolence. But this time they had mercilessly stolen something she treasured without even considering the pain they were causing. They had acted purely on selfish motives, and her anger was white-hot and relentless.

As she thrashed on her bed, all she could think of was defying her parents and rushing to Tony. The thought simmered and churned until it became an uncontrollable impulse, driving her to dress in silence, slip silently out of the house, and flee to her car.

Her hands trembled on the steering wheel as she guided the Triumph away from her parents' house and through the quiet streets of Georgetown. The night was cold and dark, and she felt a gut-wrenching loneliness, magnified by the lights shining from the houses along the way. She imagined families and friends gathered around glowing fires, enjoying a Sunday evening together while she pressed her nose to the window, the perennial outsider.

By the time she reached Tony's apartment, the dull ache in her chest had become a throbbing pain. She waited impatiently for the elevator, then pounded on his door. When he opened the door, she collapsed in his arms, her voice quavering. "I love you; I couldn't stay away. Hold me, Tony."

He held her gently in his arms, brushing strands of hair away from her face. "It's all right, *cara*. I'm here."

She knew it would never be all right, but for now it was enough just to feel the strength of his hands, the hardness of his body. Tomorrow she would face her shattering losses; tonight she allowed herself to forget.

Still holding her close, he led her into the living room and eased her down on the sofa beside him.

She looked up at him through tear-filled eyes. "I'm so sorry about this morning. . . ."

"We're together now. Nothing else matters."

"They had no right to insult you," she said.

He tenderly kissed her forehead. "Listen to me, *cara*. I love you. There's nothing your parents can do to drive me away."

Pressing herself against him, Gussie twined her arms around his neck and found his mouth, kissing him with an urgent hunger that left her weak and trembling. Suddenly her senses were running riot. She wanted him, wanted to feel his long, slender fingers play over her skin, wanted to know the sensation of his burying himself deep within her. She wanted him to possess her totally.

Tony gently lowered her back against the thick cushions, stroking her breasts, settling his hips between her thighs. Then as he slowly caressed her, she moaned and arched against the hard length of his body. "Make love to me."

"Are you sure?"

"Please."

They undressed and came together slowly and without words, savoring the joy of each touch, each cry of pleasure. Gussie gave herself completely, opening herself to his fingers, his tongue, and at last the mindless ecstasy of his penetration. Ever sensitive to her needs, Tony paced his thrusts, rising and falling, inexorably leading her to an explosion of physical release.

Afterward Gussie rested in his arms, her skin tingling, her mind drifting in a thoughtless haze.

"Are you all right, *cara*?"

"I'm wonderful." She felt him smile against her cheek and snuggled closer to his warmth. "It was perfect. I knew it would be perfect with you."

He playfully nuzzled her chin. "How did you know?"

"Because I love you."

"No regrets?"

"None." But the moment the word was out of her mouth, Gussie felt reality come crashing back with a shattering thud. She had just made love to Tony, a man she could never hope to marry. Her body went rigid as she began to assimilate the possible consequences of what she had done.

"Gussie, what's wrong?"

"I came here to . . . I never meant . . ."

Totally misunderstanding her sudden anxiety, Tony lifted her chin, forcing her to look at him. "You came here because we needed to be together. We belong together, Gussie. Will you marry me?"

Gussie felt a sickening ache in the pit of her stomach. She loved him, deeply and irrevocably, but she was terrified of being turned away from the only life she had ever known. "My parents . . . I can't . . . marry you."

Tony held her away from him, staring into her eyes. "What are you saying?"

"I'm not strong enough. I've never . . ." She lowered her eyes. "I have no choice."

"Of course you do. And once we're married they'll accept what they can't change."

She shook her head. "You don't know my father. I'd be an outcast; they'd never forgive me."

Anger lit his black eyes with a dangerous glow. "Then what are you doing here? Why the hell did you let me make love to you?"

Shrinking from his fury, Gussie twisted away from him. "Because I needed you. I needed something to remember."

He laughed bitterly. "You mean you needed a stud. That's all you ever wanted from me."

Gussie felt the life being sucked from her body, flowing like blood from her gaping wounds, leaving her an empty shell. "You're wrong," she said softly. "I love you. I'll always love you."

But Tony just looked at her with disgust, and as she gazed into his eyes, she knew she had sacrificed something precious, something she would never find again. The cost of her family loyalty would be a lifetime of regret.

A damp chill penetrated his tiny office as Ralph Edwards gathered the last of his personal belongings and carefully placed them in a cardboard box. He still found it difficult to believe he was actually retiring, shuffling off into the sunset like a used-up old man. But the town council had given him no choice. They wanted a younger, more vigorous police chief, college educated and smooth enough to relate well to the tourists. Laughing harshly, Edwards shook his head. What they wanted was a goddam public relations man, not a cop.

He had been repressing thoughts of the future for weeks, but now that he was faced with the task of cleaning out his office, his retirement seemed real for the first time. In just a few days his replacement would arrive from Boston, and Ralph Edwards would become another old relic clinging to the periphery of life.

Hot tears scalded his eyes, and he quickly reached for his hankie and blotted them away. Being caught crying in his office would be the final humiliation, a disgrace that would strip him of the last shreds of his pride. He remained immobile for a moment, staring out the window at the ocean; then as he regained control, he reached for the last folder buried in his desk drawer and thoughtfully studied it.

Circumstances had forced him to abandon the Conti case months ago, but he had never truly accepted defeat. Rick Conti was still on his mind, still intruding on his thoughts in the early hours of morning. Regulations demanded that he leave the file behind for his successor, but in a rare moment of defiance, he furtively glanced over his shoulder and then stuffed it into one of the boxes on the floor. Even old men had the right to dream, he thought. And maybe the Conti case would offer him a chance to reclaim his waning dignity.

CHAPTER
Eleven

RHETTA GREEN IMPATIENTLY STRUMMED HER FINGERS ON THE STEERING wheel while she waited to be cleared through the gates of Imperial Studios. She was nervous about her meeting with Jack Golden and could feel the perspiration breaking out under her arms, staining the wildly extravagant silk blouse she had just charged at Saks. Like her equally extravagant beige suede suit, the blouse had been a necessary expense. In a town like Hollywood appearances were everything. If you looked even slightly down-at-heel you were branded a loser, and right now Rhetta desperately needed to look like a winner.

When the guard finally waved her through the gates, she pulled into a space beside the towering glass office building and hurried inside. In the privacy of the elevator, she smoothed her hands over the soft fabric of her skirt, wishing she could lose the ten pounds that padded her middle. It was becoming increasingly difficult to squeeze herself into designer clothes and to look like a successful agent.

The elevator whooshed to a stop on the tenth floor, and when Rhetta entered the suite of offices and announced herself to a gorgeous blond receptionist, she knew Golden would keep her waiting for at least twenty minutes. It was an old power play, but it worked. By the time you finally gained entrance to the inner sanctum, you were probably intimidated.

Her prediction proved accurate when Golden appeared in the doorway precisely eighteen minutes later pleasantly smiling. "Rhetta, it's nice to see you."

"Hello, Jack." She stood and shook his hand, then followed him into his luxurious office. Obviously his fortunes had risen since she had last seen him. The chrome and glass furniture was chic and expensive and the paintings were all originals.

113

She wondered if he still remembered the old days, when he had been a hungry young director begging Rhetta Green to send him some fresh talent. Probably not, she decided. That was another thing about Hollywood—people had very selective memories.

"Would you like a drink?" he said, motioning her to a plush maroon chair.

"Bourbon on the rocks, if you have it." She had no desire for a drink, but it was part of the ritual, a prelude to business. If she refused, he would assume she was too much of an outsider to be familiar with the way things were done, or a renegade trying to demonstrate her independence. She had no intention of allowing him to make either assumption.

After a few minutes of inconsequential chatter Golden rested both elbows on his desk, signifying the start of business. "What can I do for you, Rhetta?"

"I understand you're casting *Midnight Sky*."

He nodded. "I've already signed Ken Barnes for the male lead."

"What about the girl?"

"I'm considering Angela Wade, but it's not final."

"Good, because I've got somebody for you."

His only visible sign of interest was a slight puckering of his furry brows. "Who?"

Until that minute Rhetta had been uncertain about revealing Helene's true identity, but now she sensed that Golden would never consider using an unknown and made an impulsive decision. "Helene Galloway."

"Brenda's daughter?"

Nodding, Rhetta lit a cigarette. "She's had six months with Nadia Rostoff. Wait till you see her, Jack. She has the talent to make this picture a smash."

"You must have heard wrong. I'm not in the market for tits; I need somebody fragile."

Rhetta laughed, knowing he was picturing a younger version of Brenda. "She's nothing like her mother. Here, have a look."

She passed him a glossy photograph and watched his expression evolve from bored apathy to controlled excitement as he studied the exquisite face in front of him. After a long silence, he said, "Can she act?"

"Would Nadia waste her time on a loser?"

"All right, I'll schedule a screen test for tomorrow morning, but don't get your hopes up. She'll have to make Angela Wade look like chicken shit to get the part."

"She will," Rhetta said smiling. "You can count on it."

Helene was terrified as she crossed the soundstage to join the small knot of people clustered around the set. She had studied the script Rhetta had given her until dawn, but she was still afraid of garbling her lines. Then, as Jack Golden approached her, she froze.

"Helene, I'm Jack Golden."

"I know. I . . . Where do you want me?"

Golden patted her shoulder. "Relax, kid. I'll have Bonnie take you over to makeup." He snapped his fingers, and a young woman came running. "Show Helene the dressing room and have Elena get started on her hair."

"Sure thing. Come on, Helene."

Bonnie whisked her away to a cramped little room at the edge of the set where an efficient Spanish woman styled her hair, applied fresh makeup, and helped her into a faded cotton dress. As she returned to the set, Helene concentrated on transforming herself into Nellie Howard, a vulnerable widow fighting to save her ranch from greedy cattle barons. During the course of the film she would be raped, nearly frozen to death in a brutal blizzard, and attacked by renegade Indians. Only in the final minutes of the movie would she triumph over her enemies and marry her lover.

Though the plot was typical Hollywood pap, Helene knew it would require a great deal of emotional depth to realistically portray such a tormented woman. If she failed to evoke the sympathy and support of the audience, the movie would come across as a shallow parody of a thousand other westerns.

They ended up doing two separate tests—one with the man who played Nellie's lover, the other with the greedy banker who was foreclosing on her ranch. As Helene lost herself in the role, the studio faded away and she became Nellie Howard, a lone woman fighting to preserve her heritage. Barely aware of Golden's whispered directions, she was guided by an inner voice, an inherent understanding of the character. When the bright lights finally dimmed, she stood immobile in the darkness, drained and strangely elated.

— — —

Several hours later, Jack Golden and his assistant Hy Schorr sat in a projection room viewing the screen-test film for the third time. As the screen went blank, Golden said, "What do you think?"

"The camera loves her; she's a natural."

Golden snorted. "She's a hell of a lot more than that. This kid has it. She'll rip through this town like a goddam tornado." Flicking on the light, he turned to Schorr. "I want her for *Midnight Sky*."

"She looks good, but . . ."

"What? What the hell's the matter with you, you putz? She's solid gold."

Unruffled, Schorr sucked on his pipe. "A test's one thing, how do we know she can hack the pressure of a movie?"

Golden sprang to his feet, pounding on his chest. "I feel it in here. I can smell a star a mile away. That's why I'm a director and you're still an assistant."

Schorr shrugged off the remark. "You're talking the lead in a major picture. Why not wait and try her in something else?"

"Bullshit. If I wait I might lose her. You think Rhetta Green's gonna sit and wait while we make up our minds? No way. I want this kid. Get on the phone to legal right now."

"What about Angela Wade?"

"Call her. Tell her I've got something better in the works for her."

"She won't like it."

"Make her like it. Earn your salary for once."

Schorr shrugged, then gathered up his papers and left the room. The instant he closed the door, Jack Golden turned on the projector and smiled as Helene came into focus.

Helene spent a restless night tossing and turning, wishing she had a friend or a lover to share her anxiety. She was tempted to calm her nerves with a shot of booze and actually opened a bottle of scotch before she managed to get herself under control. It would have been so easy to slip back into her old habits. She fought an internal battle every night, every time the gruesome dreams shattered her sleep. So far she had been strong enough to resist, but the bottle was always there waiting to claim her.

She was awake the entire night, and in the morning she felt shaky and slightly sick to her stomach. When she heard the unmistakable sound of Rhetta's decrepit Volkswagen sputtering into the driveway, she ran outside, every nerve in her body humming at once.

Beaming, Rhetta poked her head out the window. "You got it. Golden wants you for *Midnight Sky*."

Helene went weak all over.

"The contracts'll be ready this afternoon." Rhetta climbed out of the car and flung her arms around Helene. "This is it. We're on our way."

As Helene clung to Rhetta, a surge of panic slashed away at her elation. Her old insecurities came creeping back, and she suddenly doubted her ability to bring Nellie Howard to life. "Maybe it's too soon. What if I . . ."

Rhetta released her, looking directly into her eyes. "You promised to trust me. That's part of the deal."

"I do."

"Then believe me, you're ready for this."

Their eyes remained locked together for several seconds; then Helene smiled. "I'll try."

"Good. Now how about a cup of coffee? We have a few things to work out."

Helene rarely ventured into the kitchen, but she was reluctant to entertain Rhetta in the formal living room. It was so overdone and pretentious, rife with memories of Brenda. "Would you mind sitting in the kitchen? I hate the rest of the house. My mother . . . I'm just not comfortable . . ."

Rhetta gave her an odd look, a blend of sympathy and restrained curiosity. "The kitchen's fine."

Once they were settled at the round oak table cradling mugs of coffee, Helene relaxed slightly. Sunlight poured through the windows, casting geometric patterns on the orange tile floor. A light breeze ruffled the curtains, and the scent of freshly brewed coffee lingered in the air. There was something reassuring about the kitchen, something solid and earthy, something that made Helene feel secure.

Rhetta swallowed a mouthful of coffee, then sat back and lit a cigarette, visibly uneasy. "There's just one glitch, Helene. Jack Golden wants the Galloway name."

"Who told him my real name?"

Again Rhetta looked directly into her eyes. "I did. It was the only way I could persuade him to test you."

Helene averted her gaze and stared quietly at her hands, her outward calm masking inner turmoil. She never willingly thought about Brenda or the night that had irreversibly severed their relationship, but now the floodgates opened and strange images washed over her like a wall of rushing water.

"Helene, what's wrong?"

Drowning in her thoughts, Helene was beyond the reach of Rhetta's voice. Then Rhetta reached out to embrace her, rocking her against her chest. "Do you want to talk?"

Helene shook her head. "I can't, not about my mother."

"Jesus, was it that bad living with Brenda?"

"Not the way you think. . . . Please, don't ask me."

Rhetta fished in her purse for a hankie and gently wiped the tears from Helene's face. "Just as long as you know I'm here if you ever need to talk."

Helene nodded and reluctantly left the circle of Rhetta's arms. "Maybe someday. I'm sorry for putting you through this, Rhetta."

"It's all right. I know how it feels to hurt inside."

Looking at Rhetta, Helene saw a rare sorrow in her eyes, a lingering trace of a pain repressed but never forgotten. Then a current of awareness seemed to pass between them, bonding them in some inexplicable way. They were no longer strangers; they had quietly crossed an invisible barrier.

After a long silence, Rhetta cleared her throat and said, "What do you want to do about Golden?"

"Go ahead with the contract. I'll use my real name."

"Look, there'll be other deals. You can afford to wait."

Helene smiled weakly. "I want to do *Midnight Sky*. It's right for me, I can feel it."

"Okay, then, we'll meet at Imperial this afternoon to sign the contracts. Shooting starts in three weeks."

Helene agreed and their conversation wandered to less sensitive subjects, but as Rhetta was getting ready to leave, she said, "You can tell me this is none of my business, but why the hell do you stay in this house? Why not get a place of your own?"

Truly surprised, Helene shrugged. "I never thought about it."

"But you seem to hate this place."

"I do. I've always hated it, but a house of my own . . . I don't know."

"I've got a friend in real estate. I can have her look around a little if you want."

The idea of her own house, a house with no memories of Brenda, was immensely appealing. "Yes, tell her to look for something in the desert, something simple."

Rhetta scribbled a note to herself, then kissed Helene good-bye and hurried out to her car. As Helene stood in front of the window watching her drive away, she smiled. She had finally found a mother, a mother to love and protect her.

Three months later *Midnight Sky* was in full production, but there were multiple problems. Jack Golden was a perfectionist with an explosive temper, regularly castigating the actors for the most minor mistakes. Morale on the set was terrible, and both cast and crew dreaded the day they would leave to go on location in Montana. If Jack behaved like a maniac in the studio where he had absolute control, how would he react to the vagaries of nature and the difficulty of shooting outdoors?

Predictions of more frequent outbursts abounded, and while the older, more experienced actors had the advantage of knowing Jack would eventually produce a box office smash despite his craziness, Helene worried constantly, certain the movie would be a flop.

She also worried about her new life-style—an endless round of studio-arranged dates and parties. Intellectually she understood the need for publicity, but she detested pretending to be infatuated with a string of strange men who were interested in nothing more than being photographed with a rising star. The whole scene depressed her. She was lonely and tired, disillusioned by all the hype.

Now, seated across from Rhetta at the Polo Lounge, Helene felt conspicuous. She had wanted to meet at a less public place, but Rhetta had insisted on visibility. They hardly ever saw each other in private anymore, and Helene missed the intimacy of their quiet talks. Rhetta was her only friend in Hollywood, the only person who truly cared about her.

"So what's Jack been up to this week?"

"Sharon Sullivan left the set in tears. He called her a stupid cunt."

"Jesus, I think he's losing his mind. What about you? Have you had any trouble with him?"

Helene shrugged. "Not really."

"Then why do you look so down?"

"The night life is wearing me out. Sometimes I feel as if I need a drink just to get through the parties." Helene had confessed her weakness for alcohol months ago, and now she looked at Rhetta imploringly. "I'm so afraid I'll ruin things."

Clearly upset, Rhetta pushed the remains of her salade Niçoise to the middle of the table, eyeing it with distaste. "What about the nightmares? Are you still having trouble sleeping?"

"Jack got me some pills through the studio doctor."

Rhetta blanched. "What kind of pills?"

"Don't look at me like that. They're just mild sleeping pills."

"What the hell's the matter with you? Those things are narcotics. Golden's poisoning you just so he can get his fucking film in the can."

Her voice had risen to a shrill pitch, and she quickly glanced around the room, smiling artificially at the few people who were staring at them. Then in a softer tone, she said, "Helene, promise me you'll get rid of the pills. If you start with that crap, you'll end up a burned-out wreck."

Shaken more by Rhetta's angry outburst than by the remote possibility of becoming addicted to the little black pills, Helene nodded. "They don't help that much anyway."

Rhetta studied her in silence for a moment, then said, "Look, maybe you should see somebody, talk about whatever's bothering you."

Instantly on guard, Helene violently shook her head. A psychiatrist would pick and probe until he unearthed her memories, memories she had buried for eternity. "I could never do that, never."

"Why? It's a hell of a lot safer than pills."

"Let it go, Rhetta. I don't need a psychiatrist, and I promise I'll throw the pills away."

Sighing, Rhetta shrugged helplessly. "All right. I'll give

Jack a call, see if we can cut down on the parties. Where's he got you going tonight?''

"Marty Waltman's house. He just remarried for the third time, and his wife wants to celebrate."

"Wonderful. Why not see if you can cancel?"

"I got the word right from Jack. This is a command performance."

"Then I guess you have no choice." Rhetta reached across the table and squeezed her hand. "Be careful, Helene. If it starts getting to you, call a cab and go home."

Feeling a good deal better, Helene offered her a dazzling smile. "I'll be fine. You worry too much."

Seth Wilder slipped through the glass doors, crossed the lawn, and flopped on a chaise longue beside the pool. He was seeking a few minutes of quiet solitude, but the abrasive noise of the party filtered through the windows, disturbing the harmony of the chirping crickets and the soft swish of the water lapping at the sides of the pool. A typical Hollywood bash—loud, gaudy, and utterly boring.

Gulping down the diluted remains of his drink, Seth leaned back, regretting his impulsive decision to attend the party. He knew he had a reputation for being a loner, a thrill-seeker who lived on the edge, but even the tabloids had never linked him to the showy side of Hollywood. Seth Wilder was known as a renegade director, a thorn in the paw of the establishment. Why, then, was he here courting an asshole like Marty Waltman?

The answer was pathetically simple: Seth Wilder needed a miracle, and he needed it now. After five critically acclaimed films that had been box office disasters, his financial backing had dried up like a rain squall in the desert. Either he did something commercial to redeem himself or he gave up the ghost of his career. Artistic integrity belonged to starving dreamers and wealthy old men. In the real world, money was the only measure of success.

Lost in this thoughts, Seth was unaware of the young woman hovering in the shadows until he heard her sigh, a lonely sound that struck a chord deep inside him. Turning his head, he stared into the darkness, finally discerning the vague outline of a slender form. "Are you all right?" he asked.

She jumped as if his voice had taken her by surprise, but she remained completely silent.

"Sorry. I didn't mean to intrude. I just wanted to make sure you were okay."

Her eyes glittered in the darkness, reflecting the glow of the lights around the pool. She stood perfectly still, and he wondered if he had frightened her or if maybe she was zonked out of her mind. "Look, I'm not going to hurt you. Just tell me you're okay and I'll leave you alone."

Slowly she emerged from the shadows, warily approaching him. "The crowd was closing in on me. I had to get away for a minute."

Knowing exactly how she felt, Seth nodded. "I'm not much for parties myself."

"Then what are you doing here?"

"Business. How about you?" She sighed again, and he had a bizarre impulse to touch her, to comfort her.

"I'm doing a movie for Jack Golden. He insisted I come," she said.

"Ah, one of those deals. Jack likes to throw his weight around. I'll bet he's got you out on the town every night."

She came closer, and for the first time he had a clear view of one of the loveliest faces he had ever seen. Her features were delicately beautiful, but it was her eyes that captivated him. They were dark and wide, naked and accessible. In a town where everyone wore a mask, she exposed herself in a way that shook him to the core.

Snagging another chaise longue with his foot, he dragged it closer, then patted the canvas seat. "Sit down. Talk to me."

She moved with fluid grace, lowering herself to the chaise, offering him a tentative smile. "Are you an actor?"

"Right now I'm an out-of-work director."

"Have you done any films?"

He laughed harshly. "Five—all bombs."

She quietly studied him; then recognition flickered in her eyes. "You're Seth Wilder. You did *The Last Rose*. It was wonderful. I thought about the ending for weeks."

He was surprised and oddly disappointed by her flattery; yet there was no phony gleam in her eyes, only sincere admiration. "Did the ending bother you?"

"I knew it had to be that way, but I kept hoping . . ."

"You would have had Margot and Henri live happily ever after?"

"Probably, but then the picture would have been a fantasy, a silly love story."

"Not silly, just unrealistic."

"Is that how you see love? Unrealistic?"

Shrugging, he stared into the night. "Maybe the real thing exists somewhere out there, but not here in Hollywood. We're too good at pretending."

She lowered her eyes, and he instantly regretted infecting her with his cynicism. "This is a hell of a conversation we're having. You've got me baring my soul, and I don't even know your name."

"Helene Galloway."

"The star of *Midnight Sky*. I should have recognized you."

She shook her head. "I came out here to get away from all that. I felt so alone in there. Everybody was a stranger."

Seth felt her bewildered helplessness all the way to his gut, and it scared the hell out of him. His own emotions were buried beneath layers of contempt and mockery. He had no inclination to be touched, and yet Helene Galloway was slipping past his defenses with her vulnerable eyes and gentle smile. His rational mind told him to retreat, find his car, and go home, but some perverse part of him wanted to know Helene Galloway.

"There's a bar not far from here," he heard himself saying. "How about having a drink with me?"

"I'd like that."

"I'll get my car. Meet me out front in about five minutes."

On some level Helene knew she was dreaming, but the horrible vision seemed real—as real as the fear racing through her system. She saw the bony hands hovering above her, coming closer and closer. Her nostrils were filled with the stench of rotting flesh. She knew she was about to be tortured to death by the skeletal claws. They curled around her throat, ripping at her skin, strangling her with inhuman force. She was dying . . . dying. . . .

Then suddenly her eyes snapped open and she screamed, but instead of awakening to lonely terror, she felt powerful arms encircling her body, offering her refuge.

"Helene, it's all right. It was only a dream."

Helene softly whimpered, the horror of the nightmare still vivid in her mind. She was too muddled to identify the source of the gentle pressure on her shoulders, but intuitively she moved closer, greedily absorbing the comforting strokes. It was a long time before she looked up at Seth.

"Feeling better?" he whispered, his breath warm on her cheek.

"A little."

Fitting her snugly against his chest, he traced the fragile bones of her face with his fingers. "What were you dreaming?"

"A skeleton was killing me, choking me." She felt terribly vulnerable, afraid she might crumble. "Please stay with me. Don't leave me alone."

"Is that why you brought me here, so you wouldn't be alone?"

She remembered his tender lovemaking, the gentleness of his touch. "No. I wanted to make love to you."

Cupping her face between his hands, he looked into her eyes. "If I stay, I might hurt you. I can't give you any promises."

"I don't need promises."

His deep blue eyes were intense, shining in the darkness. "Are you sure? Will it be enough just having me here?"

"You mean you'll stay?"

He softly kissed her. "This is crazy. I'm not good at relationships, Helene."

"Me either, but I want to try with you."

"Why?" He sounded almost afraid.

"Because you're different. You make me feel . . . not so alone."

Sighing, he cradled her slight body in his arms, sifting his fingers through the black silkiness of her hair. "You're not alone, not anymore."

Helene smiled. At last she felt whole, as if she had been rummaging through the attic of her mind and had suddenly discovered the missing parts of herself, precious threads that would complete the tapestry of her life. Somehow she knew Seth Wilder was destined to fill her inner emptiness, and as she drifted off to sleep, the nightmares receded like clouds floating over the horizon.

PART
Four

Summer 1971

CHAPTER
Twelve

"I'M SCRAPPING YOUR MISS AMERICA PIECE."

Shocked, Diane looked at Ed Blake and saw an unmistakable glint of triumph in his eyes. "Why?"

"Because nobody told you to interview those dykes who were protesting outside. You turned the whole segment into a women's lib crusade."

Diane tried to control the anger welling up inside her. "I added some depth to a piece of fluff. What's wrong with that?"

Ed crossed the room and stood directly in front of her desk in an obvious attempt to intimidate her. "Nobody wants to watch that crap. You think farmers in Iowa care about a bunch of lesbos parading around on the boardwalk burning their goddam bras? The hell they do. They want to see an American tradition."

"So we just feed them another dose of fantasy? Come on, Ed. There are women out there who have something to say about beauty pageants, and they have a right to be heard."

"Forget it." He strutted over to the window, imperiously shaking his head. "I'm trashing the segment, and the next time you get any brilliant ideas remember how much this little fiasco's going to cost the network. If it happens again, I'll take it upstairs."

She was certain he had already taken it upstairs, but there was no way she could defend herself or go over his head. Since his promotion to executive producer eighteen months ago, Ed had effectively cut off all communication between staff members and the top brass. Upper management now relied exclusively on his distorted versions of events, and anyone who crossed him ended up on the unemployment line. In just a short time he had carved himself a permanent niche at the studio.

"You're being unreasonable, Ed," she said, knowing her protest was futile but unable to resist a last jab.

He spun around, his features contorted with anger. "Who the hell do you think you're talking to? One word from me and you're out of here on your ass."

"I know that."

"So knock off the bullshit. I'm putting you on the plastic surgery segment. See if you can turn in a decent piece of work." Then without even bothering to gauge her reaction, he slammed out of her office.

Diane touched her temples, gently rubbing at the beginnings of a headache. The plastic surgery piece was another trivial bit of glitz about how the rich and famous dealt with dimpled thighs and bulbous noses—just the sort of thing Ed continually foisted off on her. She was now an assistant producer, entitled to an occasional independent assignment, but Ed made sure she never got anything substantial. Those pieces he reserved for the men who religiously kissed his ass as if they were worshiping at a sacred relic.

It was remarkable how things had deteriorated since Ed took over from Jordan Carr. Under Jordan there had been consistency and some sense of fairness, but Ed played by his own rules. His promotions and demotions were arbitrary, rarely based on competence. In fact, the one thing Diane had never been able to figure out was why Ed had allowed her to remain in her position after Jordan left. She had expected to be either fired or demoted immediately. Instead, Ed had permitted her to remain an assistant producer, though he seemed to derive a sadistic sort of pleasure from harassing her. Consequently, she found herself in a perpetual state of morbid anticipation, waiting for him to end her career.

A knock on the door roused Diane from her thoughts. "Come in," she said and was relieved to see Angie step through the door carrying containers of Chinese food.

"Here you go—instant indigestion from the Pearl of China— two egg rolls and pork fried rice."

"Thanks. How about sharing with me?"

"I thought you were starved."

"Not anymore. Ed canceled the Miss America piece."

"Oh, Christ. Hold on while I get us some plates."

While Angie scurried off to the kitchen, Diane felt a small

stab of satisfaction. Hiring Angie had been a minor rebellion, one of her few victories in the long and debilitating war with Ed Blake. Instead of choosing a fresh-faced—and inexperienced—college girl as her secretary, she had defied convention by offering the job to Angie, a chubby bundle of energy who had been born and raised on the Lower East Side and who could out-type an army of sweet young things. Ed hated her, but Diane found her quick intelligence and blunt manner invigorating and had never once regretted her decision to hire her.

"All right, tell me what happened," Angie said as she swept into the room balancing plates and silverware.

"Ed accused me of desecrating an American tradition. He claims nobody wants to watch a bunch of dykes burning their bras."

"So he just scratched the whole piece?"

"You got it."

Angie wrinkled her nose. "What an asshole. I knew he was up to something. He had that funny look all week, like he was about to come for the first time in ten years."

Laughing, Diane scooped out two servings of fried rice and laid an egg roll on each plate. "I doubt he's capable."

"Not true. I hear he's been boffing Pat Reynolds from the typing pool."

"You're kidding! What would she want with an old sleaze like Ed?"

Angie gulped down a mouthful of egg roll. "What else? A promotion."

"God, I'd rather sweep floors."

Nodding her agreement, Angie helped herself to another serving of fried rice. "Men like Ed can't be trusted. How much do you want to bet she never even gets promoted?"

Diane listlessly picked at her lunch. She was too angry to eat, and the vague queasiness that had been plaguing her for the past few weeks was turning into a case of full-blown nausea.

"Hey, are you okay?" Angie said. "You look lousy all of a sudden."

"I feel kind of sick to my stomach."

"Again? That's the third time this week. Maybe you should see a doctor."

"It's just stress."

"Yeah, well too much stress and you end up with an ulcer. Why don't you go home, take the afternoon off?"

Diane shook her head, but the idea of going home and stretching out on the bed had already taken root in her mind. "Do I have any meetings this afternoon?"

"Nothing I can't reschedule. Just go home and relax."

Once Diane was settled on the blistered vinyl seat of a cab, her nausea abated, but her anger remained intact. Every time she thought of Ed Blake, she castigated herself for tolerating his terrorism. Was her ambition really worth twelve-hour days and constant abuse? She was becoming addicted to her career, and her hunger for success was devouring everything else in her life.

She thought of Joel and a marriage that had started out so bright and promising, a marriage that was now slowly deteriorating. Somehow their relationship had fallen victim to the pressures of her job and his chronic frustration. Their easy communication had dwindled to cool indifference punctuated by occasional bursts of temper. No matter how often she vowed to work harder at salvaging her marriage, she was never quite able to put things right.

Upset by the direction of her thoughts, she gazed out the open window at the traffic moving along Ninth Avenue. At lease they were living better these days. Her promotion had provided extra money to rent a third-floor apartment in a more pleasant section of Chelsea. While their building was far from luxurious, it did offer a few basic amenities such as well-lit halls and regular visits by an exterminator. She would have enjoyed a great sense of accomplishment if not for the fact that Joel heartily resented her for being able to pay the rent.

As the driver stopped at the curb, Diane handed him the fare and a tip, then climbed out of the cab and crossed the sidewalk to her building. Her legs felt too weak and unsteady to support her weight. Maybe she was suffering from more than a simple case of overwork. But the idea of being incapacitated frightened her and she quickly shoved it aside, convincing herself she was merely indulging in an advanced case of hypochondria.

She heard the frenzied screams of a quiz-show audience the minute she entered the apartment. Then she saw Joel sprawled out on the sofa staring at the television, a half-eaten sandwich in his hand, an overflowing ashtray precariously balanced on his stomach. She tried to suppress her annoyance, but the messy apartment and the sight of Joel frittering away another day drove her to distraction.

"What are you doing here? I thought you were supposed to be meeting with your agent?"

He briefly lifted his head, then turned back to the quiz show. "No sense in running all the way down there. I called him."

"And?"

"Nothing this week."

"What about next week?"

"Lay off, will you? I'm trying to watch this."

Furious, Diane stalked across the room and turned off the television. "Joel, you haven't worked in four months—*four months.*"

"So? You work enough for both of us."

"That's not fair."

He shrugged, refusing to look at her. "Bernie says it's slow right now. Things'll get better."

Her shoulders sagging, Diane slumped down on a chair. "When? You can't just sit here vegetating for the rest of your life."

"What's the matter? Getting tired of supporting your shift-less husband?"

She wanted to lash out at him, admit she was sick to death of watching him squander himself on stale dreams and empty promises, but the words died in her throat. What good would it do to add to his misery?

"You know I don't care about the money," she said carefully. "I just hate to see you so . . . so gloomy and bored."

He laughed mirthlessly. "That's the price of being a kept man. I have no pride."

"Then do something about it. There are all kinds of jobs out there."

"Cut the fucking pep talk. I'm not some kid you can con with that crap."

"Then stop acting like one."

He sat up, staring at her with angry eyes. "You're a real ball buster, you know that?"

Stunned, Diane flinched as if he had slapped her. There was

such malice in his voice, such vicious hatred twisting his mouth. He suddenly seemed like a stranger, a cruel facsimile of Joel. She looked at him, searching for some trace of regret, but his features were frozen in an ugly mask. Then, feeling hot tears burn her eyes, she ran to the bedroom and flung herself across the bed, sobbing bitterly.

An hour later, Joel quietly entered the room and sat beside her. At first she pretended to be asleep, but when he continued to stare at her, she finally opened her eyes. "What do you want?"

"I wish I knew, bright-eyes. I wish I knew how to make us both happy."

His face was pale, his eyes glassy, wet with a residue of tears. Diane felt her anger dissolve into a pool of helplessness. "Why, Joel? Why are you so unhappy?"

"Things just didn't work out the way I thought. My old lady was right. I'm a loser."

"You are not."

"No more lies, Diane. You fucked up; you married a bum. Admit it and get on with your life."

"You are my life. I love you, Joel."

Sighing, he rubbed his eyes with his fists. "You love a dream, a man who never existed. Take a good look at me the way I really am. If you stick around here, I'll drag you down right along with me."

Shattered by the thought of losing him, Diane gripped his hand. "We can work things out; I know we can. Just give it a chance."

"You're kidding yourself, bright-eyes. One of these days you'll wake up hating me for the things I've said to you and the way I've treated you. We're eating each other alive."

Suddenly it occurred to Diane that Joel might be looking for a way out, easing his conscience by forcing her to leave him. "Have you found someone else? Is that what this is all about?"

He laughed, a harsh grating noise that hurt her ears. "What woman would have me?" Then, seeing how his words had wounded her, he touched her cheek. "I love you. There's never been anybody else."

"Then we'll get past this. We still love each other. That's enough to start over."

— — —

Diane worked hard at their reconciliation. She went to great lengths to offer Joel her unconditional support despite his sporadic nastiness and stubborn refusal to look for a traditional job. On the surface their marriage seemed secure again—they made love regularly, spent a good deal of time together laughing and talking—but there were dangerous undercurrents. Joel was tense and occasionally remote. She frequently caught him looking at her in an unsettling way, as if he had something vital to say but had not yet found the right words with which to say it. Still, she continued to cling to the illusion that their marriage would survive, that their troubles were only temporary.

Her self-deception might have gone on indefinitely, but when Angie finally persuaded her to see a doctor everything fell apart.

"You're pregnant, Mrs. Elliot."

"That's impossible. I always use a diaphragm."

He offered her a kind smile. "I'm sorry it comes as such a shock, but you're definitely pregnant."

Diane struggled to breathe. "This is . . . The timing is all wrong. My husband . . ."

Clasping her hand, the doctor smiled reassuringly. "After he gets used to the idea, your husband will be delighted. A baby does wonderful things for a marriage."

Diane looked at him, amazed at his insensitivity. Where had he gotten the mistaken impression that all men would welcome the responsibility of a baby? And what right did he have simply to dismiss her fears as meaningless? He was standing there beaming at her like a benevolent grandfather and suddenly she was furious at the entire male sex.

But by the time she got home, a growing sense of wonder had eclipsed her fury. She imagined a baby, a baby she and Joel had created, and her doubts slowly vanished. Somehow she would make him see that their child was a responsibility worth accepting, a precious gift to cherish. Somehow she would prepare a warm and safe nest for their baby.

Joel was singing in the shower when she entered the apartment. At least he seemed to be in good spirits. On one of his darker days he would have been antagonistic, unlikely to appreciate his impending fatherhood. Maybe it was fate that she had caught him in a cheerful mood.

He emerged from the bathroom grinning. "I've got me a gig, bright-eyes. How about coming along to watch your husband knock 'em dead at the Village Pub?"

"The Village Pub? How did that happen?"

"It was a last-minute thing. Some poor bastard ended up in the hospital, and Bernie worked out a deal for me."

Feeling suddenly optimistic, Diane smiled. "I'd love to come, but first I have a surprise for you."

"What's up?"

"I'm pregnant."

Joel stopped dead in his tracks. "That's a lousy joke."

"It's not a joke. I saw the doctor today. That's why I've been feeling nauseated lately."

His mouth gaping open, Joel dropped to the sofa, pinching the bridge of his nose. "Jesus Christ, things are just coming together for me and you have to get pregnant?"

"Joel, I didn't plan this."

"Maybe not, but you sure as hell didn't prevent it. How could you be so stupid?"

Hurt beyond measure, Diane dumbly looked down at her hands. "It was an accident. You're as much to blame as I am."

Joel softened. "All right, so it just happened. I know some people, I'll find a doctor to get rid of it."

She gasped, her hands reflexively moving to her stomach. "No. Never! What's the matter with you? How can you even think of killing our baby?"

"How can *you* think of keeping it? We have no money, nothing to offer a kid. And what about your precious job? Do you think Ed Blake's going to wait around while you play little mother? Grow up, Diane. The last thing we need is a kid."

Horrified that he could so easily consign their child to death, she was barely able to meet his eyes. "There's no way I'll get rid of this baby."

"Fine, then you can fucking well raise it by yourself."

He stormed into the bedroom and packed a shabby suitcase. Then, not even bothering to glance in her direction, he slammed out of the apartment. The instant he was gone, Diane collapsed in a heap on the sofa, choking on her tears, wondering if he would ever come back.

After weeks of denial, Diane finally faced the truth: Joel had abandoned her, and she was solely responsible for the new life growing inside her. At first she cowered like a beaten animal, too numb and bewildered to react, but gradually some of the fear abated and she realized she had to make plans. Money was a critical problem. Her small savings would last only a few months, so it was imperative that she continue working, and that meant concealing her pregnancy from Ed Blake for as long as possible.

Once her condition became readily apparent, Ed would have a plausible reason to get rid of her. The network was still functioning in the Dark Ages, having no formal provisions for pregnant employees. Policy was left to the various department heads, and the decision about her future would automatically revert to Ed. If she wanted to retain her job, she would have to persuade him to grant her a leave of absence, but at the moment she was too unsteady to face him.

Since she was forced to keep her pregnancy a secret from everyone at the network, Rachel became her only source of comfort. They had lunch together every Saturday, and Diane lived for those few hours of closeness. All week she anticipated the pleasure of having someone to confide in, someone who cared about her. Now as they sat on her shabby sofa sharing a pepperoni pizza, she felt a familiar warmth.

"Any word from Joel?"

"No. It's over. I can finally say that without breaking down."

"That miserable bastard. I hope you're going after him for support."

Diane shook her head. "What good would it do? He has no money."

"Then let him get a job. You're too easy on people, Diane. The guy worked you over. At least nail him for support."

Sinking back against a pile of throw pillows, Diane propped her feet on the coffee table. "It's not worth the hassle. I never want to see him again."

"So you just let him off the hook? What about the baby? He owes the baby something."

"Not in his mind. He did his duty by offering to arrange for an abortion."

Rachel threw a half-eaten wedge of pizza back into the box, then lit her ritual cigarette. "How the hell did you put up with him for so long?"

"I loved him," Diane said. "Maybe too much. I practically begged to be his scapegoat."

Sighing heavily, Rachel shook her head. "Why do women always blame themselves? *You* were the victim here, remember?"

"But I was a willing victim. Joel said once that we were eating each other alive. Maybe he was right. Maybe we never had a chance. But even when things were terrible, I never thought he'd leave me. I never knew I could hurt this much."

Rachel impulsively reached out to hug her. "I wish I could make things better for you."

Diane laughed, dabbing at her eyes. "So do I. Where's your magic wand?"

"I guess I lost it somewhere."

The abject sorrow in Rachel's voice hit Diane like a deadweight plowing into her chest. "What's wrong? Has something happened with Brian?"

"Hey, you have enough to worry about without me dumping my troubles on you."

Just as Diane started to protest, the phone rang and she rushed to the kitchen, still nurturing a faint hope that it might be Joel. But when she returned to the living room, her face was ashen. "That was Helene. Brenda died last night. She had a stroke."

"My God, she just dropped dead?"

"In Spain. At a party. They thought she was drunk, so nobody called a doctor for hours."

Rachel shot to her feet and began to pace around the sofa. "How's Helene?"

"She sounded fine, not upset at all. I told her we'd fly out for the funeral, but she said it was a bad time. She's busy with her movie."

Frowning, Rachel slowed her pacing. "It's hard to imagine Brenda dead. I was always afraid she'd pull some crazy publicity stunt and blab about what happened with Rick."

"You never told me that."

"I tried not to think about it, but I kept dreaming I'd wake up one morning and see our names plastered across the front page of the *Times*. Thank God it's finally over.''

Diane looked at her in disbelief. ''It'll never be over. What if one of us cracks? What if they have to dig up the well for some reason? I can think of a hundred ways it might come out.''

Sighing, Rachel dropped to the sofa. ''So can I. And no matter what happens, we still have to live with the guilt.''

''Do you think about it a lot?''

Rachel nodded. ''It's always there in the back of my head.''

''Me too.''

They lapsed into silence. Then after a few minutes Rachel said, ''Look, I have to go. I'm meeting Brian at the library.''

It hit Diane that they had never gotten around to discussing Brian, but now they were both too preoccupied, too aware of the secret they shared. ''I'll see you next week, then,'' she said.

''We'll go out for Chinese, my treat.''

Diane accompanied her to the door, feeling an odd blend of depression and anxiety. Even though Brenda Galloway was dead, the secret would live on in their minds like a malignant cell waiting to be released.

A month later Diane realized it was futile to go on trying to conceal her pregnancy. She was receiving too many speculative glances to believe she was fooling anyone, least of all Ed Blake. He continually stared at her with a knowing look that undermined her sense of well-being. She finally decided she had no choice but to admit the truth and then engage in the inevitable battle for her job.

After squeezing herself into her favorite beige wool suit, she allowed herself the rare luxury of taking a cab uptown to work. It was vitally important that she arrive at the office looking as calm and unruffled as possible. If Ed caught the slightest whiff of her insecurity, he would make things more difficult. He seemed to derive tremendous pleasure from watching his underlings squirm.

When she arrived at the studio, she headed directly for the lavish suite that Ed had appropriated for his own use. Since his secretary was not at her desk, Diane rapped on his open door.

''Come on in, Diane,'' he said. ''What's on your mind?''

Diane felt conspicuous as she crossed the room and eased

herself into a low leather chair. Ed had a way of watching her that left her feeling self-conscious and unattractive, especially now that she was so aware of her slightly protruding stomach.

"I need to talk to you about something personal," she said.

Checking his watch, he frowned. "You'll have to make it quick. I'm due at a budget meeting in ten minutes."

Rattled by the unexpected pressure, Diane looked directly into his beady brown eyes and tried to project an aura of confidence. "I'm pregnant. In a few months I'll need a short leave of absence. Six weeks at the most."

Ed leaned back in his chair, clearing enjoying her discomfort. "Six weeks? How the hell do you plan to pull that off?"

"I'll work right up to the end."

"Forget it, Diane. I can't have you parading around here like some kind of earth mother. This is a television studio, for chrissake."

"What has that got to do with anything? I'm still perfectly capable of doing my job."

Smoothing his fingers over a jade paperweight, Ed shrugged dismissively. "A pregnant woman has no place in an office."

"Come on, Ed, that's ridiculous. Most companies have automatic maternity leaves. Why should I give up my job just because I'm pregnant?"

Under any other circumstances she would have admitted that keeping her job was absolutely essential, but she knew Ed well enough to avoid giving him any further ammunition. Since she had told only a few people about her separation from Joel, she could only hope he had no inkling of how desperate she was.

But his next words crushed her feeble hope. "What about your husband?" he said. "I can't believe he approves of you working now."

"Joel and I are separated," she said quietly.

Ed briefly lowered his head in what was obviously calculated to be a gesture of sympathy, but Diane caught a glimmer of satisfaction in his eyes. "So you need your job to pay the rent," he said.

She nodded, hating him for the way he was torturing her.

"You should have been honest with me right from the beginning, Diane," he said, smiling expansively. "I'm sure we can work something out."

He paused and Diane knew he expected her to thank him

profusely for his benevolence, but the words caught in her throat. After a few seconds of strained silence, he continued. "Of course there's no way I'll be able to send you out on any assignments—the boys upstairs would never go for that. But there's plenty of work right here in the office. Then, after you have the baby, we'll see where we stand."

Though his offer sounded more than generous on the surface, it took Diane only a moment to see through his ploy. Although he was allowing her to remain at the network, he was effectively stripping her of her position, reducing her to a clerk with an inflated salary, and she had no guarantee that she would ever be allowed to function as an assistant producer again. She was furious at the way he had manipulated her, but she had to accept his terms, at least temporarily. Once the baby was born and she was ready to resume her career, she promised herself that she would somehow beat Ed at his own sleazy game.

"Thanks, Ed," she said stiffly. "I appreciate it."

He looked at her intently, and she sensed that he knew exactly what she was thinking, exactly how much she detested him, but then he smiled, throwing her off balance. "I'm glad I was able to help," he said. "But now I have to run. I'm late for that meeting."

As Diane following him out of his office, she was hit with the disquieting realization that Ed probably believed she now owed him a substantial debt. He would expect her to behave like one of his lackeys, and she had no doubt that someday he would try to extract repayment for his dubious generosity.

At times Diane wondered if she had the strength to endure the remainder of her pregnancy. She felt tired and depressed, angry at Joel for abandoning her, discouraged by her disempowerment at work. Nothing had turned out the way she had expected, and she found it difficult to muster any enthusiasm for a future that seemed shot through with uncertainty. Only the prospect of holding her baby in her arms kept her from disintegrating.

When she went into labor on a frigid winter evening, she summoned a cab to take her to the hospital. As she huddled on the cold seat bracing herself against the pain, she felt miserably alone. Joel was gone, and their baby would be born without a father to welcome it into the world.

But the moment the doctor placed her little girl in her arms, she was overcome by an overpowering love, a sweet, piercing sensation that magically soothed her pain. As she gently caressed her tiny daughter, she promised herself that Carrie Elliot would have all the love and affection she needed. Her darling child would never suffer because Joel had chosen to reject them.

Three days later Rachel packed Diane and a squalling Carrie into a borrowed car and drove them home. Once Diane had settled Carrie into her crib for a nap, she carefully lowered herself to the sofa and sighed. "I'm so glad it's over and everything turned out okay. I was a nervous wreck these last few weeks."

"No wonder. You had nobody to lean on."

Nodding, Diane absently stroked the soft flannel receiving blanket she was holding. "It was hard not having Joel here, especially during labor and delivery, but I got through it on my own. Now I have more confidence about raising Carrie alone."

"You'll be a great mother," Rachel said. "And who knows? Maybe someday you'll meet another man."

Diane frowned, shaking her head. "I don't think so. After the mistake I made with Joel, I'd never trust myself again. I guess I'm not a very good judge of character. I just see what I want to see."

"Why are you always so damn hard on yourself? Just because Joel turned out to be wrong for you doesn't mean you have to run around in sackcloth and ashes for the rest of your life."

Diane started to respond, but the doorbell cut her off. Shrugging at Rachel, she stood and made her way to the small foyer. When she opened the door, a young female messenger flashed her a beaming smile.

"Are you Diane Elliot?"

Diane nodded and the woman passed her a thin envelope. "I've been here five times in the last four days. I was beginning to think I'd never catch you. All you have to do is sign right here and I'll be on my way."

As Diane scratched her name on the paper the messenger held out, she felt a peculiar sense of foreboding. Her first thought was that Ed Blake had finally fired her, but as she noted the unfamiliar return address on the envelope, she discounted that possibility.

Joining Rachel in the living room, she resumed her place on the sofa, nervously fumbling with the envelope. "I can't imagine what this could be," she said. Then, as her eyes scanned the neatly typed letter, she began to tremble. "It's from Joel. He's filing for divorce."

"On what grounds?"

"Mental cruelty."

Rachel looked outraged. "Is he out of his goddam mind? You can't let him get away with this."

Suddenly weary to the bone, Diane leaned back against the sofa and closed her eyes. "What's the difference?"

"Why should you take the blame? Find a lawyer and go after him for desertion. My God, I can't believe he has the balls to pull something like this."

Just the thought of an ugly courtroom battle filled Diane with dread, but she knew Rachel was right. She would be compounding the disaster of her marriage if she allowed Joel to publicly accuse of her mental cruelty without mounting a defense. "I guess I'll have to talk to a lawyer before I decide how to handle this."

"I'll ask Brian to help you find one. Once Joel sees you're willing to fight back, he'll back off."

Diane nodded, feeling too numb to reply. How could she have been so wrong about Joel? She had loved and trusted him, believed in their future together. But now she was alone with her baby, under attack by the man she had once so blindly adored. Well, she would never behave so foolishly again, she thought, never let herself be taken in by an illusion of love. She would build a life around Carrie and her work, a life that was safe from such devastating hurt.

Mick Travis hated hospitals—the antiseptic odor that was never strong enough to disguise the underlying stench of death and disease; the fear and apprehension that seemed to permeate the air. But he also felt compelled to visit his old friend Ralph Edwards. The man was dying, and much as Mick longed to avoid a direct confrontation with the ugliness of death, his conscience had been prodding him for days. Edwards was one of his few real friends, and he figured he owed him at least a few minutes of his time.

As he made his way through a maze of stark white corridors,

Mick tried to block out the disembodied voice of the intercom
and the detached smiles of the nurses. They reminded him too
much of his own mortality, the possibility that someday he
might find himself helplessly entombed in a hospital bed, alone
and afraid. He shuddered at the thought and increased his pace,
determined to do his duty and escape to the safety of a crowded
bar.

Edwards was asleep when he entered the room, a skeletal old
man hooked up to a network of wires. His cheeks looked
sunken and hollow, and his skin had a sickening yellow cast.
And the smell—the room reeked of rotting flesh. Mick was
tempted to turn and flee, but then Edwards slowly opened his
eyes and smiled. "Mick, you're here. I knew you'd come."

Inching farther into the room, Mick hoped his strained smile
disguised his horror and revulsion. "Sure. I came as soon as I
got your letter. How're you feeling?"

"Like hell, but it won't be much longer. Liver cancer goes
fast."

Mick gasped for breath as the pale yellow room seemed to
shrink around him. Beads of sweat popped out on his upper lip,
and there was a strange ringing in his ears. He thought he might
pass out as he stumbled to a chair and sank down on the spongy
cushion.

After a long silence, Edwards shook his head and said, "I
guess it's a shock seeing me this way. I forget how bad I look."

Instead of denying the truth, Mick simply sat there gulping
huge mouthfuls of warm air until the strangling sensation
slowly abated. Then he forced himself to look directly at
Edwards. "Christ, I'm sorry."

"Never mind that," Edwards said impatiently. "I have a
few things to say to you before the damn drugs put me to sleep
again. Get me the envelope out of the top drawer of that dresser
over there."

Feeling slightly more in control, Mick retrieved the envelope
and gave it to him, curious about what Edwards was so anxious
to tell him.

"This is the Conti file," Edwards rasped. "I never managed
to find out what happened to Rick Conti, but I want you to keep
trying. Solve this case for me, Mick."

It had been months since Mick had even thought about Rick
Conti's disappearance, a case that had once fascinated him but

now held little interest. He wondered why Edwards seemed so obsessed with it, and then he wondered if the cancer had impaired his thinking. "What the hell are you doing with the file, Ralph? It's police property."

A violent cough racked Edwards's emaciated body, and several minutes elapsed before he was able to speak. "I took it when the town council forced me out of office," he said breathlessly. "Nobody else cared about Rick Conti. I was the only one who ever even bothered to look for the poor bastard. Now it's up to you to find him."

Mick stared at his friend, pity welling up inside him. "You know I can't do that, Ralph. I have enough projects lined up to keep me busy for the next five years."

"But think of the book you could write—an exclusive on a celebrity murder investigation."

"Murder? You have no proof that Conti was murdered."

"No, the proof is there somewhere. Look hard enough and you'll find it."

Mick absently stroked his chin, feeling a familiar stirring in his gut, the relentless urge that drove him to investigate and expose. Brenda Galloway was dead, but her life had been one juicy scandal after another, and this lurid tale of a missing lover might arouse enough morbid curiosity to turn her biography into a smash best-seller. It was definitely a possibility worth pursuing with his publisher.

Nodding at Edwards, he said, "I'll take the file, but I'm not promising anything. We'll see how things go."

Edwards smiled wanly, but his eyes seemed suddenly brighter, more alert. "You do that. I just wish I was going to be around to hear the verdict."

CHAPTER
Thirteen

RACHEL DROPPED HER PENCIL ON HER DESK AND RUBBED HER HANDS together. The air in the church basement was frigid, and she wondered if the money saved by lowering the heat after the kids left each day was worth the discomfort. Then, glancing back at the ledger she had been studying, she knew there was no choice. Every dime was essential to the survival of the school.

Somehow over the course of the last few years she had been gently but firmly nudged into the role of administrator—keeping the books, ordering supplies, dealing with an occasional irate parent—and even though Cal swore she would someday be able to return to the classroom, they both knew it was an empty promise. As she became more and more entrenched in the business end of the struggling school, her chances of teaching again became virtually nil.

Still, she felt a rush of pride as she glanced around her shabby office. In spite of the never-ending financial crunch, the school was a resounding success, a glimmer of hope in the still turbulent civil rights movement. Though most of the white community mistrusted Cal and his Black Brotherhood, there was a growing respect for his efforts to educate the children of Harlem.

Distracted by a rustling sound, Rachel glanced into the hall and smiled when she spotted Mary Bevins. "What're you doing here? I thought you left hours ago."

Mary entered the room and gracefully perched on the edge of the desk. "I did. I came back with Cal. We have to talk to you."

Rachel shot her a curious look, but Mary just grinned and

shook her head. "Have some patience. He'll be along in a minute."

Slouching back in her chair, Rachel studied Mary. It still amazed her that they had become friends—not the kind of deep and trusting friendship she shared with Diane, but a cautious acceptance that she never would have believed possible three years ago. Somehow the night of the riot had changed everything. Since then Mary had gradually become less guarded and defensive. Now they worked together with a quiet understanding that pleased Rachel enormously.

"Good, you're still here," Cal said, his presence suddenly dominating the room. "I need a favor, Rachel."

"What?"

"I had unofficial word we might be up for a major donation from the Congress of Jewish Women. They want to meet with somebody from the school, and we decided you're the best one to handle it."

"Me? Are you crazy? I'm no good at that kind of thing."

"Then you'll have to learn," Mary said firmly. "You're our best shot."

"Why me?"

Cal and Mary exchanged uneasy glances. Then Cal said, "You're white; you speak their language."

"Come on," Rachel snorted, anger beginning to churn in her chest. "I thought we were past all that."

"Look," Cal said impatiently. "These are rich white women. If I show up at their luncheon I'll scare the hell out of them. They want to help black kids, not the Brotherhood."

"So you need me to act as a front, the token white."

Cal scowled. "You know it's not like that, but we have to play the game for the kids. These people will never give us any money if they think it links them to the Brotherhood. We'll have to keep the school and the Brotherhood separate or we'll lose our chance at all those fat contributions."

"Isn't that called selling out?" Rachel said angrily.

His wiry shoulders slumping, Cal shook his head. "It's called facing reality. We can either swallow some pride and go for the bucks to keep the school open or we can lock the door on the kids. Which is better, Rache? Would you rather just give up?"

Feeling deeply ashamed, Rachel lowered her eyes. "I'm sorry, I had no right to say that."

A rare unguarded smile lit his strong ebony features. "Why not? I've said the same thing to myself a hundred times. But I finally figured out that you either learn to compromise or you end up with nothing. And my people have already had a bellyful of nothing."

"What about the rest of the Brotherhood?" Rachel said quietly. "Do they support you?"

Suddenly Cal looked discouraged, and Mary audibly sighed. "Clay Mathis and some of the others left the Brotherhood last night," she said, her sad dark eyes fixed on Cal. "But there are enough of us to keep going. Can we count on you, Rachel?"

"Of course," Rachel said. "But I'm not sure I'm the one to do your public relations work."

Cal exhaled a long breath that seemed to echo relief. "Just give it a try, see how it goes."

"All right," she said. "Set up a meeting." She said good-bye to Mary and Cal, then threw her old wool jacket over her shoulders and made her way to the street and down the steps to the subway. Then, as the old train rattled its way toward the West Side, she was besieged by doubts of her own ability to convince a group of wealthy Jewish women to invest in a floundering school in Harlem. Why would they listen to a woman who dressed in shabby jeans and had never quite mastered the social niceties? What could she possibly say to make them understand?

Life was certainly full of ironies, she thought. All she had ever wanted was to teach underprivileged kids, and here she was preparing to make a sales pitch. But Cal was probably right, she was probably the best one for the job simply because of her white skin—no matter that she lacked the polish and the patience to cultivate potential benefactors. She was being tossed into the arena of big money, and she had absolutely no idea how to function without stumbling all over herself.

By the time she left the subway the streetlights had flickered on, and she banished her thoughts and increased her pace, uneasy in the encroaching darkness. As she hurried along Columbus Avenue toward Brian's apartment, she felt a familiar urge to see him, to tell him what had happened, but he was probably still tied up at the office. He seemed obsessed with his

work, always asking for the most difficult cases, impressing his
superiors with his single-minded dedication. She knew he
dreamed of someday becoming district attorney, and while
she understood his ambition, it frightened her as well. Every
time he mentioned marriage, she tried to picture herself as the
wife of an important political figure, but the image refused to
form in her mind. Unfortunately, the conflict between his work
and hers continually threatened their future together.

When she reached his building, Rachel hurried inside and
used her key to enter his apartment. As she carelessly tossed
her coat on the sofa, she was surprised to see Brian seated at the
kitchen table sipping a bottle of beer.

"You're home early," she said.

Smiling, he pointed to a bubbling pot on the stove. "I
finished up early at the office so I thought I'd fix us some
dinner. How does spaghetti sound?"

"Terrific," she said, as she joined him at the table. "But I
have to get home early tonight. My parents are giving me
trouble about spending so much time in Manhattan. I don't
want to alienate them any further."

His lips thinned to a frown. "I was hoping you'd stay."

Shaking her head, Rachel reached for his hand, lacing her
fingers through his. "I can't, not tonight."

He was quiet for a moment, and she felt the sharp edge of his
disappointment. They had so little time together. There were
never enough hours to share their thoughts or even their bodies.
She couldn't remember the last time they had made love
without rushing.

"I'm really not that hungry," she said softly. "I'd much
rather make love."

Brian looked at her, his deep blue eyes coming alive with a
familiar twinkle. "Since when have you been reading my
mind, lady?"

Flirting had always been slightly alien to Rachel, but she was
softer around Brian, more attuned to herself as a woman. "It's
not your mind I'm interested in."

"Then what do you say we finish this conversation in the
bedroom?"

She nodded, and he wordlessly led her to his bedroom. As
he eased her down beside him, she felt the hard length of his
body pressing against her. Then he gently kissed her, and she

willingly relinquished all awareness of time and place. Only Brian existed, Brian and a love she desperately needed to nurture and preserve.

Later she burrowed against his chest, breathing in the heady male scent of his skin. "I love you," she whispered.

"Enough to marry me?"

She drew in a quick breath, not at all prepared for the resurgence of an argument that both frightened and confused her. "You know I do, but we need more time to work things out."

Sighing heavily, he moved away from her and fumbled on the nightstand for his cigarettes. "Time won't change a damn thing."

"But what about our parents, our jobs? We have so many problems, so many differences."

"And you think time will just make those things go away?"

"No, of course not," she said, reaching across him to grab a cigarette.

"Then what the hell are we waiting for? Marry me so we can get on with the rest of our lives."

Rachel lit her cigarette, then leaned back against the pillows wondering what the rest of their lives would be like if they impulsively ignored reality and married. Would their differences eventually corrode their love? Would they someday exist in a world dominated by fights and recriminations? Just the thought of being estranged from Brian left her feeling hopelessly bereft, and yet in her rational mind she knew it was all too possible.

But what was the alternative? Somehow she knew her love for Brian was exclusive. There would never be anyone else, and without him the rest of her life would be a vast stretch of emptiness. She would still have her work and her friends, but inside she would be a hollow core of regret, a bitter woman clinging to her tattered memories.

"All right," she said in a shaky voice. "Let's get married."

Brian smiled, then gently wrapped his arms around her shoulders. "We'll make it work; I promise."

Though she was still plagued by doubts—not only about her future with Brian but also about the increasing estrangement between her and her parents, who disapproved of her relationship with an Irish Catholic—Rachel chose to believe him as she melted against his chest. No matter what happened they would have each other, and that would be enough.

Two days later Rachel's resolve wavered as she sat across from her parents at the scarred maple table. They had no idea that a man named Brian McDonald even existed and now she was about to shatter their dreams by marrying him.

"So what's wrong?" Naomi said, her eyes sharply inquisitive.

"Nothing's wrong, Ma. I just have something to tell you."

Naomi glanced at Sol and shook her head. "I knew there was trouble coming. She's never home, never sleeps in her own bed."

"Shush, let her talk."

Although Rachel had been searching for the right words all day, she was suddenly speechless as she stared at her parents. How could she rip their world apart like this? She felt sick with guilt, but a mental image of Brian finally persuaded her to go on.

"I've been seeing someone. I'd like to bring him home so you can meet him."

"Who is he?" Naomi said. "Where did you meet him?"

"At school, a few years ago. I'm in love with him, Ma."

Naomi was suddenly silent, seeming almost reluctant to hear anymore, but Sol stiffened as if he had already perceived a threat. "So tell me about this man, Rachel. Is he a Jew?"

"No," she said quietly. "His name is Brian McDonald. I love him. I'm going to marry him. Please try to understand."

"Then we have nothing more to say." His usual gentle expression was gone, replaced by an unyielding mask that rendered him a stranger. "If you marry this man, I'll consider you dead."

Naomi gasped, closing her plump fingers around his arm in a restraining gesture. "Wait, Sol. Think about what you're saying. Let's meet him. Maybe he'll convert. Maybe—"

"No," Sol said quietly, his weary eyes intently focused on Rachel. "All these years I looked the other way when my daughter pretended to be somebody else. I told myself it was all right, that young people have to test the waters, that someday she would find out what it means to be a Jew. But I can't look the other way anymore."

"Please, Pop, don't make me choose between you."

He shook his head, a look of ineffable sadness passing over his face like a shadow. "You've already chosen, so go to your goy. My daughter is dead."

Suddenly looking like an old man, he spared one last haunting glance at Rachel, then stood and left the room. As she watched him disappear, Rachel felt a terrible crushing sensation in her chest, a pain so intense it robbed her of breath. Gazing at Naomi, she said, "Why is he doing this, Ma?"

"He's the father. The father does what he thinks is right."

"What about you? What do you think?"

Naomi shrugged helplessly. "What do I care about right? I don't want to lose my only child."

"Oh, Ma, it doesn't have to be this way. Talk to him. Get him to change his mind."

Sadly Naomi shook her head. "You heard him. There's nothing else to say." She leaned over the table, gripping Rachel's hand with astonishing strength. "It's up to you now. Please forget this man, Rachel. I beg you."

Though Rachel felt an instinctive urge to blurt out the words that would erase the suffering from her mother's eyes, she knew there was no going back. She had chosen a life with Brian. "It's too late, Ma," she said softly. "I love him."

Naomi dropped her hands to her lap. "Then it's best you pack your things and go tonight."

Their eyes met, and Rachel suddenly felt weak as a lifetime of memories flitted through her mind like pages of a scrapbook—her bas mitzvah, countless Passover seders, times that had woven her family together like threads in a tapestry. Only now the pattern would change. Rachel Hannah Weiss was dead.

"Ma, I'm so sorry," she said, her brown eyes glimmering with tears.

"I know, Rachel, I know."

"Will you meet me in the city sometime? We could see each other without Pop knowing."

"Thirty years I've been married to your father. I won't start lying to him now, not even for you."

Rachel nodded, both hurt and ashamed. She had no right to pit her parents against each other, but she desperately wanted Naomi to offer some frail hope that someday the wound might

heal. "I'll write to you, Ma," she said. "You can't stop me
from writing."

Sighing deeply, Naomi stood and tenderly embraced her.
"Take care, Rachel."

Rachel tried to cling to her mother, but Naomi slowly moved
away, leaving her alone in the kitchen. As she looked around
the familiar room, she was overwhelmed by the discordant
silence. There should have been yelling and screaming, anything but this quiet resignation. How was it possible for a
family simply to disintegrate as if it had never existed?

Three weeks later Rachel stood in front of the mirror trying not
to squirm as Diane adjusted the numerous tucks and folds of
her stylish blue silk dress. "I can't wear this thing," she said.
"I look ridiculous."

"Stop saying that. You look beautiful."

Frowning, Rachel stared at her reflection. Diane had subdued her curly hair and softened her features with cleverly
applied cosmetics, but instead of feeling more attractive,
Rachel felt uncomfortable with herself, like an impostor
concealing her true identity behind a mask of powder and lip
gloss. She fleetingly wondered what Brian would think when
he saw her. Oddly enough, it bothered her that he might prefer
this slightly altered version of the woman he was about to
marry.

"Quit fiddling with your dress," Diane said. "You'll have
it a mess of wrinkles before we even get to the church."

Dropping her arms to her sides, Rachel backed away from
the mirror and began to pace around Diane's tiny bedroom.
"I'm so nervous. I never thought I'd be this nervous."

Diane gently touched her shoulder. "Come on in the kitchen.
We have time for a quick drink before Carrie's baby-sitter gets
here."

"Great. I'll smell like a lush at my own wedding."

"Well, at least you won't be pacing like a caged animal."

Rachel followed her to the kitchen and gingerly sat on the
edge of one of the cheap chrome chairs. As she watched Diane
pour two glasses of wine, she rummaged in her purse for her
cigarettes, wondering how she would ever get through the rest
of the day.

"This whole thing was supposed to be so simple," she said. "No fuss, no religious ceremony."

"Are you having second thoughts about being married by a priest?"

Rachel shrugged. "I try not to think about it. My parents would be so hurt if they knew."

After passing her a glass of wine, Diane joined her at the table. "Does Brian know how you feel?"

"Not really. He tried not to pressure me, but I saw how worried he was by the idea of upsetting his parents. I love him, Diane. How can I cause him that kind of pain?"

"What about you? You just went through the same kind of pain."

"That's different. My parents never would have accepted him even if he had converted. But . . ."

"What?"

Tears shimmered on Rachel's dark lashes. "I miss them. I wish they were going to be there today." She laughed hoarsely. "Can you picture that? Naomi and Sol in a Catholic church?"

"Look, there's still time. Maybe you should call them. Maybe they'll reconsider."

"Never. As far as they're concerned I'm already dead and buried." Though it hurt her to admit it, Rachel knew she had spoken the truth. "I'll never see them again," she said quietly. "I knew that when I chose to marry Brian."

Diane wordlessly embraced her, offering physical comfort when there were no words to diminish the pain. After a long time, Rachel lifted her head and smiled weakly. "I think I just ruined my face."

Nodding, Diane returned her smile. "You look like a raccoon. We'd better make some repairs. It's getting late."

As they walked to the bedroom, arms linked, Rachel tried not to think about all the precious things she was leaving behind, all the empty places in her heart.

The air inside the church was cool and faintly redolent of incense. Sunlight filtered through the stained-glass windows, illuminating the altar in soft shades of heather. As Rachel stood beside Brian at the marble communion rail, she felt over-whelmed by the unfamiliar surroundings. It all seemed unreal, as if she had suddenly become part of a surrealistic painting in which everything was distorted.

She found it difficult to believe that this ceremony would unite her with Brian for the rest of her life. Even though she no longer practiced her faith, somehow she had always assumed she would be married beneath a canopy, surrounded by her family. Instead she was about to recite her wedding vows amid a roomful of strangers.

Feeling vulnerable, she glanced at Diane and felt reassured by her presence. Suddenly she regretted her decision not to invite Gussie and Helene. At the time it had seemed so much easier to avoid a lot of painful explanations, but now she felt incomplete. Losses. Why did a day that should have been filled with such joy and happiness have to represent so many losses?

Only marginally aware of the ceremony proceeding around her, Rachel was startled when the priest asked her to repeat her vows. She glanced at Brian; then, comforted by his gentle smile, she suppressed her apprehensions and softly pronounced the words that would bind them together forever.

CHAPTER
Fourteen

GUSSIE WAS SEATED AT HER DRESSING TABLE, LETHARGICALLY STARING out the window, when her mother rapped on her door and entered her room. "Honestly, Augusta," she said, frowning as she noticed that Gussie was still wearing her rumpled silk peignoir. "You were supposed to be ready for your fitting fifteen minutes ago. Gabriella is downstairs waiting for you."

"I'm not up to a fitting today. I have a splitting headache."

Her frown increasing, Elizabeth crossed the room and gingerly sat on the edge of her daughter's bed, taking care not to wrinkle her ivory linen suit. "Have you taken your medication?"

"Yes, Mother, but it's not working. You'll have to tell Gabriella to come back another time."

"That's impossible. It would be terribly rude after she came all the way out to the house. I'm afraid you'll just have to put up with the discomfort."

Gussie momentarily considered pursuing the argument, but a furtive glance at her mother convinced her that it would be a futile gesture. Gabriella was currently the darling of Washington, a young designer who had maneuvered herself into the enviable position of choosing her own clients, and Elizabeth would die rather than risk offending her.

"All right, Mother. I'll be down in a few minutes."

"Do hurry, dear. After all, this is your wedding dress. You want to show the proper amount of enthusiasm."

As Elizabeth gracefully stood and left the room, Gussie idly wondered what constituted the proper amount of enthusiasm. Was there a formula? A Richter scale to help you judge whether or not you were suitably enthusiastic over your own wedding? How absurd, particularly in her case, she thought.

155

She found it difficult to dredge up even the slightest bit of enthusiasm at the prospect of her imminent marriage to Richard Chandler.

Thinking back, Gussie tried to identify the exact moment when she had abdicated control of her own life, and as always she came to the same conclusion. She had never recovered from her affair with Tony. Ever since then she had been afflicted with a debilitating inertia that had allowed her parents to seize control of her future.

And the culmination of their substantial efforts was her impending marriage. After nearly three years of what could only be described as a mechanical courtship, Richard had finally proposed, sounding more like a businessman suggesting a mutually beneficial merger than a prospective husband. Yet it was his very detachment that had ultimately persuaded Gussie to marry him.

Since she had always known she would eventually be pressured into wedding a suitable man, she had settled on Richard because he seemed so totally uninterested in any sort of emotional intimacy. He needed a wife of impeccable breeding who would be an asset to his career and would never publicly embarrass him. In return, he offered the numerous benefits of a socially acceptable marriage and an affluent life-style. It would have been a perfect bargain except for the disquieting fact that Gussie remained hopelessly in love with another man.

For three years she had been trying to overcome her obsession with Tony De Costa, to no avail. He continued to haunt her dreams like a wonderful fantasy that was always just out of reach. She vividly remembered the musical lilt of his voice and the feather-light touch of his fingers caressing her skin. But most of all, she was haunted by sweet memories of an all-consuming love.

Sighing, she rubbed her throbbing temples, forcing herself to evict Tony from her thoughts and concentrate on her breathing. Deep cleansing breaths sometimes relieved the discomfort of her recurring headaches, though this time the pain was more acute, pulsing with each beat of her heart. She had been on edge for weeks, and now with the wedding only ten days away, she felt a panic that seemed to fuel the almost constant pounding in her head.

Unfortunately, there was no time to indulge either her pain or her anxiety. Unless she made an appearance downstairs within the next few minutes, Elizabeth would be rapping at her door again, this time erupting in righteous anger. Slowly rising from the chair, Gussie walked to the bathroom and turned on the shower, gearing herself up to play the role of an enthusiastic bride-to-be.

Later that evening Gussie and Richard were alone on the patio after enduring a long and tedious dinner with her parents. Richard was in an unusually expansive mood, rambling on about a bill he was sponsoring in the Senate, while Gussie tried to appear marginally attentive.

"Anyway, I expect to have it out of committee by the end of next week," he said.

Gussie sighed, finding it increasingly difficult to conceal both her boredom and the discontent that had been fermenting inside her for weeks.

"Augusta, what's on your mind? You've been distracted all evening."

Feeling a perverse need to annoy him, she deliberately broached a subject that had been a constant source of friction between them. "It's my job. I want to keep working after we're married."

"How many times do we have to discuss this?" he said irritably. "Last week you agreed to quit that ridiculous job, and I intend to hold you to your word."

"Why? What difference does it make if I work?"

Shaking his head, he pursed his lips in a way that made him look repulsively feminine. "I'm a United States senator. I don't want my wife wasting her time on some menial little job over at the Smithsonian."

Gussie had never taken much pride in her work, viewing it as an escape rather than a career, but she was furious at his casual disdain. "Of course not. You'd much rather have me doing menial little jobs at home."

He seemed momentarily bewildered by her sarcasm. Then his eyes narrowed, and his expression turned frigid. "Just what are you trying to say, Augusta?"

"Will you please call me Gussie?" she snapped. "Augusta makes me feel a thousand years old."

"Fine," he said, glaring at her. "But since I assume that's not the real issue here, why don't you tell me what's really bothering you?"

She briefly flirted with the idea of just blurting out the truth—that she had grave doubts about marrying him, that she dreaded the prospect of making love to him—but it was too late to voice any second thoughts. Her mother and a crew of hired assistants had been planning the perfect wedding for months, and it would be sacrilegious even to speculate on what would happen if the bride suddenly changed her mind.

Still, Gussie felt compelled to voice the terms of their tacit agreement, to remind him that love had never been a part of their bargain. "Are you sure this marriage is what you want, Richard? You know I care for you, but maybe that's not enough."

He reached for her hand and lightly stroked her wrist. "I stopped believing in adolescent professions of undying love a long time ago, Gussie. No matter what the poets say, a solid marriage is based more on common goals and interests than on raging hormones. I'm certain we can build a good life together."

Though it was precisely what she had expected him to say, Gussie was disappointed by his dispassionate appraisal of their future. But what right did she have to judge him? She was a willing partner in their bloodless covenant.

"I just wanted to be sure you understood."

Sliding his chair closer, he wrapped his arm around her shoulders and pressed a few perfunctory kisses on her lips. "Believe me, I have no reservations," he whispered. "And I hope we've settled this once and for all."

Gussie nodded, but as she leaned into his embrace she realized that nothing had really been settled. He still expected her to devote herself completely to the task of being his wife—a thought that stirred profound feelings of claustrophobia.

Sunlight poured through the windows, seductively luring Gussie from sleep. As she opened her eyes, she was greeted by the cheery sound of birds warbling in the oak trees and the sweet fragrance of roses drifting on the breeze. She remained perfectly still, absorbing the glorious June morning, but a few seconds later the shrill ring of her telephone shattered the peace.

She picked up the handset without hesitation, only to be greeted by an unfamiliar male voice.

"Hello, I'm trying to reach Gussie Tremain."

"Who's this?" she said, disgruntled that a stranger had managed to unearth her private number.

"Never mind that. Just do yourself a favor and get Gussie on the line."

Rattled by his rudeness, Gussie was silent for a moment. Then she said, "This is Gussie Tremain. Who are you?"

He laughed, a thoroughly disagreeable sound. "My name is Mick Travis. I'm writing a book about Brenda Galloway."

Gussie gasped, instantly recognizing his name. He was a ruthless journalist who had built a career on writing unauthorized biographies rife with lurid details and titillating speculation. Suddenly feeling imperiled, she scavenged her mind for some way to get rid of him, but before she was able to collect her thoughts, he said, "I'd like to meet with you and your college friends sometime next week."

"Why? We hardly knew Brenda."

"You knew her daughter," he replied. "well enough to spend a weekend at her Hyannis hideaway."

Now Gussie was certain he was fishing for something, and she was wary of inadvertently assisting him. "That was four years ago," she said at last. "And I never saw Brenda again after that."

"But you were there the night her boyfriend disappeared," he persisted. "I have copies of the police reports."

Gussie felt weak with fear. Why would he be interested in Rick Conti unless he suspected something? Maybe he had already guessed the truth or even discovered the body. She shivered uncontrollably as horrid visions of prison raced through her mind.

"So what d'you say, Gussie? Are we on for next week?"

Wildly searching for a plausible reason to refuse him, Gu hesitated for a moment, then said, "I'll need time to touch with Diane and Rachel. And I'm getting marrie Maybe we can meet after the wedding."

"No dice, Gussie. I'm on a tight deadline here. Monday in New York?"

"That's impossible. I'm too busy."

He emitted another unpleasant laugh. "I'll be at the Mirage on West Forty-eighth on Monday, in case you change your mind."

"No. Wait a minute—"

"See you Monday, sugar."

She listened incredulously as he hung up on her. Then, closing her eyes, she collapsed against the pillows, her chest heaving with each labored breath. She had succeeded in putting the nightmare of Hyannis behind her for a while, but now it was back, threatening to destroy her. She knew for a certainty that if Mick Travis ever discovered the truth, he would relish the opportunity to expose her as an accomplice to murder.

Early Monday morning Gussie left Washington, driving the cream-colored Cadillac Eldorado that had been an engagement present from Richard. She had always preferred sporty little convertibles, but now she appreciated the powerful engine as she sped toward New York and her dreaded appointment with Mick Travis.

She found it difficult to believe she was actually on her way to meet a man who might someday send her to prison, but after numerous discussions on the telephone with Diane and Rachel, she had finally agreed that it would be a dire mistake to ignore him. He had already invaded their lives, and now their only alternative was to discover precisely where his investigation was headed.

Feeling her stomach lurch, Gussie focused on the passing landscape in a vain effort to distract herself, but the scenery along the New Jersey Turnpike was a depressing conglomeration of oil drums and dismal factories. Then she saw the New York skyline looming in the distance, and her heart began to dance against the walls of her chest.

By the time she had parked in a crowded lot and walked the blocks to the bar Mick Travis had mentioned, her yellow drenched with perspiration. She could feel the mois- on her breasts, and her face was slick with a film of andered if Mick Travis would suspect her simply appearance.

l and Diane standing in front of the bar n. Diane looked sleek and sophisticated in a simple raw silk dress; Rachel looked somewhat nunnish in a khaki shirt and low-heeled leather pumps.

"Thank God," Rachel said. "I was afraid you'd be late. We need a few minutes alone before he gets here."

"Let's go inside where it's cool," Gussie said as she lightly embraced Rachel and then Diane. "I'm melting."

Rachel led them through the glass door into the dark interior of the bar. As Gussie sat down on a wooden chair, she quickly scanned the dim corners of the room for a man who might be Mick Travis, but the only other customers were a group of men in three-piece suits, and she felt a rush of relief. She desperately needed time to repair her frazzled composure.

They remained silent until a waiter took their order and returned with their drinks. Then Rachel hunched over the table and whispered, "I still can't believe this is happening. Maybe we should have refused to meet with him."

Diane shook her head. "He would have hounded us until we agreed. I did some research on Mick Travis. He has a reputation for being a real bastard."

"Then we'll have to be very careful not to give him any reason to suspect us," Gussie said. "Maybe if we can convince him we have no scandalous dirt for his book, he'll leave us alone."

Rachel and Diane nodded, but Gussie felt her own anxiety escalate to an unbearable pitch. No matter how much they pretended otherwise, they all knew they were about to be subjected to a grueling inquisition. Then a man entered the lounge, and she knew she was looking at Mick Travis. Short and slightly paunchy, he had a thatch of sandy hair and was wearing a neatly pressed tan suit. Surprisingly, there was nothing at all sleazy about him, at least nothing overt. "Here he comes," she whispered.

"Ladies," he said, smiling faintly, "I'm Mick Travis."

After a tense silence, Rachel mumbled a cursory introduction while Mick snagged a chair with his foot and joined them at the table. He seemed to sense their wariness, and instead of wasting time on superficial amenities, he said, "We may as well get right down to business. I'm writing a book about Brenda Galloway, and I need some information. You three were there the night Rick Conti went for a walk on the beach and never came back. What happened to him?"

Diane shrugged, but instead of seeming coolly indifferent, she looked like a snail stripped of its protective shell. "We have no idea, but you already know that if you've read the police reports."

Beckoning to the waiter, Mick ordered a whiskey and water and casually slouched back in his chair. "I know what you told the cops, but your story has a few flaws. Why the hell would a loser like Conti just disappear when Brenda was taking such good care of him? It doesn't make sense."

"Maybe not," Gussie said shrilly. "But we certainly had no way of knowing what was in his mind. He was a complete stranger to us."

Mick pulled a notebook out of his pocket, scribbled a few lines, and aimed his accusing gaze at Gussie again. "So you're asking me to believe he just up and vanished without a word of explanation?"

"That's right," she replied.

"Come on, gimme a fucking break. I figure Conti is either dead or in hiding. Which is it?"

Afraid to glance at Rachel or Diane, Gussie mutely stared down at the table, her nerves all vibrating at once. Her mouth felt pasty, and when she tried to swallow, her throat ached with the strain. Knowing she was incapable of speech, she helplessly waited for someone to break the unbearable silence.

Several seconds passed as Mick slowly routed his gaze around the table. Rachel averted her eyes while Diane stared off into the dark recesses of the room. Finally Rachel cleared her throat and said, "We told the police everything we know about Rick Conti."

"I don't buy that for a minute," he said in a harsh voice edged with contempt. "Something strange went on at that beach house, and I plan to dig around until I find out exactly what it was. If you girls are smart, you'll save me the trouble."

Rachel adamantly shook her head. "You're wasting your time. We have nothing to tell you."

His face now suffused with anger, Mick abruptly stood and shoved his chair aside. "You haven't seen the last of me, ladies. And if you happen to talk to your friend Helene, you can tell her I'll be in touch. Maybe she has a better memory than you do."

As he stalked out of the bar, Gussie reflexively started after him, but Rachel restrained her. "Let him go," she said.

"Are you out of your mind? God knows what Helene will do if he badgers her."

"I know, but there's no way we can stop him from trying to see her. We'll just have to warn her about him."

Resuming her place at the table, Gussie exhaled a long breath. "What are we going to do? He won't stop looking until he finds something."

"We have to stay calm," Rachel said. "Remember, nobody else knows what happened. Unless one of us tells him the truth, he has nothing but suspicions."

"God, I *hope* that's all he has," Diana said. "He seemed so determined."

"Ruthless," Gussie added.

"Maybe, but he needs facts to put the pieces of the puzzle together," Rachel said. "And he'll never come up with anything on his own."

Draining the last drops of her wine, Gussie struggled to convince herself that Rachel was right, but her rationalizations all fell short of relieving her fears. Much as she wanted to believe she was safe from exposure, she knew there was always a chance that Mick Travis would come across an obscure bit of evidence that would allow him to unravel their entire story.

Gussie was married on a magnificent June morning within the cool marble elegance of the Arlington Episcopal Cathedral. Several hundred prominent guests filled the solid oak pews, and a small army of reporters and photographers waited outside, primed to take pictures of the bride and groom the moment they emerged from the shadowy interior of the church.

Although there had been a great deal of pre-wedding publicity, the ceremony itself was a dignified display of pomp and tradition. The rich contralto voice of opera singer Eileen Carter led the choir in a variety of hymns, clusters of gardenias and pink roses saturated the air with a sweet fragrance, and the bride was exquisite in a cloud of white satin. It had all the elements of a fairy-tale wedding, but as Gussie knelt beside Richard at the altar listening to the priest extol the virtues of marriage, she fought an impulse to scream in protest.

Then suddenly the ceremony was over, and she was march-

ing down the aisle, a beaming Richard holding her arm in a
proprietary grip. At that moment it dawned on her that Gussie
Tremain no longer existed. She was now a Chandler, tethered
to Richard for the rest of her life.

When the wedding party had reassembled in the vestibule,
Diane and Rachel rearranged the gossamer layers of Gussie's
veil while the frenzied wedding consultant organized a receiving line. By the time the guests began to trickle out of the
church, Gussie already felt the strain of her artificial smile, but
Richard looked elated as he genially accepted the good wishes
of friends and political associates.

After what seemed like hours of inane conversation, the last
guest finally passed through the receiving line, and the wedding party moved outside for a short photo session. Gussie
continued to smile mechanically as the press went about the
business of taking pictures, but then she caught a glimpse of a
man standing at the edge of the crowd and every bit of blood
in her body seemed to rush out of her head at once. Mick Travis
was watching her with all the intensity of a hunter stalking his
prey.

Feeling dizzy, she gulped a mouthful of fresh air, but her
heart was pounding so hard she was afraid she might faint.
Stumbling against Richard, she grabbed his arm in a frantic
attempt to steady herself.

"Augusta, what's wrong?" he said, turning to face her.

"I don't feel well. Please . . . help me to the car."

Suddenly Gussie was surrounded by a solicitous crowd, and
her view of Mick Travis was mercifully cut off as Richard
whisked her away to the waiting limousine. Once they were
settled on the soft leather seat, he carefully inspected her face.
"Are you all right? Maybe you should see a doctor."

Closing her eyes, Gussie weakly shook her head. "I'll be
fine in a minute. It must have been all the excitement. I felt
faint."

Richard gently stroked her cheek. "Just lie back and relax."

Gussie nodded again, keeping her eyes tightly closed to
discourage him from any further conversation. She was in no
condition to explain her odd behavior, not when her mind was
reeling with terrifying visions of Mick Travis. Why was he
stalking her? What did he want?

She fought to control her fear; but it was like a wild thing clawing away at her insides, poised to escape if she relaxed for even a second. Somehow she had to contain it before Richard began to suspect she was suffering from far more than a simple case of wedding-day jitters. She felt his eyes roving over her face, and suddenly the air in the limousine seemed hot and stale, heavy with the sickening sweetness of her bouquet.

"Here we are, Gussie," Richard said as the driver passed through the security gate and entered the sprawling grounds of Foxwood, her parents' estate. "Maybe you'd like a few minutes to freshen up before the party starts."

Surprised by his unusual display of sensitivity, she nodded. "I'll need Rachel and Diane to help me with my dress. I'm a little rumpled."

Richard turned to look out the rear window. "They're in the car right behind us. Wait here and I'll get them. Then we'll help you up to your room."

But a quick escape proved impossible. Elizabeth and Robert were visibly upset, fluttering over Gussie like nervous sparrows, while several of the guests seemed intent on getting a closer look at the stricken bride. By the time Rachel and Diane managed to spirit her away to the privacy of her room, Gussie was bursting with impatience.

"Did you see him?" she cried, slamming her bedroom door. "He was right there on the church steps."

"We saw him," Rachel said grimly.

Gussie stormed across the room to the window to look out at the guests assembling in the garden. "What do you think he wants?"

"He was probably just sending us a message," Diane said. "Letting us know he has no intention of backing off."

"So now what do we do?" Gussie said. "How do we get rid of him?"

Carelessly disregarding her delicate organdy gown, Rachel flopped down on the edge of the bed. "All we can do is ignore him. If he tries to contact us, we refuse to have anything to do with him."

Gussie felt fear stirring inside her again. "And what if he keeps following us?"

After a brief silence Diane said, "We'll just have to hope he runs out of patience."

Shifting her gaze to Rachel, Gussie said, "What about Helene? Have you gotten in touch with her yet?"

"She's shooting on location in Mexico, remember? Maybe I can find out where she is and call her tonight after the reception."

Gussie nodded. "Good. We don't want him tracking her down before we've had a chance to warn her."

At that point, Elizabeth knocked on the door and insisted that they join the reception already under way in the garden. She looked appalled when she saw their tense expressions, but Diane managed to reassure her with an earnest smile and a promise to appear downstairs in a few minutes.

As her mother disappeared into the hallway, Gussie blotted her flushed face with a hankie. "Look at me, I'm a mess. I can't go downstairs like this."

"Come on. I'll help you with your hair," Diane said, retrieving a silver-backed brush from the cluttered dresser. "Then I want to call home and check on Carrie. I hate leaving her overnight with a sitter."

Startled, Gussie turned to stare at her. It was still vaguely disconcerting to think of Diane as a mother, especially since she was no longer married to Joel. Gussie wondered how she had survived the death of so many of her dreams. Then she thought of Tony, and suddenly she understood: you never really managed to find all the missing pieces of the puzzle; you simply learned to live without them.

Brilliant sunlight streamed through a canopy of oak trees as Gussie stood at the edge of the lush garden watching her wedding reception unfold. An enormous white tent sheltered numerous buffet tables laden with every imaginable delicacy from fresh lobster to an irresistible array of French pastries. Several well-stocked bars had been set up along the periphery of the garden, and strains of popular music drifted from a temporary bandstand. Most brides would have been delighted with such a lavish affair, but Gussie was finding it increasingly difficult to keep her smile in place.

Still reeling from the shock of seeing Mick Travis outside the church, she was also having trouble accepting the idea that her marriage was now an accomplished fact. All along she had been secretly hoping for a last-minute reprieve, but suddenly she was faced with the crushing reality of spending endless years with Richard, endless years of stilted conversations and unwanted obligations. A sobering thought. A thought best consigned to the most inaccessible reaches of her mind.

Turning her attention back to the party, Gussie noticed Rachel and Brian gyrating on the temporary dance floor and stared in amazement. She had never seen Rachel dance, never seen her so easy and comfortable with a man. Life was certainly unpredictable, she thought. Rachel had always been involved with her causes, not at all interested in frivolous emotions like love, and yet here she was married and obviously deeply in love with her husband.

Feeling a sharp twinge of envy, Gussie stopped a passing waiter and helped herself to a glass of Dom Pérignon. This was definitely not the time to speculate on love or on what might have been if only she had possessed the courage to defy her parents and run off with Tony. She was married to Richard now, and she had to forget her girlish dreams and concentrate on her new role as his wife. Any other course would be perilous to her sanity.

"It's time to cut the cake, dear," Elizabeth said, coming up beside her. "Then you and Richard can be on your way."

Gussie flinched at the thought of being alone with Richard. He had every right to expect her to welcome his lovemaking, or at least to tolerate his touch without shrinking away, but how could she allow him to penetrate her body when his presence there would violate her sweet memories of Tony?

Several hours later Gussie stood in the center of an elegant room at the Plaza Hotel staring at the bed, her heart wildly thudding in her chest. Suddenly she was acutely aware of her body. Every nerve seemed on edge as she reluctantly crossed the room and slipped between the satin sheets.

Then she heard Richard in the bathroom performing his nightly rituals, and she blushed profusely. Listening to him gargle and flush the toilet struck her as obscene. Much as she had obsessed over the sex act itself, she had never even considered the other intimate aspects of marriage, the embarrassing realities of living together.

Uncomfortable with such thoughts, she blocked them out of her mind. Richard would be emerging from the bathroom any minute, and she had to prepare herself for his inevitable invasion of her body. But the instant the bathroom door opened, she froze.

Dressed in a ridiculously pretentious red silk robe, Richard approached the bed, his thin smile even more unappealing than usual. "Would you be more comfortable with the lights out, Augusta?" he said.

Gussie mutely nodded, stifling an urge to scream.

His eyes raked over her face and down her neck to her bare shoulders as his smile became a leer. He continued his vile inspection for a long moment; then he dimmed the lights and climbed into bed beside her. As the mattress dipped slightly beneath his weight, Gussie went rigid.

But Richard seemed unaware of her reticence. As he leaned over to kiss her, he lifted her nightie and closed his fingers around one of her breasts, fondling her nipple. After a few minutes, he skimmed his hand along her belly and carefully probed her dry interior with his finger. She willed herself to respond, but there was no gush of warm fluid, no softening of her internal tissue.

He continued to massage her for what felt like hours. Then he shrugged out of his robe and touched himself, gathering moisture on the tips of his fingers and smearing it over her flesh. She recoiled at the sensation, but he was already climbing on top of her, penetrating her with mechanical precision.

Gussie felt nothing as he thrust into her again and again. She had expected pain, but instead she felt a strange detachment, as if her mind and body had somehow become separated. Then, his body heaving, he collapsed on her breasts and she felt a rush of relief.

A moment later he rolled away from her and turned on the light, cold fury glittering in his eyes. "How many men have there been before me, Augusta?"

Stunned by his crudeness, Gussie just stared at him, her green eyes wide with disbelief.

"How many? I want to know."

She drew the sheet up to her chin, shielding herself from his accusing glare, but she felt naked and defenseless. "Richard, this is . . . How can you ask me such a thing?"

His expression bitter and unforgiving, he said, "Humor me. I want to know exactly what kind of slut I married."

Tears brimmed in her eyes, then spilled down her cheeks. She was shocked by his deliberate cruelty, the malice contorting his thin face. She felt like a child accused of having committed a disgraceful act, but somehow she found the courage to meet his frigid gaze. "Stop it, Richard. You have no right to treat me this way."

He looked at her with distaste. "All right, Augusta. Since you seem unwilling to discuss your past lovers, I won't press you. But I want you to understand something. If you ever cause me even a moment of embarrassment, you'll regret it for the rest of your life. You're my wife now, and I damn well expect you to live up to your obligations."

Anger pulsed through Gussie, but there was guilt there, too. Guilt and the numbing realization that she was married to this man, her future irrevocably linked to his. And what sort of future would they have if he viewed her as a promiscuous tramp? Hating him for forcing her to defend her decency, she whispered, "There was only one man . . . a long time ago. I've never been with anyone else."

Richard studied her as if he had the power to see right through her. Then he smiled, a cold dispassionate smile. "I believe you. We'll never speak of this again. Good night, Augusta."

Horrified by his insensitivity, Gussie watched him roll on to his side and turn off the light. He seemed completely impervious to her feelings, her need to be held and comforted. She stared at the sliver of light slipping between the draperies and wondered what kind of a man she had married. Then she heard the soft sound of his breathing and wondered how she would endure the rest of her life.

CHAPTER

Fifteen

AT FIRST HELENE WAS DELIGHTED WITH THE SPACIOUS VILLA THE STUDIO provided for the cast in Acapulco, but she quickly tired of life in a tropical paradise. She found the heat and humidity oppressive, and the lush vegetation reminded her of a jungle growing wildly out of control, the colors too vivid, the sweet fragrances too intense. She began to dread each new day in Mexico, but she was stranded until her film was completed. And Jack Golden appeared determined to sabotage his own production.

They were already three weeks behind schedule, and Jack was taking his frustrations out on the entire crew. His tantrums and vile outbursts created an almost paranoid atmosphere. Cast members expended more energy avoiding his wrath than producing a quality film.

But what troubled Helene most was her forced separation from Seth. They had never been apart for more than a few weeks and she was finding it increasingly difficult to survive without him. She longed for his touch, the shelter of his arms in the darkest hours of the night.

As she stood on the patio gazing out at the twinkling lights of the city, Helene felt an overwhelming weariness, but she was afraid to go to bed for fear of encountering the demons that had once haunted her sleep. They seemed so close, hovering right on the fringes of her dreams, and she feared it was only a matter of time before they penetrated the fragile barrier of her resistance.

Feeling chilled despite the hot breeze, she slowly crossed the patio to her bedroom. She considered joining the rest of the cast downstairs, but she was afraid she might be tempted to ease her tensions in a bottle of scotch. Instead, she sat on the edge of her bed, picked up a framed photograph of Seth, and pressed it to her cheek, imagining the warmth of his skin.

She remained that way, lulling herself into a dreamy daze, until a sharp rap on her door plummeted her back to reality.

"Helene, you have a phone call, babe."

She recognized the raspy voice of one of the assistant directors and hurried to the door. Maybe Seth had sensed her loneliness and reached out to her. "Who is it, Dave?"

"Beats me, sweetheart. But if you want any privacy you better take it in the den."

After returning his smile, Helene ran down the sweeping staircase to the den. As she curled up on one of the leather chairs and picked up the telephone, she felt a warm tingle of anticipation, but she tensed the instant she heard Rachel's voice.

"Helene, thank God. I've been trying to get through to you for the last hour."

Instantly alert, Helene tightened her slender fingers around the receiver. "Why? What's wrong?"

"Nothing terrible, but we have a problem. A man named Mick Travis is writing a book about your mother. He plans on getting in touch with you, and we thought you should be prepared."

"A book? What kind of book?"

"One of those disgusting biographies. He knows about Rick disappearing, Helene. He suspects . . . He has all the police reports."

Helene blinked as strange visions floated through her mind. She felt dizzy and short of breath, terrified that the hazy images would suddenly solidify and become real.

"Helene, are you okay? Say something."

"What am I going to do?"

"Try to avoid him, but if he manages to corner you, just tell him the truth, tell him you don't remember anything."

Helene felt cold all over, as if her blood had turned to ice water. Maybe this man, this Mick Travis, would somehow force her to remember, to see the visions more clearly. Then she shook her head in mute protest. If she allowed them to surface, the memories would devour her like ravening beasts.

"No, I have to stay away from him. He might . . . I don't want to talk to him at all."

"Then you'll have to be on guard every minute. He's ruthless, Helene."

"Does he know where I am?"

"Probably not, but I'm sure he'll be there waiting when you get home."

Despite the trembling in her hands, Helene felt her panic diminish slightly at the thought of home. Seth would be there. And Rhetta. She wouldn't have to fight Mick Travis alone. "Thanks for warning me," she said. "I'll be okay."

Rachel heaved a deep sigh of relief. "Good. Call me when you get back to the States."

"I will." Helene paused for a moment, suddenly feeling an aching void inside. "How was Gussie's wedding? I wanted to be there. Sometimes I think I'll never see you again."

"I know. I hate being so far apart. The wedding was beautiful, but we all missed you."

Tears misting in her eyes, Helene recalled the past, the laughter and the caring, the friendship that had once seemed immune to the ravages of time and distance. "I'll come to New York one of these days, I promise."

"Great. Take care, Helene."

Helene reluctantly replaced the receiver, hating to break the frail contact with her past. For a long time she sat perfectly still, staring out the window into the darkness of the garden, fear churning in her chest. Then the wild sounds of a party in the living room lured her to her feet. She needed warmth and gaiety to block out the fear and fill the hollowness inside. She needed to forget the nightmares waiting to claim her.

A week later Jack Golden and Hy Schorr were closeted in the small bungalow at the rear of the villa watching the dailies. When the final scene faded from view, Golden turned on the light and slammed his fist on the table. "Jesus Christ, that Galloway bitch is fucking up the whole goddam picture. What the hell am I going to do?"

Hy thoughtfully stroked his chin. "She needs help, Jack. I hear she's drunk every night."

"Help? I'll give her help. I'll make sure she never works again."

"That won't get your picture in the can," Hy said calmly.

"Maybe you should talk to her, try to figure out what's bothering her."

Jack shot him a scathing look. "What am I? Some kind of shrink?"

"Maybe not, but if you let things go on this way we'll both be out of work."

Since there was no denying the truth of that, Golden retreated into moody silence, his eyes dark and remote. After a long time he said, "So what do I say to her, for chrissake?"

"See if she has a problem. Ask how you can help. But be nice, Jack. You have to be nice. Start screaming and you'll just make things worse."

Golden sprang to his feet, crossed the room to the window, and raised the bamboo shades. When he turned back to Hy, his face was as red as the flowers on his gaudy Hawaiian shirt. "Jesus, I hate this shit. I should have listened to my old man and gone to med school."

Hy laughed cynically as Jack glared at him and then stormed out the door.

In the seclusion of her room, Helene poured herself another shot of scotch and sat on the bed. Her eyes burned, and there was a raw ache in her throat as she drained the glass in one desperate gulp. Maybe tonight she would sleep. Maybe tonight the scotch would chase away the nightmares.

She was just about to curl up on the bed with there was an impatient knocking on her door. She dragged herself across the room and was shocked to find Jack Golden pacing in the hall.

"Do you have a few minutes? I want to talk."

Uneasy about allowing him to invade her personal space, she shifted her weight from one foot to the other, trying to think clearly. He looked so intense, hawkish in the dim light. She hesitated for another moment, then stood aside and permitted him to enter.

Jack seemed equally uneasy as he perched on the edge of a wicker chair, and his discomfort made Helene feel more secure, more in control. She sat across from him and forced herself to wait for him to speak.

"Look, Helene," he said at last. "I just saw the dailies, and we have a problem. They stink."

Flinching as if he had punched her, Helene inclined her head, avoiding his angry scowl.

"You're not giving me your best. What's wrong?"

She felt her lips begin to quiver and hated herself for her weakness. Crying in front of Jack would be an unbearable humiliation. But the tears were already there, glimmering in her huge black eyes.

"Jesus Christ, what the hell are you crying about?" he shouted. "I'm not here to persecute you. Just tell me what's wrong so we can get on with the picture."

Helene buried her face in her hands, unable to quell a flood of tears. "I . . . haven't been able to sleep. . . . I have these awful nightmares."

"So you get loaded every night and then turn in a crappy performance the next day. This has to stop, Helene. I want you to see a doctor. He can give you some pills to help you sleep."

Helene shook her head, remembering how Rhetta had warned her about the little black capsules. "No, no pills."

"Then pack up and get out. You're fired."

His voice echoed through her mind like a gunshot, sharp and precise, aimed to kill. She met his gaze and winced at the unvarnished fury she encountered. "Jack, please . . ."

"What do you want me to do? Let you screw up my picture? No way, baby. You'd better see a doctor, because if I have to replace you I'll sue you for every penny you've got. You'll never work again."

Helene implored him with her eyes, but his mouth remained molded in a grimace and she knew he was dead serious. She imagined herself exiled from Hollywood, a pariah branded too unreliable to finish a film. Just the thought left her feeling dead inside. She had to save her career.

"Okay, Jack, I'll see a doctor."

Jack smiled, clearly pleased by her unconditional surrender. "Good girl. You just rest now. I'll have a doctor here first thing in the morning."

Nodding listlessly, Helene accompanied him to the door and then flopped across the bed like a rag doll, tears trickling down her cheeks.

In the morning, a Mexican doctor came to her room and spent a few minutes examining her. He was a trim man, neatly dressed in a white suit that complemented his bronze complexion and soft brown eyes. She wanted to trust him, but when he tried to question her about the source of her nightmares, she retreated inside herself. Eventually he handed her a vial of pills and left her alone.

That night Helene discovered that the tiny white pills miraculously extinguished her nightmares. Suddenly she was able to sleep again and the next day she felt calm and focused on her work. Jack stopped ranting, and the cast seemed to breathe a collective sigh of relief as they turned their attention back to the business of making a movie.

Helene returned to Los Angeles a month later, weary and drained, but relieved that she had completed the picture with no further incidents. Rhetta met her at the airport, and as they hurried through the crowded terminal to a waiting limousine, Helene said, "I did it, Rhett. I survived another picture with Jack Golden."

Rhetta smiled, but remained oddly silent until they were seated in the spotless white limousine. Then she fixed Helene with a piercing gaze and said, "What happened down there? You look rotten."

"I'm just tired. You know Jack; he never lets up for a minute. And I missed Seth. It was awful being apart for so long."

Rhetta continued to stare at her. "I heard some rumors, Helene. Are you drinking again?"

Feeling like a little girl caught peeking under the bathroom door, Helene slumped down in the seat, averting her eyes. "I had a few drinks to help me sleep, but that was weeks ago. I'm fine now." Then she remembered the vial of pills stashed in her purse and felt even guiltier. Rhetta might understand her drinking, but never the pills. "Now that I'm home, I'll be okay. I promise, Rhett."

Rhetta impulsively hugged her. "Christ, I was worried about you."

Helene returned her embrace, resolving to flush the pills down the toilet. She was safe now, safe with Seth and Rhetta, she no longer needed a narcotic to kill her nightmares. But then Rhetta fractured her tenuous confidence by saying, "*Promises* goes into production in two weeks. They want you at the studio for your final fittings tomorrow morning."

"Tomorrow?" Helene echoed. "But I'm so tired. I need some time alone with Seth." She twisted her fingers into a knot on her lap as she envisioned the next few months—rushing to the studio at dawn and then collapsing at the end of each day. Suddenly she felt like a rat trapped in a maze, blindly running herself into a frenzy.

Rhetta had warned her about stretching herself too thin, but the prospect of playing the lead in *Promises*—the part of a woman obsessed with her married lover—had been irresistible. It was a role with almost unlimited potential, an opportunity to display depth and intensity. Only now the opportunity seemed less appealing in the face of the sacrifice it would require.

"What's wrong?" Rhetta said.

"I should have listened to you about *Promises*. I'm not ready. I need a break."

Rhetta looked distraught. "It's too late for that, Helene. There's no way you can back out now without getting yourself into a nasty legal mess."

"I know," Helene said. Then, responding to the anxiety emanating from Rhetta like a cloying perfume, she manufactured a smile. "Don't pay any attention to me, Rhett. I'm just tired. By tomorrow I'll be ready to roll again."

Rhetta nodded, and Helene rested her head against the window and closed her eyes, forcing her mind to go blank.

Moonlight painted the bedroom in soft shades of silver as Helene clung to Seth, her body still warm and moist from their lovemaking. She felt him smile against her cheek and reached out to touch her finger to his lips. "I missed you," she whispered. "God, I missed you so much."

Sighing, he held her closer. "I know. Every day was hell. I love you, Helene."

His words kindled a wonderful warmth deep inside Helene, which slowly seeped through her entire being. In the beginning Seth had been so remote, so afraid of letting himself care, but somehow she had penetrated his shell and exposed an inner reservoir of love. Now as she snuggled against him, listening to his heart beat, she wished she could remain cradled in his arms forever. But the reality of another separation loomed at the edge of her awareness like a dark cloud.

"Do you really have to go to Rome next week?" she said softly.

He gently rubbed her back. "You know I do, but I'll only be gone a few weeks, maybe a month."

Another month without him seemed interminable. Every selfish instinct urged her to beg him to stay, but she bit back the words. He was finally receiving the recognition he deserved from the film industry. How could she ask him to sacrifice his dreams?

"Will you be okay alone, Helene?"

She detected the deep river of concern in his husky voice, and again she was forced to battle her own selfishness as she imagined the empty days and lonely nights without him. Her fears would have a chance to slither out of the dark corners of her mind and turn her dreams to nightmares; her body would feel dry and barren without his gentle touch. But she restrained the helpless tears gathering in her throat. "I'll be fine," she said.

Seth softly kissed her, his hands moving over her lithe body in a silent affirmation of love. As she cuddled against him, she felt safe and protected. Then he was inside her, trembling with each powerful thrust, and her anxieties ebbed in a rush of glorious sensation.

Rhetta slid into her brand-new Lincoln, grinning as she felt the buttery softness of the leather seat against her thighs. After driving sputtering wrecks for years, she reveled in the unfamiliar luxury, but her delight went far beyond a simple infatuation with creature comforts. There was something prestigious about a Lincoln, something that assuaged a gnawing need to prove to the world that Rhetta Green had succeeded.

Utterly pleased with herself, she turned the key in the ignition and headed out of town toward the isolated ranch that Helene shared with Seth Wilder. As the glitzy landscape of Beverly Hills yielded to the rugged terrain of the desert, her thoughts drifted to the strange attachment between Helene and Seth. They seemed to share something much deeper than the shallow affairs that abounded in Hollywood. Maybe not love—Rhetta had lost her illusions about love a long time ago—but something more than just a casual exchange of body fluids.

Then, as Rhetta left the highway and gingerly guided the Lincoln down the rutted road that led to the ranch, a niggling worm of doubt inched into her thoughts. Helene had been moody and depressed ever since Seth left for Italy. She seemed to be in a daze, just going through the motions of living, and that disturbed Rhetta. Much as she hated to think about it, she knew Helene was always vulnerable to the lure of the bottle.

Frowning slightly, she chided herself for allowing morose thoughts to sour a beautiful morning. Seeking a diversion, she gazed out the window at the profusion of wildflowers in the fields surrounding the ranch, slashes of vibrant color in a sea of straggly grass. Then she spotted Helene standing on the porch of the weathered house and waved as she pulled the Lincoln to a stop in the driveway.

Helene smiled and ran down the steps, her ebony hair whipping around her face in the warm breeze. She looked incredibly young and fragile against the backdrop of the endless blue sky and the distant mountains.

"Rhett, what are you doing here?"

"I brought some papers for you to sign. Then I thought I'd take you out to lunch."

"I'd like that. Sundays always seem so long when Seth is away."

Rhetta climbed out of the car and accompanied Helene into the rambling old house. The airy rooms had all been renovated, but they retained the rugged flavor of a working ranch, earthy colors and natural wood tones enhanced by rustic oak furniture. Rhetta privately thought it was insane to live so far from the amenities of Beverly Hills, but Helene seemed completely content.

"I can see why you get lonely out here," she said. "All this quiet makes me nervous."

Helene laughed. "I like the quiet, but I'm lost without Seth. I miss him so much, Rhett."

"I know." Rhetta gently squeezed her hand. "Are you making it through the nights okay?"

Shrugging, Helene brushed a wisp of hair away from her face and Rhetta noticed how pale she was. Her skin looked thin, almost translucent.

"I'm not drinking, if that's what you mean. But I'm not sleeping much either. I never do when I'm alone."

Curious as she was, Rhetta refrained from probing. She knew Helene was tormented by dark secrets, but something always stopped her from voicing her questions. Maybe some secrets were simply better left alone.

After a brief silence she hugged Helene and said, "What do you say we get out of this place? You can sign the papers at the restaurant."

Helene smiled wanly. "Great, let's go."

Helene felt much more relaxed after a leisurely lunch and some easy conversation, but she tensed when they left the restaurant and a bright red Corvette pulled out of the parking lot behind them and tailgated them all the way back to the ranch.

"Who the hell is that?" Rhetta muttered. "If he comes any closer he'll be right up my ass."

Nervously glancing over her shoulder, Helene tried to identify the driver of the sleek red car, but a cloud of dust obscured her vision. "I don't know, but he has no right to be here. This is a private road."

"Damn jerk is probably lost."

Helene doubted that, but she remained silent, trying to ignore the tingle of alarm skittering along her nerve endings. When the Corvette stopped behind them in the driveway, she felt a terrible sense of foreboding as a strange man hoisted himself out of the car. He was short and stocky, and his stance was aggressive, intimidating. Suddenly Helene knew Mick Travis had finally found her.

She groaned softly, and Rhetta swiveled to face her. "What's the matter?"

"That man, get rid of him, Rhett."

Rhetta seemed bewildered by the note of panic in her voice. "Who is he? Do you know him?"

Struggling to force words past the lump of fear in her throat, Helene nodded. "Mick Travis. He's writing a book about . . . my mother."

"Jesus Christ." Rhetta scrambled out of the car like a marionette jerked into motion by invisible strings, but she was too late. Mick Travis was already peering into the passenger window at Helene, a look of smug satisfaction on his face.

"Hello, Helene," he said. "My name is Mick Travis. I'm

writing a biography of your mother, and I'd like to ask you some questions.''

Helene crumpled on the seat, glancing from Rhetta to Mick, her eyes filled with anguish.

"If you want to interview Miss Galloway, you'll have to request an appointment through my office," Rhetta said firmly.

Mick eyed Rhetta with contempt, dismissing her as if she were nothing more than an irritating mosquito buzzing around his head. Then he turned back to Helene. "Look, why not make this easy on yourself? Give me a quick interview right now and I'll leave you alone."

Feeling an overwhelming helplessness, Helene huddled against the door and lowered her head, childishly wishing for the power to make herself invisible.

"What do you say, Helene?" he persisted.

Rhetta glared at him. "Maybe you didn't hear me, Mr. Travis. Nobody interviews Helene without my permission. Now I suggest you get the hell out of here before I call the cops."

Mick scowled, his pasty complexion mottled with blotches of angry color. "That would be a big mistake, lady. Helene has a few skeletons in her closet, and unless she wants the whole damn world to know about them, she'd better talk to me."

Helene jerked convulsively as a rush of blood roared in her ears and the world began to spin wildly out of control. She blindly fumbled for something solid to latch on to, but her hands just fluttered in the air like useless wings.

After a moment of crackling silence, Rhetta advanced on Rick, her hands balled into fists at her sides. "Take your ugly threats and get lost, buddy."

Clearly shocked that his efforts at intimidation had failed, Mick seemed at a loss for words. His face was twisted with rage, but the only sound to emerge from his mouth was an incoherent grunt.

"And don't even think about coming back," Rhetta said through clenched teeth. "There's no way I'll let you near Helene."

Again Mick appeared at a loss, as if he had vastly underestimated the strength of his opponent and was now unsure how to proceed. He shot Rhetta a poisonous glare and then focused on Helene. "You'll regret this," he snarled. "When I find out what happened to Rick Conti, I'll nail your ass to the wall."

Casting one last venomous glance at Helene, he shoved Rhetta out of his way and stalked to his car. A few seconds later the Corvette vanished in a cloud of dust.

Rhetta just stood there in the hot desert sun, visibly shaken, her chest heaving. Then something seemed to spur her into action and she rushed to Helene. "Good God, are you okay?"

Helene violently shivered. Rhetta's voice seemed to be coming from a great distance, faint and indistinct. She strained to understand the garbled words, but everything was jumbled in her mind.

"It's all right, Helene. He's gone."

Helene felt so weak she could only nod. Rhetta hesitated briefly, then gently helped her out of the car and led her into the house.

Helene allowed Rhetta to steer her to the living room and settle her on the plump corduroy sofa, but suddenly the space that had once seemed like a refuge no longer felt quite so safe. Mick Travis had violated her sense of security, stripped it away as if it were nothing more substantial than a flimsy bit of gauze.

"Everything's okay now," Rhetta said, sitting beside her on the sofa. "Just take it easy."

Her kindness struck a chord deep inside Helene, but instead of feeling reassured, she was reminded of how much she needed Seth. She had never needed him more, but he was thousands of miles away, completely lost to her. Panic began to claw at her again and she burrowed against Rhetta like a frightened animal.

They remained that way for what seemed like hours. The sun pouring through the windows paled, and a cool breeze ruffled the filmy white curtains. At last Rhetta drew away and sighed. "We have to make some plans, Helene. I want you to come home with me tonight."

Helene slowly sat up, rubbing her eyes. "No. I'll feel better here. Will you stay with me, Rhett?"

"Sure, if that's what you want. Tomorrow we'll hire a bodyguard and some security people. We have to be ready next time Travis tries to get to you."

Helene cringed. Suppose Mick Travis was hiding some-where out in the desert waiting for the cover of darkness to creep back to the house. She had trouble finding her voice. "You . . . you think he'll come back?"

Suddenly Rhetta looked uncertain. After a long pause, she said, "Probably, but this time we'll be prepared. That bastard will never get near you again, Helene."

Though Helene wanted desperately to believe her, icy fingers of fear continued to grip her heart. What if Mick Travis succeeded in trapping her alone? She was terrified of what she might say if she lost control and her unconscious mind suddenly took over and began spewing out the horrible visions that appeared in her nightmares. She closed her eyes and let out a muffled sob.

"Helene, tell me why you're so afraid," Rhetta said.

Helene trembled, her slender hands clenched in her lap. "Something happened at my mother's beach house a few years ago. A man disappeared." Her voice faded to a reedy whisper. "I only remember bits and pieces. I'm not sure how much of what I remember is real."

"What do you mean?"

"My nightmares . . . Reality is all tangled up with my nightmares."

Rhetta looked increasingly grim. "How much does Travis know?"

Shrugging, Helene stammered, "I guess he thinks Rick Conti was . . . murdered."

"Was he?"

"No . . . I don't know." She felt a brutal pounding in her head and clasped her hands over her face. "I don't remember."

Rhetta wordlessly embraced her, rocking her against her chest as she sobbed. Then she led her to the bedroom and tucked her into the brass bed. Helene tried to lose herself in sleep, but the instant Rhetta left her alone, her eyes snapped open and her mind filled with a frightening vision of Mick Travis.

She fought the nightmare images for as long as she could, but they seemed to consume her and finally she slipped out of bed and stumbled to the bathroom. As she reached up to open the medicine cabinet, she caught a glimpse of herself in the mirror and paused. Her eyes were swollen and bloodshot, mirroring her inner panic. She looked like a caricature of a madwoman. Averting her eyes from the disturbing picture of herself, she opened the cabinet and closed her fingers around the forbidden vial of pills.

All rational thought seemed to flee her mind as she greedily swallowed a tiny white pill and gulped down a glass of water. She was driven by a primal need to find a respite from her pain. Nothing else mattered.

Mick Travis sat at his desk, simmering with anger after a vehement argument with his editor. Time had run out on the Galloway book. Either he turned in a complete manuscript or the publisher was prepared to sue him for breach of contract.

Leaning back in his chair, he bitterly remembered the months he had wasted dogging Helene Galloway. In the beginning he had been certain that she would eventually crack under pressure, but then a platoon of bodyguards had made it impossible for him to get close to her. His standard battery of tricks had failed abysmally, and he was left with a mediocre book and a festering desire for revenge.

But for the moment his only option was to turn in the manuscript minus the sizzling climax he had anticipated. Instead of a stunning revelation of murder and intrigue, his book was destined to be just another scandalous celebrity biography, and even the fact that it would add considerably to his fortune was of scant consolation.

He had become obsessed with the idea that Rick Conti had been murdered. He now understood why Edwards had been fascinated with the case. There was something morbidly intriguing about the thought of a famous actress and four young women killing a man and then hiding the truth for years, something that incited a fanatic desire to expose them. But for now, at least, they were beyond his reach.

Grunting with displeasure, he inserted a sheet of paper into the typewriter and began the last chapter of his book. But as his words filled the pages, his mind remained fixed on the idea of someday unveiling five beautiful women as merciless killers.

PART
Five

Winter 1979–1980

CHAPTER
Sixteen

DIANE WATCHED ED BLAKE OVER HER MUG OF COFFEE, WONDERING JUST how long he intended to toy with her. She was awaiting his approval of a controversial piece that would expose rampant drug abuse among New York City cops, a report that had the potential to win her an Emmy nomination. But Ed had been stalling for weeks. Now she was seated across from him in his luxurious office feeling like a supplicant.

"All right, Diane," he said. "I'm giving you a tentative go-ahead on the drug piece, but I want you to know I have some pretty strong reservations."

Refusing to let her annoyance show, she returned his level gaze. "Such as?"

"You're trusting the word of a drug dealer, for chrissake. What makes you so sure he's not conning you?"

"An ex–drug dealer, Ed. Vic has been clean for over a year. And he has tapes of his conversations with at least twenty cops."

Ed drummed his fingers on his desk, drawing her attention to his perfectly manicured nails. On any other man she might have found them attractive; on Ed they struck her as just one more affectation. She quickly looked away before he caught her staring at him.

"Okay, start putting things together, but be careful on this one, Diane. If it blows up on you, I won't be able to save your ass."

Diane was barely able to conceal her excitement. Though she had been a producer for three years now, she had been given only a few meaty assignments. Ed always bypassed her in favor of one of his male lackeys. In fact, she was certain she had only been promoted because the network had been under

187

pressure to conform to new affirmative action standards. But none of that mattered now. She finally had an opportunity to distinguish herself.

"What kind of time line are we talking about?" she asked.

"At least six months. I haven't even presented it upstairs yet, and with a proposal like this I'm sure there'll be some static."

Instantly suspicious, Diane wondered if Ed might be playing some devious game, keeping her in line with promises he never intended to honor. She looked at him, trying to see beneath his smooth facade, but he was much too adept at deception to allow his thoughts to register on his face.

"Six months seems like a long time," she said at last. "I've already done most of the research."

Ed snorted. "You're never satisfied, are you? I'm going out on a goddam limb for you, and you're still bitching."

Taken off guard by such a direct attack, Diane simply sat there staring at him. After a few seconds of uncomfortable silence, he said, "Look, do you want to do the piece or not?"

She understood then that she was being given an ultimatum: accept his terms or there was no deal. "All right, I'll get started on the pre-production work."

"Fine, but don't schedule the shoot until I give you the word. In the meantime I'm putting you on the Disney segment. See if you can track down a few of the original Mouseketeers."

Though the idea of tracking down former child stars was less than appealing, she nodded agreeably. There was no point in antagonizing Ed when he was finally giving her a crack at something substantial.

"Keep me up to date on both pieces," he said by way of dismissal. "And I'll need a firm budget on the drug segment before I can give you a final approval."

Nodding again, Diane picked up her empty mug and quickly left his office, conscious of his gaze burning into her back. She always wondered what he was thinking when he stared at her in that disconcerting way.

After a stop at the coffee machine, she hurried back to her own office and closed the door, anxious to relish her victory in private. But Angie, now her production assistant, burst into the room, her face alight with curiosity. "So what happened? The suspense is killing me."

"We have tentative approval on the drug piece."

Angie beamed. "I don't believe it. Eddie boy finally came through."

Still vaguely suspicious of Ed's motives, Diane shrugged. "It looks that way, but you can never be sure with Ed. He might change his mind next week."

"No way. We're going to snag an Emmy on this one; I can smell it."

Diane smiled at her unwavering enthusiasm. "Then I guess we'd better get started. Why don't you pull the files while I work on the budget?"

Angie nodded and started for the door, but she paused when the telephone rang. "D'you want me to get that?"

"Please. I'm not available unless it's the President."

Angie grinned and reached for the phone, but a moment later she said, "I think you'd better take this; it's the nurse from Carrie's school."

Feeling a flash of apprehension, Diane quickly grabbed the receiver. Then as she listened to the voice on the other end of the wire, her entire world seemed to heave and crumble. Suddenly there was a crushing pressure in her chest, robbing her of breath.

Angie was at her side instantly. "What's wrong?"

Diane struggled to speak. "It's Carrie. She . . . she collapsed on the playground. They rushed her to the hospital."

"My God. Let's get out of here. We'll catch a cab downstairs."

As Angie sprang into action, Diane reflexively reached into her desk and grabbed her purse. Everything around her faded to a dull gray, and she was conscious only of her own terror, the awful fear squeezing her insides like a vise.

The ride downtown seemed interminable, a blur of fuzzy images seen through the smudged window of a cab. When they finally arrived at the hospital, Diane filled out a sheaf of forms; then joined Angie in the dingy waiting room. The peeling walls were painted a dull green, and the matching Naugahyde furniture was cracked and torn. Several people sat hunched on the shabby chairs, lost in their own thoughts. Only a disheveled old man muttering passages from the Bible breached the pervasive silence. A sickening wave of helplessness washed over Diane as she sat beside Angie on a sagging sofa and joined the quiet vigil.

An hour later an owlish-looking young doctor appeared in the doorway, squinting through thick wire-rimmed glasses. "Mrs. Elliot?"

Trembling all over, Diane bolted to her feet. "Yes, I'm Mrs. Elliot. How . . . how is Carrie?"

He crossed the room and rested a comforting hand on her shoulder. "I'm Dr. Schuman, and Carrie is stable. There's no immediate danger."

Diane soaked in his words like a thirsty sponge, but her relief died a quick death. Something was still dreadfully wrong. "What happened? Why did she collapse?"

"We're not sure yet, but it looks as if she might have a heart problem. We'll know more after we see the test results."

"My God, she's only nine years old. How can she have a heart problem? This is crazy! I want you to call her pediatrician."

Ignoring the hostility in her voice, he gently patted her shoulder. "I already have. Carrie told us his name. He's with her right now."

As her irrational anger faded, Diane dropped down on the sofa, ashamed of her outburst. "I'm sorry. I didn't mean to imply—"

"Forget it," he said. "You're upset."

Diane just nodded, knowing she was dangerously close to hysteria. Tears blurred her vision, and the lump of fear in her throat was growing to enormous proportions. Angie reached for her hand, but she was well beyond such simple comfort.

"When can I see her?" she whispered.

"In a few minutes. Right after you talk to Dr. Shipman."

Diane relaxed fractionally when she saw Carrie's pediatrician in the corridor. He was a white-haired man with enough wrinkles to attest to his years of experience. Just the sight of him instilled in her a sense of confidence.

"Diane," he said, striding toward her, "let's go out in the hall where we can talk in private."

Feeling wobbly, Diane followed him out to the corridor, where he motioned her to a wooden bench. She tried to ignore his grave expression as he sat beside her and said, "I just saw the test results. Right now everything points to a heart problem.''

She flinched at the dreaded words. "What kind of heart problem? Is it serious?''

"It's too soon to make a diagnosis, but I think we're looking at an atrial septal defect, a hole between the chambers of the heart."

"Oh, God." Diane felt as if all the air had suddenly been sucked out of her lungs.

"Now don't panic," he said quietly. "It sounds more ominous than it is. We have the technology to go in and do a surgical repair if that becomes necessary."

Diane found his assurances less than comforting. Heart operations were dangerous. Deadly. The thought of someone cutting into Carrie's chest chilled her to the bone.

"I've arranged a consultation with a cardiac surgeon," he went on. "Michael Casey is one of the top men in the field. We'll know more after he examines Carrie in the morning."

Diane was dazed. She knew she should be hurling questions at him, but an aching need to hold Carrie in her arms overshadowed everything else in her mind. "May I see her now?''

"Certainly, but only for a few minutes. I've sedated her, and I'd like her to rest as much as possible."

He summoned a nurse, and a moment later Diane was ushered into a stark white room. She hesitated in the doorway, crushed by the sight of her little girl lying in a huge hospital bed, a network of wires and tubes running into her thin arms. Suddenly the nightmare was undeniably real.

A few seconds elapsed before she was steady enough to approach the bed. Then as she looked down at her sleeping child, her own heart lurched in her chest. Carrie looked so fragile, so unnaturally still. Her unruly mop of carroty hair seemed to accentuate the sickly whiteness of her skin; her tiny face was pinched and drawn. Diane felt an ineffable sadness. Why Carrie? Why her beloved child?

As she leaned over the bed and gently adjusted the sheet, she thought of Joel and her sorrow turned to fierce anger. What sort of monster abandoned his own flesh and blood without so much as a backward glance? Even now she found it difficult to comprehend his selfishness. But oddly enough she felt a peculiar regret as she remembered their last encounter on the courthouse steps.

She had been nearly blinded by whirling snow as she stood outside the courthouse, afraid of confronting Joel but even more afraid of allowing their marriage to dissolve without some sort of requiem. Even though she had persuaded him to drop his charges of mental cruelty, their amicable divorce had been a hollow victory. She still felt a need to resolve the past before she could even begin to think about the future.

When Joel emerged from the courthouse, his threadbare topcoat drawn tightly against the buffeting wind, she had slowly approached him. She'd expected to see anger and hostility in his vibrant green eyes, but instead she saw a terrible bleakness, and hope flared in her heart. Maybe he regretted his actions; maybe now he realized his life was incomplete without his wife and child.

"Why d'you want, bright-eyes?" he had said, his breath curling like wispy smoke rings in the frigid air. "The show's over; it's time to go home."

"Why, Joel? Why did you do this to us?"

He looked at her intently, and she thought maybe she had finally reached him, but then his eyes went blank. "What the hell do you want from me? Just let it go, Diane."

Angry now, she began to tremble. "What about Carrie? Don't you even want to see your own child?"

Shaking his head, he slowly turned away from her, looking like an old man as he trudged down the steps and melted into the swirling storm. And much as she wanted to hate him, something inside her still mourned the death of their love.

Her thoughts rudely scattered when Carrie stirred and slowly opened her eyes. "Mommy?"

"I'm here, sweetie. How do you feel?"

"Funny. I fell down at school. Dr. Shipman said I passed out."

Diane gently caressed her pale cheek. "I know, but everything's okay now. You just rest."

Carrie was soon asleep, her red eyelashes falling like crescents across her soft white cheeks. Choking back a sudden rush of tears, Diane gently kissed her and then slowly left the

room, feeling as if she had left an essential part of herself
behind.

Early the next morning Diane awaited Dr. Casey in a cluttered
office adjacent to the emergency room. She wore a chic gray
wool dress, and her auburn hair framed her face in a halo of soft
curls, but the ravages of a sleepless night were clearly visible
in her haunted eyes. She had lain awake for hours imagining
the risks and complications of heart surgery. Now she was
about to have her worst fears confirmed.

She was so engrossed in her troubled thoughts that she
jumped when a raven-haired man strode into the room,
extending his hand. "Mrs. Elliot, I'm Michael Casey."

As Diane shook his hand, a myriad of impressions assaulted
her at once. He was tall and moved with an easy confidence.
His features were strong and well defined, but it was his brown
eyes that riveted her gaze to his face. They were so intense, at
once alluring and intimidating. She found it impossible to look
away.

She was still staring at him when he crossed the room and sat
behind the green metal desk. "I've just examined Carrie," he
said quietly. "I'd like to run a few more tests, but basically I
agree with Joe Shipman. It looks like an atrial septal defect."

"A hole . . . in the heart?"

"Between the chambers of the heart. Here, let me show
you." He reached into the pocket of his white lab coat, pulled
out a small notebook, and sketched as he spoke. "The heart is
divided into four chambers. The upper two are called atria; the
lower two are the ventricles. A septal wall separates the two
sides. The right side receives deoxygenated blood and routes it
to the lungs; then the left side gets it back again and pumps it
through the body."

He pointed to the sketch. "An opening between the two atria
is supposed to close at birth, but occasionally it doesn't. We
call that an atrial septal defect. In such cases the arterial blood
mixes with the venous blood and puts a strain on the heart."

It all sounded terribly frightening to Diane, like a death
sentence. Tears stung her eyes as she said, "So what happens
now? Is Carrie going to die?"

His intense dark eyes were soft with compassion. "We can

repair the hole surgically, and the odds are good that Carrie will be able to lead a completely normal life.''

''But isn't that risky?''

As he went on to describe the procedure, Diane felt increasingly hopeful. Somehow she trusted this stranger with the compelling eyes and strong-looking hands—hands that seemed capable of performing miracles.

''So if you want to go ahead with the surgery, I can schedule it for next week.''

Diane nodded and slowly rose, conscious now of taking up too much of his time. But he surprised her by saying, ''I just hit you with a hell of a lot of information, Mrs. Elliot. Do you have any questions?''

''Not now. I'm so worried about Carrie that I can't think straight.''

He smiled kindly. ''Of course you are. That's understandable. But feel free to call me anytime.''

Diane was touched by the sincerity in his voice. Many doctors were insensitive, even arrogant, but there was a kindness about Michael Casey that rendered him utterly human. As their eyes met, she felt the force of his quiet understanding soothe some of her fears. Then, bewildered by a strange impulse to hurl herself into his arms and sob, she quickly left the room.

''Let's give him a few more minutes,'' Angie said. ''Maybe he got caught in traffic.''

Diane could only imagine the sort of traffic their informant had encountered at midnight on the Lower East Side. He was nearly an hour late, and her stomach muscles tightened as she gazed around the sleazy coffee shop. Flickering fluorescent lights flashed on the grease-splattered walls, and the air reeked of fried onions and cigarette smoke. A grossly fat man sat at the counter leering at the two hookers beside him, and a ragged old woman muttered a litany of obscenities as she rummaged through her tattered shopping bag. Diane wondered what had ever possessed her to agree to meet Vic Loomis in such a squalid place. Much as she wanted to conclude her research on the drug piece, she was rattled by such a close brush with the seamy underbelly of the city.

Stirring her lukewarm coffee, she looked across the table at Angie. "I hope he's not backing out on us."

"So do I, since I was the one who got you mixed up with him."

Sighing impatiently, Diane shook her head. "That's ridiculous. Your brother put me in touch with a source; that doesn't make you responsible."

"Well, let's just hope he gets here soon. I don't feel all that safe in this crummy joint."

Diane nodded and lapsed into silence, her thoughts drifting to Carrie and her impending surgery. She had been trying to subdue her anxiety all week, but it continued to plague her, thriving like a weed in the fertile soil of her imagination. She never quite forgot that in just a few days she might face the most devastating loss of her life.

"Here he is," Angie whispered.

Diane glanced up and saw Vic Loomis pause for a moment and then slink into the coffee shop. As the bright lights illuminated his fleshy face, she noticed how dirty he looked with his black hair drooping over his forehead in oily clumps and his unkempt beard shadowing his chin. He reminded her of a wild animal, cunning and dangerous.

"Vic, we were just about to give up on you," Angie said.

He shrugged, not bothering to apologize.

"Did you bring the tapes?" Diane said, eager to conclude their business and return to the safety of her familiar neighborhood.

"No way. I'm holding on to them."

Annoyed, Diane momentarily forgot her nervousness. "But you agreed to turn them over to me."

He looked at her, his cold brown eyes completely expressionless "I changed my mind."

"Come on, Vic," Angie said. "What the hell's going on here?"

"Look," he said, furtively glancing over his shoulder. "I'm burning a bunch of cops. No way I'm letting them tapes out of my hands."

Diane began to panic at the thought of her story just falling apart. "Will you at least make some copies?"

His eyes narrowed suspiciously; then after a long pause he

nodded. "I'll be in touch when they're ready." He quickly left the coffee shop and vanished into the night like a phantom.

"I don't like this, Angie," she said. "Why is he so nervous all of a sudden?"

"Who knows? Maybe the guy is a little paranoid."

Suddenly Diane was tempted to scrap the entire piece. Vic Loomis was too unreliable. But when she remembered the potential rewards of producing such an important story, she suppressed her doubts. This might be her only opportunity to prove herself to Ed Blake.

A cold rain had been falling since dawn, and thick gray clouds hung over the city like a shroud on the morning of Carrie's surgery. As Diane climbed out of a cab and hurried into the hospital, she braced herself against the driving wind and tried to banish the nagging thought that the dismal weather was an omen.

Inside the lobby, she was surprised to see life going on as usual while her entire world was teetering on the brink of disaster.

Instead of heading directly to the cardiac unit, she heeded an impulse to visit the chapel, but as she slipped into the tiny room, she was overwhelmed by the silence and the hollow feeling inside her. Her childhood faith had wilted and died like an untended garden. Now she was a stranger in the house of God.

She gazed at the plain oak altar, then slid into a pew, and folded her hands in her lap, and tried to pray. But all she felt was a great gulf of nothingness.

Blinking away tears, she stared down at her hands, wondering if Carrie's heart problem might be some sort of retribution. Was God or Fate cruel enough to punish a child for the sins of her mother? Was Carrie about to sacrifice her life to atone for the death of Rick Conti?

She raised her eyes to the plain wooden cross suspended from the ceiling. Then, searching the deepest recesses of her soul, she found the words to beg for mercy and forgiveness.

That evening Diane huddled on a chair in the waiting room, reluctant to leave the hospital even though the surgery had been over for hours. She felt utterly drained, but she also felt a staggering sense of relief. After a week of unbearable tension, the worst of the nightmare was behind her.

Shifting on the shabby chair, she gazed out the window at the inky sky and shivered. Suddenly the waiting room seemed cold and dreary. Rachel and Angie had gone home hours ago, and now she felt isolated. There was something infinitely sad about being alone in a hospital waiting room, something that evoked all sorts of unfulfilled longings.

Tears trickled down her cheeks, and she roughly rubbed them away with a rumpled tissue. Then, sensing another presence in the room, she looked up and saw Michael Casey standing in the doorway. He was still wearing blood-splattered scrubs and his chiseled features looked weary, but the glowing intensity was still there in his dark eyes.

"Mrs. Elliot," he said softly, "what are you doing here so late?"

She shrugged, afraid to trust her voice. Seeming to sense her mood, he strode across the room and lowered his lanky frame into one of the sagging chairs. "You look tired," he said. "Go home and get some sleep. Carrie is doing fine."

A picture of her bedroom flashed through her mind, her haven that now seemed more like a lonely cell. She shook her head. "I think I'll stay here. I don't want to be alone right now."

She tensed the moment the words popped out of her mouth. Dear God, why had she revealed such a personal thought to a stranger?

But he just nodded as if he understood the complex feelings roiling inside her. He was silent for a moment. Then he smiled and said, "Listen, I was just about to go out for some dinner. How about joining me?"

Flushing to the roots of her hair, Diane shook her head. His invitation was clearly inspired by pity, and yet some lonely part of her wanted to accept. She had to force herself to meet his eyes. "I'm sorry. I'm not very hungry."

Instead of simply accepting her refusal and leaving her to her solitude, he said, "Then come along and have a drink. We could both use some company tonight."

She studied his face, suddenly aware of a trace of uncertainty in his eyes. "All right," she said. "I'd like that."

He grinned and the uncertainty disappeared like a shadow on a cloudy day. "Give me twenty minutes to shower and change," he said. "I'll meet you right here."

She nodded, but as he left her alone, she felt a stab of alarm. What was she doing thinking of Michael Casey as a man—a man with dimensions?

As Michael stood in the shower, hot water beating on his back, he wondered why the hell he had practically coerced Diane Elliot to have dinner with him. He rarely acted so impulsively, but then, he rarely found himself so attracted to a woman. Something about her fresh face appealed to him. She was nothing at all like the ultrasophisticated women his friends had been thrusting at him ever since Janet's death. He was weary of that entire scene, the artificial conversations, the clever little games, and ultimately the practiced sex that left him unfulfilled. He had no idea why he thought Diane Elliot might be different, but somehow he did.

Closing his eyes he summoned a mental picture of her, slender yet subtly sensual, curly auburn hair and striking blue eyes. He liked her looks, but he was more intrigued by her sensitivity, the alluring blend of warmth and reticence in her smile. She was more than just a cookie-cutter version of a thousand other women. He sensed that Diane Elliot was well worth knowing, but there was a reserve about her that might prove difficult to penetrate.

He stepped out of the shower and toweled himself dry. As he stood in front of the mirror shaving, he hoped his beeper would remain silent at least through dinner. He needed a few hours of relaxation, a few hours away from the constant stress of the cardiac unit. Then, as he slipped into his shirt, he felt an unfamiliar sense of anticipation at the prospect of spending an hour or two with Diane.

Diane was surprised when he led her into a family restaurant in Little Italy. Bunches of plastic grapes hung from a trellis on the ceiling, and murals of Venice adorned the walls. Somehow she would have expected him to be more at home in a trendy West Side pub.

"The scallopini is excellent," he said.

She smiled, realizing she was hungry after all. "That sounds good."

An elderly Italian waiter took their order and returned shortly with a chilled bottle of wine. As Michael filled her goblet, Diane felt a sudden twinge of guilt. She had no business enjoying herself while Carrie was sick. But as she mentally chided herself, her loneliness came rushing back and unwanted tears pooled in her eyes.

"It's all right," he said quietly. "I checked on Carrie right before we left the hospital."

"I know, but I just can't seem to . . . I'm sorry, everything seems to be catching up with me at once."

He reached across the table and gently closed his strong fingers around her hand. His touch was warm and soothing and for a moment she just let herself enjoy the unexpected comfort. Then she slowly met his eyes. "You're a kind man, Dr. Casey."

A smile tugged at his lips. "Then how about calling me Michael?"

"Yes, of course. And you call me Diane."

Smiling again, he nodded and released her hand. Her skin seemed to shrink at the loss of his warmth, and she felt an unsettling flash of déjà vu. She had experienced this same profound sense of connection with Joel, but it had been nothing more than an illusion, an illusion that had come dangerously close to ruining her. So why was she allowing herself to respond to Michael Casey when experience warned her to retreat?

"I imagine this whole ordeal has been especially hard on you," he said. "Carrie tells me you're divorced."

"Yes, I am." She paused and then surprised herself by saying, "Sometimes things come up and I'm afraid I won't be able to handle them alone, but I always seem to manage. This was a rough one, though. I still feel pretty shaky."

"How long have you been alone?"

"Nine years. Joel left me before Carrie was born." Again she was surprised by her peculiar inclination to reveal so much of herself to a stranger. "And you?" she said, anxious now to shift the conversation away from herself. "Have you ever been married?"

"My wife died five years ago." Something seemed to dim in his eyes as he gazed at the candle flickering in the center of the table. "It was a car accident."

"I'm sorry," she said softly. "That must have been terrible for you."

He was silent for a long time, staring at the dancing flame. Then finally he looked at her and said, "At first the shock kept me going. I was too dazed to feel much of anything. When the fog started to clear, I worked. I stayed at the hospital until I was too wiped out to think. Then one night I woke up in a cold sweat, shaking all over. I thought I was having a coronary, and it hit me that I was throwing my life away. After that I started trying to put myself back together."

"And now?"

He shrugged. "Now I've pretty much come to terms with things."

"But you haven't remarried?"

He shook his head. "I've never really gotten close to anyone else. Maybe it's different when you're older, harder to let your guard down."

Diane nodded thoughtfully and he said, "How about you?"

"I stopped thinking about marriage when Joel left me."

His dark eyes reflected curiosity, but instead of pressing her, he chuckled and said, "I don't know how the hell we got off to such a gloomy start. Tell me about your job. Carrie says you work in television."

Diane began to describe her job. She tried to keep him at a distance, but she found herself responding to his perceptive comments. By the time the waiter appeared to clear the table, she was appalled to realize she had been rattling on about Ed Blake and the frustrations of constantly struggling to prove herself for nearly an hour.

"I'm sorry," she said. "You must be bored to death."

"Not at all. Your drug piece sounds fascinating."

As the waiter filled her coffee cup, Diane conjured up a mental image of Vic Loomis and frowned. "My informant is very nervous all of a sudden. I'm afraid the whole thing might fall apart."

He started to respond, but the intrusive whine of his beeper cut him off. Suddenly his eyes were dead serious as he shoved his chair away from the table and sprang to his feet. "Please excuse me, I'll be right back."

Diane watched him thread his way through the maze of tables to the telephone, sheer terror filling her chest, cutting off her supply of air. How had she forgotten Carrie for even a minute? Feeling a wave of dizziness, she bowed her head and clenched the arms of her chair to ground herself.

By the time Michael returned, her face was ashen and her lips were quivering. He looked at her and quickly rounded the table and stood beside her. "Diane, it's all right. It was just a routine request for a medication change."

It took her a moment to make sense of what he was saying. Then she went limp all over, deflating like a punctured balloon. "I thought . . . something had happened to Carrie."

He brushed his fingers over her cheek. "Carrie is fine."

"I'm sorry, Michael," she whispered. "I'd like to go home now."

"Of course, just let me take care of the check."

As she watched him summon the waiter, her crushing panic began to dissipate and she felt strangely alone again. Then to her disgust, she realized she was crying.

Michael maneuvered his Mercedes out of Little Italy and headed uptown, occasionally shifting his eyes away from the road to glance at Diane. She still looked upset, and her voice sounded strained as she directed him to stop in front of a stately row house.

"Would you like to come in for a drink or a cup of coffee?"

"Are you sure? You've had a hell of a long day."

"I'm too wound up to sleep. I'd appreciate the company."

Nodding, he climbed out of the car and hurried around to open her door. As they crossed the sidewalk to the imposing Federal-style house, he was surprised by the aura of elegance. Potted evergreen shrubs adorned the high stoop, the long narrow windows gleamed in the moonlight, and the elaborately carved oak door was polished to a rich satin sheen. "Yours?" he said.

"I bought it three years ago. I hated living in apartments. It always seemed so temporary."

As she led him through the front door and into the living

room, he was engulfed by a sudden feeling of warmth. Fat leafy plants hung from the ceiling and crowded the wide window-sills. A brown corduroy sofa and two matching chairs were clustered around a brick fireplace, and an Oriental carpet covered most of the polished hardwood floor. It was an inviting room, casual but appealing.

"What would you like to drink?" she asked.

"Scotch if you have it."

She nodded and left the room. After a moment he followed her, stopping just short of the kitchen. As she stretched to retrieve the bottle of scotch from a cabinet above the sink, he noticed her breasts straining against the soft fabric of her dress and fleetingly fantasized making love to her. Then he saw her hand tremble, and he crossed the room in three steps and gently enfolded her in his arms.

At first she resisted his touch, her eyes reflecting surprise and maybe a trace of fear. But as he crushed her against his chest, she seemed to dissolve in his arms, softly crying. It had been a long time since he had used his body to comfort a woman and he had forgotten how vulnerable it left him. Yet the feeling was revitalizing, a rebirth of his senses.

When her tears finally abated, she looked up at him, her lips slightly parted. He stared at her for a long moment, then slowly lowered his head and pressed his lips to her mouth. Again she was hesitant at first, but as he deepened his kiss, he felt her respond with a hunger as fierce as his own. Drawing her closer, he delighted in the warmth of her body, the sweet scent of her skin.

As he moved his hand to her breast, she seemed to tense for a second. Then she mutely took his other hand and led him to her bedroom. He was acutely aware of what was about to happen, and though his body ached to make love to her, some small portion of his rational mind warned him to go slowly. She was defenseless right now, desperately seeking comfort, but later she might hate him for taking advantage of her. And that bothered him. Suddenly he knew with startling clarity that he wanted much more than an urgent coupling.

"Diane, are you sure?" he whispered.

"Yes. Oh, God, yes."

His doubts vanished in a pulsing haze of desire. He eased her down on the bed, stripped away her clothes and then his own, starved to feel the softness of her skin pressing against him. Moonlight streamed through the windows as his hands played over her body, discovering and arousing. Then she touched him, and he lost the last shreds of his control. Groaning, he entered her in a single thrust, shuddering as she closed around him, warm and moist.

Later he held her in his arms, his heart thudding in his chest. "Are you all right?" he murmured.

She nodded, but he felt her stiffen slightly. Lifting her chin with his finger, he stared into her clear blue eyes. "Talk to me. Tell me what you're feeling."

"I'm not sure. I've never done anything like this."

"It's all right," he whispered. "I want more than just sex, more than just one night."

"How can you say that? You don't even know me."

He caressed her face, trailing his thumb over the delicate bones of her cheeks. "I feel as if I've known you forever."

"Please, Michael, I'm not ready to discuss this right now. Just hold me."

He drew her into the circle of his arms, and a few minutes later she was asleep. As he listened to the gentle rhythm of her breathing, he realized that the pattern of his life had just abruptly shifted. Suddenly he was no longer alone. Diane Elliot had filled the coldness in his heart.

The next morning Diane sat at her desk staring out the window, remembering Michael Casey and his lovemaking. She tried to find the whole thing repugnant, an impulsive mistake to be regretted and forgotten, but she was unable to lie to herself. Sex with Michael had been more than just a physical act of release. She had felt an alarming emotional intimacy as well.

Sighing, she thought back over the past nine years. She had been relatively happy, lonely at times, but never enough to consider a serious involvement with a man. Now suddenly she was feeling this unwelcome attachment to Michael. She was already beginning to have hopes, expectations that would invariably lead to dependency and caring, all of the things Joel had used against her.

Michael was different, she reminded herself, stronger and more mature, a man rather than a selfish boy. But there were just too many risks. He wanted more from her than just a quick affair. He had made that abundantly clear last night and then again this morning. But she was afraid of being hurt.

A sharp rap on her door interrupted her reverie, and she looked up as Angie entered the room carrying two mugs of coffee and a newspaper.

"How's Carrie?" she said, setting one of the mugs on the desk in front of Diane.

"Good. I stopped at the hospital on my way here. She was wide awake and begging for ice cream."

Angie grinned. "What a kid. In three weeks she'll be racing around on her bike again."

Nodding, Diane fought the guilt that had been licking at her all morning. She had impulsively slept with a virtual stranger, and she had momentarily forgotten Carrie in a flood of sexual gratification. The memory shamed her.

"Hey," Angie said, "did you see the *Daily News* this morning? The Galloway summer home in Hyannis burned to the ground."

Diane jerked to attention.

"Here, have a look." Angie handed her the paper and then flopped into a chair.

As Diane focused on a picture of the charred rubble that had once been a magnificent summer home, her heart thudded in her chest. She shuddered as her mind re-created the gory details of a night of horror that had changed her life forever.

"Diane, are you okay?"

"I'm fine, just a little shocked. What started the fire?"

"An electrical storm. Luckily no one was hurt. Your friend Helene was in California, and the staff got out in time."

Still dazed, Diane said, "God, I hope this won't stir up a lot of new gossip." She recalled the furor Mick Travis had created with his vile book about Brenda Galloway. He had not uncovered a single shred of evidence regarding the disappearances of Rick Conti, but his nasty speculations had aroused a great deal of morbid curiosity. Just the thought of all that ugliness resurfacing frightened her.

Angie shook her head. "I doubt it. All that crap about

Brenda Galloway and her missing boyfriend is ancient history."

"I hope you're right," Diane said, but inside she was quaking, wondering if it would ever be over, if she would ever feel secure again.

CHAPTER
Seventeen

RACHEL CLOSED HER BRIEFCASE AND FASTENED HER SEAT BELT AS THE small commuter jet began its descent to La Guardia Airport. She looked out the window at the glittering lights of the city, eager now to be home. There was something disheartening about spending so many nights in anonymous motel rooms.

As she braced herself against the jarring motion of the plane, she thought back over the last few years, regretting some of the changes in her life. In a way it was gratifying to be considered an expert on the education of minority children—she was now in a position to raise both money and public awareness—but she was paying a tremendous price for the privilege. The little snags in the fabric of her marriage were slowly becoming irreparable flaws.

Shaken by such an unwelcome thought, she tried to banish it from her mind, but it had already taken root. Brian vigorously resented her frequent trips to Albany and Washington, her endless committee work, and her association with Cal and the Brotherhood. But those were just superficial conflicts that disguised the deeper layers of their discontent, the internal wounds that would spread like cancers if they were ever bared to the light of day.

When the plane landed, Rachel grabbed her briefcase and hurried into the terminal, but by the time she had retrieved her suitcase and flagged down a taxi, evening had faded to night. Glancing at her watch, she frowned. Brian would be furious. They were due to attend a political dinner at the Plaza in less than an hour, and she was already anticipating his disapproval, the taut set of his jaw that had recently become so familiar.

A short time later she climbed out of the cab in front of their West Side brownstone, pausing on the sidewalk to gaze at the house they had shared for the last seven years. Light filtered through the tall windows, spilling into the street, and she felt an inner warmth as she pictured her two daughters, Amy and Jess. She loved them with a ferocity that frightened her at times, the same fierce and consuming love she felt for Brian.

Swallowing the lump in her throat, she hurried into the house and followed a trail of tinkling laughter to the kitchen. Jess and Amy were seated at the cluttered table stuffing themselves with cookies while Brian stood at the sink rinsing dishes, looking totally incongruous in his neatly pressed tuxedo.

When he noticed her standing in the doorway, his blue eyes turned frigid. "Nice of you to remember you have a family."

"Brian, I'm sorry. The meeting ran longer than I expected, and I missed my flight."

She wanted to say more, to penetrate the cold wall of his anger, but the girls scrambled out of their chairs and hurled themselves at her. "Mommy," Jess shrieked, "you haven't finished my elf costume, and I need it for the school play next week."

"And Johnny Duncan smashed my Raggedy Ann lunch box," Amy cried, sticking out her lower lip. "I had to use an ugly old brown bag today."

Rachel dropped to her knees, gathering them against her chest, kissing one dark head and then the other. Jess was nearly seven, tall and sturdy, with an eager smile and flashing brown eyes. Amy was a year younger, quieter and less sure of herself. She had deep blue eyes like Brian and fine Irish features. As Rachel hugged them to her breast, breathing in their sweet scent, she felt a love so pure and complete it momentarily stunned her.

"Mommy," Jess said impatiently, "what about my costume?"

"I'll finish it tomorrow night, I promise." Then, smiling at Amy, she said, "And I'll pick up a new lunch box on my way home from work tomorrow. How does that sound?"

"Okay," Amy agreed solemnly. "Can we watch TV now?"

Rachel checked her watch. "Just till the baby-sitter gets here, then it's time for bed."

Squirming out of her embrace, they raced to the den, leaving her alone with Brian. There was a strained silence as she struggled to her feet, feeling clumsy and awkward. "I really am sorry," she said.

He wiped his hands on a dish towel, then tossed it on the counter, his anger still clearly visible. "Great. You're sorry. That fixes everything."

Hurt by the bitterness in his voice, she searched his face for a hint of tenderness, but found only accusation. "What else do you want me to say? I tried, Brian, but I missed the plane."

He just shook his head, as if he no longer cared enough to argue. "Look, there's no time to get into this right now. We're already late."

Somehow his indifference hurt even more than his anger, but instead of lashing out at him, she mutely nodded and rushed upstairs to their bedroom. As she closed the door and stripped off her clothes, it came to her that she was afraid of a confrontation, afraid she might blurt out words that would irretrievably damage their marriage. They knew each other so well, every sore spot and hidden weakness. It would be so easy to deliver a mortal blow.

She padded across the rose-colored carpet to the bathroom and turned on the shower. She tried to banish her thoughts, but her mind returned to them the way her fingers would have worked at a deeply embedded splinter, persisting in spite of the pain. She had once been so certain of their love, certain enough to sever every link with her past. But now she understood that love was extremely perishable, always hostage to the little disappointments and unconscious cruelties that somehow managed to become unforgivable atrocities.

As she started to climb into the shower, she caught sight of herself in the full-length mirror and paused, startled by the gaunt woman staring back at her. She had never thought much about her appearance, maybe because she had always known she was plain. Even as a child she had never played at being coy or cute, but now she was truly shocked by her thinness, the sharp angles of her face. She wondered if Brian still had any desire to make love to her.

Then, stung by the sudden presence of such glaring insecurities, she stepped into the shower and mindlessly scrubbed herself.

When she emerged from the bathroom wrapped in a fleecy towel, Brian was standing in front of his dresser fiddling with his tie. Ignoring him, she put on fresh cotton panties, then rifled through the closet in search of her white crepe evening gown. But as she removed it from its protective plastic bag, she noticed a spot on the bodice and swore under her breath.

"What's the matter?" Brian said, glancing at her.

"I forgot to have my dress cleaned. There's a stain on the front."

"So wear something else."

She shook her head, oddly embarrassed, as if she had somehow failed as a woman. "I don't have another gown. I'll have to wear a cocktail dress."

"Jesus Christ, you know how important this dinner is. How could you forget to get your goddam dress cleaned?"

All Rachel could do was stare at him, at the bright color suffusing his face, the disgust in his eyes. She remembered a time when those eyes had been filled with love and laughter, but now everything had changed. Feeling a terrible heaviness in her chest, she said, "Don't worry. Nobody will notice."

"Maybe not, but I was counting on you to be here on time tonight and to dress like the wife of a future district attorney. You don't seem to give a damn about my career anymore."

Rachel sucked in a sharp breath. "You know that's not true."

"Horseshit. You've made your priorities pretty clear. I need an appointment to even talk to you these days."

"That's not fair," she said. "I have responsibilities. You knew that when you married me. Now all of a sudden you want a brain-dead Barbie doll."

Brian laughed, a harsh bark that seemed to lacerate her flesh, drawing fresh blood. "What I want is a wife. Look at this place; it's a fucking disaster. Our cleaning lady sits on her ass swilling gin all day, and you're too busy to come home. I'm sick of it, Rache. I'm sick to death of living this way."

As Rachel looked around the room, she wondered how Brian could reduce their marriage to a pile of dirty laundry and a rumpled bed. But of course those were just the symbols of his unhappiness.

"This isn't about a messy house, Brian. Say what you really mean."

At first she thought he intended to ignore her. He sat on the bed, raking his fingers through his thick blond hair, but then he looked at her, his eyes distant and shuttered. "Why the hell should I bother? Nothing ever changes around here."

"Maybe that's because I always have to guess at what you're thinking. You deliberately shut me out."

"That's garbage, Rache. If I shut you out, it's your own fault. You don't give a damn what I have to say."

"No, Brian . . ." She broke off, hurt and angry, unable to find the words to reach him. She wondered when they had become strangers, hoarding their feelings like misers. Suddenly the tension between them seemed unbearable. She blindly rushed across the room, sat on the bed beside him, and clutched his hands as if they were a lifeline.

"Why are we doing this to each other?" she whispered hoarsely. "I love you, Brian."

A myriad of emotions flashed in his eyes—pain, doubt, anger—but there was love there, too, and she felt a resurgence of hope. "Is it too late to work things out?"

"God, Rachel, you know I love you." He reached for her, pulling her against his chest. "I never meant to hurt you."

She tried to lose herself in the feel of his arms tightly wrapped around her shoulders, but a nagging inner voice reminded her that this was only a respite. Their love was still under siege, threatened by countless hidden hurts and disappointments.

Sunday mornings had become something of a ritual. After a bracing run through Central Park, Brian showered and dressed, then drove the girls to Queens for a visit with his parents. In the beginning, Rachel had accompanied them, but over the years she had manufactured a variety of excuses to avoid encounters with his family. Now he just assumed she would remain at home, and he found he actually preferred it that way.

As Amy and Jess chattered in the back seat, Brian considered the strained relations between Rachel and his parents. Johnny and Mary had just never accepted her, and Rachel had done nothing to ease the tension. Not that he blamed her. His parents were good people, but they lived in a narrow world dominated by church and family. In their eyes, Rachel was an aberration—a working mother, a white woman involved in the civil rights movement. No matter how much he might wish things were different, reality told him his wife and his parents would always be at odds.

After parking in front of the brick row house, Brian helped Jess and Amy out of the car, then followed them up the steps, listening to their childish laughter ring out in the frigid morning air. Right now they loved visiting their grandparents, but it was only a matter of time before they detected the hostile under-currents between the adults. Jess was already asking why Rachel never came along on their Sunday outings.

Mary McDonald opened the door, her round cheeks flushed with happiness. She was wearing a white apron over a plain cotton dress, and her silver hair was tucked into a neat bun at the nape of her neck. She looked the part of a grandmother, not at all concerned by the wrinkles etched into her face or the slight stoop of her shoulders.

She kissed the girls, then pecked Brian on the cheek. "Come on in out of the cold. You don't want to take a chill."

As Brian trailed her into the house, he greedily inhaled the familiar scent of fresh cinnamon rolls and coffee, a scent that reminded him of countless other Sunday mornings. Mary always served cinnamon rolls after mass, a reward for another week of righteousness.

Johnny McDonald was sitting at the table paging through the *Daily News,* but he quickly dropped the paper and opened his arms to the girls. His florid face beamed with pleasure as they rushed to hug him.

"So how are my two beauties today?"

Amy giggled. "You're silly, Gramps."

"Silly, am I? Well, no cinnamon rolls for you, little lady."

Always in competition, Jess tugged at his red flannel shirt. "Guess what, Gramps? I was an elf in the school play."

"And I'll bet you were a fine elf, too."

Jess nodded sagely, then shifted to look at Mary. "Can we play upstairs?"

Mary nodded as she handed them each a cinnamon roll. "But be careful on those steps, you hear?"

Once they disappeared, Johnny lit his pipe and shot Brian a belligerent look. "So what's the story? When do the girls start their religious instruction?"

Irritated by his father's stubborn refusal to abandon an

argument that had been raging for years, Brian shook his head. "Forget it, Dad. We're not raising the girls in the church."

"No, I can see that. You're raising them to be heathens." Johnny glared, his red cheeks darkening to an unhealthy shade of purple. "Me own sweet granddaughters are looking at an eternity in hell."

"That's enough, Dad. And if you ever say anything like that to the kids, you'll never see them again."

Chastened, Johnny sat back sucking his pipe while Mary nervously fluttered over the stove, clearly upset by the conflict. Stifling an urge to smooth things over, Brian aimlessly glanced around the cozy room.

As he took in the cheery yellow wallpaper and the plants flourishing on the windowsill, he felt a disquieting unrest, a sudden awareness that something was missing from his own life. Looking at his mother, he remembered the warmth and security of his childhood, the sense of home and family that seemed to emanate from Mary McDonald. He had never consciously appreciated those things, but now he felt a poignant longing for the past, a longing that was somehow connected to his own marriage.

He usually went to great lengths to deny such unsettling thoughts, but every now and then they poked through his defenses like weeds. Much as he loved Rachel, he had needs she seemed incapable of meeting. Her indifference to his career wounded and irritated him. She never even tried to play the political game, never went out of her way to ingratiate herself with party regulars or to stifle her liberal rhetoric. At times he found himself thinking of her as a political liability, but that made him feel like a disloyal bastard. Somehow he had to vanquish the doubt and resentment that ate away at him like corrosive poisons. He had to reconcile with Rachel because the alternative was unthinkable.

Dawn was just ribboning its way across the indigo sky when Mick Travis slipped into his Corvette and drove toward the charred remains of the Galloway summer home. Though the air was frigid, his excitement seemed to insulate him from the cold. After years of obsessive but futile investigation, he finally had an opportunity to search the house and grounds for proof

that Rick Conti had been murdered by a group of merciless
women.

In a way it pleased him that all of the women had achieved
a degree of fame and success. That would render their public
disgrace more shocking and much more gratifying. His interest
in exposing them as murderers had now become an obsessive
desire for vengeance. He felt like a judge preparing to dispense
long overdue justice.

A pale winter sun was just peering over the horizon as he
stopped the Corvette in front of the skeletal remains of the
house. For years the majestic house had been protected by an
army of guards, but now it stood alone and vulnerable, like a
naked old whore no longer able to conceal her secrets.

Mick sat there for several minutes, reliving his countless
attempts to sneak onto the grounds only to be discovered and
rudely turned away by the security force. Now a random act of
nature had miraculously provided him with a chance to search
for the clues that would unravel the mystery. His excitement
flared as he climbed out of the car and made his way across the
lawn to the house.

But a week later he was still searching, still sifting through
the rubble. His bones ached from cold and exertion, yet he
stubbornly clung to the belief that the truth was there, waiting
to be uncovered.

It was nearly dusk when he knelt on the ruins of what had
once been a redwood deck. Aiming his flashlight at a pile of
debris, he shoved a few boards aside and began to pick through
the ashes. Then he saw a glint of gold, and his heartbeat
accelerated. Slowly he reached for the glittering object and
lifted it to the light, his hand trembling as he realized he was
holding a medallion—a gold medallion flecked with what
looked like dried blood.

Leaning back on his haunches, Mick emitted a low grunt of
satisfaction, a primal sound of victory that seemed to violate
the early evening stillness. At last he had something to
substantiate his suspicions. Intuitively he knew the medallion
had belonged to Rick Conti, just as he intuitively knew he now
had a weapon to use against four vicious murderers.

As he studied the medallion, he considered his options,
immediately discounting the idea of turning it over to the
police. Even if they were able to prove that the dried blood

belonged to Conti, there was still no concrete evidence that he had been murdered. But just the sight of the medallion might be enough to scare a guilty woman into making a confession.

Smiling, he carefully tucked it into his pocket, his mind already engaged in plotting the final chapter of the mystery.

Rachel hung up the phone and turned to Brian, tears shining in her eyes.

"What's wrong?" he said.

"That was my cousin Yetta. My father's dying."

Brian had been dressing for work, but he quickly tossed his shirt on the bed, walked to her side, and enfolded her in his arms. "God, I'm sorry, Rache."

Slumping against his chest, she sobbed as bittersweet memories assailed her. She had never healed the breach with her parents. Now it was too late. Sol was dying.

"I'm going home," she said in a raspy voice. "I have to see my father."

"Are you sure? It's been so long. What if they turn you away?"

Rachel felt a numbing chill, an inner coldness that mirrored her thoughts of death. "I won't let them, not now. But I don't want to face this alone. Come with me, Brian."

In the long silence that followed, Rachel actually felt his withdrawal. Then at last he said, "That's not a good idea. I have no right to be there."

"You're my husband. That gives you the right."

He moved away from her and sat on the bed. "Look, this is no time to start pushing. I'll stay here with the kids."

"Brian, I need you," she said, desperate to make him understand, but he just looked at her with a blank expression, as if he were completely indifferent to her pain.

"How can you do this to me?" she asked.

"Christ, what do you expect? I've never even met your father. Now all of a sudden you want me to show up at his deathbed."

Anger burned away some of her pain. "This has nothing to do with my father. Do it for me, Brian."

He shook his head. "I'm sorry, Rache. I can't." Abruptly he grabbed his shirt and walked into the bathroom, leaving her feeling alone and empty, her faith in his love shattered.

— — —

A few hours later Rachel emerged from the subway station and stood immobile on the sidewalk, dazed by the familiar yet strangely altered landscape of the Grand Concourse. Nothing was quite as she remembered. The apartment buildings looked shabbier, litter blew along the street like tumbleweed, and there were no friendly faces in the crowd. She felt displaced, as though she were viewing a familiar scene through a dirty lens.

She remained rooted to the sidewalk for several minutes. Then as she slowly walked the few blocks to her childhood home, she tried to envision her father, but the image was cloudy and unclear. By the time she arrived at her parents' deli, she was trembling.

The glass door was locked and her heart thumped with anticipation as she fumbled in her purse for the worn brass key. Moments later she was standing alone in the deli, breathing in the tangy scents of pastrami and pickled herring, listening to the steady hum of the cooler and the hiss of the radiator. She was engulfed by memories, vivid portraits of her childhood that were impressed upon her mind like precious bits of antique lace.

As her eyes grew accustomed to the dim light, she slowly made her way to the stairs, feeling dizzy and breathless. What if her parents rejected her, treated her like an unwelcome stranger?

When she reached the wooden door at the top of the stairs, she hesitated, afraid to enter and reluctant to knock. Her entire body was trembling like a blade of grass caught in a brisk wind. She stood there for a long time, then opened the door and entered the warm kitchen.

Naomi was sitting at the table, her face buried in her hands, but when she heard the door opening, she glanced up, her faded brown eyes widening in disbelief. Time seemed to stand still as she stared at Rachel, her lips moving in a silent litany, her gnarled fingers clutching her chest. Then she whispered, "Rachel."

Rachel blindly rushed across the room and knelt beside her mother, raw sobs filling her throat. Suddenly she felt like a child again as Naomi gently hugged her, softly crooning in Yiddish. There were so many words waiting to be spoken, explanations and recriminations, but for just a moment, Rachel allowed herself the comfort of her mother's touch.

An eternity seemed to pass before Naomi finally drew away, tears glittering on her wrinkled cheeks. "Rachel, I'm glad you came home, daughter."

Her words were simple, but they filled Rachel with wonder and relief. "I heard about Pop, and I couldn't stay away anymore," she said hoarsely. "Will he see me, Ma?"

Naomi rubbed her eyes wearily, and Rachel noticed how much her mother had aged. Her features seemed sharp and gaunt, and her gray hair was sparse, barely covering her scalp. But her eyes were still just as piercing.

"Maybe, now that he knows this is his last chance to talk to his daughter. He never said your name, but every day he missed you. Every day he regretted what he did."

Rachel smiled sadly. "How do you know that, Ma?"

"After all these years, I know my husband."

As she looked at her mother, Rachel was suddenly ashamed of her own selfishness. Naomi was losing the man she had loved and depended on for nearly forty years. "Are you all right, Ma?" she said thickly. "How long has Pop been sick?"

Sighing, Naomi reached into her pocket for a hankie and blotted her swollen eyes. "Six years ago he had a heart attack. The doctors wanted to operate, fix some of the clogs in his arteries, but Sol said no. I think he was afraid. Then he had another attack and it was too late. His heart was damaged. There's nothing they can do to save him."

"Are you sure? Did you get a second opinion? Diane is seeing a heart surgeon. I'll call him."

Naomi shook her head. "No, Rachel. Your father's dying. They only let him leave the hospital because he wanted to die at home."

All at once reality punctured the illusions Rachel had been fabricating in her mind. "How long does he have?" she asked.

"A few more days."

Rachel sucked in a ragged breath. "Can I see him now?"

Naomi nodded, gripping Rachel's hand. "Come, we'll go together."

As Rachel followed her mother through the familiar rooms, she struggled with the memories that surrounded her like a fog. She saw her father everywhere, hunched over the table sipping tea, reading his Yiddish newspaper in front of the television, studying the Torah in the quiet dining room. This was his home, and his spirit seemed to float in the air, reminding her of his presence.

She tensed when they reached the bedroom, afraid her father would turn her away. "Maybe you should tell him I'm here," she said.

"No, it's best if you just go in, Rachel."

Rachel glanced at Naomi, absorbing the anxiety on her creased face, and suddenly her legs felt rubbery and her heart began to beat in a hard tattoo. But before she had a chance to turn and run, Naomi shoved her into the dim room.

She was instantly enveloped by the stench of death, a sickening odor of decay. Then she saw her father lying in the center of the double bed, looking more like a skeleton than a man. His face was gaunt, his eyes had sunk deep into their sockets, and his mouth was just a thin slash between his hollow cheeks. She thought he was unaware of her presence, but as she approached the bed, he called her name in a weak thready voice. "Rachel, is that you?"

"Yes, Pop. I came home to say good-bye." She waited for words of condemnation, but they never came. After a long moment she crossed the room and carefully sat on the edge of the bed, her eyes riveted to his face.

"It's been such . . . a long time, Rachel. I was . . . wrong to send you away."

Feeling her throat fill with tears, Rachel struggled to speak. "I'm here now. Nothing else matters."

"Come closer. Let . . . me look at you."

Rachel leaned over as her father reached out to stroke her face, like a blind man, his wasted fingers seeming to memorize her features. "So many good years . . . we threw away," he rasped. "So many years I was too proud . . . to admit I made such a terrible mistake. And your mother . . . how she suffered because of me."

"Forget the past, Pop."

He sighed, releasing a frightening gurgle deep in his throat. "The past is all I have left. In a few days I'll be in my grave."

Rachel was tempted to deny his words, but she saw the stark truth written in his eyes and simply nodded, preserving his dignity.

There was a long silence while he labored to breathe. Then he said, "So tell me, has your . . . husband made you happy?"

This time Rachel succumbed to the temptation to lie. As she thought of Brian and their dying marriage, she knew she had to spin an illusion of happiness to comfort her father. "Yeah, Pop. And we have two beautiful little girls, Amy and Jess." She fished in her purse and drew out her wallet. "I have pictures of them."

As Sol held the picture in his trembling hands, a film of tears shimmered in his eyes. "Such precious ones. They smile . . . just like you."

Just then Naomi slipped into the room and Sol held out the photographs, his ravaged face suddenly more alive. "Naomi, come see your grandchildren."

Slowly making her way to the bed, Naomi took the pictures and sank down on a chair, greedily studying each one. When she finished, she set them on the night table and sighed. "Tell me about them. Tell me everything."

Soft lamplight bathed the room as Rachel brought her daughters to life for her parents. Sol dozed occasionally, but Naomi perched on the edge of her chair like an inquisitive bird, drinking in each detail. When Rachel paused, weary and hoarse, her father touched her hand. "You're . . . a good daughter, Rachel. Now I can die in peace."

"I love you, Pop."

But Sol was already asleep, the shadow of a smile still lingering on his lips.

"He loves you too, Rachel," Naomi said softly. "He never stopped loving you."

Sol died in his sleep three nights later. He simply slipped away, almost willingly relinquishing his hold on life, and though Rachel felt a deep well of grief, she also felt restored by their time together.

She sat shiva with Naomi in the tiny living room, rediscovering the Jewish roots that still seemed to be an essential part of her. Even after living in another world for nine years, she felt the pull of the faith she had abandoned so casually.

But even as she struggled to resolve the past, she remained troubled by her deteriorating marriage. Brian refused to attend

Sol's funeral, and her anger was sharp and fierce, fueled by the unrelenting hurt that had settled in her heart. As she climbed into her narrow bed each night, she wondered if she and Brian would be able to paste their marriage back together or if the wounds were simply too pervasive to heal.

CHAPTER
Eighteen

GUSSIE DREW HER SILK ROBE MORE TIGHTLY AROUND HER WAIST AS SHE stared out the window at the barren winter landscape. Everything looked so stark against the dull gray sky, withered and lifeless. She shivered slightly, then turned away from the depressing view, but her melancholy seemed to follow her like a shadow.

Glancing around the bedroom she shared with Richard, she frowned at the sight of his keys and wallet neatly laid out on the dresser. He was always so fastidious, so precise and predictable. His entire life was a carefully orchestrated production, and she was simply another bit of scenery.

She had no idea why that bothered her so much. Her marriage was nothing more than a contract, and Richard had scrupulously lived up to his obligations. They resided on a country estate surrounded by every imaginable luxury, and they were icons of Washington society. She should have been deliriously happy or at least marginally content. But in truth she was miserable.

Gussie hated her life, dreaded rising each morning to face the sterile sameness, the crippling boredom. Somehow she had lost her sense of self. She had become so adept at playing a role that she no longer had a clear picture of the woman beneath the facade. Where was Gussie Tremain? Where was the young girl who had loved a dark-eyed man with such boundless passion?

Feeling a familiar throbbing in her head, Gussie sat on the bed and listlessly rubbed her temples. It always shocked her to realize she was still in love with Tony, still wondering what her future might have been like if she had just indulged in one reckless action. But no matter how much she fantasized, she was always forced to return to the reality of her life with Richard, a life that had become increasingly intolerable.

Her thoughts scattered as Richard hurried out of the bathroom naked, his hair still damp from his shower. She continued to massage her temples, hoping to avoid conversation, but he seemed insensitive to her pain.

"I thought you were having lunch with your mother today, Augusta."

Gussie nodded. "I have a headache, but I suppose I'll go anyway."

"I'm sure you'll feel better if you get out. Just be sure you're home in time to dress for the fund-raiser tonight."

The thought of another tedious evening in a smoky hotel ballroom left Gussie feeling put upon and resentful. "I'm really not up to it, Richard. I think I'll stay home."

He seemed to puff up with indignation. "People expect to see you there, Augusta. You know this is going to be a rough campaign. I need your support."

Gussie stared at him, feeling a wave of revulsion. His sagging stomach reminded her of a soft white pillow, and his limp penis dangled between his legs like a shriveled hot dog. Closing her eyes for an instant, she swallowed the bile in her throat, then said, "I hardly think I'll ruin your campaign by missing one dinner."

"Maybe not, but I want you beside me. God knows I don't ask much else of you."

His voice was laced with sarcasm, and Gussie knew he was referring to more than just her reluctance to attend a political dinner. She was tempted to pursue the argument, but the thought of a nasty scene was just too exhausting.

"All right, Richard," she said wearily. "What time should I be ready?"

He pursed his lips into a thin smile. "We'll leave at eight."

Gussie nodded, then abruptly stood and made her way to the bathroom. Richard's mechanical smile had taken on enormous proportions in her mind, symbolizing everything she detested about him. She knew it was insane to obsess over something so petty, and yet she was unable to block that smile out of her thoughts.

By the time she showered and fixed her hair, Richard had left for his office and the bedroom was pleasantly quiet. She took her time dressing, then sat at her delicate mahogany desk and poured herself a cup of coffee from the steaming pot the maid had left there earlier.

As she savored the rich dark brew, she paged through the paper, pausing to read a review of a Molinari exhibit at a trendy Georgetown gallery. While modern art had never particularly appealed to her, she suddenly had a strong desire to view the strong colors of a Molinari painting. After checking her watch, she impulsively decided to cut her lunch with Elizabeth short and treat herself to a brief respite from the dull pattern of her life.

Elizabeth was seated in the blue and white breakfast room when Gussie arrived at her parents' house. Her pale silver hair was swept into an elegant bun, and she wore a simple sea green dress that enhanced the color of her eyes. She was nearly sixty but she was still a vision of youth and beauty.

Gussie forced herself to smile at her mother, but Elizabeth was far too perceptive to be fooled.

"What is it, dear? You look troubled."

"I had another headache this morning, but it's better now."

Elizabeth sighed, looking vaguely annoyed. "Have you seen the doctor lately? There must be something he can do for you. Maybe the headaches are connected to your infertility."

Easing herself into a white wicker chair, Gussie inhaled a calming breath, but her sudden flash of anger was too potent to be denied. "That's absolutely absurd."

"Not necessarily, Augusta. I think you should ask your doctor about it."

Gussie laughed bitterly. "Mother, I'm not infertile. Richard had a vasectomy fifteen years ago. He just never bothered to tell me."

Just then one of the maids entered the room, balancing a tray in her plump hands. Elizabeth shot Gussie a quelling look as the servant carefully set out plates of shrimp salad and a chilled bottle of Chenin Blanc. But the moment she disappeared, Elizabeth picked up the threads of their conversation.

"Surely you're not serious. I can't believe Richard would do such a thing."

"Believe it, Mother. You'll never have a grandchild, at least not as long as I'm married to Richard."

Elizabeth paled. "Please, Augusta, don't even joke about such a thing."

Gussie felt betrayed. Instead of damning Richard for his cruel and deliberate deceit, Elizabeth was worried about the possibility of a divorce staining the family name. Confiding in her mother had been a mistake, but she found it impossible to abandon a topic that continued to cause her untold misery. "Would you really blame me for divorcing him? He deliberately lied to me, Mother."

Elizabeth looked distressed. Suddenly there were fine lines around her mouth, and her hand trembled almost imperceptibly as she delicately speared a piece of lettuce. "Divorce is out of the question. You know that."

"Why? People get divorced all the time."

"Not in our family. We have an image to uphold. I hate to even think of all the nasty publicity a divorce would create."

Gussie realized that she was engaging in a useless argument, but she stubbornly persisted. "So I'm supposed to stay married to Richard even though I'm miserable?"

Clearly struggling to control her anger, Elizabeth said, "I'd hardly call you miserable, Augusta. You have a wonderful life, a devoted husband, a beautiful home. Many couples choose not to have children these days."

"But Richard never gave me a choice. He deliberately hid the fact that he had a vasectomy."

Elizabeth set aside her fork and leaned over the table, her aristocratic features molded in a rigid mask. "Listen to me, Augusta. Every marriage has its disappointments, but you learn to live with them. You have no alternative. Divorce is totally unacceptable."

It irritated Gussie that her mother still felt free to treat her like a child. Then it occurred to her that in many ways she was a child, caught somewhere between adolescence and true independence. She had allowed her parents and then Richard to dominate her life. Now they expected her to comply with their wishes, to graciously set aside her own dreams and behave like a dutiful wife, forever trapped in a web of her own making.

Rattled by this new and unsettling insight, Gussie felt a rising panic. The room seemed to shrink around her, cutting off her supply of air.

"What's the matter, Augusta? Are you ill?"

Gussie looked at her mother, but instead of seeing Elizabeth, she saw a silver lioness, fresh blood dripping from her gaping jaws. In the blink of an eye the horrible hallucination disappeared, and Gussie wondered if she was losing her mind.

"Augusta, are you all right?"

Swallowing a huge gulp of air, Gussie shook her head. "I need some fresh air. I'll call you later, Mother."

As she ran from the room, Gussie heard Elizabeth frantically calling her name, but she blindly rushed out of the house and climbed into her car, her heartbeat drumming in her ears.

After spending an hour aimlessly driving through Georgetown, Gussie finally parked in front of the Whitman Gallery. She was no longer interested in the art show, but the idea of going home was oppressive. Her mind was spinning with a wild jumble of thoughts, and she felt too shaky to begin sorting them out. She needed a diversion, and at the moment the Molinari exhibit seemed the simplest alternative.

Inside, the gallery was noisy and crowded. High heels clicked on the polished parquet floor, champagne flowed in a continuous stream, and the air reeked of wealth and an intoxicating blend of costly perfumes. As Gussie wove her way through the modishly dressed crowd, she felt old and matronly in her rose-colored suit. There was an aura of youth and energy in the air, and she was completely out of touch.

She had a sudden urge to escape to the protective anonymity of her car, but a quick exit would have been too conspicuous. Acutely uncomfortable, she drifted toward a huge canvas done in shocking shades of red and orange and tried to appear engrossed.

But the garish painting failed to evoke even a spark of interest, and she soon found herself gazing around the room. When she noticed a dark-haired man standing in a corner, her breath caught in her throat. After so many years of lonely fantasy, Tony De Costa had suddenly materialized like an apparition.

She blinked to clear away the confusing vision, but when she opened her eyes, he was still there, firmly rooted in reality. And while every instinct warned her to slip away before he noticed her, she remained completely still, watching him with a compelling intensity.

He was talking to an older man and casually cradling a glass of champagne in his long bronze fingers. Even from a distance his hands were beautiful, slender yet strong, moving with an artless grace. She vividly remembered those hands stroking her breasts, awakening them to sensation.

Feeling her cheeks flush, she lifted her gaze to his face, his chiseled nose and lush full lips. His hair was still inky black, but now there were threads of silver at his temples. He looked even more dashing, more vital and exciting. She recalled the sheer pleasure of making love to him. Then, shaken by such forbidden thoughts, she turned away, determined to leave the gallery as quickly and unobtrusively as possible.

But as she crossed the room, her gaze returned to his face, and their eyes connected. She saw his surprise and then a flash of desire, a primal look of yearning that lasted only a second. But it was enough to stimulate and alarm her.

Her rational mind warned her to escape, but she remained paralyzed, incapable of motion. As she watched him slowly walk in her direction, the entire scene took on a dreamlike quality.

"Gussie," he said, "how nice to see you."

As he closed his warm hand around her fingers, Gussie felt dizzy. She struggled for words, but none came, and after a long silence she finally managed to say, "Tony, it's been such a long time."

She was aware of his dark gaze on her face, but she was afraid to meet his eyes for fear that he would peer into her soul and see that she had never stopped reliving their time together. Feeling transparent, she tried to erase any trace of emotion from her face as she lifted her eyes to his. "Are you still living here in Georgetown?"

"When I'm not traveling on company business. My father died last year, and I've inherited some new responsibilities."

"I'm sorry . . . about your father."

He studied her for a long moment, then lightly squeezed her hand. "You have no reason to be afraid of me, Gussie."

Memories of their last hours together rushed into her mind. She remembered his lovemaking, his soft words and gentle touches, and then she remembered his anger. Still, she knew she had no reason to be afraid of him. She was afraid of herself, of the turbulent emotions swirling inside her.

"What a strange thing to say. I'm not afraid of you."

He simply smiled. "Good, then have a drink with me."

"No, I'm sorry. I have to be getting home."

"There's a bar right next door. We'll only be a few minutes."

Gussie felt herself weakening, giving in to an irresistible urge to appease an inner longing. "All right, just a quick one."

After looping her arm through his, Tony led her through the noisy gallery to the street. She was keenly aware of his closeness, the exotic fragrance of his cologne, and the nubby texture of his wool jacket. As they entered the bar, she feared she was making a dangerous mistake, and yet her heart fluttered in anticipation.

He remained silent until they were settled in a secluded booth sipping glasses of zinfandel. Then he looked at her intently, his dark eyes glimmering in the shadows. "I read about your marriage. Are you happy with Richard Chandler, Gussie?"

She caught a ragged breath, surprised by his bluntness. "Yes, of course I am. Richard and I have a lot in common."

"Do you love him?"

His intense gaze seemed to strip away her defenses, leaving her helplessly naked. "Please, Tony, this is . . . You're upsetting me."

Slowly he reached across the table and brushed his fingers across her hand, evoking vivid memories of other, more intimate touches. "Why, *cara*? Why are you running from the truth?"

"What are you talking about?"

He laughed softly. "This attraction between us. You feel it, too. I know you do."

Gussie weakly shook her head. "You're wrong. I'm married."

"To a man you've never loved. You married Richard Chandler just to please your parents."

"No . . . Leave me alone, please."

"I want to see you again, Gussie."

Seized by a longing so fierce it seemed to radiate from her very soul, Gussie shot to her feet, fighting frantically to hold on to her will to resist. Terrified of encountering his alluring black eyes again, she hesitated for a moment, then blindly rushed out of the bar, knowing she was just a breath away from an unthinkable mistake.

As Mick Travis watched Gussie leave the bar and run to her car, he idly wondered if the prim Washington matron was having a hot affair. Not that it had any relevance to the Conti case, but after writing so many steamy books, his mind just naturally gravitated in that direction. And Gussie definitely had the look of a woman involved in something suspicious.

As soon as she started her car, Mick shifted his Corvette into gear and followed her through the streets of Georgetown, carefully maintaining his distance. Though he had been trailing her for two days, he was certain she was oblivious to his presence. There was something perversely gratifying about spying on a murderess. But much as he enjoyed his little game, he knew it was almost time to make his presence known. Gussie Tremain Chandler was about to have her complacency shattered by a simple gold medallion.

A dense layer of smoke hung over the ballroom of the Mayflower Hotel like a dull gray cloud. Dinner and the requisite speeches were over, but Richard was still circulating among his supporters, pumping hands and smiling officiously. As Gussie watched him from her place on the dais, she was reminded of a clown performing for an audience, bowing and scraping, hiding behind a painted grin.

Frowning with distaste, she turned her gaze away from Richard and sipped her tepid wine. He would be furious at her for neglecting to work the crowd, but she was too preoccupied to feign an interest in his campaign. Her encounter with Tony was still burning in her mind like a slow, hot fire.

She flushed as she recalled his fingers lightly caressing her hand. Suddenly her fantasies were no longer just the unfulfilled yearnings of a woman trapped in a life of regret. But much as she ached to see him again, her ingrained sense of duty ran strong and deep. An affair was inconceivable.

Yet every time she tried to dismiss Tony from her thoughts, she found herself clinging to her memories with an incredible tenacity. It seemed like an ironic twist of fate that he had reappeared in her life when she was so unhappy and discontent. At another time she might have had a stronger will to resist him, but now she felt disillusioned and weak, devastated by the prospect of a life without children. Richard had betrayed her, and in some way that made it easier to entertain thoughts of infidelity.

Stunned by the realization that she was actually considering an affair with Tony, Gussie furtively glanced around her, afraid her thoughts were visible on her face. She felt hot and sweaty, all her nerves strumming at once. Then as she picked up a napkin and fanned her face, she heard a familiar raspy voice, a voice that sent shock waves pulsing through her system.

"It's been a long time, Gussie, but I told you we'd meet again." Mick Travis slid into the empty seat beside her and flashed her a sinister grin.

"What are you doing here?" she hissed. "This is a private party."

Digging in his tuxedo pocket, Mick produced a battered press pass and smugly waved it in her face. "I'm part of the press crew, sugar."

"You're not a reporter. Get out of here right now or I'll call Security."

He laughed, then leaned back in his chair and lazily lit a cigarillo. "I don't think you want to do that, Gussie. You and I have a little unfinished business to settle."

"I have no business with you." She glared at him, hoping to disguise her raging fear behind a disdainful manner, but he seemed impervious to her efforts to intimidate him.

"Then maybe you'd rather talk to the cops."

Alarmed, Gussie glanced around the room again. Richard would be outraged if he caught her even speaking to a disreputable man like Mick Travis, but she was too upset by his threat to just send him away. "All right," she said. "But not here. I'll meet you outside in a few minutes."

He scowled, then stood and kicked his chair aside. "A few minutes, Gussie. I'm not a patient man."

Gussie watched him disappear into the crowd, panic flaring inside her. What now? What did he want after all this time? She fleetingly wondered if he intended to blackmail her. Trembling uncontrollably, she sprang to her feet and elbowed her way through the crowd.

After pausing to claim her sable coat, she went directly to the hotel lobby, lowering her head to avoid drawing attention to herself. The last thing she needed was a nosy reporter following her outside.

A cold blast of air hit her as she stepped out into the moonless January night. Mick was hovering in the shadows like some malevolent creature of darkness. Shivering, Gussie steeled herself against the fear licking at her insides and slowly approached him.

"All right," she said. "What do you want?"

Eyeing a curious doorman, Mick led her into a patch of darkness where the night seemed even more ominous. "I want to talk to you about Rick Conti."

"Why? You've already written your nasty little book."

Anger glowed in his eyes. "And you thought that was the end? You thought you could get away with murder?"

"Murder?" she gasped. "You're out of your mind."

But there was nothing insane about his accusing gaze. He was looking at her with an alarming certainty, like a prosecutor already sure of a guilty verdict. Terror thudded through her bloodstream.

Then Mick withdrew a gold medallion from his pocket and dangled it in front of her. "Does this look familiar, Gussie?"

Gulping, Gussie shook her head.

"Brenda Galloway had it made for Rick Conti. It took me weeks, but I finally tracked down the jeweler."

Gussie mutely stared at the brilliant disk glittering in the glow of a streetlight. She had never seen it before, and yet her fear escalated.

"What's the matter, sugar? Does it bother you to see the medallion Conti was wearing the night you killed him?"

"Killed him? This is ridiculous! I'm going inside."

Mick suddenly looked dangerous. "Not yet. There's something else I want to show you." He cradled the medallion in his palm and lifted it to the light. "Those rusty spots are dried blood, Gussie. Proof that you murdered Conti."

Shrinking away from him, Gussie wildly shook her head. "You're just looking for a disgusting story."

"I found this medallion at the old Galloway place in Hyannis, right under the ruins of the deck," he went on. "The game is over, sugar. You may as well confess."

"I haven't done anything wrong."

His lips curled into a nasty sneer. "I'm going to nail you and your friends for murder, Gussie. Think about that. Then, if you decide you want to talk, give me a call.''

''Go to hell.''

He laughed maliciously, then turned and stalked into the darkness, leaving Gussie feeling like a hunted animal.

A week later Gussie was still on edge, but conversations with Diane and Rachel had substantially reduced her panic. She now realized that the blood-splattered medallion was nothing more than circumstantial evidence. Even if Mick Travis followed through on his threat to involve the police, there was no tangible proof that Rick Conti had been murdered. Still, she continued to obsess over the possibility that the medallion might eventually lead to the excavation of the abandoned well.

She shivered as she imagined being dragged off to prison. Even now the memory of Rick Conti lying on the deck in a puddle of blood remained clear in her mind, each graphic detail preserved as if in a photograph. Over the years she had lulled herself into believing the danger of exposure had diminished. Now suddenly the threat was real again.

Closing her eyes, she rested her head against the pillows and tried to focus her thoughts on the day ahead. Richard was out of town, and she was scheduled to represent him that evening at a dinner sponsored by the American Cancer Society. Not a very stimulating prospect, but at least she would be too busy to dwell on Mick Travis and the incriminating medallion.

She climbed out of bed and started for the bathroom, but paused when she heard a soft rap on the door. ''Come in,'' she said sharply, irritated by the intrusion.

Her maid entered the room carrying a single red rose wrapped in cellophane.

''This was just delivered, Mrs. Chandler.''

Gussie tried to appear indifferent, but inside she was a mass of nerves. ''Thank you, Annette. Just leave it on my desk.''

''Yes, ma'am. Will you be wanting breakfast?''

''Not now. I'll buzz you if I need anything.''

The instant the maid was gone Gussie hurried to her desk, removed a small white card from the nest of cellophane, and quickly read Tony De Costa's lunch invitation, her heart vibrating with excitement.

Much as she had imagined a love affair with Tony, she had

never seriously considered acting out her fantasies. They were
sweet lingering dreams, safe because they existed only in her
mind. But now he was inviting her to bring her fantasies to life.

It was impossible of course, she told herself. Seeing him
again would mean taking an unthinkable risk. Still, she yearned
for his touch, the musical sound of his voice, and the hard
strength of his body. As she held the rose to her cheek, inhaling
the sweet fragrance, her mind reeled with enticing memories.

She remained motionless for several seconds, torn by doubts
and indecision. Then she gently placed the rose on her desk and
picked up the telephone. There was nothing wrong with
enjoying a simple lunch and perhaps collecting a few more
previous memories to cherish.

When Gussie spotted the old fieldstone inn, her mouth went
dry and a thin vein of perspiration trickled down her cheek.
Then she saw Tony sliding out of his gray Mercedes and her
fingers tightened on the steering wheel. There was still time to
escape. But instead of fleeing to safety, she was drawn
inexorably forward, as if fate had somehow intervened and
sabotaged her sense of reason.

Time seemed suspended as Tony approached her car. Sunlight glinted in his ebony hair, illuminating his strong features
and the clean line of his jaw. Gussie felt a familiar stirring in
the pit of her stomach, a dizzying blend of nervousness and
arousal. Then suddenly he was opening the door, reaching for
her hand.

"*Cara*, you're here."

A feeble voice of caution whispered in her mind, but she was
already lost in the seductive web of his touch. Instead of
warning him not to expect anything from her, she simply
nodded as he helped her out of the car.

"I feel as if I've been waiting forever to see you," he said
softly.

"Tony . . . please."

Smiling, he took her arm. "It's just lunch, Gussie. Anything
else will be on your terms."

"There can't be anything else, you know that."

"Then let's enjoy our lunch. Come inside, the restaurant is
delightful."

— — —

A few hours later, Gussie pulled into the parking lot of a quiet roadside motel and watched Tony get out of his car and go to the office. She felt weak with anxiety, but she now realized their lovemaking was inevitable, as necessary and elemental as breathing. Meeting him for lunch had been just a prelude to the culmination of her fantasies.

Tony emerged from the office and entered one of the rooms. She waited a few moments, then hurried to join him, her heart lurching wildly in her chest. She was risking everything to steal a few hours with the man she loved, but what if reality paled in the face of her memories? What if her body was no longer able to respond after so many nights of mechanical sex with Richard?

Assaulted by doubts, she paused at the door, vulnerable and afraid. Then suddenly Tony was standing in the doorway, smiling tenderly. "Don't be afraid, *cara*. I love you. I've always loved you."

Her doubts slipped away as he drew her into the room and hugged her close. She felt as if she had reached a critical destination of the spirit, an end to her lonely isolation. At last she was exactly where she belonged.

Lowering his head, Tony softly kissed her, his warm mouth tasting faintly of wine. Her body greedily arched against him, and he groaned, a husky sound of need and love. "I've imagined this so many times, Gussie. I nearly drove myself crazy."

"And I never stopped thinking about you."

He gazed down at her, and she saw the unvoiced question in his eyes, the lingering trace of pain. "I made a terrible mistake," she murmured. "I left you because I was afraid of my parents."

He smiled again, his eyes soft with understanding and forgiveness. "It's all right, *cara*. I should have realized, but I let my anger blind me."

"And now it's too late. This is all we'll ever have."

She felt him stiffen. "I want more, Gussie. I want you to be my wife."

Thoughts of Richard edged into her mind, troubling thoughts of duty and obligation. "I love you, Tony, but I'm married to Richard. Nothing can change that."

"Divorce him. We've already lost too much time."

Gussie drew away from him, feeling a wave of coldness seep through the layer of warmth he had created with his touch. "This is a mistake. We'll only end up hurting each other again."

Gently lifting her chin with the tip of his finger, he gazed into her eyes. "No, it's not a mistake. Right now I want you enough to accept whatever you can give me."

Gussie melted against him again, certain that their love would never be appeased by something as transitory as an affair, but wanting him too much to allow reality to shatter her beautiful illusion.

CHAPTER
Nineteen

HELENE STOOD IN A SECLUDED CORNER OF THE LAVISH GOLD AND WHITE living room watching the spectacle going on around her.

It was a typical Hollywood party—noisy, crowded, and fueled by generous amounts of liquor and cocaine. But instead of feeling lost amid the glitz and glitter, she felt as if she were floating on air. The top brass of Imperial Studios was assembled at the palatial estate of producer Howie Rodman, to celebrate the stunning news that Helene had received an Oscar nomination for her role in *Shadowed Lives*.

Smiling radiantly at a passing waiter, Helene picked up a fluted goblet of champagne and cradled it in her slender hands. She rarely drank these days, but this was a magical night, a night she wanted to absorb and remember for the rest of her life. Despite all the predictions of doom, she had returned from the edge of destruction and had salvaged her career.

As she sipped her champagne, she remembered her long struggle with the little white pills, the days and nights of mindless craving. Now it hardly seemed real, but she had been desperate then, driven by an insatiable need. She had slowly descended into a bottomless pit of despair, and only Seth and Rhetta had loved her enough to stop her insane crusade to destroy herself.

But tonight she was a star again. Tonight she felt hope blossoming inside her like a tender seedling. Maybe the cravings would always be there, but tonight she believed she possessed the will to resist them.

Then, forcing her thoughts away from the past, she smiled as she spotted Rhetta weaving her way through the crowd, her black dress billowing around her stocky legs. She still wore her drab gray hair gathered in a tight knot at the base of her skull, but the creamy pearls at her throat were stylish and expensive, a tribute to her success.

"Here you are," she said, hugging Helene. "I've been looking all over for you. How does it feel to be the star attraction?"

Helene smiled, her black eyes shining. "It feels good, Rhett. Only sometimes I think I'm dreaming."

Laughing, Rhetta fumbled in her beaded evening purse for her cigarettes, then lit one with a pricey Cartier lighter. "Hardly. Jack Golden just grabbed me outside the bathroom to tell me he wants you for the lead in *Deadly Obsession*."

Helene remembered her last disastrous film with Jack Golden and flinched. Most of the details of those hot weeks in Mexico were a blur in her mind, but she still vividly recalled the pills and the booze, the endless nights of dissipation.

"What did you tell him?" she asked, the first pangs of anxiety beginning to stir in her stomach.

"I told him to get the hell out of my way and let me pee."

Helene burst into laughter. "You're something else, Rhett."

Grinning, Rhetta flicked some ashes into a delicate Waterford ashtray. "Well, I'm not about to let a prick like Golden rush us into anything."

Helene nodded. "I want to keep working, but I'm not sure I could handle another movie with Jack."

"So we'll tell him no. We have plenty of offers. Take some time and think about what you want to do next."

Nodding again, Helene nervously smoothed her hands over her white sequined dress. Only minutes ago she had felt marvelous, but now she was edgy and uncomfortable.

"Hey, are you okay?" Rhetta said.

"A little jittery all of a sudden."

Rhetta reached for her hand. "Come on, relax. You're doing fine. Not to mention that you look terrific in that dress."

Helene felt her confidence return in a rush. She was still too thin—her bones seemed to stick out like fragile twigs—but the glittering dress made her feel beautiful again.

"I won't fall apart on you, Rhett," she said softly. "Those days are over."

"You're damn right they are. Now what do you say we check out the food? I hear it was catered by Earl Moss himself."

— — —

It was nearly dawn when Helene kicked off her flimsy white sandals and curled up on the plush bucket seat beside Seth. Still savoring the lingering glow of the party, she glanced at his strong profile in the ghostly light of the dashboard. "I feel so good, I hate to see the night end."

Seth glanced at her, his deep blue eyes oddly serious. "We made it, Helene. This is a whole new beginning."

Helene felt the force of his love and understanding wash over her like a gentle tide. They had been through hell together, and now they shared something even more elemental than love—they were survivors of her addiction.

"I love you," she murmured.

He reached out to stroke her hand. "Maybe this is lousy timing, but I've been thinking . . . how would you feel about getting married?"

"But you—"

"I know. I always thought of marriage as a trap, but not now, not with you."

Helene understood precisely what he was feeling. Suddenly marriage seemed right and natural. They belonged together.

"When?" she asked.

Seth threw his head back and laughed. "As soon as we can arrange it."

Helene leaned over to brush her lips across his cheek, but the sudden glare of headlights momentarily blinded her. A second later her vision cleared, and she saw the other car barreling toward them.

"Seth, be careful!" she screamed.

But her terrified cry was absorbed by the screech of metal crushing metal.

Helene moaned as the familiar dream played through her mind like an endless movie. She was imprisoned in a stark white room surrounded by strange sounds and unpleasant odors. And there was pain—sharp, unremitting pain.

"Helene, open your eyes. Come on, look at me."

There was something familiar about the low, gravelly voice, and Helene fought to open her eyes, but the bright light was blinding.

"That's right, Helene. Try again to open your eyes."

This time when her eyes snapped open Helene forced herself to look in the direction of the voice. She saw the vague image of a woman standing over her. Then she blinked and the vision sharpened.

"Rhetta," she whispered.

"Thank God," Rhetta said.

"Where . . . am I?"

"In the hospital. Don't you remember the accident?"

Helene closed her eyes again. Her head felt light and feathery, and she still seemed to be drifting in the foggy residue of the dream. Nothing made sense. "What accident?"

Rhetta gently touched her shoulder. "That's not important now. How do you feel?"

"Fuzzy. Everything hurts."

"I'll get the doctor. You rest. I'll be right back."

As Rhetta bustled out the door, Helene struggled to sit up, but a burning pain exploded in her head and she fell back against the pillows. Clearly something terrible had happened to her. Why was it all a blank? She willed herself to remember, but it hurt too much to think, and she finally abandoned the effort.

She was lying perfectly still when Rhetta returned accompanied by a strange man wearing a spotless white coat. The lower half of his face was hidden by a bushy black beard, but his brown eyes seemed kind. He smiled as he approached the bed. "Hello, Helene, I'm Dr. Perez. How are you feeling this morning?"

"Awful. What happened to me?"

"You were injured in a car wreck. You have a slight concussion and some nasty bruises, but you should be fine in a few days."

"Why don't I remember?"

He smiled again, a warm reassuring smile. "You will. Some temporary confusion is common in head injuries. Just give yourself a little time to heal."

He placed his stethoscope on her chest. "I'd like to examine you now," he said. "Then if everything looks okay, I can give you something for the pain."

Feeling a sudden jolt of alarm, Helene stiffened. "No . . . no drugs."

He stared at her for a moment, his eyes full of silent

sympathy and understanding, then he nodded. "That's up to you, of course. Let me know if you change your mind."

Though his examination lasted only a few minutes, Helene felt weak and disjointed by the time he left the room. The throbbing in her head was worse and she wanted desperately to sleep, but scattered memories were floating through her mind like swirling particles of dust.

She closed her eyes and tried to concentrate, slowly piecing the fragments together. Then suddenly she saw the other car hurling out of the darkness, and she screamed.

Rhetta rushed to her side. "Helene, what's wrong? Are you all right?"

"The accident . . . I remember the accident." She licked her dry lips. "What happened to Seth?"

Rhetta quickly looked away, but Helene caught a glimpse of the pity in her eyes and her heart began to flutter. "Where is he? I want to see him."

"Not now. You need to rest."

"Tell me!" she shrieked.

Rhetta was silent for a long moment. Then she said, "Seth died in the crash."

Trembling, Helene shook her head. "No, you're wrong. We're getting married, Rhett. We decided last night. Maybe we'll go to Las Vegas . . . to one of those little chapels."

"Baby, he's dead," Rhetta said huskily, her eyes filling with tears as she leaned over the bed and gently drew Helene into her arms. "I'm so sorry."

Helene flinched at her touch, feebly attempting to shove her away. "Seth wouldn't leave me alone. You're lying."

Fiercely clinging to Helene, Rhetta shook her head. "You're not alone. I'm here. I'll take care of you."

Helene viciously fought the truth, but as a numbing cold settled in her heart, she knew she was alone again, alone with the ghosts of her past and her shattered dreams of the future. Closing her eyes, she helplessly sobbed as the cold seeped into her heart.

Rhetta pushed her way through the heavy glass doors and entered her elegant suite of offices, but instead of pausing to admire the mauve walls and sleek smoky gray furniture, she slumped down on a chair and absently stared at her secretary.

"How's Helene?" Millie asked anxiously.

Blotting her bloodshot eyes with a damp hankie, Rhetta shook her head. "Terrible. I'm afraid she'll never get over this."

Millie sighed heavily. "Poor Helene. They were so happy together. It was like a fairy tale, Rhett."

Rhetta swallowed a sharp retort. Even death was romantic in Hollywood, she thought, just one more tragic ending to one more love story. "I have a lot of work to do," she said abruptly. "Hold my calls unless it's an emergency."

Clutching the arm of her chair, Rhetta heaved herself to her feet and made her way to her private office. She had always felt a sense of peace in the bright airy room surrounded by Impressionist prints and delicate porcelain figurines. But now their beauty seemed at odds with the grim horror of death.

After slowly crossing the room, Rhetta sat at her desk and stared down at her hands. Years of easy living had made them soft and fleshy, just like her sagging chin—glaring reminders of her own mortality.

Unsettled by her thoughts, she rummaged in her desk for a bottle of bourbon and poured some into her empty coffee mug. Death always unleashed all sorts of unbidden thoughts. Swallowing a mouthful of the smooth liquor, she waited for the warmth to blossom in her throat, then sat back and forced herself to concentrate on the funeral arrangements.

She knew Helene would want something simple and dignified, but Hollywood would demand a production worthy of a famous director. There was no such thing as simplicity, when loss and pain had generated so much ghoulish curiosity. Even though Seth had been a fiercely private man, his death would be a public spectacle.

Disgusted, Rhetta picked up a pencil and started to jot down some notes on a yellow pad, but a few seconds later Millie buzzed her on the intercom.

"I'm sorry to bother you, Rhett, but there's a Diane Elliot on the phone. She says she's Helene's friend."

Rhetta recognized the name. She had listened to Helene wistfully recount stories of her college days enough times to have a clear mental picture of her three old friends. "Put her on."

There was a click and then a soft voice came over the wire.

"Ms. Green, my name is Diane Elliot. I heard about the accident and I've been trying to get in touch with Helene all day, but the hospital refuses to put my calls through. Do you know how she is?"

Rhetta felt a sudden burst of anger. What the hell gave Diane Elliot the right to be so concerned after all these years? Maybe she was just another ghoul looking for a little vicarious excitement. Rhetta was tempted to rudely brush her off, but then she thought of Helene and softened. Right now Helene needed friends, and there was always a chance Diane Elliot might be sincere.

"She has a few minor injuries, nothing serious," she said at last, still conscious of a need to protect Helene.

After a brief silence, Diane said, "Is she up to visitors? I talked to Rachel and Gussie this morning, and we'd like to fly out there unless you think it would be too much for Helene."

Surprised, Rhetta cradled the phone against her shoulder and lit a cigarette. A gut instinct told her to trust this woman with the gentle voice, but she was also innately cautious. "You haven't seen Helene in years. Maybe you should plan your reunion for another time."

Diane inhaled sharply. "We're not planning a reunion, Ms. Green. We care about Helene, and we know how much she must be hurting. We want to be there."

Suddenly ashamed of her suspicions, Rhetta blew out a stream of smoke and said, "Sorry, but I had to make sure you were coming for the right reasons. When can I expect you?"

"Tomorrow afternoon."

"Helene will have been discharged from the hospital by then. Let me know your flight number, and I'll have a limo waiting at the airport. You can stay at the ranch."

"Are you sure? Maybe it would be better if we stayed at a hotel."

"She'll need her friends, Mrs. Elliot. Right now Helene is hanging on by a thread."

Besieged by an almost unbearable sadness, Rhetta quickly concluded the conversation and leaned over her desk, pressing the heels of her hands to her throbbing temples. She wanted so much to help Helene, but deep in her heart she knew there was nothing she could do. Some wounds were just beyond healing.

— — —

Helene opened her eyes and felt a sense of peace. She was nestled in her own bed, moonlight dancing on the walls, an early evening breeze drifting through the windows. Then she reached for Seth, and reality came rushing back with a hollow thud.

Seth was dead.

She touched his pillow, smoothing her hand over the cool cotton pillowcase. She ached to feel him lying there beside her, but all she felt was an emptiness so vast it seemed to swallow her.

Sobbing, she buried her face in his pillow, breathing in the lingering scent of his woodsy soap. How could he be dead when his essence still filled the room? She could almost see him, his dark hair tousled by sleep, his blue eyes twinkling in the clear morning light, but when she tried to touch him, the vision evaporated like a wisp of smoke.

She moaned as something seemed to snap inside her, a last frail thread of hope. Seth was really gone, and she was alone with her memories, alone and afraid. Drawing her knees up to her chest, she shivered even as the warm desert breeze wafted through the windows.

She was still huddled on the bed when Rhetta softly knocked on the door and entered the room. "Are you awake, Helene?"

Helene turned on a bedside lamp. Her eyes were red and swollen, and tears matted her silky black hair.

Rhetta crossed the room and stood at the foot of the brass bed. "You have company. I thought you might need some help getting dressed."

Helene stared at her with glazed eyes, overwhelmed by the thought of facing the polite sympathy of acquaintances who were really no more than strangers. "Not now, Rhett. Send them away."

Then she caught sight of three faces in the doorway, faces that seemed to rise from her memory like ghosts suddenly granted mortal substance. Certain she was hallucinating, she tried to force the strange images from her mind. But instead of fading, they became more distinct. Rachel edged into the room, Diane and Gussie following close behind her. As Helene silently watched them, she felt a slight crack in the dark curtain of her despair. "You came," she said.

Rachel nodded. "We wanted to be with you."

Tears filling her eyes, Helene held out her slender arms. Rachel ran across the room and sank down on the bed, pulling Helene against her chest. "God, I'm so sorry," she said.

Helene clung to her, burying her face in the warm hollow between her breasts. "I've lost everything, Rache."

"No, you'll get over this," Rachel said fiercely. "Right now you're going through hell, but someday you'll get over this."

She was wrong, but Helene had no words to describe the eerie feeling that her soul had left her body to follow Seth into eternity, leaving a hollow shell behind. Instead, she drew away from Rachel and looked at Diane and Gussie.

"I'm so glad you're here," she said quietly.

They started to approach the bed, but Rhetta waved them away. "Why don't you get dressed, Helene? We'll all be more comfortable in the living room."

Helene recognized the ploy to force her to leave the security of her bed, but she was too weary to argue. "All right. I'll be out in a minute."

Looking relieved, Rhetta quickly ushered the others out of the room while Helene struggled to her feet. Her head still ached and she felt slightly woozy, but she ignored the discomfort as she limped to the closet and grabbed a pair of faded jeans and an old white cotton sweater.

As she gingerly slipped the sweater over her head, she considered how odd it was to see her friends here at the ranch. They belonged to another time and place, a dim corner of her memory where they remained perpetually young, the way she remembered them at Brentwood. But they were all so different now.

Rachel was thinner, her thick brown hair still a curly halo around her face, but now there was an unfamiliar sadness in her eyes. She seemed oddly subdued in her simple black skirt and severely tailored blouse.

But Diane had blossomed like a brilliant flower. Her vivid blue dress was sleek and sophisticated, and her eyes radiated a new confidence. She was no longer a shy young girl bubbling over with impossible dreams. Life in the city seemed to have transformed her.

Gussie, too, seemed different. She was still uncommonly beautiful, but there was a brittle edge to her smile. She looked

almost too perfect in her high-fashion beige suit and impecca-
bly applied cosmetics, like a glossy mannequin. Always
slightly remote, she now seemed inaccessible.

As Helene tugged on her jeans, she suddenly felt uneasy.
These women were her oldest friends, but they were strangers
in many ways. Lost years separated them like a gaping chasm.
They had not seen her in the throes of her addiction or in the
aftermath of her terrifying nightmares. Their lives had taken
vastly different twists, and yet they were here to console her.
They still cared.

Fresh tears welled in her eyes as she made her way to the
living room where lamplight cast a warm glow on the bleached
oak floor. Diane and Gussie were curled up on the sofa while
Rachel stood beside Rhetta in front of the bay windows staring
out into the black desert night. Their muted voices rose above
the clatter of the crickets and the occasional hoots of a barn
owl. It was such a peaceful scene. Suddenly Helene longed to
join them, to momentarily fill the emptiness with the comfort
of their presence.

Rachel stared out the window, unnerved by the absence of city
sounds—the steady rumble of traffic, the honking horns and
wailing sirens. Out here the night seemed to go on forever,
unbroken by flashing neon signs or lights beaming from
apartment windows. It was eerie somehow, the silence and the
darkness.

Feeling edgy, she turned away from the window and noticed
Helene hovering in the doorway. She looked frail and wounded,
deep purple smudges discoloring the tender skin beneath her
eyes. Rachel watched her pause for a moment, then make her
way to a brightly upholstered chair and collapse like a rag doll.

Rhetta hurried to her side, but Helene held out a hand as if
to ward her off. "I'm okay, Rhett," she said. Then, glancing at
the others, she smiled weakly. "Is there anything you need?
Fresh drinks or a sandwich?"

"Not right now," Diane said. "We had an early dinner on
the plane."

Helene nodded, and a heavy silence settled over the room.
Feeling almost embarrassed, Rachel sat down and folded her
hands in her lap. All day she had been thinking of Helene,
imagining her pain and grief, but now she felt like a voyeur

intruding on a stranger at a moment of tragedy. She wondered if it would have been kinder just to send flowers, sparing Helene this uneasy encounter with her past. Maybe their mission of mercy was really an unwelcome invasion of privacy. No. She doubted that. Many years had passed, but the bond of closeness was still there. And right now Helene needed them.

Rachel sprang to her feet and crossed the room, then dropped to her knees on the floor beside Helene. "This is crazy," she said. "Why the hell are we sitting here like strangers after all we've been through together?"

Helene stared at her with dead eyes. Then her pale face seemed to come alive, and she smiled a sweet sad smile. "We'll never be strangers," she said softly.

"Then talk to us. Let us help you."

Helene was silent for a long trembling moment, tears spilling down her cheeks. In the soft light her fine features reminded Rachel of delicate china, lovely but fragile, maybe too fragile to absorb such a shattering blow.

"There's so much you don't know," Helene said at last. "Seth saved my life. I'm not sure I can go on without him."

"What do you mean?" Diane said.

Helene brushed at the tears glistening in her dark eyes. "You knew I had a drinking problem for a long time. Then, a few years ago . . . I started using sedatives to block out my nightmares. They made me feel so good, like I was in control again. Then all of a sudden everything fell apart. I needed uppers to get out of bed in the morning. I messed up at work. But none of that mattered. All I cared about was the drugs."

Sympathy glowed in Gussie's wide green eyes. "How did you shake the habit?"

Helene smiled faintly. "Seth and Rhetta saved me. They never gave up on me even when I gave up on myself."

"Why did you hide it from us?" Rachel said.

Helene shrugged. "I was ashamed. I hated always being the weak one."

"Weak? What are you talking about? You beat a goddam drug habit?"

Helene shook her head. "There's no such thing as beating a drug habit, Rache. Right now I'm straight, but tomorrow . . ."

Rachel was both touched and alarmed by the uncertainty in Helene's voice. Drug addiction was dark and deadly, but now she understood that Helene had lost much more than a lover. In a very real way Seth Wilder had been her salvation.

"How can we help you?" she said.

"You're here. Right now that's enough."

Choking back tears, Rachel flung her arms around Helene, holding her close, loving and cherishing her. Then suddenly Diane and Gussie were there too, their bodies pressed together. And for just a moment there was no more pain.

A brilliant sun and flawless blue sky seemed to mock the very idea of a funeral, as a huge cast of Hollywood luminaries gathered at Forest Lawn cemetery for the burial of Seth Wilder. As Diane stood silently beside Gussie and Rachel, she was amazed by the almost festive atmosphere. Hundreds of fans pushed and shoved behind police barricades, straining for a glimpse of their favorite celebrities, while members of the press scrambled for the best camera angles. Somehow the aura of frenzied excitement struck Diane as obscene, a violation of the solemnity of death.

Forcing herself to focus on the polished oak casket, she tried to pray, but she was too distracted to concentrate. She felt hot and uncomfortable in her black linen suit, and the overpowering scent of the lavish floral arrangements was sickening. Dabbing at a trail of perspiration trickling down her cheek with a rumpled tissue, she longed to escape to the blessed coolness of the shiny black limousine waiting at the curb, but the prominent actor delivering the eulogy seemed enthralled by the sound of his own voice.

Then, appalled by her selfishness, Diane shifted her gaze to Helene and felt a sharp tug in the center of her chest. She looked so frail and defenseless, her simple black dress seeming to engulf her like a shroud. Pale and listless, she was clinging to Rhetta, a haunted expression on her lovely face. Diane wondered what tortured thoughts were playing through her mind. Helene had seen so much tragedy in her life, so much loneliness and sorrow. But this was worse—this loss might very well destroy her.

Diane shuddered at her grim thoughts, chilled by an eerie premonition of doom. Quickly forcing her attention back to the service, she listened to the actor conclude his eulogy, then watched Rhetta lead Helene to the coffin, where she placed a single blood red rose.

Everything seemed to stand still for a moment. Then the crowd appeared to exhale a collective breath and all hell broke loose. Cameras whirred and morbidly curious fans pressed against the barricades, their voices loud and abrasive. Diane looked at Gussie and Rachel, and they simultaneously rushed to Helene.

"We have to go now, Helene. The service is over," Rhetta said as she gently tried to lead Helene away from the grave.

"I can't leave him, Rhett."

"You have to. It's time to go home."

Helene shook her head, her slim hand still resting protectively on the coffin.

After a quick glance at the surging crowd, Diane stepped forward and wrapped her arm around Helene's waist. "Come on, Helene," she said softly. "We'll go back to the ranch, and you can rest."

Helene resisted for a moment. Then she mutely allowed Diane and Rhetta to steer her toward the waiting limousine. But the fans and reporters were relentless, converging on them like hungry buzzards.

"What now, Miss Galloway? Are you going back to work right away?"

"Is it true you tried to kill yourself the night Seth died?"

"Were you and Wilder secretly married?"

Horrified by such blatant cruelty, Diane helplessly looked to Rhetta for direction, but Rachel was already insinuating herself between Helene and the reporters, her eyes glowing with fury. "That's enough," she shouted. "Have a little respect."

Some of the reporters had the decency to move back a few paces, but most of them continued their pursuit, blocking the route to the limousine. Rachel hesitated for an instant, then plowed through the center of the crowd, opening a path for Helene.

By the time they reached the car, Diane was nauseated and dizzy, overwhelmed by such rabid aggression. Then as she settled herself on the cool leather seat, she heard Gussie gasp.

"My God, look over there," she said, gesturing toward the swarm of reporters. "It's him—Mick Travis."

Diane swiveled on the seat and glanced out the window, her breath catching in her throat when she spotted Mick Travis lounging against the trunk of a palm tree, insolently smiling. There eyes met, and his smile turned into an evil grin as he raised his hand in a mocking salute.

Paralyzed by shock, Diane just stared at him, but Rachel immediately leaned forward and rapped on the glass partition, ordering the chauffeur to pull away from the curb. Once Mick was no longer visible, she nervously lit a cigarette and said, "What the hell is he doing here?"

"I told you he was stirring up trouble again," Gussie said. "Now that he has that damn medallion, he'll never leave us alone."

"What more can he do?" Diane said. "He already wrote his book."

Rachel shook her head. "This has nothing to do with the book. I think he's obsessed with the idea that we killed Rick Conti. He wants to see us punished."

There was a moment of silence. Then Helene let out a low wail that seemed to rise from deep in her soul. Her body went rigid and her eyes looked wild and unfocused, like those of an animal seized by some sort of primitive fear.

"Helene, what's wrong?" Rhetta said. "Talk to me."

But Helene remained stiff and mute, her tortured black eyes the only visible measure of her panic.

"Rick Conti," Rachel whispered, glancing at Diane and Gussie. "We never should have mentioned him in front of her."

Diane nodded, suddenly aware of how indiscreet they had been, not only by mentioning Rick but by talking so freely in front of Rhetta. After all these years they were becoming careless, and that thought sent a prickle of alarm racing along her nerve endings. "You're right," she said. "We're upsetting Helene."

Gussie started to protest, but Rachel shot her a warning look and they lapsed into a strained silence that lasted until the limousine arrived at the ranch and Rhetta ushered them inside.

"I'll help Helene to bed. Then I'd like to talk to you," she said.

"Of course," Diane said, feeling a new surge of alarm. "We'll wait for you in the living room."

Nodding, Rhetta guided Helene down the hall, and Diane followed Rachel and Gussie into the sunny living room. Once they were seated, Rachel said, "God, that was stupid. I forgot she was even there."

Diane wrung her hands. "We're getting careless, and with Mick Travis following us again that's the last thing we can afford. I wonder how much Rhetta knows. What are we going to say to her?"

Crossing her long elegant legs, Gussie smoothed her fingers over a crease in her stylish black silk dress, managing to look glamorous even after hours in the hot sun. "Even if Helene hasn't told her anything, she's probably read Mick's book. We'll have to be very careful. God knows what a woman like that might do if she ever learned the truth."

Rachel frowned. "What the hell does that mean?"

"She could blackmail us," Gussie said impatiently. "Or sell the story to one of those awful tabloids."

Scowling, Rachel stood and began to pace. "That's ridiculous. Rhetta would never do anything to hurt Helene."

"You don't know that. How can you trust a complete stranger?"

Irritated by their senseless bickering, Diane started to protest, but Rhetta suddenly burst into the room and flopped on the sofa. "You're right, Rachel," she said quietly. "I'd never do anything to hurt Helene. But I need to know what that bastard Travis is up to so I can protect her."

Rachel looked at Diane and Gussie. Then she sat down beside Rhetta and lit a cigarette. "Have you read his book?"

"Of course, but that was years ago. What is he after now?"

"Revenge. He found a gold medallion at the old Galloway mansion in Hyannis. Now he thinks he can prove Rick was murdered."

"And he believes Helene is the killer," Rhetta said flatly.

Diane shook her head. "Not just Helene—all of us."

Rhetta was silent for a long time. Then she cleared her throat and said, "So how do we get rid of him? Helene is in no shape to handle this right now."

Diane had been bracing herself for a barrage of probing questions, but now she realized Rhetta had absolutely no interest in discovering the truth. Maybe she was afraid of finding out Helene was a murderer, or maybe she was just too loyal to care. Whatever her reasons, Diane felt a palpable sense of relief.

"All we can do is avoid him," Gussie said, finally entering the discussion. "Eventually he'll give up and leave us alone."

"That's not good enough," Rhetta said. "I'm hiring a security service first thing in the morning. If that son of a bitch even tries to get near Helene, I'll be ready for him."

Just the thought of dealing with Mick Travis again filled Diane with dread, and she wondered if the constant shadow he cast over their lives was the price of their crime. Maybe he was destined to expose and punish them, and all their feeble attempts to avoid him were merely delaying an inevitable confrontation with the sins of the past.

Then, deeply troubled by her thoughts, she struck them from her mind and forced herself to concentrate on the conversation flowing around her. But she knew her relief was only a temporary respite. Deep inside, her fears were still churning and festering, always there to remind her of her guilt.

Huddled on her bed like a beaten animal, Helene listened to the conversation echoing from the living room, her head whirling with horrible images of blood and death. Long repressed memories were suddenly right there at the surface of her mind. She fought to exorcise them, but they were strong, much stronger than her battered will to deny them.

Recoiling from a vivid picture of Rick Conti lying on the deck, his body drenched in blood, she frantically rubbed her eyes as if the sheer pressure of her hands might erase the gory vision. But the horror persisted, becoming more real by the second. Her heart beat wildly in her chest as she rolled to the edge of the bed and staggered to the bathroom. There was only one way to blot out the images, one way to save her sanity.

Though the bathroom was bathed in shadows, Helene needed no light to guide her to the vial of pills stashed in the toilet tank, the pills she had secretly acquired from Dr. Perez. Now she understood why. She had been afraid to leave the hospital without them: she was still an addict, still dependent on drugs to numb her fears and lull her into a state of mindless oblivion.

She opened the brown plastic bottle, and shook two pills into her hand. She stared at them for a minute, her rational mind crying out in protest. Then the craving tightened in her stomach like a fist and she quickly swallowed them, not even bothering with water.

Helene knew then that she was lost. Seth was dead, and the nightmares of her past were rising from the darkness to haunt her. This time there would be no salvation.

CHAPTER
Twenty

DIANE FROWNED AT THE PAPERS SCATTERED ACROSS HER KITCHEN TABLE, then tossed her pen aside and closed her eyes. Her drug piece was scheduled to air in just three weeks and there were countless details to resolve, but the alluring sound of Michael and Carrie laughing in the backyard was too tempting to ignore. Pushing her chair away from the table, she stood and walked to the window to gaze out at the small patch of grass where Michael was tossing a ball to a giggling Carrie.

Completely engrossed in their game, they were unaware of her presence, but something inside Diane seemed to melt as she watched them. Carrie looked strong and sturdy, her carroty hair whipping around her face in the warm spring breeze, her eyes glowing with happiness and excitement. It was hard to believe she had ever been so close to death.

And Michael—so vital and energetic, his infectious laughter ringing out in the clear morning air. Diane had been denying her feelings for weeks, but now as she quietly studied him, she knew she was in love, deeply and irrevocably in love. Even bitter memories of Joel and his betrayal failed to crush the new warmth flowering in her heart.

Still, the thought of opening herself so completely to another person scared her. Loneliness was something she understood. She knew how to survive long dark nights and rainy Sunday afternoons alone, but she doubted she had the reserves to survive another brutal rejection. This time she was hopelessly vulnerable.

But Michael was nothing at all like Joel, she reminded herself. It was unfair of her to compare them. So why did she persist in resurrecting the past every time he mentioned marriage?

She turned away from the window as Michael strode into the room with Carrie at his heels. There was something endearing about his flushed cheeks and rumpled dark hair, something boyish and appealing. It always surprised her to see how easily he shed the role of brilliant heart surgeon.

"Michael's taking us to the zoo this afternoon," Carrie squealed.

Laughing, Michael ruffled her tangled red hair. "Hold on a minute, kiddo. We have to check with the boss before we make any definite plans."

Carrie grinned at him, then turned pleading eyes on Diane. "Please, Mom, we haven't been to the zoo in ages."

Diane glanced at the mountain of papers piled on the table, feeling a familiar pressure in the pit of her stomach. There was so much work to be done, but it was such a beautiful spring day, warm and sunny, the scent of lilacs floating on the breeze. Suddenly an afternoon at the zoo seemed irresistible.

"All right," she said, smiling. "But we aren't going anywhere until you clean your room, it looks like a disaster area."

Carrie let out a shrill whoop of delight, then shot Michael a devilish grin. "See? I told you she'd say yes."

His warm brown eyes glittering with mischief, Michael nodded solemnly. "You sure did, kiddo. I guess I owe you a bag of popcorn."

"What are you guys up to?" Diane said, routing her gaze from Carrie to Michael.

Carrie started to squirm. "Nothing. We just—"

"Made a little bet," Michael said.

Looking relieved, Carrie nodded, then ran for the foyer. "I'm going to clean my room now," she shouted over her shoulder. "See you later."

Diane watched her scurry away, feeling a tugging sensation in her heart. Carrie was bursting into bloom like a spring bud, thrilled by the idea of a man in her life. She had never once fussed about not having a father, but Diane sensed how much she longed for a real family and silently damned Joel for his selfishness.

"Why so sad all of a sudden?" Michael said, wrapping on arm around her shoulders.

"I was thinking about how selfish Joel was to go off and forget about Carrie. I'll never forgive him for that, Michael."

"Have you ever tried to get in touch with him? Maybe he regrets what he did."

Diane shook her head, remembering how cold and indifferent Joel had been that day on the courthouse steps. "No, Joel was always good at putting anything unpleasant out of his mind. I'm sure he never even thinks of Carrie."

Drawing her closer, Michael pressed his lips to her cheek. "Then he's not worth your unhappiness. Carrie's better off without him."

"I know that, but I hate seeing her suffer for my mistake. No child deserves to be tossed aside like an old newspaper."

"Hey, you have no reason to feel guilty," he said, cupping her face in his hands. "You've done a great job with Carrie, she's a happy, well-adjusted kid."

Diane gazed into his expressive dark eyes, losing herself in his warmth and caring. This strong, sensitive man was in love with her, and the thought filled her with wonder. Raising her hand, she gently skimmed her fingers along the firm line of his jaw. "What would I do without you?" she said.

He chuckled. "I'm not sure, but as long as you're thinking along those lines, how about marrying me?"

Tensing slightly, Diane waited for the familiar doubts to spring up in her mind like a flock of wildly screeching birds. But this time there was only blessed silence. She felt no encroaching panic, no smothering pressure. And suddenly she wanted more than an affair with Michael Casey—she wanted to spend the rest of her life with him.

"It won't be easy," she said cautiously. "We're both so busy with our work and Carrie might . . ."

He tightened his arms around her, crushing her against the hard wall of his chest. "Are you saying you want to marry me?"

She hesitated. There was still time to change her mind, still time to come up with a refusal that would leave both their egos intact. She forced herself to remember Joel and the awful price she had paid for loving him, but somehow the hurt she had been nourishing like a poisonous weed was no longer strangling her heart with bitterness. All at once she felt free.

"If you'll have me," she said.

Michael looked into her eyes for what seemed like an eternity. Then he slowly lowered his head and kissed her, silently reaffirming his love.

As Diane nestled into his arms, she felt her inner coldness warm to his touch. She had been alone for so many years, but now her heart filled with hope.

"Have I told you how much I love you?" she murmured.

"Tell me again just so I'm sure I'm not dreaming."

Laughing, she drew away from him and lightly kissed his chin. "I wish we were alone. I'd rather show you."

"Later," he said. "Right now we have a wedding to plan."

"Now?"

Suddenly he looked serious. "I don't want to wait, Diane. We know what we want. Why put it off?"

"But I'm so busy with the drug piece. Maybe this summer . . ."

Michael shook his head. "There'll always be something. If we don't set a date, we'll just drift along the way we are, and I don't want to waste any more time."

The urgency in his voice puzzled her until she remembered the accident that had tragically ended his first marriage. Then she thought of Helene, and she was certain that time was too precious to squander. "You're right. We'll get married as soon as we can make the arrangements."

A smile flashed from his mouth to his eyes. "What about two weeks from today right here?"

She imagined standing beside him in her cozy living room, surrounded by Carrie and a few close friends. "That sounds perfect."

Sweeping her into his arms again, Michael held her so tightly she could feel his heart beating strong and steady against her breasts, and she knew with startling clarity that this time she had made the right choice.

Two weeks later Diane sat in front of her mirrored dressing table marveling at her reflection. Gussie, with her magic satchel of cosmetics, had transformed her. Her skin looked soft and dewy, and her blue eyes seemed to glow like a bright morning sky. She knew it was silly, but she felt like a giddy young girl on the verge of some wonderful new discovery.

"You look great," Rachel said as she came out of the

bathroom and plopped on the bed. "Wait till Michael sees you."

Diane blushed profusely. "I feel a little foolish going through all this wedding nonsense at my age."

"That's ridiculous," Gussie said. "Age has nothing to do with it. Every woman deserves at least one perfect wedding."

"And one perfect marriage," Rachel added quietly.

Hearing the sorrow in her voice, Diane swiveled to face her. "What's wrong, Rache?"

Rachel sighed. "Weddings kind of get to me these days."

"Are you and Brian still having problems?"

Shrugging, Rachel pretended to be engrossed in a speck of lint on the bedspread. "Things have been better," she said finally. "But I don't want to think about that now, not today."

There was a long silence. Then Gussie gracefully sat on the edge of the bed beside Rachel, her green eyes bright with tears. "Rachel's right, this is a terrible time, but I . . . I need to tell you something."

"Gussie, what is it?" Diane said.

"Richard and I . . . I'm in love with another man." Gussie described her long repressed love for Tony and her dismal life with Richard. "So Tony and I are having an affair," she said, delicately dabbing at her eyes with a lace hankie. "He wants me to leave Richard, but I . . . I'm not sure I have the courage. Richard can be so vindictive, and my parents . . . There's never been a divorce in our family. They'd never forgive me."

"Forget your parents and forget Richard," Rachel said. "What do *you* want?"

Gussie shrugged. "I'm not sure. I love Tony, but I just can't imagine myself really leaving Richard." She glanced at Rachel, a wistful expression on her face. "I've never been strong like you. I care too much what other people think."

Instead of blurting out a quick response, Rachel picked up a bright pink throw pillow and hugged it to her chest. After a long pause, she said, "I thought I was strong when I married Brian. I thought he was all I needed, but now . . ."

"What?" Gussie asked.

Rachel seemed lost in her own thoughts for a moment. Then she looked at Gussie. "Sometimes things don't turn out the way you think they will."

Gussie slid off the bed and walked to the window to stare out at the tiny yard. "It's strange. I've always been so careful, but now I'm risking everything and I can't seem to stop myself. I have this crazy feeling that if I let Tony slip away, I'll never have another chance at happiness."

"Then maybe the risk is worth it," Diane said.

"I don't know. I'm so confused, nothing makes sense anymore." Gussie turned away from the window and pressed her hankie to her eyes. "This is terrible. I'm ruining your wedding, Diane. But you're my closest friends. I had to tell you."

Diane felt a rush of love and sympathy that made her throat ache. After all these years they still needed one another in times of trouble. No matter what happened in the future, these women would always be a part of her life.

"You haven't ruined anything," she said, rising to embrace Gussie. "I'm glad you're here."

Rachel joined them in the center of the room and flung her arms around their shoulders. "Helene should be here, too."

Diane felt the ache in her throat intensify. "I called her three times," she said, "but I couldn't persuade her to come. Maybe the idea of a wedding is just too painful for her right now."

Rachel moved away and looked at Diane, her sharp features softened by a gentle smile. "Enough of this schmaltz. It's almost time for your wedding."

Diane nodded. Then as she imagined Michael waiting for her in the living room, a giddy grin spread across her face. This was a new beginning, maybe the most wonderful day of her life.

Baskets of daffodils and hyacinths filled the air with the sweet scent of spring as Diane slowly crossed the living room and joined Michael in front of the tall windows. Only moments ago she had been breathless with anticipation. Now she felt shy and hesitant as his gaze swept from the cluster of gardenias in her hair to her filmy blue dress. Then he smiled, and her heart seemed to swell with happiness.

As the judge began the ceremony, Diane tried to engrave every detail in her memory. Her marriage to Joel had been a cursory affair held in an anonymous room at the courthouse, but this time her loved ones were here to share her joy. Carrie was beside her, looking deceptively ladylike in a white voile dress trimmed with tiny hand-embroidered violets. Rachel and Gussie were standing off to her right, and Angie was sitting in front of the fireplace with a group of Michael's friends. Her only regret was that her father had not lived to witness her happiness. Alden Henderson would have approved of Michael, she thought.

Then suddenly the judge was leading them through their vows and the ceremony was over. Flashbulbs popped, and a chorus of voices shouted congratulations as Michael leaned forward to kiss her, love shining in his eyes like a brilliantly burning candle.

Married. She and this wonderful man were married. . . .

On a sunny morning just a week after her wedding, Diane hurried into the kitchen and poured herself a mug of coffee. Mornings had always been hectic, but now they were frenzied. Michael had an affinity for long scalding showers, and Carrie had suddenly developed an unprecedented interest in her appearance, fussing with her hair and staring at her freckled face in the mirror for hours. By the time they were both dressed and out of the house, Diane invariably felt frazzled. Much as she adored being married to Michael, there were still a few adjustments to work out.

Inhaling a calming breath, she flicked on the television and sat at the table to unwind for a few minutes before she left for the studio. Her drug piece had aired last night, and she was feeling a keen sense of satisfaction. This time Ed Blake would be forced to recognize her accomplishment. The piece had come across as a well-researched look at an escalating problem among urban cops. After years of grunt work she had finally produced something important.

Then suddenly a familiar face appeared on the television screen, and she leaned over the table to listen more closely, a sickening sense of dread settling in her stomach like a lead weight. This couldn't be happening. She had to be dreaming. But as she intently watched Vic Loomis recant his story on national television, she felt her career crumbling around her like a building besieged by a wrecking ball.

—   —   —

Ed Blake impatiently jabbed the intercom, shouting at his secretary. "Where the hell is Elliot? I told you I wanted to see her the minute she got here."

"Sorry, Mr. Blake. Diane's not in yet. I tried her at home, but she's not there, either."

Ed gulped back his fury, then went on in a more rational tone. "Keep trying. And check with Angie. See if she knows anything."

"Right away, Mr. Blake."

Ed turned off the intercom and leaned back in his chair, forcing himself to inhale a few deep breaths. Now that he finally had Diane Elliot where he wanted her, his adrenaline was pumping in anticipation of their confrontation, but she was off somewhere hiding. A typical woman—always stirring up trouble, but too cowardly to face the consequences.

Well, this little screwup was going to cost her plenty, he thought with relish. And ironically the whole thing had just fallen into his lap. He had spent years plotting to be rid of her, and now fate had intervened and provided him with a perfect opportunity to discredit her, maybe even oust her, if top management heeded his recommendations.

Suddenly feeling a good deal better, he lovingly stroked the flawless surface of his desk. He could afford to delay his gratification for a few more hours. Things were going to work out beautifully. Even if she managed to hold on to her job, any further advancement would be unthinkable. She was at a dead end, and he intended to make damn sure she understood what her ambition had cost her. Maybe Jordan Carr was beyond his reach, but Diane Elliot had just become a sitting duck.

After hours of aimless wandering, Diane stepped off the elevator and made her way down the long corridor to her office, acutely conscious of the way people seemed to be avoiding her, as if her disgrace might taint them in some way. Feeling like a pariah, she hurried to reach the seclusion of her office, but Ed's secretary intercepted her at the door.

"Ed's been waiting to see you all morning," she said, looking embarrassed. "He'll have my head if I let you escape."

Much as she had been hoping for a few minutes to compose herself before she faced Ed, Diane nodded and followed his secretary across the hall to his lavishly appointed suite of offices. As she waited to be ushered into the inner sanctum, she felt a terrible heaviness in her chest, a premonition of disaster.

"Go right in," his secretary said.

Steeling herself for an unpleasant scene, Diane slowly entered Ed's private office, wondering if this would be their final battle.

Ed was sitting at his desk, his meticulously groomed hands folded in front of him. As Diane looked at him, she suddenly noticed how little he had changed over the years. His fine brown hair was a bit thinner and there were a few wrinkles around his eyes, but his skin was still pink and baby soft and his gray suit and red paisley tie were right out of a fashion magazine. She imagined Ed vainly preening in front of a mirror and felt a wave of revulsion.

"Where the hell have you been all morning?" he snapped.

"I needed some time alone," she said, desperately trying to quell the defensive note in her voice.

"Then I assume you saw your precious Vic Loomis on television this morning telling the whole goddam world how he conned us."

Hating him for the gleam of triumph in his narrow brown eyes, she nodded.

"I warned you about him, Diane. But you were too damned stubborn to listen. Now we're in a legal mess that could cost the network millions. I've already had calls from the mayor and the police commissioner. We'll face a dozen slander suits—not to mention that we're the laughingstock of the industry. Great job, Elliot. You really fucked up."

"My God, you're acting as if I did it on purpose. This was a solid story, Ed. I have tapes to back up every one of our allegations."

Slamming his fist on his desk, he shouted, "Those tapes are worthless without Loomis to back them up, you know that."

"Someone must have threatened him. Maybe if I talk to him—"

"Forget it," Ed said abruptly. "All we can do now is cut our losses. Next week we'll go on the air with a public apology and pray that the fucking mayor decides to back off."

"And what about me?" she said in a quiet voice. "What happens to me?"

His eyes fixed on her, and as always she felt dehumanized, like a specimen in a laboratory. She knew he was aware of her discomfort, but he continued to watch her, savoring his advantage. His eyes remained on her for so long that she felt a crimson stain spread across her face and beads of perspiration break out along her upper lip. Then at last he said, "You're through here, Diane. You might manage to save your job, but with a thing like this on your record, you'll never be taken seriously again."

She had been preparing herself for this all morning, but hearing Ed confirm her worst fears was still a massive blow. "I have a contract," she said, "and I'll fight you every step of the way if you try to let me go."

He shot her a scathing look as he stood and strode to the window. "You can fight all you want," he said. "If the boys upstairs decide to get rid of you, you're out of here."

"You're really enjoying this, aren't you?"

Turning to face her, he smiled maliciously. "What the hell do you expect? Right from the beginning you barged in here like some kind of female crusader looking to fight your way to the top. You're damn right I'm enjoying this."

Diane was stunned by his contempt. She had always sensed the resentment lurking behind his oily smile, but she was shocked to realize that his hatred had been festering like a boil just beneath the surface of his skin for years.

"You were never qualified to be a producer," he went on. "But once we got hit with all that affirmative action crap, we had no choice but to promote you."

Furious now, she glared at him. "That's bullshit, Ed. I've done a good job here, but you and your little boys club made sure I never had a chance at anything important. You deliberately stuck me with silly pieces of fluff so I'd never get ahead."

His face contorted with anger, but instead of responding to her accusation, he resumed his place behind his desk as if to remind her of his authority. "Watch it, Diane," he said at length. "You're in no position to make any wild allegations."

She tried to resist his effort to intimidate her, but at the same time she realized she was totally at his mercy. He was the one ensconced behind the polished desk, the one empowered to smash the tattered remains of her career to shreds. The only thing that might appease him now would be her complete and utter humiliation, but the thought of an unconditional surrender disgusted her. She remained silent.

He stared at her as he absently stroked his chin. Then after clearing his throat, he said, "All right, there's no point in beating this thing to death. It'll probably be a few weeks before any decisions are made about your future here. In the meantime I want you to help out in research."

"Research? But I . . . What about my segment on health insurance?"

"Forget it. As of now you're a research assistant. If you don't like it you can resign and save us all a hell of a lot of trouble."

Stiffening, Diane ignored his challenge and nodded. "I'm going home for the rest of the day. I'll report to research in the morning."

Ed shrugged indifferently, and Diane quickly turned and left his office, fighting a choking sensation. She had been so dedicated to her career, working endless hours to prove herself, and now it was disintegrating like an ancient sheet of parchment. Her own ambition and Ed Blake were conspiring to strip her of the dream that had sustained her for so many years, and there was absolutely nothing she could do to save herself.

CHAPTER
Twenty-one

EVENING SHADOWS FELL OVER THE CHURCH BASEMENT AS RACHEL checked her empty office for the last time. Her desk and files had already been shipped to the new building on 121st Street, but she still felt a need to spend a few minutes alone with her memories. So much of her life had been tied up in this room, so many hopes and dreams. She could almost hear the echo of eager young voices spilling from the classrooms, happy sounds of joy and laughter. But now it was time to move on, time to build new dreams.

Glancing at the peeling blue walls and scuffed linoleum, she felt a strange sort of regret. Though the new building was bright and airy, large enough to accommodate at least a hundred more children, there was something sad about leaving the past behind. So many good things had happened here. An impossible dream had become a reality. A struggling school had grown and prospered against tremendous odds. And somehow in the midst of all the chaos, she had found an incredible sense of peace and belonging.

She brushed at the tears pooling in her eyes, wondering why she was working herself up this way. No matter how many good things had happened here, it was still just a place, a pile of bricks held together by crumbling mortar. In a few days the new building would be safe and familiar and all this melancholy would seem ridiculous.

Clearing her throat, Rachel forced her memories to the back of her mind and resolutely started for the door, but she paused when she heard the sound of footsteps in the hall. A moment later Cal burst into the room, clearly surprised to see her crying like a mourner at a fresh grave.

''Rache, what're you doing here? What's the matter?''

Rachel shrugged, embarrassed by her silly tears. "Nothing, I just came for a last look around."

"Why are you crying?"

Smiling faintly, she said, "I'm not."

"Bullshit. What's wrong?"

As she looked at his familiar face, his dusky skin and alert black eyes, she remembered their first hostile encounter all those years ago and felt another surge of emotion. "Memories," she said softly. "This place has so many memories."

He nodded. "We did some good work here, good things for the kids. Now we're going on to something better."

"So why am I crying? I must be getting old, afraid of changes."

Bursting into laughter, he crossed the room and put his arm around her shoulders. "Never. You're just mellowing."

Mellowing. In a way the word seemed appropriate. They had all mellowed over the years, softened and learned to bend without breaking. Even Cal was softer now. Still committed to the cause, but not as rigid, not quite as uncompromising. Somehow they had found a way to survive in a crazy world.

"Maybe you're right," she said thoughtfully. "But it's still scary to get older. I see myself acting more like my mother every day. God, I even warn my kids about cleaning off toilet seats before they sit."

Cal laughed again, and Rachel felt a deep tenderness spring up inside her. He was one of her oldest friends, and right now she needed his reassurance. "I really am scared, Cal. Sometimes I wake up at night and start thinking about the future and I panic. I'm not always so sure what's right anymore. Everything looks gray instead of black and white."

She was referring to far more than the situation at the school, and he seemed to understand that. He reached for her hand and gently squeezed her fingers. "Join the club, Rachel. When I look in the mirror every morning, I'm still not sure who that guy is looking back at me. I see all that gray hair, and I wonder how the hell I ever got so old."

Comforted by the warm pressure of his hand, she smiled. "I wish I could just stop time so everything would stay the same."

"You'd be bored out of your mind in a week."

She thought of Brian and the increasing coldness between

them and shook her head. "Right now a little boredom doesn't sound all that bad."

Cal looked at her, seeming to see beyond her glib words. "D'you want to talk about it?"

She was tempted to pour out all her hurts and disappointments, but an unwavering loyalty to Brian stopped her. What right did she have to reveal the intimate details of their lives to another man?

"Not this time," she said. "But thanks for caring."

Nodding, he released her hand. "Then I guess I'll get on home. This has been one hell of a long day."

"Go ahead. I'll lock up when I leave."

Once she was alone, Rachel felt suddenly uneasy. The lengthening shadows seemed more formidable without Cal's sturdy presence. Then she heard a rustling noise in the hall and a tingle of alarm slithered along her spine.

"Cal? Is that you?" she shouted.

There was no response, and her heartbeat accelerated as she inched her way to the door and peered into the darkness. "Cal? What's going on?"

Again there was no response, but now the silence seemed fraught with danger, an eerie absence of sound that prickled the hairs at the back of her neck. "Who's there?" she cried, her mouth dry with fear.

"It's only me, sugar."

Rachel froze as Mick Travis stepped out of the shadows, his lips twisted in a wicked grin. "You're a hard lady to catch alone."

"What do you want?"

"You know what I want, Rachel," he said, his hot breath fanning her face. "I want to know what happened to Rick Conti."

She started to back away, but his hand shot out, grabbing her arm in a crushing grip. "Not so fast, sweetheart. You're not going anywhere till I get some answers."

"Leave me alone," she said, sheer terror reducing her voice to a pitiful squeak. Mick looked menacing in the dim light, strong and powerful, a glint of madness in his eyes. Maybe his obsession had driven him insane. Maybe he was contemplating rape or even murder. Shivering, she fought to free herself, but his grip was like an iron band around her arm.

"I'll never leave you alone, Rachel. I'll never let you forget what you did."

"What are you talking about? I haven't done anything."

He jerked her hard against his chest. "Cut the crap. You and your friends killed Conti. I want to know how and why."

"You're crazy."

"Not as crazy as you are if you think you can get away with murder."

Rachel stared into his accusing eyes, feeling as if she were tumbling down the side of a mountain, faster and faster, plunging toward a gaping hole in the center of the earth. She nearly blurted out the truth, but a lingering shred of sanity prevailed and she violently lashed out at him, at last breaking free of his punishing grip.

"Stay away from me!" Her face was slick with sweat, and her breath was coming in ragged gasps. "I'll never tell you anything, you bastard."

Instead of backing away, he pressed so close she felt the heat emanating from his body. "How long do you think you can live with the guilt, Rachel? One of these days you'll crack like an egg, and I'll be right there to see that you get what's coming to you."

She realized then that he was driven by a twisted need for revenge and that this sick game he was playing would never end. Only now the rules had subtly changed. Instead of simply trying to intimidate her, he was turning her guilt against her, using it as a weapon to force her to confess.

"I have nothing to feel guilty about," she said, her voice cracking. "Just accept that and get the hell out of my life."

He shook his head. "I don't believe you, not for one fucking minute. You killed a man, lady, and I'm going to prove it, no matter how long it takes me." Hate flashed in his eyes as he stared at her. "I'll be back, Rachel. And I'll keep coming back until I see you and your friends in hell for what you did."

Eyes wide with fear, Rachel watched him melt into the shadows like a phantom. Only the stale scent of his sweat and a lingering trace of musky after-shave assured her that he had been there at all. That and the terror curling around her heart. She had always hoped that Mick Travis would eventually tire of his pursuit, but now she knew he was truly obsessed. And her own nightmare would never end.

— — —

Rachel tried to put Mick Travis out of her mind, but he was always there on the periphery of her thoughts like a stain that refused to fade. A few days after his visit, she was still so nervous and distracted that she left piles of unpacked cartons strewn about her new office and hurried outside to catch a breath of fresh air.

It was a gorgeous spring day. Even the mean city streets looked fresh and clean in the dazzling sunlight. People who had been cloistered in their stuffy apartments all winter flooded the sidewalks, a tide of ebony faces chatting and laughing. Street vendors were back at their corners, and the balmy air smelled of barbecued ribs and hot dogs. Harlem seemed to be emerging from a long hibernation, pulsing with new life after a cold, dreary winter.

As Rachel stood in the doorway watching the surge of humanity parade past her, she was seized by an urge to join them, to lose herself in the happy beat of the crowd. Completely dismissing the work stacked on her desk, she slung her purse over her shoulder and blended into the throng of people moving along Lenox Avenue.

At first her steps were quick and rigid, but as her tension began to ebb, her muscles relaxed and her pace slowed. She found herself growing hot, as if the sun were burning through her blue cotton blouse to warm her insides. For the first time in days she was able to push Mick Travis out of her thoughts and simply enjoy the glorious afternoon.

She walked for hours, pausing frequently to gaze into shop windows or listen to the street musicians. Then as the sun began to sink below the horizon and the breeze turned chilly, she headed for home, feeling a good deal better.

But her sense of well-being quickly waned when she found Brian seated at the kitchen table with Cleatus McDonald and three of his political cronies. They seemed to be involved in a heated discussion and she was instantly wary. On the surface Cleatus was always guardedly pleasant, but she sensed his underlying hostility toward her liberal political sympathies. Now his unexpected appearance in her kitchen struck her as a threat.

"Where the hell have you been?" Brian said irritably. "I've been trying to call you all afternoon."

Embarrassed by his abruptness in front of his uncle and three virtual strangers, Rachel felt a flash of anger. "Why? What's wrong?"

"Joe De Fazio died this morning."

"My God, what happened?" she said, finding it difficult to imagine the pudgy district attorney dead.

"Heart attack," Cleatus said. "Went down like a tree."

Rachel turned to look at him, offended by his crudeness. He was such a mass of contradictions—a dignified judge in public, a crass tyrant in private. "I'm sorry to hear that," she said. "What happens now?"

"That's what we're trying to decide," Brian said. "The party wants me to run for his spot in November."

Stunned, Rachel sank down on an empty chair, absently noticing the whiskey bottle in the center of the table. The whole scene suddenly reminded her of an old movie, a gang of corrupt political bosses meeting over a few shots of booze to decide the fate of the city. Only this was no movie. These sharp-eyed men were plotting to make Brian the next district attorney.

"But you're too young," she stammered. "You said it would be years before you'd be in a position to run."

"That was yesterday. De Fazio was a shoo-in to be re-elected, but now the field's wide open. This is my chance, Rachel. Fate or whatever the hell you want to call it just dumped an opportunity right into my lap."

"And that's what we want to talk to you about," Cleatus said, sweeping his fingers through his thick mane of silver hair. "If Brian's going to win, he'll need you behind him all the way. Do you understand what I mean?"

Rachel understood him all too clearly. She was a political albatross, much too liberal for the tastes of old party regulars, much too plain and blunt. Cleatus was asking her to change colors like a chameleon, and Brian was just sitting there letting him. She felt betrayed, as if her husband had just plunged a knife into her back.

"What did you have in mind, Cleatus? Are you suggesting I have a lobotomy?"

There was a burst of laughter from the three strange men, but Cleatus frowned and Brian glared at her. "For chrissake, Rachel, this is no joke. I'm asking you to help me get elected. Is that too much?"

His anger was like a snake winding around her chest, crushing the breath from her lungs. "I don't know," she said quietly. "What does that mean? Exactly what are you asking me to do?"

Suddenly Brian looked bewildered, as if he had not yet figured out precisely what he wanted from her, but Cleatus quickly jumped in to fill the void. "This is going to be an uphill fight all the way. People are disgusted with politicians; they don't trust us anymore. If we want to win, we'll have to convince the voters that Brian is the one man they can trust to clean up the city. We need you to help him establish his image as a good solid family man, a man with a vested interest in getting the scum off the streets."

He paused to sip his whiskey, then went on in a booming voice that belied his age. "That means public appearances, Rachel. Saying the right things to reporters, keeping your radical ideas to yourself. You'll have to learn to play the game."

"You mean I'll have to pretend to be somebody else."

Brian thumped his fist on the table. "Jesus, why do you have to make everything a moral issue? I'm not asking you to compromise yourself. All I want is your support." He stared at her for an instant, his blue eyes dark and brooding. Then he leaned over the table and pinned her with a fierce gaze. "Unless you're against me. Is that the problem here? Do you think somebody else could do a better job?"

"No, of course not. It's me. I'm just not sure I'm cut out to be a political wife." She glanced at Cleatus. "And I've never been any good at playacting."

"Then you'll have to learn," Cleatus said. "Either that or sabotage your own husband. And I can't believe you'd want to do a thing like that."

Rachel felt trapped and defensive, hating Cleatus for deliberately pitting her against her husband. She looked at Brian. "If you decide to run, you know I'll support you."

Brian smiled, but it was only a ghost of a smile. "Great. I knew I could count on you."

Rachel waited for something more, a flicker of warmth in his eyes or a softening of his unnatural smile, but his expression remained cool and aloof, and finally she stood and pushed her chair aside. "If you don't need me anymore, I think I'll go upstairs and rest."

"Sure, go ahead," Brian said. "Maybe we'll take the kids out for a pizza later."

Rachel nodded, then forced herself to smile at Cleatus and his cronies before she hurried out of the room.

Upstairs she heard Jess and Amy playing in the den, but instead of stopping to hug them as she usually did, she quietly made her way to her bedroom and closed the door. Then, after stripping off her skirt and blouse, she stretched out on the unmade bed and stared at the network of fine lines crisscrossing the ceiling. Why was she so upset by the prospect of Brian running for district attorney? He had certainly never made any secret of his aspirations, but they had always seemed distant and far away. Now suddenly he was asking for her support, asking her to conceal her true self behind a Barbie-doll smile.

And that hurt beyond measure. After all these years her husband was telling her she was inadequate, an obstacle to his career. Dear God, was that how he really thought of her? Pain closed around her heart like a tight fist. Maybe Brian no longer loved her. Maybe he was only preserving their marriage out of a sense of obligation. And maybe she was a fool for feeling this terrible wrenching sorrow.

Shuddering, Rachel drew the rumpled sheet up to her chin, but the thin cotton did nothing to relieve her chills. This coldness came from within, bubbling up from a well of hurt and anger. She fleetingly wondered if she should just pack her bags and leave. But a second later she realized that was impossible. Leaving Brian would be like cutting herself in half. She would never be complete without him.

So there was really no choice. If she wanted to save her marriage, she would have to swallow her hurt and do whatever was necessary to support her husband. The alternative was simply unthinkable.

Over the next few weeks, Rachel struggled to repair the fissures in her marriage, but Brian seemed inaccessible. Completely immersed in his campaign, he was rarely home, and the few hours they spent together were strained and uncomfortable. She began to hate her own artificial smile and the forced optimism in her voice, but she feared her pretenses were the only glue holding their relationship together.

Her mind was filled with those troubling thoughts as she absently gathered the dirty laundry strewn about the bedroom and sorted it into haphazard piles. It was a lovely Saturday morning, clear and bright, robins chirping in the spindly maple tree outside the window, but she felt edgy and irritable. Then she heard Brian whistling in the shower and some of her tension eased. Maybe today she would find a way to reach him. Maybe today they would begin to put things back together.

Infused with new hope, she picked up a rumpled pair of jeans and routinely checked the pockets, but instead of coming up with a handful of loose change, her fingers closed around a cold metal key attached to a plastic tag. Surprised, she pulled it out and cradled it in her hand, blankly staring at the logo of a midtown hotel.

Dazed, she slumped down on the bed, holding the key so tightly that it left little white indentations in her skin. Cheating. Brian was cheating on her. Her mind conjured up obscene visions of him making love to another woman, and she felt a wave of nausea rise in her throat. Brian in love with someone else—the thought was like a hot iron searing her flesh.

Turning the key over in her hand, she wondered what to do. She was tempted to slip it back into his pocket and hope the nightmare would go away, but she was no good at pretending, no good at concealing her feelings.

Her mind was still whirling when Brian emerged from the bathroom, a towel casually tossed over his shoulders. She tried to contain herself, but hurt and anger blunted her ability to reason. "Who is she?" she asked.

Brian looked puzzled. "What are you talking about?"

"This." In a sudden fit of fury, she flung the key at him, hitting him in the chest. "Who is she, Brian?"

"Oh, Jesus," he hissed. "Where the hell did you get that?"

Rachel laughed bitterly. "Your pocket. You were too stupid to get rid of it."

He flinched, then seemed to crumble as he sank down on a chair and buried his face in his hands. "She's a friend from the old neighborhood," he said quietly, making no attempt to deny her accusation. "I ran into her at the courthouse, and we stopped for a few drinks. I never meant for it to go any further.''

"But you just happened to have an affair with her.''

"I'm sorry, Rachel. God, I'm so sorry.''

Now that the brutal truth was out in the open, Rachel wished she had never voiced the question that had just smashed her life into thousands of jagged pieces. But it was too late to retreat. "Are you in love with her?'' she asked, the words filling her throat, vibrating there like trembling hummingbirds.

"No, it's over, but . . .''

"What?'' she said, mortally afraid of his answer.

"It's us, Rachel. I love you, but I'm not sure I can live with you anymore. You were right all those years ago; we're too different. I feel as if I'm being torn apart.''

"So you found yourself a girlfriend,'' she said dully. "Did it help, Brian? Did you feel better after you screwed her?'' His face flushed bright red, and she felt a little jolt of satisfaction. "Is that how you solve your problems now? Lie and cheat.'' Sobs filled her throat. "I trusted you, Brian. I trusted—''

He rushed to her side and tried to embrace her, but she shoved him away, repelled by his touch.

"Rache, I'm sorry. I never wanted to hurt you. I just . . . I was so confused. I felt as if my life was falling apart.''

Rachel looked at him blankly, sickened by his pathetic effort to justify his behavior. "Get out, Brian,'' she said quietly. "Pack your things and get out.''

"What good would that do? We have to settle this, try to work it out.''

Rachel inhaled a ragged breath. "It's already settled. Our marriage is over. There's nothing more to say.'' Then, turning away from him, she started for the door, afraid to look back, afraid she might weaken and beg him to love her again.

During the next few days Rachel cared for Amy and Jess and forced herself to go to work, but each night when she slipped into bed, she was tormented by thoughts of Brian and her broken marriage—painful thoughts that left her feeling hollow.

Though her anger had slowly faded to a dull ache, the hurt was still an open sore. How could she go on without Brian? How could she face each new day knowing their life together was just a memory?

Crying softly, she kicked her legs free of the tangled sheets, rolled to her side, and drew her knees up to her chest. She wondered if the pain would ever stop, if she would ever feel whole again.

Despite his betrayal, she still loved him, still longed to feel him lying beside her in the quiet hours before dawn. They shared a past, years of loving and caring. How could she just erase those things as if they had never existed?

Rachel, lost in thought, was startled when a long shadow suddenly arched across the bedroom floor. She instinctively cried out, then looked up and saw Brian approaching the bed.

"I have to talk to you, Rachel," he said quietly.

"Leave me alone. I'm not interested in anything you have to say."

Ignoring her harsh words, he sat on the edge of the bed and gently touched the trail of tears trickling down her cheek. "Then why are you crying?"

"Because I . . ." Her voice faded away in a rush of fresh tears. Just seeing his beloved face tore at her very soul.

"These last few days have been hell, Rachel. My life is nothing without you. I want to come home. I want to try again."

Some hungry place inside her had been yearning to hear those words, yet she was afraid to trust him, afraid to let him know how much she loved him. "It's too late," she choked. "There's nothing left."

He groaned, a sad cry of loss and pain. "I don't believe you. I know how much I hurt you, but I won't let you throw everything away like this. Give us another chance."

"Why?" she said caustically. "So you can cheat on me again?"

"So I can make things right. We have a lot of fixing to do, but I love you, Rachel. I never stopped loving you."

He was crying now, tears running down his face and falling on her hands like gentle rain. "Forgive me, Rachel. Please forgive me."

Something softened inside her. His tears seemed to wash away the hard core of hurt and anger in her chest, cleansing her of bitterness. Maybe all they had was hope, but right now it was enough.

''Are you sure?'' she whispered. ''Are you sure you still want me?''

He nodded, his eyes shining with love as he leaned forward to kiss her, a tender kiss filled with hope and promise. And Rachel opened her heart and let herself begin to forgive.

CHAPTER
Twenty-two

GUSSIE SHIFTED SLIGHTLY ON THE NARROW EXAMINING TABLE, HATING the indignity of lying there exposing her insides to Dr. Alexander Whitten. There was something inherently unnatural about a virtual stranger peering between her legs, probing at her most sensitive flesh with cold metal instruments.

"All right, Mrs. Chandler," he said. "You can get dressed now and I'll see you in the office in a few minutes."

Gussie watched Dr. Whitten cross the room to the sink and wash his hands, idly wondering what sort of man would choose to spend his life inspecting an assortment of breasts and vaginas. Then, remembering why she was sprawled out on his examining table like a gutted chicken, she clenched her fists into tight balls at her sides. This was much more than a routine examination. Something was terribly wrong.

After completing his ritual cleansing, Dr. Whitten hurried out of the room, his officious nurse trailing behind him. The instant they were gone, Gussie slid off the table and quickly dressed, feeling a good deal less vulnerable once her nakedness was concealed beneath her tailored blue suit. She inhaled a deep breath, then walked out to the reception area and followed the nurse to Dr. Whitten's private office.

"Have a seat, Mrs. Chandler," the nurse said, pointing to a red leather wing chair. "The doctor will be right with you."

As the nurse hustled off, Gussie sat on the edge of the chair and glanced around the doctor's office, finding the blatantly masculine decor oppressive. All that leather and massive walnut furniture seemed too dark and forbidding, reeking of male authority. But maybe that was precisely the image the doctor wanted to project.

Lost in her own thoughts, she jumped when the door opened

and Dr. Whitten strode into the room and took a seat behind his desk. He was a tall man with pale blond hair and thin aristocratic features. She had never really noticed before, but now his formal manner and impersonal smile reminded her of Richard.

"Let me assure you that you're in excellent health, Mrs. Chandler," he said. "I found nothing at all abnormal."

"Then why am I having these problems?"

"Quite frankly I'm surprised you didn't figure it out yourself. You're pregnant."

Gussie gaped at him, feeling an insane urge to burst into hysterical laughter. Pregnant! She had abandoned all hope of ever having a child, and now she was pregnant by her lover. It was almost too much to assimilate.

"My practice is strictly limited to gynecology," Dr. Whitten went on "But my nurse will schedule you for an appointment with one of my associates As I said, you're in good health and I don't anticipate any problems."

As the reality of her situation slowly sank in, Gussie began to feel light-headed. It took every bit of her willpower to leave his office without stumbling. By the time she reached the parking lot and slid behind the wheel of her Eldorado, her hands were trembling and her heart was thundering in her chest.

There was only one choice, she told herself. Much as she detested the idea of abortion, she could hardly present Richard with undeniable evidence of her infidelity. But how could she kill her baby, a baby she already ached to hold in her arms? And how could she betray Tony that way?

She started the car and drove home, relieved that Richard was away on a campaign trip. If she had to face him now she might fall apart like a shattered piece of crystal. He was such a vindictive man. She had to be absolutely certain what she was going to do before she confronted him.

Once she was alone in her bedroom, she stripped off her clothes and stood in front of the mirror studying her naked body. Her stomach was still firm and flat, no visible signs of the life growing inside her. But soon her condition would be readily apparent. Richard and her parents would know beyond a doubt that she had been an unfaithful wife. And Tony. Dear God, how would she explain this to Tony?

She sat down on the bed and covered her face with her hands. An abortion would allow her to go on with her life, preserving both her marriage and her love affair with Tony. But the very idea of destroying her child sent an ice cold bolt of pain racing through her body. No matter how terrible the consequences might be, she desperately wanted this baby.

And beyond that, she desperately wanted to divorce Richard and marry Tony. She loved him even more now that they had created this miracle of life. They belonged together. But Richard would never see things her way. Even if he agreed to a divorce, he would find some way to punish her for her faithlessness.

Completely engrossed in her thoughts, Gussie let out a sharp cry when the door flew open and her mother sailed into the room wrapped in a cloud of Joy. "Good God, Augusta, where are your clothes?"

Stunned, Gussie stared at her for a moment, then scurried to cover herself with the sheet, terrified that Elizabeth would somehow discover her pregnancy. "What are you doing here, Mother? Who let you in?"

"Your maid. She said you were ill, so I came up to make sure you were all right. I certainly never expected to find you naked. If your servants see you like this, they'll have it all over Washington."

"I'm in my bedroom, Mother, not parading through the White House."

Elizabeth sniffed as if she had just caught a whiff of an unpleasant odor. "I should think you'd have more modesty. We certainly never raised you to be so . . . so uncouth."

Struggling to curb her irritation, Gussie wondered what her mother would say if she knew she would soon be the grandmother of a bastard.

"Why are you here, Mother? I wasn't expecting you."

Still looking aggrieved, Elizabeth sat on a tufted velvet love seat and carefully crossed her slender legs. "Since Richard is away, I thought you might like to join us for dinner. Your father was complaining just this morning that we haven't seen you in ages."

Gussie cringed at the thought of spending an evening with her parents. She was in no condition to play the part of dutiful daughter. "Not tonight, Mother. I've had a headache all day."

Elizabeth frowned. "Really, Augusta, these headaches of yours are wearing rather thin. It would probably do you a world of good to get dressed and leave the house for a few hours."

"Sorry. We'll have to make it another time."

Not accustomed to defeat, Elizabeth fixed Gussie with a withering stare. "Sometimes I just don't understand you," she said. "You have such a wonderful life, and yet you behave as if you're constantly being put upon."

"What makes you think I have such a wonderful life, Mother?"

Sighing, Elizabeth shook her head. "I don't know why I bother talking to you. You seem determined to find fault with everything these days."

Her imperious tone and the undisguised disapproval in her eyes triggered a dark and unreasoning anger in Gussie, an anger nourished by years of unvoiced resentment. "What do you expect?" she snapped. "I'm miserably unhappy, but then, you've never cared the slightest bit about my happiness, have you?"

Looking at once shocked and wounded, Elizabeth stiffened her shoulders. "What in the world are you talking about? Your father and I have always gone out of our way to see that you were happy. How can you be so ungrateful?"

Now that she was finally venting her anger, Gussie felt a strange exhilaration, as if an internal abscess had suddenly been lanced, purging her body of a virulent poison. "Is that why you all but forced me to marry Richard? Because you were so concerned about my happiness?" She laughed harshly. "Well, you were wrong, Mother. My marriage is a sham. I can hardly stand to be in the same room with him. His touch makes my skin crawl."

Elizabeth fanned her face. "Stop this at once. You're raving like a madwoman."

Gussie shook her head. "I'm not mad. I'm just telling you the truth."

Elizabeth seemed to falter. Her mouth dropped open and her slim manicured hands went limp in her lap, but it was only a transitory weakness. A second later she resumed her iron mask of dignity. "There's no point in continuing this discussion while you're so out of control," she said in a low voice. "But

I'm warning you, Augusta, be careful. You have a position to uphold, and even one foolish indiscretion could cause a scandal.''

Something inside Gussie snapped like a rubber band. Even now her mother refused to recognize her suffering, refused to offer comfort. "This is unbelievable!" she cried. "I just told you I'm miserable and you're worried about a scandal. What's wrong with you? I'm your daughter! Don't you care about me at all?"

Even in the face of Gussie's accusations Elizabeth remained cool and impassive, her refined features devoid of emotion. After a long moment she stood and smoothed her hands over her slim gray skirt. "This unpleasant scene was totally uncalled for, Augusta. You owe me an apology."

Silence seemed to vibrate in the air between them. Then Gussie looked at her mother and shook her head. "No . . . not this time. I won't apologize for speaking the truth."

Elizabeth stood rooted to the floor, her flawless complexion as pale as parchment, her eyes wide with disbelief. Several seconds elapsed before she regained her poise and regally walked to the door. "We'll talk about this later," she said icily. "In the meantime, I suggest you get yourself under control and think about some of the awful things you've said."

Choking on her own rage, Gussie helplessly watched her mother float out of the room like a queen. But only a moment later she felt a familiar longing rise up inside her. Even now she ached to have Elizabeth look at her with love and respect. God, what was wrong with her? Why was she always groveling for a few crumbs of approval?

Hating herself for her weakness, she jumped up and slammed the door, appeased by the crash that resounded through the house. No matter what her mother thought, she had a right to some happiness. This time nothing would stop her from divorcing Richard and spending the rest of her life with Tony and their baby.

A few days later Gussie was close to panic as she sat in the formal living room awaiting an audience with Richard. Just the thought of facing him and demanding a divorce sent little shivers of apprehension up and down her spine. Although she was certain he had never loved her, he did consider her an accessory to his public image. And that image would be tarnished by a divorce.

Clasping her hands in her lap, she tried to calm herself by gazing out the window at the fiery sunset. It had been an unusually hot day, and now the sky was ablaze with vivid shades of red and orange. But the lovely view did nothing to blunt her anxieties. All she could think of was Richard and the dreadful ordeal of ending her marriage. Then she heard his footsteps in the foyer and felt herself tense all over.

"All right, Augusta," he said irritably. "This better be important. You know what a hellish week I've had."

Gussie watched him cross the room to the marble bar and pour himself a shot of Chivas Regal. Despite the heat, he was wearing a white summer suit and a blue silk tie, as if he expected to be photographed.

"Well, are you going to get on with this dire conversation or just sit there staring at me?" he said, turning to face her.

She met his cold, expressionless eyes and felt her resolve weaken. How would she get through the next few minutes? Much as she had carefully rehearsed her speech, she knew her words would emerge in an inarticulate jumble. But if she failed to tell him now, she might never find the courage to approach him again. "I've been unhappy for a long time, Richard," she said. "We married for all the wrong reasons, and I can't go on pretending anymore. I want a divorce."

Instead of reacting with shock or anger, he looked at her for a moment, then ambled over to the brocade sofa and sat down. "A divorce?" he said. "You must be out of your mind, Augusta. This is an election year."

Too stunned to respond, Gussie felt as if she had stumbled into some strange twilight world where everything was distorted. Richard was supposed to be shouting and threatening retribution. Why on earth was he just sitting there calmly sipping his drink?

"I'm sorry you're unhappy," he went on. "But you know the rules as well as I do. Divorce is impossible."

"I don't care about the rules. I want a divorce."

Sighing, he shook his head. "That's your problem, Augusta. You refuse to accept reality. We're public figures, and we have to live by certain standards. We have a perfectly adequate arrangement, and I see no reason to make any changes.''

Gussie lurched forward in her chair, her head beginning to pound. ''Richard, you're not listening to me. I don't love you. Our marriage is over.''

His mouth curled in a thin sneer. ''Love never had anything to do with our arrangement, my dear. Why worry about it now?''

''Because I . . . I'm in love with someone else.''

There, Gussie thought with relief, he finally knew the truth. But as she watched him puff up with fury, she suddenly felt like a child playing with matches. She had just started a dangerous fire and she had no idea how to put it out.

''Are you telling me you've been unfaithful?'' he said, his eyes hard and menacing.

She nodded, the drumming in her head so loud she could hardly hear him. ''I'm pregnant, Richard.''

There was a silence so thick and pervasive it seemed to fill the room. Then Richard made a strangling noise in his throat as he pounded his fist on a cherry end table, smashing a precious Rosenthal figurine. ''You bitch! I'll kill you for this.''

In all their years together Gussie had never seen him so enraged, and she was frightened. Reacting to a primal instinct to shield her baby, her hands flew protectively to her stomach, but he made no move to physically assault her.

''I warned you about other men,'' he shouted. ''I warned you about embarrassing me.''

Gussie swallowed convulsively, grimacing at the bitter taste of her own fear. ''I never meant for this to happen. I love Tony, but I never meant to cause you pain.''

Richard pinned her with a hard glare that simmered with malignant hatred. ''Pain? That's hardly the word to describe what I'm feeling right now, Augusta. If I thought I could get away with it, I'd choke you to death. Nothing in this world would give me greater pleasure.''

Gussie felt her heart bound up into her throat as she watched him shoot to his feet and cross the room, stopping directly in front of her. ''What do you think, Augusta? What are my chances of murdering you without getting caught?''

''Richard, stop it. You're scaring me.''

He laughed, a coarse bray that made him sound slightly mad. "That's too bad, because I'm just getting started, my dear. How long have you been cuckolding me?"

Gussie vainly struggled to sink deeper into the sofa, wishing it would swallow her.

"What's the matter, Augusta? Squeamish all of a sudden?" He pitched forward, grabbing her by the shoulders, his bony fingers digging into her flesh. "Answer me. How long have you been fucking your lover?"

"A . . . a few months."

"Who is he?"

His face was only inches from hers. She could smell the liquor on his breath, see the tiny hairs growing out of his nostrils. She wondered if he actually intended to kill her. Then suddenly he was shaking her, rattling her like a rag doll. His grip on her shoulders briefly intensified, then he seemed to lose his momentum and suddenly she was free as he staggered back to the sofa.

"You disgust me," he said, little specks of spittle glistening on his lips like dewdrops. "But I'll never give you a divorce. Do you understand me, Augusta? If you try to end this marriage, I'll ruin you."

Gussie shook her head. "Why can't you just let me go? My God, I'm having another man's baby!"

He flopped down on the sofa, picked up his glass, and drained it in one gulp. "It's very simple, my dear—politics. Right now a divorce would hurt my campaign. And even more important, I've come to depend on your father's support."

Horrified by his cold-bloodedness, she glared at him. "You can't force me to stay, Richard."

"Is that so?" he said. "Well, let me tell you something. If you so much as step out that door, I'll have no choice but to expose your dirty little affair. Everyone in Washington will know what a whore you are. And you can be damn sure your parents will never forgive you for dragging the Tremain name through the mud. Is that what you want, Augusta? To live like an outcast?"

Gussie blanched, feeling the first stirring of doubt. She tried to reassure herself by thinking of Tony and the baby, imagining them living together in blissful happiness, but the loving fantasy quickly faded as she imagined what it would really be like.

An ugly divorce would be humiliating. Richard would paint himself as an innocent husband betrayed by a promiscuous wife, and the gossips would rip her reputation to shreds. But it was the thought of being cut off from her parents that filled her with anxiety. God in heaven, she was thirty-three years old and still mortally afraid of severing the umbilical cord. Why was she letting Richard blackmail her?

She felt a wave of self-loathing as she realized she was actually considering staying with Richard. Love and happiness were finally within her grasp, but she was too weak to reach out and grab them. Once again she was being forced to choose between Tony and everything else she cherished.

"Well, Augusta, have you reconsidered your position?" Richard said.

"Please . . . don't do this to me. Let me get a quiet divorce and marry Tony. I'm begging you, Richard."

His eyes turned hard and cruel again. "Not a chance. If you marry your lover, you'll pay the price."

"But what kind of life will we have together? How can you still want me?"

He burst into laughter. "Want you? You totally misunderstand. Right now I can hardly stand the sight of you."

"Then let me go."

Sighing, he shot her a disgusted look. "This conversation is getting very boring. Make up your mind, Augusta. What are you going to do?"

Gussie felt a great black void open up inside her as all her hopes and dreams slowly died. There was no point in lying to herself any longer. She was afraid to leave Richard, afraid to face the consequences of her love for Tony. But this time she had something to cling to. "What about my baby?" she whispered.

"You'll abort it, of course."

"No. If I stay, I'm keeping my baby and I'll expect you to accept it as your own. Those are my terms, Richard."

He silently stared at her, seeming to measure her resolve. At last he nodded. "But you're to end your affair immediately. And if I ever find out you've been unfaithful again, I'll destroy not only you but the child as well. I mean that, Augusta. I'll have you declared an unfit mother and you'll never see your precious baby again.''

"There's no need to threaten me," she said stiffly. "No matter what you think, I'm not a tramp. I love Tony. There'll never be anyone else.''

"Then we have an agreement. I'll move my things into one of the guest bedrooms tomorrow. Right now I'm going to my club. I'll spend the night there.''

Relieved that he no longer intended to share her bed, Gussie nodded wearily, but as she watched him leave the room, she felt a raging sense of grief spring up inside her. She had just condemned herself to a lifetime without Tony, a lifetime of loneliness and regret. And even her baby would never completely fill the empty space in her heart.

Gussie pulled to a stop in the motel parking lot and hunched over the steering wheel, fighting back tears. Today was the last time she would ever see Tony, the last time she would ever be touched as a woman or know the exquisite feeling of being loved. Today was a day of mourning.

Even the rain pelting the windshield mirrored her mood. All morning the sky had been thick with billowing gray clouds. Now the eerie darkness seemed almost like an omen as she drew her raincoat around her chest and wondered where she would find the strength to walk away from Tony.

After days of anguish, she had finally decided to keep her pregnancy a secret from Tony. He would never let her go if he even suspected she was carrying his baby. She was riddled with guilt for deceiving him. Denying him the right to love his child seemed inhumanly selfish, a crime that would forever haunt her. But what choice did she have? She was a liar and a cheat, and now she was reaping the bitter harvest of her sins.

She slid out of the car and hurried past the old fieldstone inn to the tiny cabin she had come to think of as theirs. Tony opened the door the instant she knocked and drew her into his arms. "God, I've missed you," he murmured. "It seems like forever since I've held you.''

Too distraught to speak, Gussie pressed her face against his chest, memorizing the fresh scent of his skin, the feel of his

slightly damp shirt against her cheek. These memories would
have to sustain her through endless long and sleepless nights.

"What is it, *cara*?" he said. "Why are you trembling?"

Until that moment Gussie had been planning to make love to
him one last time. Now she knew she had to tell him the truth
at once, before she succumbed to the urgent need to soothe her
hurt in the loving warmth of his body.

"Something's happened," she said. "We have to talk."

Suddenly looking anxious, he pulled her into the room and
closed the door. "Tell me."

Gussie removed her coat, then sat on the edge of the bed,
absently skimming her fingers over the familiar orange patch-
work quilt. "Richard knows about us."

Tony inhaled sharply. "I'm sorry, *cara*. It must have been
terrible for you, but maybe this is for the best. Now we can get
on with our lives."

"No . . . you don't understand," she said. "I can't see
you anymore. He threatened me. I have . . . no choice."

His black eyes blazed with anger. "That bastard! I'll kill him
for threatening you." He crossed the room to join her on the
bed and cradle her hand in his. "Forget his threats, *cara*. I'll
never let him hurt you."

She shook her head. "There's nothing you can do. If I
divorce him, he'll ruin me . . . turn my parents against me. I
have to stay with him."

Tony stared at her. Then, as she watched in horrified
fascination, awareness dawned in his eyes, and his entire face
contorted with an anger so fierce it stunned her.

"What the hell are you saying?" he shouted. "I thought you
loved me! I thought you wanted to marry me."

"I do love you!" she cried.

He looked at her with disgust. "You don't even know the
meaning of the word."

Gussie flinched as he jerked his hand away and lurched to
his feet, his beloved features still twisted by the pain and rage
of her betrayal. She felt his anger crackling in the air around her
like lightning seeking a target. This was worse than she had
imagined . . . much worse.

"I should have known," he said bitterly. "You're still the
same spoiled little girl you were ten years ago. How could I

have been stupid enough to believe you had become a woman?''

Then, casting her a last dark and piercing look, he grabbed his raincoat and started for the door. ''I pity you, Gussie. You're nothing but an empty shell.''

''Tony, wait!'' she cried, but he was already gone, leaving her alone with her memories and a heart shattered beyond repair.

CHAPTER
Twenty-three

RHETTA WATCHED IN HORROR AS HELENE TRIPPED OVER A THICK electrical cable and tumbled to the floor in a boneless heap. A second later Jack Golden raced onto the set, wildly waving his arms.

"That's it!" he screamed. "Get her the fuck out of here. She's too goddam drunk to work."

Rhetta wove her way through the maze of equipment and sank to her knees beside Helene. "Helene, are you okay? Come on, baby, look at me."

Helene slowly opened her eyes, but they were dazed and bloodshot, and her breath reeked of alcohol. "I'm sorry," she murmured. "I . . . I must have lost my balance."

"Bullshit!" Golden shouted. "You're loaded again. You're a goddam lush, and you're screwing up my picture." Looking at Rhetta, he pointed to Helene as if she were a worthless pile of rubbish. "Take her home and get her cleaned up. If she's not sober and ready to work tomorrow morning, she's fucking fired."

"Jack, not now," Rhetta said harshly. "Threats won't help anything."

"This is no threat, sweetheart," he snarled. "She shows up here drunk again, she's finished. Now get her the hell out of my sight."

Much as Rhetta wanted to argue, she knew he was right. They were only two weeks into production, and already Helene was caving in under the pressure. Her drinking was completely out of control, and the pills . . . the pills were poisoning her. Feeling a dull heaviness in her chest, Rhetta glanced at Jack and nodded. "I'll see that she gets some sleep. Things have been a little rough since Seth died."

Jack just snorted, then stalked away shaking his head.

Hating him for his callousness, Rhetta leaned over Helene and gently touched her cheek. "I'll take you home now," she crooned. "You'll feel better once you rest."

Helene blinked, still looking dazed. "Why is Jack so mad at me, Rhett? It was a mistake. I didn't mean to fall."

Rhetta forced herself to smile. "You know Jack. He's always mad about something. Come on, let's get out of here. Grab my arm and I'll help you up."

Once Helene was asleep, Rhetta went to the kitchen and poured herself a shot of bourbon. Then, sitting at the polished oak table, she lit a cigarette and kicked off her shoes, her eyes bright with tears. She had been lying to herself for weeks, but after the scene at the studio this morning, she knew Helene was critically ill, slowly killing herself with booze and pills.

And she had no idea how to stop her.

Picking up her glass, Rhetta gulped a swallow of bourbon, holding her breath as it burned its way down her throat. God how she hated this helpless feeling. She loved Helene like a daughter, and here she was just standing on the sidelines watching her wither and die. But how did you make someone want to live? How did you fix a heart ravaged by such an unbearable loss?

Maybe it was impossible. Maybe Helene was already beyond help, fated to destroy herself. Rhetta felt her chest constrict at the thought. There had to be some way to pull her back from the edge.

But Helene was so fragile and vulnerable. She rarely spoke of Seth these days, and yet the ghost of his presence was always there in her haunted black eyes. And heaven only knew what tortured thoughts filled her mind. She seemed lost and alone, slipping through life like a shadow.

As Rhetta drained the last drops of bourbon from her glass, she heard a sound and glanced up, surprised to see Helene standing in the doorway. She looked almost ethereal in a filmy white nightgown, her black hair tumbling over her shoulders, her face so thin and pale it seemed incandescent.

"You're supposed to be resting," she said.

Smiling faintly, Helene joined her at the table. "You didn't have to stay, Rhett. I'm okay now."

Rhetta looked at her shaking hands and glassy eyes and felt a sudden gut-wrenching fear. "No, you're not okay," she said. "You're killing yourself with booze and drugs. You need help, Helene."

Helene shook her head. "I don't want any help. Just leave me alone."

"I can't do that. I love you too much to let you destroy yourself. There are clinics where they can help you sober up, help you deal with losing Seth."

Helene slumped over the table. "Can they bring him back to me?"

Her despair seemed to engulf the room like a black cloud of misery and desolation. Rhetta remained motionless for a moment, then she sprang to her feet and wrapped Helene in her arms.

"No, baby, nothing can bring him back, but maybe they can make things better. Give them a chance. Let them help you."

"It's too late."

"No, it's never too late," Rhetta insisted vehemently. "But you have to be willing to try."

"What about Jack and the picture? I can't just walk out on him."

"The hell with Jack," Rhetta said. "We have to do what's best for you. Let me make a few calls. We'll find a good place, I promise."

Helene lifted her head, her eyes full of helplessness. "All right, whatever you want."

Instead of a rush of relief, Rhetta felt a sharp ache in the pit of her stomach. Helene had agreed only because she no longer cared enough to fight, and in a way that was even more frightening than her addiction.

"And how did you feel when your mother died, Helene?"

Helene looked at the earnest young psychiatrist sitting across from her and tried to figure out what he wanted her to say. He was such a sincere man. She always felt guilty for disappointing him, but she was totally incapable of digging into her unconscious and blurting out her most secret thoughts.

"I really didn't feel much of anything," she said at last. "We were never very close."

"Why do you think that was?"

She shrugged. "I guess we just never had anything in common."

Dr. Wolfe shoved his thick wire-rimmed glasses up over his forehead and stared at her intently. "You've been here at Evergreen a month now, Helene, and you're still resisting treatment. Why?"

Suddenly he no longer seemed affable. His mouth was set in a stern line, his level gaze deadly serious. Helene felt her respiration quicken. Why was he pressuring her?

"I'd like to go back to my room now," she said.

"First I want you to tell me why you're afraid to open up to me."

Helene wrung her hands. They felt cold and stiff, like blocks of ice. All the black places in her mind seemed to be humming at once, sending a strange sort of energy pulsing through her head.

"Why are you here, Helene?" he persisted. "Do you really want help or are you just going through the motions?"

"Leave me alone," she said. "I'm tired. I can't think."

He leaned back in his chair, his penetrating green eyes fixed on her face. "You're hiding again. Every time I get too close, you run away."

Helene looked down at the bright orange and yellow tweed carpet. He was right. She was here at Evergreen because she loved Rhetta too much to disappoint her. But in her own mind she knew she was hopeless. She was already dead inside.

"All right, Helene," he said kindly. "We'll try again tomorrow."

She wanted to tell him he was wasting his kindness and caring on a corpse, but the words refused to form. Instead, she mutely nodded and hurried out of his office.

Once she reached the corridor, she slowed her pace and smiled wanly at one of the other guests. No one here was ever referred to as a patient. Evergreen was more like an elegant hotel than a sanitarium. Each suite of rooms was unique, decorated with original oil paintings and custom-designed furniture, every amenity to make the wealthy guests feel pampered and content.

But the luxury was only an illusion, a gracious facade to conceal the ugliness of tortured souls fighting madness and addiction. No amount of elegance could hide the piercing screams that echoed through the stillness of the night or the ravaged faces of addicts craving drugs.

Helene entered her suite and closed the door. Late afternoon sunlight flooded the sitting room with a golden glow, but her chills intensified as she sat on the plump beige sofa and nervously plucked at a throw pillow. During the day she was almost always able to keep her dark thoughts at bay, but as evening shadows loomed on the horizon her demons seemed to slither out of the darkness like creatures of the night.

God, she wanted a drink. Just one to chase away the ghosts, but there was no alcohol at Evergreen, no drugs of any kind. Only the memory of sweet oblivion.

She shifted on the sofa, tucking her legs beneath her as she anxiously searched the sky for the first streaks of purple. Her nightly terrors were so much worse now. Not only was she tormented by memories of Seth but she was also starting to remember other things, horrible things that left her weak and trembling. All the ghosts she thought she had buried for eternity were returning to haunt her.

Shuddering again, she stood and slowly walked to the window. She parted the gauzy white curtains, then pressed her forehead against the cool glass and watched as shadows swallowed the sun.

Hours later Helene lay perfectly still on the bed as forgotten memories rose from some dark inner hell to fill her mind. Suddenly everything was clear. All the vague images that had played through her nightmares for so many years were now sharp and precise. She was seeing her past with crystal clarity, and the pain and horror were nearly unbearable.

But there was also a certain peace in finally knowing the truth. At last she understood why she had chosen to escape with drugs and alcohol, why her life had been full of such inner turmoil. And at last she understood why she was beyond salvation.

Then as she stared at the ceiling, she began to feel a strange contentment, an acceptance that flowed over her like a gentle tide of warm, comforting water. There were no more black places in her mind. Suddenly she saw her own destiny, and all her fears receded.

Completely calm now, she turned on the bedside lamp and

picked up the telephone to order a limousine. Then she slipped out of bed, crossed the room, and sat at the fine Chippendale desk. Tears blurred her vision as she wrote two letters, one a simple business matter, the other a purging of her soul.

It was nearly dawn when she made her way to the nurses' station. Only one weary nurse was sitting behind the desk, her feet propped up on an open drawer. When she noticed Helene, she sat up straight and rubbed her eyes. "Is something wrong, Miss Galloway?"

Helene smiled. "No, but I've decided to leave. My limo should be here any minute."

Suddenly the nurse looked wide awake. "Leave? It's five o'clock in the morning. You can't leave now."

"I'm not a prisoner here, Miss Jenkins. I can leave anytime I want," Helene said softly.

"Of course . . . but you . . . you really should talk to Dr. Wolfe first. Why don't I call him?"

"That's not necessary. I've already made up my mind. I'll send someone for my things. Good-bye, Miss Jenkins."

Smiling gently, Helene turned and walked down the corridor to the lobby where she saw the lights of the limousine glowing beyond the glass doors. A security guard stared at her with undisguised curiosity, but made no move to stop her as she dropped her letters in the mailbox and then left Evergreen behind forever.

A new morning was bursting over the horizon as Helene dismissed the driver and entered the ranch house, her nostrils flaring at the familiar scent of dried herbs and sun-bleached wood. It felt so good to be home, sheltered within the sturdy walls of the only place where she had ever been happy. As she moved through the quiet rooms, she picked up a bottle of scotch from the bar and slowly made her way to her bedroom.

Frail sunlight slanted through the bamboo shades, painting the rough white walls in soft shades of pink and heather. Everything looked fresh and clean in the pure morning light, almost like a benediction. She felt Seth all around her, but now there was no pain, only a deepening serenity.

She sat on the edge of the bed, placed the bottle of scotch on the nightstand, and rummaged in the drawer for her Valium. She felt no fear as she swallowed all of the pills left in the bottle, washing them down with scotch. Then she reached for a framed photograph of Seth, looked into his beloved eyes and softly implored him to come to her.

And as the sun rose higher in the sky, she felt his presence close around her like a blanket, soft and gentle, filled with love. All the hurt was gone, and the lonely little girl living in the attic of her mind was finally at peace.

CHAPTER
Twenty-four

FEELING LIMP AND SOGGY IN THE OPPRESSIVE HEAT, DIANE SCRAMBLED out of a wheezing cab and crossed the hot pavement to the Preston Building, then exhaled a sigh of relief as she entered the cool lobby. All around her people were hurrying to the elevators intent on reaching their offices, but she moved listlessly through the crowd, dreading another day of tension.

She had received no formal word on her position at the network. She was still in possession of her office, but she had been stripped of her duties as a producer. Ed Blake delighted in assigning her to mundane research projects, and she had no idea how long it would be before the top brass reached a decision regarding her future.

The strain of waiting was beginning to fray her nerves. She felt irritable and out of sorts, snapping at Michael and Carrie for the slightest transgressions. At times she was actually tempted to resign and steer her life in a new direction, but sanity always prevailed. She loved her job, and she remembered the years of struggle it had taken to breach the barriers of sexual discrimination. There was no way she would simply walk away without a fight.

She stepped off the elevator and headed directly to her office, avoiding the crowd gathered at the coffee machine. Since her disgrace, she felt too conspicuous to mingle. Perhaps it was all in her mind, but she sensed a wariness among her colleagues, a certain reluctance to associate with someone who might cast a shadow on their own careers.

She breathed a sigh of relief when she reached the privacy of her office, but a moment later Angie burst through the door, looking frantic. She held out a crumpled sheet of paper. ''This just came over the AP wire. I thought you'd want to see it right away.''

Feeling a dark sense of dread, Diane reached for the paper and quickly read the short press release. Then, slumping against the wall, she gripped her chest and emitted a low cry that seemed to emanate from the very depths of her being.

''Diane, sit down before you collapse.''

Jamming her fist against her mouth to stifle her own eerie cries, Diane staggered to a chair, her legs buckling under her. ''Helene is dead.'' She repeated the words over and over, but they had no meaning.

''Just take it easy,'' Angie said. ''I'll call Michael for you.''

Diane weakly shook her head. ''No, don't do that. I'm all right now.'' Tears brimmed in her eyes, then spilled over and ran down her cheeks. ''I just can't believe she's dead.''

''God, I'm sorry,'' Angie whispered. ''What can I do for you?''

''I'd like to be alone for a few minutes.''

Angie nodded. ''Sure. I'll be right outside. Call if you need anything.''

Once she was alone, Diane buried her face in her hands and sobbed. There was so much to be done. She had to call Rhetta Green and find out the grim details, then notify Rachel and Gussie so they could make arrangements to fly to California. But at the moment all she could do was cry as precious memories of Helene filled her mind.

Rachel elbowed her way through the crowded terminal at JFK, nervously checking her watch every few seconds. Traffic leaving the city had been hell, and she was late meeting Diane. Her heart pumping wildly, she pushed past a group of Japanese tourists and broke into a run.

When she had finally reached the gate, Diane was hovering by the jetway looking frazzled. She seemed to wilt with relief as Rachel came bounding up beside her. ''Thank God. I was afraid I'd have to leave without you.''

''Sorry, the traffic was miserable.''

Their eyes met for a long moment and then everything else faded away as they reached for each other. ''Why?'' Rachel said hoarsely. ''Why the hell did she have to kill herself?''

"I don't know," Diane said, "but we should have suspected. We should have done something."

As Rachel was about to reply, a young woman wearing an airline uniform tapped her on the shoulder. "Excuse me, ladies, but you'll have to board now."

Moving away from Diane, Rachel dabbed at her tears. She had been fiercely repressing her grief all day, but now it engulfed her. Sweet, gentle Helene was really dead and nothing would ever be the same again. They had started out four young women bound by a unique friendship. Now there were only three.

Gussie climbed out of the limousine in front of the Beverly Hilton Hotel and waited for the chauffeur to retrieve her luggage. She was still queasy after the long flight, and there was an unpleasant metallic taste in her mouth, the bitter taste of grief.

She tried to force her mind to go blank as she followed the doorman into the lobby, signed the register, and boarded the elevator, but thoughts of Helene continued to plague her. Suicide seemed like such an unnatural act, irrational and repellent, and yet she was unable to quell her morbid curiosity. What had Helene been thinking when she swallowed the pills? Had she been frightened by the prospect of death or simply relieved to be escaping the horror of her life?

Appalled by her thoughts, Gussie stared straight ahead until the elevator whooshed to a stop on the seventh floor. Only minutes ago she had been eager to see Diane and Rachel, but now she felt apprehensive as she left the elevator and approached their suite. Everything seemed so strange and out of kilter now that Helene was dead.

She stood at the door for a moment, then hesitantly knocked. An instant later Rachel and Diane were both hugging her at once.

"We thought you'd never get here," Diane said.

"The flight seemed endless," Gussie replied. "All I could think about was Helene."

Rachel squeezed her tight, then released her. "Let's go inside. We could all use a drink."

Once they were seated in the living room, Gussie slipped out of her shoes and rested her head on the arm of the sofa, her queasiness now a full-blown case of nausea.

"Gussie, what's wrong?" Diane said. "You look awful."

Gussie glanced at her for a moment, then dashed for the bathroom and knelt on the cold tile floor in front of the toilet. Good heavens, even now her body was reminding her of the new life growing inside her.

"Hey, are you okay?" Rachel said, rapping lightly on the door.

"I'll be right out," Gussie mumbled as she weakly stood and splashed cold water on her face, fighting a wave of dizziness.

When she emerged from the bathroom, Rachel looked at her sharply, then said, "What's going on? Are you sick?"

This was such an odd time to tell them about her pregnancy, Gussie thought. Helene was dead, and they were all immersed in this terrible grief. She considered just glossing over the truth, but then she realized how much she needed their support. Resuming her seat on the sofa, she sucked in a deep breath and said, "Not sick exactly. I'm pregnant."

"Pregnant?" Diane said. "But I thought . . ."

"It's not Richard's baby," Gussie said flatly. "Tony and I . . . I'm carrying his child."

"Oh, God," Rachel said. "What are you going to do?"

Gulping back tears, Gussie said, "I'm staying with Richard. He agreed to accept the baby as his own."

"Why don't you leave him?" Diane said, her blue eyes wide and incredulous. "I thought you were in love with Tony."

Suddenly Gussie regretted having told them the truth. Now she was forced to defend herself, and in her own mind she was still struggling to justify what she had done. "Richard threatened to publicly disgrace me. I was afraid to leave him."

"And Tony?" Rachel said. "Does he know about the baby?"

Gussie shook her head, misery welling up inside her. Every day she fought to strike Tony from her heart and mind, but her love was like a brand seared into her soul. No matter how hard she tried to wash it away, it would always be a part of her.

"I thought it was better to make a clean break," she said. Then sickened by her lie, she blurted, "No, that's not true. He would have hated me even more if he'd known about the baby. I . . . I just couldn't face that.''

"Oh, Gussie, I'm sorry," Diane said.

Gussie glanced from Diane to Rachel, knowing she was unworthy of their sympathy. "I know what you must think of me," she said. "I did a terrible thing to Tony. I'll never stop hating myself, but I . . . I'm too weak to fight Richard.''

She lost all control then, and sobbed bitterly as Rachel and Diane sat beside her on the sofa, trying to comfort her. "Who the hell are we to judge you?" Rachel said. "You did what you had to do. There's nothing more to say.''

"That's right," Diane murmured, gently embracing her. "All we care about is you. There's just the three of us now. We have to be there for each other.''

Her words seemed to fill the room, echoing from every empty corner, a quiet reminder of Helene and the reason they were together. Gussie burrowed against Diane, aching inside. "In my mind I know she's dead, but I keep hoping it's a horrible mistake. It all seems so unreal.''

Rachel sat up and reached for the pack of cigarettes on the coffee table. She lit one and then slouched back against the arm of the sofa. "And we'll never really know why she did it.''

"I'm sure it was losing Seth," Diane said. "Rhetta told me Helene had started abusing drugs and alcohol again. Her life just fell apart when he died.''

Shooting to her feet, Rachel began to pace. "Why didn't she come to one of us? It's driving me crazy to think she went through something like that alone.''

Gussie shook her head. "I don't think it was just Seth," she said quietly. "Helene murdered a man. All these years she pretended it never happened, but I'm sure . . . I think she committed suicide because of Rick Conti.''

Rachel swirled to face her. "You don't know that. It was probably Brenda who killed him. She just blamed Helene to save her own skin.''

"Maybe," Gussie conceded. "But whatever happened, Helene was never the same after that night.''

There was a long silence; then Diane sighed and said, "I guess we'll never know for sure.''

Rachel shrugged. "What difference does it make? It's too

late to change anything. Helene is gone. There's not a thing we can do to help her.''

There was another silence, but this time they avoided looking at one another as memories seemed to flow between them like an electric current. Gussie blinked at the picture that arose in her mind, four young women standing in the rose garden at Brentwood, their faces bright with hope. Then the picture swirled and changed, and she had a vivid image of Rick Conti lying dead on the deck, Helene crumpled beside him, mutely staring into the darkness. It was all so clear, a night of horror that had irrevocably altered the course of their lives.

And now Helene was dead. Gussie found herself wondering if her death was the final chapter or if more tragedy awaited them. Perhaps they were all destined to pay a price for the part they had played in the murder of Rick Conti. Perhaps this was only the beginning.

Closing her eyes, she tried to convince herself that such dire thoughts were simply a reaction to the shock of Helene's suicide. Right now she was insensible with grief, but once the funeral was over and she returned home, these crazy notions would dissipate. They had to—she was already coping with more unhappiness than she could handle.

''What time is the service tomorrow?'' she said, anxious to shatter the gloomy silence.

Rachel paused in her endless pacing. ''Noon at the cemetery. Then we have an appointment to meet with Helene's lawyer at three.''

Gussie felt a tingle of alarm. ''Her lawyer? Why? What would he want with us?''

''Who knows?'' Rachel replied. ''Rhetta Green called a few minutes before you got here and said he had some business to discuss with us.''

Gussie found the thought of meeting with Helene's lawyer disturbing, though she had no idea why. ''Do we really have to bother? Tomorrow will be stressful enough without sitting through a lot of legal nonsense.''

''It's the least we can do for Helene,'' Rachel said sharply.

When Diane nodded her agreement, Gussie abandoned the argument, but she still felt uneasy. Then her mind returned to her earlier thoughts of sin and retribution, and a shiver slid

down her spine. She had a bad feeling about tomorrow, a very
bad feeling.

Mick Travis leaned against the scabby trunk of a gnarled elm
tree avidly watching Helene Galloway's funeral service. He
was positioned far enough away to avoid any conflicts with the
massive security force, but he still had a fairly good view of the
mourners. And they were all there. The three surviving
conspirators were huddled together beside the grave holding
hands like lost little girls.

They looked so innocent in their sorrow. He almost felt a
pang of pity, but he quickly reminded himself that they were
heartless killers. And Helene Galloway was dead because she
could no longer live with her guilt. He was sure of that, but
instead of appeasing his lust for revenge, it only inflamed his
desire to see the others punished.

Shoving his hand in his pocket, he fingered the gold
medallion, which he had come to think of as an amulet, a charm
that would one day lead him to the truth. But despite the
medallion and his obsessive investigation, the truth always
remained just beyond his reach.

In his more rational moments, Mick knew he should just
give up and forget his insane thoughts of revenge, but then the
hate would boil up inside him again like smoldering lava.
Those women deserved to be exposed and punished. And he
was the only one who cared enough to pursue them.

As the service ended and the crowd began to disperse, Mick
watched his prey pause for a moment at the grave, then begin
the short walk to the waiting limousine. He was tempted to
confront them just for the sheer pleasure of seeing them
squirm, but he resisted the impulse. There was too much
security, and he had no inclination to be rousted by a burly cop
for harassing the mourners.

This time he had no choice but to let them escape, but one
day those three bitches would be completely at his mercy. One
day the grisly truth would rip their perfect lives to shreds.

Diane blinked away tears as she glanced around the well-
appointed waiting room, wondering why prominent Beverly
Hills attorney, Douglas Halvorsen, had insisted on this meeting, especially today when they were all so shaky. What could

possibly be important enough to intrude on their grief this way?

Then, glancing at Rachel and Gussie, who were seated across from her, she fought to steady herself. They were both on the verge of collapse. The funeral had been worse than they had ever imagined, so final and irrevocable. Helene was now interred beside Seth for all eternity, but her death still seemed like a surrealistic nightmare.

"Our appointment was at three," Rachel said. "Where the hell is he?"

Checking her gold Cartier watch, Gussie frowned, then turned to the pretty blond receptionist. "Is Mr. Halvorsen aware we're here?"

"Yes, Mrs. Chandler. We're waiting for Rhetta Green. I'm sure she'll be here any minute."

"Rhetta?" Rachel muttered. "What does she have to do with this?"

"I have no idea," Gussie said, fanning her face with a slim manicured hand. "But I don't like it. We never should have agreed to come. I told you that yesterday."

Just then Rhetta slipped into the room, her face sunken and pale, her black dress seeming to hang from her shoulders like a shapeless sack. "Sorry I'm late," she said in a husky voice. "There were some last-minute details at the cemetery."

Diane looked at her and felt a rush of pity. They were all suffering the pain of losing Helene, but the pain must have been even worse for Rhetta, almost like that of a mother losing a child. Rising from her chair, she impulsively held out both hands to the older woman. "Are you all right?" she said softly.

Tears misted Rhetta's eyes. "No, I'm not. I don't know how the hell I'll get along without her. She was . . . Helene was special."

Feeling impotent, Diane nodded. "If there's anything . . ." She faltered, her words seeming to freeze in her throat as she realized how empty they sounded in the face of such anguish.

But Rhetta smiled wanly. "Maybe someday I'll come to New York. You can tell me all about Helene when she was young. I'd like that."

"Anytime," Diane said, squeezing her fingers. "Anytime at all."

Rachel and Gussie had remained seated, but now they stood

as the receptionist approached them. "Mr. Halvorsen will see you now, ladies. If you'll just follow me."

They trailed her down a long corridor to a spacious corner office where an older white-haired man sat behind an intricately carved mahogany desk. He stood when they entered the room, extending his hand to Rhetta. "Hello, Rhetta. I'm sorry about Helene. It was quite a shock."

"Yes, it was. If I had only known she . . ." Rhetta briefly closed her eyes and shook her head as if to gain control of herself. Then she looked at the lawyer and frowned. "What's this all about, Douglas? Why the hell did you have to see us today?"

"I'll get to that in a minute," Halvorsen said. "First I think a few introductions are in order. Would you do the honors, Rhetta?"

Rhetta performed the introductions and then sank into a mahogany armchair. Once the others were seated, Halvorsen resumed his place behind his desk. "Would anyone like a drink before we begin?"

"No, thanks," Rachel said. "We're all anxious to get this over with."

Halvorsen seemed reluctant, but at last he opened a manila folder, thumbed through the contents, and withdrew a sheet of ivory stationery. "I received this letter in the mail yesterday morning. Apparently Helene wrote it a few hours before she took her life. She specifically requested that I gather you together for a reading immediately following her funeral."

Diane's flesh prickled at the idea of Helene coolly and deliberately writing a letter before she killed herself. Then she glanced at Rachel and Gussie and saw horrified disbelief on their faces.

"If you have no objections," Halvorsen went on, "I'll read the letter now. Then I'll try to answer any questions you might have."

"That's fine," Rachel murmured. "Do you mind if I smoke?"

Halvorsen shook his head and shoved a large jade ashtray across his desk. Then after clearing his throat, he began to read. " 'Dearest ones,' " he said. " 'By now the service is over and you all know I chose to end my life rather than go on feeling this awful loneliness. Seth was everything to me, and without him I'm lost. I really did try to put myself back together at the clinic, Rhetta, but there was nothing left, and finally I realized I was beyond salvation. Please try to forgive me. I love you all, and I hate the idea of causing you pain.' "

Rhetta sniffed, and Halvorsen paused. "I know how hard this is," he said kindly. "But please bear with me."

"Is there much more?" Gussie said, her cheeks the color of wax. "I'm not feeling very well."

Lowering his head, Halvorsen avoided her eyes. "I'm afraid . . . there's quite a bit more. Maybe you'd like me to pause for a few minutes so you can visit the ladies' room."

"No, go ahead," Gussie said weakly.

Diane felt jittery. It was eerie listening to words Helene had written just before her death, eerie and frightening.

Halvorsen began to read again: " 'Maybe it will help you to know that I'm not afraid of dying. I've never been religious, but these past few weeks I've felt Seth's presence all around me. I know we'll be together again and I'm not afraid.

" 'But I have a terrible secret to confess before I die, a secret I've blocked out of my mind for twelve years. I killed Rick Conti. I made love to him because I wanted to hurt my mother. Then he rejected me, and I stabbed him.' "

"Oh, my God," Rachel murmured. "She really did kill him. I was so sure Brenda had lied to us."

Diane gripped the arms of her chair until her knuckles were white as she remembered that hot night in Hyannis. She could still see Rick lying in a bloody heap, hear the dull thud of his body hitting the bottom of the well. Everything was startlingly clear, as if it had happened only yesterday.

"Go on," Gussie said in a strangled voice. "Read the rest of the letter."

Halvorsen nodded grimly and resumed his reading: " 'I guess the truth was so awful that my mind just shut it out. Even in my nightmares I saw only bits and pieces of what had happened. Then Seth died, and that seemed to trigger something. All of a sudden I started remembering—I murdered a man and you, my dearest friends, protected me all these years.

" 'Now I'm begging you to understand why I have to confess. I can't die with this on my conscience. I can't let Rick Conti lie at the bottom of that well forever. I've written a letter to the Hyannis police telling them exactly what happened, and I've instructed Douglas Halvorsen to mail it immediately after my funeral. I know how difficult it will be for you to face the publicity, but I made it perfectly clear that you had nothing to do with the murder.

"'Please forgive me and always remember how much I love you. Helene.'"

There was a stunned silence, then Gussie shot Douglas Halvorsen a horrified look. "Good God, I hope you didn't mail that letter."

"A messenger service picked it up a few hours ago," he said quietly.

"Are you crazy?" she shouted. "How could you do that to us?"

Pinching the bridge of his nose, Halvorsen looked drawn and weary. "I had no choice, Mrs. Chandler. I had to obey the law."

Diane glanced from Halvorsen to Gussie, but their faces were all blurry, like shapes in a kaleidoscope, spinning and whirling, constantly changing form. "So . . . so what happens now?" she stammered. "Will . . . will we be arrested?"

"No, of course not," Gussie shrieked. "Helene was out of her mind. We'll prove she was unstable . . . a junkie."

"Gussie," Rachel said sharply, "that's enough."

Halvorsen cleared his throat. "Please try to calm down," he said. "You've just had a shock, but it won't help to argue among yourselves."

Rhetta had not uttered a single word, but now she furiously lashed out at Halvorsen. "You bastard! It was your job to protect Helene. Do you have any idea what the press will do with this? My God, they'll crucify her."

"I'm truly sorry, Rhetta, but as I said, I had no choice. I was bound by law to follow Helene's instructions."

Glaring at him, Rhetta shook her head in disgust. "Since when does a lawyer give a damn about the law? You're in this for the publicity, Douglas. You want to see your name splashed all over the papers. You might even make the evening news."

Halvorsen looked both wounded and annoyed that she had dared to question his ethics, but his voice remained calm. "I'll forgive that insult because I know you're under a great deal of stress, Rhetta. But let me assure you that my only interest in this matter is professional. I have no need of gratuitous publicity." He turned to Diane. "I believe you had a question about your own legal position, Mrs. Casey."

Struggling to find her voice, Diane wondered if she really wanted an answer to her question. What if he said they were likely to serve long prison terms? What if the police were already primed to arrest them? Feeling smothered, she said, "Do you think . . . Will we be charged with conspiracy?"

Gussie groaned, but Halvorsen ignored her as he continued to fix his gaze on Diane. "I doubt that very much. Helene made it clear in her letter that you had nothing to do with the actual murder. You became aware of the crime only after the fact, so there's no basis for a charge of conspiracy."

"But we helped Brenda dispose of the body," Rachel said. "And then we lied to the police."

Halvorsen picked up a silver letter opener and absently rubbed the pad of his thumb along the dull blade. "You have to understand that I'm not well versed in Massachusetts law, so I can speak only in general terms, but in my opinion you're most vulnerable to a charge of obstruction of justice. In essence that's what you did by hiding a body and then lying to the authorities."

"My God," Gussie cried. "Obstruction of justice is a felony. We'll go to prison."

"That is highly unlikely, Mrs. Chandler," Halvorsen said. "You probably won't even be indicted. Prosecutors are always leery of cases like this. There are no living witnesses against you and, as you pointed out earlier, Helene had a long history of mental instability. Any good attorney could probably cast enough doubt on her credibility to win an acquittal."

He smiled faintly at their relieved expressions, then went on. "Perhaps if you were longtime criminals the state might be inclined to try to make a case against you, but you're all upstanding citizens. They have no reason to believe you represent any threat to society."

"So that's it?" Rachel said. "You don't think we'll have any legal problems?"

"None of any consequence, but I advise you to hire an attorney. There'll be an inquest, and you'll need representation. I imagine the publicity will be troublesome as well."

Diane had been quietly listening, her relief mounting with

every word, but now her heart began to pound again and she felt a tightening in her chest. Publicity. They might not go to prison, but the publicity would ruin them. Then she thought of her tenuous position at the television studio, and knew beyond a doubt that Ed Blake finally had the weapon he needed to destroy her.

"There must be something we can do to stop the publicity," Gussie said in a nervous rush. "What about a gag order?"

Halvorsen chuckled. "I'm afraid not, Mrs. Chandler. We have a free press in this country, and they'll be out in force to cover this story. My best advice is to avoid them as much as possible."

"But . . . I can't afford to be involved in a scandal. My husband is running for reelection, and my parents . . . my parents will never forgive me."

Looking uncomfortable, Halvorsen gathered the papers on his desk and replaced them in the manila envelope. "I really wish I could do something to help you," he said. "But unfortunately I have no control over the media."

Her face ashen, Rachel said, "How much time do we have before the story breaks?"

Halvorsen shrugged. "A few days at most."

"I have to get to the airport," she said, bolting to her feet. "Brian is running for D.A. If he reads about this in the paper, he'll hate me."

Rattled by the urgency in her voice, Diane felt a deep sense of foreboding. They were all at critical junctures in their lives, and this scandal might very well destroy them. After all this time, they were finally being called upon to atone for their sins.

CHAPTER
Twenty-five

DIANE PAID THE DRIVER, THEN CLIMBED OUT OF THE CAB AND STOOD ON the sidewalk in front of her home. Everything looked exactly the same as it had two days ago—the pots of geraniums scattered on the stoop, the highly polished front door—but somehow everything was different. In just two days the entire fabric of her life had been ruptured, and she wondered if she would ever be able to repair the damage.

As she trudged up the stoop, she dreaded telling Michael the truth about her past. Their marriage was still so new, like a tender seedling struggling to take root. What would he think of her? How would he feel about a wife who had shoved a human body to the bottom of a well long ago on a hot night in Hyannis?

She fished in her purse for her keys and unlocked the door, then quietly entered the house. Michael was sprawled out on the sofa in the living room reading a medical journal. She had been half hoping he was still at the hospital. Now there was no delaying the moment of truth.

"Diane!" he said. "Why didn't you call me? I would've picked you up at the airport."

She forced a smile, containing an urge to fling herself into his arms and pretend the past few days had never happened. "I shared a cab with Rachel," she said wearily.

Michael looked at her for a moment, his sensitive dark eyes seeming to absorb all the pain and fear she was feeling. Then he scrambled to his feet and rushed to embrace her. "Are you okay?" he said, hugging her close.

She tried to hold back her tears, but as she stumbled into the warm circle of his arms, harsh grating sobs filled her throat. "Oh, Michael . . . it was so awful."

Instead of attempting to comfort her with meaningless words, he simply held her, gently rubbing her back as she cried. But even while her body found solace in the tender sanctuary of his arms, her mind remained riveted to the past, and at last she drew away from him. "Michael," she said, "I have something to tell you."

"You look exhausted. Can't it wait until morning?"

"No. I'll go crazy if I don't tell you now."

He looked worried as he sat beside her on the corduroy sofa. His black hair was tousled and he wore an old faded pair of jeans, but she had never found him quite so appealing and she tried to engrave his image in her mind. By tomorrow he might very well be out of her life, hating her for concealing such a damning secret.

"We met with Helene's lawyer this afternoon," she said quietly. "He read us a letter she left."

"A suicide note?"

"Not exactly." She looked into his depthless dark eyes and felt herself coming apart. "I . . . I don't know how to tell you this."

He reached out and trailed his fingers over her cheek, those strong fingers that were capable of restoring a failing heart. If only they had the power to wipe away her past.

"I love you, Diane," he said. "Nothing you tell me will change that."

Though she desperately wanted to believe him, she knew some sins were unforgivable. She imagined his shock and horror when he learned the truth. Then, because she was too drained and frightened to prolong the ordeal, she slowly confessed her secret.

"In a few days the whole world will know the truth," she concluded, ashamed to meet his eyes. "I'm so sorry for embarrassing you."

In a quick movement he pulled her into his arms and fiercely hugged her. "Christ, why did you face this alone? Why didn't you tell me?"

"I was afraid," she said simply.

"Did you really think I'd love you any less? My God, Diane, don't you know you can trust me?"

Suddenly she did. She knew she could trust this man with

her very life. Even if she lost everything else, she would still have the priceless gift of his love. "I should have known," she said softly. "But the secret was so much a part of me, something I had to hide from everyone, even you."

Michael pressed his lips to her forehead. "We'll get through this, Diane. Whatever happens, we'll get through it together."

Resting in his arms this way she almost believed him, but a sly inner voice reminded her of all the trouble ahead—the lurid publicity, the inquest into Rick's death, her shaky position at the studio. Her life was filled with uncertainty.

"I'll probably lose my job," she said. "Ed Blake has been waiting for something like this. He finally has the weapon he needs to discredit me completely."

Michael continued to hold her, smoothing his hands over her back in a steady rhythm. After a time he said, "Maybe you can beat him to the punch."

"What do you mean? I don't want to resign, Michael. Even if I lose in the end, I refuse to give him the satisfaction of knowing he forced me to quit."

"I'm not talking about resigning. What if you go over his head, meet with the bosses, and offer to give the network an exclusive interview in exchange for keeping your job?"

At first the idea struck her as absurd, but the more she thought about it, the more plausible it became. Ratings meant everything in the television industry, and her own personal account of the tragedy would surely draw a large audience. Maybe enough to spare her job. She felt a burst of optimism, but the buoyant sensation quickly ebbed as she thought of Rachel and Gussie. She could never exploit them that way just to save her own skin. Looking up at Michael, she shook her head. "Even if the network agreed, I couldn't do that to Rachel and Gussie."

"Once the story breaks, every sleazy tabloid in the country will be scrambling to print the most outrageous lies. An interview will give you a chance to set the record straight."

Diane considered that, then shook her head again. "What about Helene? I'd feel like a ghoul talking about her suicide on television."

Moving away from her, Michael sat up and looked directly into her eyes. "Have you seen the evening news lately?" he said quietly.

"No, not since—"

"Helene's suicide has been one of the lead stories every night. They covered everything from her drug and alcohol abuse to her funeral."

"God, why did they have to violate her like that? They had no right to portray her as some kind of . . . drug-crazed alcoholic."

Michael drew her close again, cradling her head against his shoulder. "No, they didn't, but you knew the real Helene. In a few weeks all this publicity will die down, and you'll still have your memories."

She nodded. Then, hating the reporters who had so viciously stripped Helene of her privacy even in death, she said, "Do you think it would help if I went on the air and told the truth? Or would I be exploiting her memory just like those other vultures?"

"Never," he said gently. "You loved her. She was your friend."

Her mind reeling, Diane tried to sort out her conflicting feelings. Was it selfish to barter such personal secrets for a chance to salvage her career? Would Rachel and Gussie view it as a betrayal? Dear God, they had all lost so much already. "I don't know what's right anymore," she said.

"Why not talk to Rachel and Gussie? Ask them how they feel about it."

"Maybe I'll call them in the morning," she said. But as she nestled against his chest, she was still plagued by doubts. Where would this nightmare end? Would they ever really be free of their secret?

Shadows played over the familiar kitchen as Rachel wearily sat at the table in the dark and buried her face in her hands. Brian and the girls were asleep, and the house seemed oddly silent without the echo of their voices. A fierce loneliness settled over her, reaching all the way to the marrow of her bones. Why was life so full of sad endings and broken dreams?

Tears stinging her eyes, she remembered her wedding day, the day she had promised herself to Brian. God, they had been so young then, so certain of their love. But over the years their hopes and dreams had slowly withered like autumn leaves, then dropped to the ground one by one. And now her secret would deliver the mortal blow to their marriage.

All evening she had been searching for words to tell Brian the truth without killing his love for her, but no such words existed. She was guilty not only of concealing a murder but also of deceiving her husband. Now he was about to become a victim of the truth; his dreams would be crushed by scandal.

Rachel tensed as she heard a sound, then looked up and saw Brian standing in the doorway, his beloved face illuminated by the warm glow of the hallway light. "Rachel, what're you doing sitting here all alone in the dark?"

Rachel tried to find her voice, but there were too many tears. She just looked at him, her mouth helplessly trembling.

"Christ, what's the matter?"

He hurried to her side and cupped her tear-ravaged face in his hands. "What is it? Talk to me."

At last finding her voice, Rachel stared into his clear blue eyes and said, "There's something I have to tell you. I . . . did a terrible thing . . . a long time ago." She paused, the muscles in her face all working at once. "Helene . . . killed a man . . . and Diane and Gussie and I . . . we hid his body in a well."

"Rache, what are you talking about?"

In a strangled whisper she blurted out the story of Rick Conti and the night that was forever embedded in her memory. "So you see . . . now it will all come out. You'll be dragged into the scandal. I'm sorry, Brian. I know you must hate me. I'll give you a divorce . . . anything you want."

Brian stood completely still, his eyes fixed on her face, his skin pale as death in the dim light. She felt lost and bewildered, free of the secret at last, but so alone.

Then Brian dropped to his knees beside her and gently slipped his arms around her waist. "I love you, Rachel," he said softly. "I spent the last two days thinking about us, about how much I need you. My life would be hell without you."

"But you could lose the election because of me."

He shook his head. "You and the kids are all I need. I forgot that somewhere along the line, but I'll never let it happen again, Rachel. I promise."

It seemed like a miracle, being held in his arms, feeling his

hard body pressed against her, solid and secure. At last the
nightmare was over. Brian knew the truth and he still loved her,
still needed her in his life. No matter what happened, they were
together, the way they were meant to be.

Pulling away slightly, she looked at him and smiled. "I
prayed this would happen, but I was afraid to let myself
believe."

His eyes were clear and bright in the darkness, beaming with
love. "Believe," he said tenderly. "And this time it's forever."

Gussie climbed into a cab at Dulles Airport and slumped down
on the hot Naugahyde seat, wincing as the throbbing in her
head intensified.

"Where to, lady?" the driver said in a bored voice.

"I . . . I'm not sure. Could you just drive around for a few
minutes."

He turned, eyeing her suspiciously through the Plexiglas
shield. "D'ya know what that's gonna cost ya?"

"Just drive. I don't care what it costs," she said impatiently.

"Sure thing, lady. It's your dime."

Turning away from her, he revved up the engine, then
squealed away from the curb and merged with the traffic
heading out of the airport. Gussie settled herself on the hard
seat, closed her eyes, and tried to think. It was ludicrous to ride
around aimlessly in a cab. She should just go home, face
Richard with the truth, and worry about the rest of her life later.
But an inner voice—the same voice that had been constantly
echoing through her mind for the last two days—relentlessly
urged her to forget Richard and run to Tony.

Her close encounter with death had given her a new
reverence for life. She now saw herself as she really was, a
lonely woman anticipating endless years in a barren marriage.
Such a waste of precious life. Such a foolish sacrifice. What
had made her believe her parents and her social position were
more important than her love for Tony?

And now there was the baby to consider. Tony had a right to
know and love his child. Instinctively she knew he would be a
wonderful father, just as he would have been a wonderful
husband if she had found the courage to defy her parents and

marry him. Her courage had failed her later, too, when she was given a second chance and succumbed to cowardice again. Now it was too late. Tony probably hated her.

But suddenly she knew she had to try to make him understand how much she loved him.

Tapping on the Plexiglas shield, she gave the driver Tony's address and then sat back and closed her eyes again, clinging to the frail hope that maybe this time her dream would come true.

Tony opened the door and was stunned to see Gussie standing there looking up at him, her huge green eyes seeming to dominate her pale face. He felt a thrill of pleasure, then quickly shoved it aside. This was Gussie, the woman who had twice betrayed him. "What are you doing here?" he said.

"I . . . I'd like to talk to you."

Anger stirred in his gut as unbidden memories drifted up from his subconscious—memories of her laughter, the silkiness of her skin, the light in her eyes when she smiled. Christ, what kind of fool was he to still feel this burning love? Why did this woman have such power over him? She was shallow and selfish, incapable of love, and yet he still dreamed of her, still wanted her.

"There's nothing more to say, Gussie," he said coldly. "Go home to your husband. I'm not available for stud service anymore."

"Please, Tony," she said. "Please . . ."

He tried to harden himself to her plea, but a second later he found himself stepping aside, wordlessly inviting her into the apartment.

She brushed past him and made her way to the living room. Tony followed, her scent floating around him like a familiar cloud, feeding his starving senses. Even now he found her lovely beyond measure. Even now he longed to make sweet lingering love to her.

Disgusted with himself, he watched her gracefully sit on the sofa and cross her slender legs. Now that he was recovering from the initial shock of seeing her, he wondered what the hell she wanted. Their affair was over; she had made that abundantly clear.

"All right, Gussie," he said. "What do you want?"

She hesitated briefly and then, in a quavering voice, said, "Helene Galloway killed herself. Did you know that?" He nodded and she went on in a rush. "Her death made me realize that life is precious. . . . I made a terrible mistake, Tony."

A glimmer of hope flickered inside him, but he savagely snuffed it out, reminding himself that Gussie was capable of the most treacherous betrayal.

"I love you," she whispered.

He laughed harshly. "Come on, Gussie. No more games. Just tell me why you're here."

Her shoulders sagged and her eyes were bleak, but she continued to look at him as if she were afraid to break the frail contact between them. "I'm here because I love you. Maybe it's too late, but I had to let you know."

Tony stared at her, hope warring with disbelief. He knew he'd be a fool to trust her, but would he be more of a fool to send her away without even trying?

She said, "Is it too late for us, Tony?"

He felt like a man lost in the desert, parched and weak, suddenly spying a cool green oasis in the distance. Was it real or only a mirage he had conjured up in his desperation?

He sat beside her on the sofa. "Is it real this time, *cara*? Are you ready to spend the rest of your life with me?"

She nodded. "But there's something I have to tell you. Then if you still want me, I'll spend the rest of my life with you."

As Gussie watched suspicion replace the joy on Tony's face she died a little inside. She had to make him understand about Rick Conti. To lose him now would be unbearable. "A long time ago I was involved in something," she said. "I was very young, just out of college."

Relief glowed in his dark eyes. "Forget the past, *cara*. It doesn't matter."

"But it does. You see, I . . . I did a terrible thing, and now the whole story is going to come out. Soon the whole world will know."

"What terrible thing did you do?"

Inhaling a deep breath, Gussie looked into his eyes and bared her soul, purging herself of the guilt and fear that had been festering inside her for so long. When she finally finished, Tony drew her into his arms and held her as she sobbed.

"It's all right," he said softly. "Let it go. You've suffered enough."

"How can you say that after what I did?"

"You were young and frightened, trying to protect your friend. It was a tragedy, but it's time to forgive yourself."

"Can . . . can you forgive me? Not just for this, but for everything?"

"I already have, *cara*."

He lowered his head and kissed her, his warm lips seeming to infuse her with life and hope. Then she remembered the baby and moved away from him. "There's something else," she said. "I'm pregnant, Tony. I'm going to have your baby."

His arms dropped to his sides as he stared at her. "Is that why you came back to me? Did your husband object to raising another man's child?"

"No, I came back because I love you, but even if you had sent me away, I was going to tell you about the baby. After Helene died, I realized I could never keep you from knowing your child. Life is too fragile."

He smiled very gently, all the anger gone from his eyes. "I love you, Gussie. Will you divorce Richard and marry me, let me be a father to our baby?"

"Yes," she said simply, feeling a wonderful serenity, a wonderful sense of belonging. At last she understood the gifts of love and trust and sharing. And at least she truly understood the power of dreams.

Late the next afternoon Diane stepped off the elevator on the twentieth floor of the Preston Building and entered the office of Howie Bloomenthal, a senior vice president. She was surprised that he had agreed to talk with her, since network officers rarely met with underlings without first going through the chain of command.

"Go right in," Mrs. Casey, the secretary said. "Mr. Bloomenthal is waiting for you."

When Diane entered the plush office, Howie Bloomenthal was seated behind his sleek oak desk smiling pleasantly, his bald head gleaming in the bright light streaming through the windows. "Good afternoon, Diane," he said as he rose and held out his hand.

"Hello, Howie. Thank you for seeing me on such short notice."

He pumped her hand, then motioned to a leather armchair. "Have a seat. Ed Blake should be here any minute."

Diane nearly choked as she sank into the chair and folded her hands in her lap. How could she have been naive enough to believe Bloomenthal would see her without involving Ed? She thought she had been so clever by contacting him directly; now she felt like a fool.

An instant later Ed breezed into the room. He oozed charm as he effusively greeted Bloomenthal, but when he turned to Diane, his beady eyes were full of animosity and suspicion. "This is a surprise, Diane," he said as he selected the chair closest to Bloomenthal and made himself comfortable. "I thought you were still in California."

"I got back last night," she said, her voice sounding strained even to her own ears. Ed was watching her with an irritating intensity, as if he had already figured out her plan and was just biding his time, waiting for the appropriate moment to launch his attack.

"I hate to rush things," Bloomenthal said. "But I'm due at a meeting in a few minutes. What did you want to talk about, Diane?"

Diane had rehearsed her speech all night, but now her mind went blank. She became completely unnerved when she caught sight of Ed sitting there like a hyena salivating over a fresh carcass.

Still, she had no choice but to go ahead. "I'm sure you've heard about Helene Galloway's suicide," she said finally.

Both men nodded, and she went on. "Before she died, Helene sent a letter to the Hyannis police confessing to a murder she committed twelve years ago. The story will break sometime today."

"Very interesting," Ed said impatiently. "But what the hell does that have to do with us?"

"I was there in Hyannis with Helene on the night of that murder. I helped conceal the body in an abandoned well."

Bloomenthal sucked in an audible breath. "Diane, you've just confessed to a crime."

"I know that, Howie, but I'm fairly certain I won't be

prosecuted. The problem is the publicity. I'll be at the center of a scandal.''

Ed pitched forward in his chair. ''And some of the dirt will invariably rub off on the network. This is a serious matter, Diane. I hope you understand that.''

Repressing a flood of revulsion, Diane forced herself to look directly into his gloating eyes. ''That's why I'm here, Ed. I have an idea that might allow us to avoid some of the negative publicity.''

''So do I,'' Ed snorted. ''Resign and spare us all a nasty mess.''

Diane glanced at Bloomenthal, silently imploring him to intervene. She was beginning to feel an aching certainty that Ed would prevail. He was so good at manipulating situations to his own advantage, and she had just presented him with a perfect excuse to get rid of her.

But then Bloomenthal cleared his throat and said, ''That suggestion is a bit premature, Ed. I'd like to hear what Diane has to say.''

Ed tensed for a moment, then flashed Bloomenthal one of his oily smiles. ''Of course. I guess I overreacted there for a minute. Go ahead, Diane. Fill us in on the details of your idea.''

Now that she was the center of attention, Diane felt even more apprehensive. Her palms were drenched with sweat, and there was an irritating tickle at the back of her throat. She wondered if she had the strength to get through the next few minutes. Suddenly everything she had worked so hard to achieve hung in the balance. If she failed now, her career would be a smoldering pile of ashes and Ed Blake would have the satisfaction of witnessing her blistering defeat.

She paused for a moment, carefully gathering her thoughts. Then she described the murder and the events of the past few days, ending with a detailed explanation of her plan to appear on the evening news. When she finished, Ed looked triumphant, though Howie Bloomenthal's expression was unreadable.

''Forget it, Diane,'' Ed said maliciously. ''You're out of your mind if you think we'll put you on national television just so you can save your ass.''

"Hold on, Blake," Bloomenthal said abruptly, his jowly face flushing. "I think it's a good idea. We'll string the interview out over three nights, keep the viewers tuned in for more. Is that all right with you, Diane?"

Diane glanced at Ed, swallowing a nervous laugh as she watched him squirm. Suddenly he reminded her of a particularly unpleasant insect trapped in a glass jar.

"That's fine," she said, turning her attention back to Bloomenthal.

"Good. We'll get on this pronto. I'll call Pete Fianelli down in the newsroom and tell him you're on your way."

Realizing she had just been dismissed, Diane stood and started for the door. Then, feeling a spurt of reckless courage, she impulsively turned back to Bloomenthal and said, "Maybe this is poor timing, but I was wondering if you've reached any decision about me."

"Decision? What are you talking about?"

"My mistake on the Vic Loomis segment. Are you keeping me on as a producer?"

"That was settled two weeks ago. You made a serious error, but your record here has been outstanding. Of course we're keeping you on. What made you think otherwise?"

Diane looked at Ed, fury pumping through her bloodstream. The sadistic bastard had deliberately tortured her by prolonging her uncertainty.

"Ed led me to believe you were considering letting me go," she said, taking great pleasure in the way Ed suddenly looked pale and sick. "He assigned me to help out in research until you made your decision."

Bloomenthal turned on Ed, his already florid face darkening to a deep crimson. "What the hell's going on here, Blake?"

"She's just trying to stir up trouble," Ed shouted, his hatred for Diane spewing forth like venom. "She's always been a troublemaker, right from her first day on the job."

"That's enough, Ed. We'll discuss this at the board meeting tomorrow morning," Bloomenthal said. Glancing at Diane, he held out his hand. "I'm sorry for the misunderstanding, but I assure you that your job is secure."

Diane shook his hand, barely able to contain her elation. Ed would undoubtedly manage to survive the board meeting with his position intact—after all, he was still a male—but she had survived as well. And perhaps someday the balance of power would shift and her dream of becoming executive producer would become a reality.

She smiled brilliantly at Howie Bloomenthal, then floated out of the room feeling like a young girl again, her future a long winding road full of love and happiness and success.

Epilogue

GUSSIE POPPED THE CORK ON A BOTTLE OF DOM PÉRIGNON, AND FILLED three fluted goblets. The inquest into the death of Rick Conti was finally over, and she was spending the night with Diane and Rachel in a posh Hyannis hotel. It had been a grueling few days—press everywhere, the public straining for a glimpse of the three star witnesses—but in the end the prosecutor had opted not to press charges against them. At last they were free to resume their lives without fear of being exposed as accomplices to murder.

"I can't believe it's really over," Rachel said, picking up one of the goblets and cradling it in her hand. "We're not going to jail, and we don't have to hide from that damn Mick Travis anymore."

"Did you see him outside the courthouse?" Diane said. "He looked so disappointed I almost felt sorry for him."

Gussie wrinkled her nose. "Heaven forbid. He would have been overjoyed to see us all behind bars. Now he'll have to start persecuting someone else."

Laughing, Diane reached for one of the delicate crystal glasses, but as she held it in her hand, her laughter slowly died. "Helene should be here," she said softly. "It feels wrong to be celebrating without her."

Gussie nodded, her own happiness ebbing as memories of Helene floated through her mind like gentle ripples on a pond. Such beautiful memories, but so sad, so ineffably sad.

"She is here," Rachel said in a thick voice. "Somehow I know she's here with us." Raising her glass, she gazed out the window at the sun sparkling on the ocean. "Rest in peace, Helene."

As Gussie lifted her goblet in silent tribute to Helene, she suddenly felt a quiet sense of serenity, as if a loving hand had gently touched her soul and soothed her grief. Then she imagined she saw Helene standing on the beach, young and happy, her face bathed in golden sunlight. The vision only lasted a second, but in her heart, she knew Helene had truly been there.

And she knew then that the nightmare was really over. They were all free to dream again, to love and hope and search for happiness.

The sizzling new novel by the bestselling
author of <u>BLACK TIE ONLY</u>

Julia Fenton
BLUE ORCHIDS

"A dazzling page-turner. I was swept away by all the
glamour, fame and rivalry of two unforgettable sisters."
—Maureen Dean, bestselling author of <u>Washington Wives</u>

"Delightfully decadent...kept me turning pages late,
late into the night!"   —Rex Reed

It was the most eagerly awaited, star-studded premiere of
any Broadway musical ever. But for Valentina and Orchid it
would be much more. Each found success as recording
artists: Orchid had always struggled for stardom, but Valentina
captured the spotlight with her dark exotic beauty and
crystal voice. A bitter jealousy tore them apart, but tonight
they will reunite, and once again the eyes of the world will
be upon them, at a performance that will make or break
their dreams, and determine their destiny, for once and for
all . . .

___0-515-10875-8/$5.99 (Available July 1992)